A
MURDER
IN THE
MAKING

Books by Victoria Laurie

COACHED TO DEATH

TO COACH A KILLER

COACHED IN THE ACT

COACHED RED-HANDED

COACHING FIRE

A TRINKET FOR THE TAKING

A MURDER IN THE MAKING

Published by Kensington Publishing Corp.

A
MURDER
IN THE
MAKING

VICTORIA LAURIE

KENSINGTON PUBLISHING CORP.
kensingtonbooks.com

KENSINGTON BOOKS are published by

Kensington Publishing Corp.
900 Third Avenue
New York, NY 10022

All Kensington titles, imprints and distributed lines are available at special quantity discounts for bulk purchases for sales promotion, premiums, fund-raising, educational or institutional use. Special book excerpts or customized printings can also be created to fit specific needs. For details, write or phone the office of the Kensington Special Sales Manager: Kensington Publishing Corp., 900 Third Avenue, New York, NY 10022. Attn. Special Sales Department. Phone: 1-800-221-2647.

KENSINGTON and the KENSINGTON COZIES teapot logo Reg. US Pat & TM Off.

Library of Congress Control Number: 2025939899

ISBN: 978-1-4967-4252-0

First Kensington Hardcover Edition: December 2025

ISBN: 978-1-4967-4254-4 (ebook)

10 9 8 7 6 5 4 3 2 1

Printed in the United States of America

The authorized representative in the EU for product safety and compliance is eucomply OU, Parnu mnt 139b-14, Apt 123
Tallinn, Berlin 11317, hello@eucompliancepartner.com

A MURDER IN THE MAKING

CHAPTER 1

Lightning crackled across the sky, the light skittering along my bedroom walls and ceiling, illuminating shadows that were best left in the dark.

I reached over to my phone on the nightstand, lifting it to eye level. "Two a.m." I sighed. It was *hours* before dawn and well before I could justify being awake and going about my day, finding any excuse to keep busy. Occupied. Purposeful.

My to-do list was getting dangerously short because I'd attacked it with vengeance every morning, afternoon, and evening the past few weeks. I'd cleaned gutters, painted the basement, sorted through closets, emptied, cleaned, and rearranged every cupboard, hung shelving in the garage, donated old items to charity, organized my trinket collection, and I was now down to scrubbing the grout in the bathrooms and recalking any weak spots.

And I'd be willing to do it all over again plus any other unsavory chore simply to avoid thinking about what I couldn't stop thinking about.

Him.

As in Grant. Isaac. Barlow.

Gib.

I sighed again and rolled over, punching the pillow next to me in a small tantrum of frustration.

And longing.

Why? Why am I thinking about him again?!

Lightning pulsed into the room. Thunder roared seconds later.

I love the sound of thunder. I love how it begins with a crack like a branch breaking in the wind only to gain momentum and volume, the sound reverberating through the walls and windows, undulating along the landscape only to die in an echo.

I wondered for a moment how many thunderstorms I've lived through.

Thousands.

The math worked. Figuring fifteen to twenty thunderstorms a year, about average for southeastern Virginia, which had a similar climate to the parts of Europe I'd lived in, over the course of two hundred years. At a bare minimum I've lived through *at least* three to four thousand thunderstorms. Maybe more.

And even though I couldn't remember all of them, or even most of them, of the ones I did remember, I couldn't say that during any of them I'd ever felt this lonely.

This sad.

This . . . heartbroken.

Dovey Van Dalen, you are being ridiculous! I told myself.

And I was. But that didn't help me push away all the feelings weighing heavily upon my heart.

I missed him.

I simply . . . missed . . . him.

Rolling over again, I stared up at the ceiling, waiting for another lightning strike. I didn't have to wait long. Light sprayed across the room, dancing to the beat of the pelting rain.

I clenched my fists, wanting to alter reality in a way that

didn't leave me feeling so bereft, but I'd been over it and over it and there was no solution possible that could leave me even remotely hopeful.

I'd studied the problem dozens and dozens of times, and in no scenario that I imagined could I find a solution that worked.

Gib was an unbound. A mortal. Someone untouched by magical ability. He worked for the FBI, which meant interacting with him wasn't simply risky; it was suicide.

For him more than me.

Elric Ostergaard, my lover, my employer, and my spellbinder, would never abide a suspicious unbound snooping into mystic business. As much as I wanted things to be different, the fact was that I *am* a mystic. I'm bound by a magical spell that grants me special powers beyond physics and chemistry, and a youthfulness that defies the imagination.

I mean, here I am, two hundred years old, yet I don't look a day over thirty. And in my home are small treasures imbued with magical elements that make them quite useful to a mystic like me.

For instance, there's a candle in a candlestick on my dining room table that, when lit, can burn for years and years while giving even the darkest rooms a bright yellow glow.

And there's a snow globe on my nightstand that predicts the weather. Before turning out the light several hours ago, a silver glitter had tumbled about its interior, letting me know that what'd been a drizzle-filled day would continue to heavier rainfall overnight.

There's also a bronze cuff in my jewelry case that lends me superhuman strength. When I wear it, I can lift a horse. And I know that because once, in 1858, I *literally* plucked my horse from out of the mud where her hind legs had become stuck.

But none of the magical trinkets in my home could alter the

fact that I longed for a man who could never fit into my world, while a man who'd literally *created* my world held on to his romantic interest in me like a charm he found lucky.

In the weeks since I'd stopped all communication with Gib, I'd spun about at a frantic pace, tackling that to-do list with vigor just to keep from standing still long enough to think about how much I missed Gib's smile. His voice. The cut of his biceps, chest, and waistline where his sweater clung to him like it adored him as much as I did.

The swagger in his gait.

The smell of his aftershave.

The gravel in the sound of his voice.

The long scar along his right index finger.

The fact that he is drop-dead gorgeous but holds no airs.

The way he smiles crookedly before delivering a wry bit of wit.

The times his whole face lights up at the sight of a homemade cheese Danish.

The way he understands fashion in the same way that I do—as a form of flirtation.

The slope of his brow hovering over gray eyes that turn to silver if the light is just right.

I missed all these small things and the sum of their total. And I'd never felt so lonely in all my two hundred years on this planet—one-hundred and eighty of which had been spent happily in the company of another man. But now, that relationship felt stale and past its prime and I dreaded the day that Elric would ask me how I felt about us. My binding spell would compel me to tell him the truth—it quite literally wouldn't allow me even the smallest of lies where my feelings were concerned, and then he'd know for certain what I'm sure he already suspected. That I loved Elric, but I was no longer *in* love with him.

I was in love with someone else. And if Elric asked me who

that someone was, I'd be compelled again to answer him truthfully, and *that* meant that unless I got over my feelings for Gib, he was in mortal danger because Elric wouldn't stand for a competitor. Killing Gib was something he could easily fit in between his morning coffee and his first business meeting.

I doubted he'd need to be closer than a mile away to all but obliterate Gib's very existence. And I'd be responsible. His death would lay firmly at my feet.

With another sigh I rolled onto my side to stare hopelessly out the window. The sounds of thunder and flashes of lightning had moved off into the distance as the storm traveled northeast, but the loud patter of rain remained.

"It's the rain," I muttered. Gib and I had bonded on a rainy day weeks ago, and the fact that we'd sparked a flame for each other during an investigation into a deadly magical trinket from my world being used to murder people in his hadn't dampened that flame one iota.

Rolling to the other side to glance at the snow globe only deepened my misery. The globe showed the weather three, six, nine, twelve, and eighteen hours in advance. I'd once watched it flash snow, sleet, rain, rainbows, and a bright moon all in one go, but right now it simply displayed a fluttering of silver confetti on repeat, meaning it'd still be raining eighteen hours from now.

I'd have at least eighteen more hours to be reminded of that rainy day with Gib.

Sitting up in bed I reached for my phone. I hadn't taken a proper vacation in years. "Someplace sunny," I mused, opening the search engine. "Anyplace that doesn't resemble D.C."

A rustle to my left let me know that Bits, my enchanted little hedgehog, was stirring in his felt-lined bed. No doubt, all the noise of the storm and my own agitation were keeping him awake. "Sorry, picklepuss," I whispered. "I'll try to be quieter."

A pink nose appeared from the felt to sniff the air, as if testing the truthfulness of that statement.

I went back to the phone screen. There was a flight leaving for Bali at noon. "Bingo," I whispered. "And three seats left in first class."

I was about to click on the seat I wanted when an incoming text overrode the image on the screen.

It's nights like these that make me wish I hadn't already cashed in that rain check.

Missing you.

I stared at the screen, my heart hammering away in my chest. How had he known I was awake? *Had* he known? Or was the storm the reason we were both awake and thinking of each other?

Tears stung my eyes, and I dropped the phone into my lap. The enthusiasm for a vacation vanished, and all I wanted to do was curl up under the covers and feel sorry for myself. Not something I'm accustomed to, mind you, but the situation called for it.

I spent the next several hours contemplating a response, everything from "Hope you're well," to "Stop texting me!" to "I miss you too."

My mind kept circling back to that last one, and I'd grabbed my phone at least twenty times prepared to tap that message out, but the image of Gib dead on the ground, bleeding from a self-inflicted gunshot wound, kept me from making that mistake.

I'd once watched Gib die, and there hadn't been anything I could do about it except rewind time, after which I'd barely managed to avoid watching him die a *second* time.

The first time had been hard enough. It'd destroyed me. It'd been a pain beyond anything physical I'd ever experienced, and in my two hundred years I've experienced *excruciating* physical pain, which still hadn't compared to those moments after I'd watched the life seep out of Gib's beautiful silver eyes.

I couldn't go through that again, and if I reached out to him, if I even *responded* with anything more than silence, then I'd be risking that very thing.

I'd never recover if Elric murdered him, of that I was certain.

By six a.m. I was ready to leave the bed. Even with the remaining items on my to-do list, it wasn't as if I had anything pressing to attend to—it'd been a slow couple of weeks for investigations—but I was nothing if not disciplined, and getting up at six was routine for me.

Still, there was little enthusiasm for it.

Donning leggings and a tank top, I made my way to the basement, where the treadmill—aka the dreadmill—awaited me.

I hate running inside. I barely tolerate running *outside*, but my profession—mystic investigator of missing magical trinkets—called for a certain physical fitness. I couldn't even count the number of times I'd had to chase down an unbound determined to keep his or her new magical toy, and sometimes things got quite physical, which is why I'm also trained in a variety of martial arts.

But this morning the dreadmill was exactly what I needed.

I ran steadily for an hour and a half—ten miles. By the end I was soaked in sweat, my legs felt like rubber, and I badly needed coffee, but mentally at least, I felt better. A little less melancholy and a little more determined to stay strong.

Heading back upstairs I noticed Bits was up, and currently digging into the Cheerios box, which was laying on its side on the counter with a large bulge in the center and the distinct sound of crunching coming from inside.

I smiled and shook the box gently. "Scoundrel."

The crunching stopped. I giggled and tipped the box up, peeking inside. Whiskers covered in Cheerios dust and two black eyes stared innocently back at me. His expression seemed to say, "I have *no* idea how I got here!"

I laughed and set the box back down on its side. "Have at it, Bitty, but I'm making pancakes."

Rustling from the interior of the Cheerios box let me know I'd piqued his interest, and his nose appeared from the lid, sniffing the air.

"Blueberry," I added, moving around the island to open the fridge and retrieve the milk, eggs, blueberries, and butter I'd need to create a breakfast feast for us.

When I turned, Bits was on the island, licking the Cheerios dust off his paws, an eager glint in his eye. My head swiveled from the box on the counter next to the fridge then back to the island, and I shook my head.

I'd never actually seen Bits teleport himself from one place to another. He always waited for my back to be turned, but someday, I vowed, I'd witness it firsthand.

Just obviously not today.

I chatted at him for the next several minutes, stirring the ingredients and setting the skillet on the stove.

"What should we do today, Bits?" I asked him, feeling less inclined by the second to do anything involving my to-do list.

His gaze flickered from the griddle back up to me and his expression seemed to say, "We're eating pancakes, woman!"

I laughed and tapped the top of his thorny head. "Yes, yes, but *after* that. Or more specifically, what should we plan to do after I check in with Hyacinth?"

Hyacinth is Elric's new assistant. She'd replaced his former assistant—and Hyacinth's identical twin sister—Sequoia a few months earlier when Sequoia had "retired." I didn't know the particulars around Sequoia's permanent absence, but in the mystic world, "retirement" is synonymous with "dead."

As there'd been no move that I could discern on Elric's part to avenge her death, I had to conclude that Sequoia's demise had met with Elric's approval, which was why it puzzled me that he would replace her with her twin sister, but then it was rumored that Sequoia and Hyacinth had never been especially close, so perhaps Hyacinth's mourning period had been short-lived.

Being Elric's personal assistant was a coveted job, after all.

If I were being honest, which this morning I was inclined to be, I didn't much like Hyacinth. But I had somewhat liked her sister, even though Sequoia had always had an agenda—common among mystics—but hers always seemed to me to be especially pronounced. I'd never understood why Elric had trusted her in the first place, except for the fact that he'd been the one who murdered the twins' binder—which in effect, set them free. They could never be controlled by their binding spell again.

Creating that debt had perhaps left him feeling more secure about Sequoia's intentions than perhaps he should've.

As for Hyacinth, she was about as likely to betray Elric as she was to throw herself to one of Jacquelyn's dragons. The outcome in both scenarios would've been the same. Painful and decidedly not quick.

In answer to my question, Bits's gaze once again darted back and forth between me and the griddle. It was good to know that he was solely focused on the most important part of the day ahead—breakfast.

I sighed and flipped the pancakes. "Won't be long now," I assured him. He wiggled his nose.

An incoming text pinged my phone and I began to reach for it but hesitated. If it was another text from Gib, I didn't know if I'd have the willpower to let it go unanswered.

Bits made his usual impatient chuffing noises while eyeing me sternly.

"It might be work," I told him, and I crossed my fingers that it was. I needed a case to get my mind off my heartache.

It turned out that the text was from my best friend and fellow mystic, Ursula Göransdotter.

Good morning, stranger. Thought I'd check in with you as I haven't heard from you in the past few days. No doubt you're still hiding yourself away, moping.

I sighed and replied: **Am I that transparent?**

Only to me. Let me pull you out of that funk and take you to lunch today. There's that lovely bistro at the north end that serves that marvelous lobster bisque you love.

I didn't reply right away, mostly because I didn't want to go anywhere or do anything that would require me to make much of an effort with my appearance, which wasn't a good look on me, but Ursula was spot-on; I was in a definite funk, and I wanted to stay there for a while.

Please say yes, came the next text.

I smiled. She knew me too well.

Yes, I replied, rolling my eyes.

Ursula sent back a few celebration emojis and instructions to meet her at the bistro at one o'clock. Another impatient chuff from Bits had me setting the phone down to turn off the burner.

"More for you, Bitty," I told him, plating only one pancake for myself, leaving the other entirely for him. The lobster bisque was indeed a favorite of mine, and it was so rich and creamy, I was glad I'd gotten in the ten-mile run.

After cleaning up the breakfast dishes and collecting a decidedly pudgier Bits, I headed upstairs to select an outfit.

"Goodness, I haven't been out in public in *weeks*," I told Bitty, setting him on the carpeted floor of my walk-in closet. He eyed me skeptically and I added, "The grocery store and the hardware store don't count, and you know it. Now, what shall I wear?"

Bits stood up on two feet to sniff the air, wobbling a bit as he considered the choices in front of him. He then tucked himself into a ball and rolled slowly forward, stopping just underneath a pair of silk, candy-apple red, pleated slacks. I moved to the slacks and took them off the rack. "Bold choice, Bitty. Are we really doing bold for my first outing in weeks?"

Bits was already in motion again, rolling to the opposite side of the closet to pause right underneath a carmine-red mohair sweater with a mock turtleneck and wide sleeves. Cropped at the waist, it was an exquisite piece I'd picked up a decade earlier but had worn only a few times, so it still looked new.

"Red on red, eh?" I asked him. He was certainly pushing it given the funk I'd been in, but in his 170 years as my personal stylist, he'd never steered me wrong.

Bits made a chuffing noise again, then formed a ball for a third time and rolled right over to my extensive shoe collection. I knew which cranberry patent leather booties with a pointed toe he'd stop in front of before he did.

"I take it you'd like me to stand out in the crowd today, eh, picklepuss?"

Bits unfurled himself and rose up on two feet again, sniffing the air impatiently while I hesitated taking the sweater from its place on the rod.

I glanced doubtfully to my left, where I could see a corner of the window, peppered with raindrops, the weather continuing to accurately reflect my snow globe's prediction.

I *wanted* to dress in charcoal grays and black accents, but Bits was perhaps right on target in that what I probably needed was a great big dose of eye-popping color to counterweigh the dull and dreary day.

I took the sweater off the hanger and walked the few steps over to him. Reaching for the booties, I gave in. "Okay, okay. You win. I will not shy away from color today, Bitty."

When I had the booties in hand, however, I glanced down only to find the place he'd literally just been occupying . . . empty. He'd vanished.

Behind me I heard a scuffling sound and a glance over my shoulder showed me that he'd merely teleported himself into his felt snuggle located on top of my nightstand.

I chuckled. "Someday, you prickly beast, I'm going to catch you in the act."

Bits made another chuffing noise. Obviously, he doubted it.

CHAPTER 2

After parking a few meters from the entrance to the bistro, I pulled Luna's visor down to check that my bold red lipstick—appropriately named Vixen—hadn't smeared or stained my teeth.

Luna is my Porsche 718 Cayman in arctic gray. She was a birthday gift to myself, and she was still brand-spanking new. I adored the car and especially appreciated that the good-sized vanity mirror, lit with soft lighting, was enhancing some of my best features.

My mother was a celebrated beauty back in Copenhagen in the early 1800s. My father—a wealthy merchant—had reportedly paid a hefty price for her even though, technically, she should've gone to him with a sizable dowry.

My grandfather, however, hadn't been an especially agreeable man so much as he'd been an especially greedy one. He'd raised three exquisitely beautiful daughters to the ripe old age of fifteen and auctioned them off one by one, each one's price increasing in value as their beauty became more and more celebrated.

My mother had been the most beautiful of them all. In personality she was affectionate, thoughtful, and loving, and her death when I was only ten devastated me. We were so close, both in personality and in looks. Side by side, I could've easily passed for a younger version of her. As I grew older, there were people among the town that hadn't heard of her passing that often mistook me for her.

Little had changed of my features in the past 18 decades; Throughout all those years I'd kept my wavy dark blond hair long and wore colors that complemented the warm ivory glow of my skin tone.

My brow was high but a pronounced widow's peak kept it from feeling out of proportion, and the rest of my face angled nicely into a pleasing heart shape.

My eyes were rather deep-set, but their light blue irises glowed from the depths, especially in the right light.

I also had my mother's nose and lips—perky and full. The last bit of good fortune she'd bestowed on me was a double row of straight, strong, white teeth.

On occasion, I've been accused of putting on airs, but the truth is that I've never felt more than a moment or two of insecurity because, in a strange way, the face staring back at me in the mirror has always been more my mother's than mine. Seeing her there looking back at me often fills me with comfort. I adored Mama, and even after all this time, I still miss her deeply.

Fluffing up my hair a bit and dotting a little more red lipstick on my lips, I sat back to reassess my appearance. I smiled in satisfaction. Why I didn't wear red more often was perhaps its own miscalculation.

Reaching for the umbrella on the passenger seat, I glanced quickly at my watch, noting that I was running late, but then, Ursula was *never* on time, so I had still likely beat her here.

It'd been a while since I'd seen my dear friend—scratch that, my *best* friend. At least a few weeks, which was another oversight I was finding myself happy to rectify today. I hoped that she'd been having a bit of fun with her on-again, off-again love interest, Dex—a mystic I genuinely like, save for the fact that, while he treated Ursula like a queen whenever they were together, we all knew he was in love with his partner, Esmé Bellerose.

Esmé and Dex were thieves who'd officially become employees of SPL Inc. (Elric's business front) several weeks back—right around the time I'd first met Gib, in fact.

While Elric had assigned me to investigate the theft of trinkets by the unbound, Esmé and Dex stole trinkets from *other* mystics to add to Elric's personal collection.

Ursula is also employed by SPL, and I am perhaps the only other mystic besides Elric who knows what she does for him, and that is a secret I'll gladly take to my grave. Suffice it to say that Elric's wife, Petra Dobromila Ostergaard, has been losing a few IQ points the past decade, making her just a wee bit less able to outsmart her husband.

My best friend is significantly older than me, and it's rumored that Elric is responsible for her binding, which I know happened perhaps in the early eleventh century. Ursula remembers little of her homeland or her parents and siblings. The longer a mystic lives, the less likely it is that they'll remember their unbound days. She firmly believes, however, that she came from the Duchy of Brittany because she distinctly remembers the news of the death of Duke Geoffrey I, who ruled over her homeland in the early 1000s, reaching her village, and the fear that Geoffrey's son, Alan III, was too young to stand against other rebellious counts in the region who would've thought nothing of trampling the village—loyal to Geoffrey and Alan—on their way to stake a claim for power.

It was near that time when she was bound, leaving the troubled, turbulent world of the unbound behind.

For much of her early life as a mystic, she made her living as an artist—both a painter and a sculptor—talent which allowed her to float among the various mystic courts, collecting gossip to report back to Elric as his loyal spy. A job that very nearly had her beheaded a time or two.

Along with being a talented artist, my friend is also a rather famous potion specialist—she can brew a love potion that you'll remember fondly *forever*. She's also a respected linguist, fluent in perhaps fifty different languages.

Dumb, she ain't.

However, a celebrated beauty in her own right, she definitely *is*.

Since the 1960s she's been constantly compared by nearly every unbound of a certain age to Brigitte Bardot, and I have to chuckle each time an unbound mentions this because in 1978 Ursula attended a cocktail party where Ms. Bardot was present, and it's rumored the movie star left early because she could no longer claim to be the most beautiful woman in the room once Ursula arrived.

As I reached the entrance to the bistro, the door was held open for me by an elderly gentleman on his way out. He tipped an imaginary hat as I smiled and thanked him. Heading to the hostess stand I wasn't surprised to see the restaurant's sparse lunch crowd. The rain was keeping everyone indoors, chained to their desks today.

"Hello," I said, greeting the hostess.

Her eyes flickered over me. "Wow," she said, before I could say more. "Your look is *exactly* the color we need in here today. I'm so *sick* of this rain!"

I laughed lightly. "I wish I could take credit for selecting this ensemble, but my stylist did all the work."

"Professional stylist?"

I winked conspiratorially. "Of a sort. Anyway, I'm probably the first of my party here. I'm meeting a friend, and the reservation might be under her name, Ursula Göransdotter."

Ursula had chosen her surname to honor her mystic mentor,

Göran the Terrible, who, according to Ursula, was only terrible to his enemies.

"Oh yes," the hostess said. "They've arrived. This way."

My brow furrowed slightly when the hostess referred to Ursula as "they" but then I thought about it. Using the "they" pronoun as a default was rather clever and helped to avoid the potential for insult.

I followed along as we wound a circuitous route through the restaurant all the way to the back right corner and, sitting in the booth, there *they* were.

And by "they" I mean Ursula *and* Gib.

His back was to me as we approached, but there was no mistaking that copper blond hair, those gorgeously broad shoulders, and that seductive aftershave.

My breath caught and I stopped in my tracks as a tightfisted panic clenched in the center of my chest. Should I turn tail and walk straight back out of this restaurant and never speak to Ursula again?

I mean, she *knew* I'd been doing my level best to avoid Gib. She *knew* how hard the past month and a half had been for me, and how many weak moments I'd had, holding my phone, staring down at it, my finger hovering over the keyboard unable to think of anything to text him, but wanting to simply connect with him again. But for his own safety, I couldn't. And she *knew* that too.

"Dovey!" I heard Ursula call, and my gaze snapped up from the hold it had on Gib's broad shoulders to find hers, locked on me, a smile plastered to her lips and a scoundrel's glint in her eye.

I will kill you, I mouthed right before I noticed Gib stiffen, then turn his head sharply.

I couldn't help but stare at him, reading every emotion that flashed across his face like the lines in a poem we'd both been reciting.

Surprise, to see you,
Relief, you are near,
Desire, I keep for you,
Hurt, you made clear,
Hope, I still have for us,
But loss I still fear . . .

Then, after those first fleeting moments, Gib adopted a brief, forced smile, calming the tumble of emotions reflected in his eyes and expression.

I quickly mirrored him, before focusing fully on the other person at the table.

"Ursula," I said flatly, offering her only the slightest nod. She'd set me up and she'd no doubt set Gib up too, given the way he'd stiffened when Ursula had called to me. My best friend was a scoundrel of the highest order.

Smiling winningly back at me, she pretended not to notice the fury in my eyes, jumping up from her seat to wrap me in her arms, squeezing me tight. "It was for your own good," she whispered.

I patted her numbly on the back and pulled away. I'd have to think up an excuse—a reason not to stay—but as I turned to nod and smile politely at Gib, all semblance of intelligent thought went right out the window when he stood up to offer me a warm smile and his hand.

Dressed smartly in navy blue jacket, turtleneck, and poly-blend joggers, he'd styled his all-navy-blue attire with suede, sand-colored fatigue boots and the cologne that had haunted my dreams. I took his hand, and he covered it with his other one. "Looks like I still had some credit in the rain check account after all," he said with a wink.

I wanted to cry . . . as in, I *literally* wanted to cry, and my eyes did, in fact, water a bit. I'd been awful to Gib. I'd ghosted this lovely man, disappearing from his life without explanation, knowing I'd hurt him terribly, and yet here he was holding my hand both gently and warmly, effortlessly evaporating the awkwardness from this encounter.

I swallowed hard and cleared my throat. "It's nice to see you, Gib."

"Nice to be seen, Dovey."

Ursula waved to her side of the booth. "Dovey, take a seat next to me. Gib arrived just before you and we were catching up."

I released my grip from Gib's hand, but his lingered for a moment on mine and that same spark of chemistry rippled along my skin, stirring that familiar desire I seemed to always have whenever he was nearby.

With a slight squeeze he let go and I moved to the booth to take a seat. Ursula then tucked in next to me—no doubt to make sure I didn't try to escape before we ordered lunch.

She's a sneaky mystic; I'll give her that.

Turning in her seat to toggle her index finger up and down at me, she said, "You look beautiful, by the way. Red is so your color, Dovey."

I felt a blush touch my cheeks. "Thank you."

Ursula was attired in mint-green silk pants and a low-neck, cream sweater that felt quite optimistic on this dreary spring day.

Before I could compliment her, however, our server appeared at the table and asked for our drink order. We chose iced teas all around. After she'd left, an awkward silence ensued, into which Ursula said, "How's work, Dovey?"

My gaze pivoted between Ursula and Gib—Ursula knew, of course, that I worked as a mystic investigator, retrieving trinkets from the unbound when those magical objects fell into nonmagical hands. But Gib thought I was an ordinary P.I., which was a decent enough cover for an unbound to believe, but it still wouldn't allow me to talk as freely about my work than if it'd just been me and Ursula for lunch.

"Slow," I told her. "Not a lot of cases need my attention right now."

She nodded like she fully understood, then pointed to Gib. "Right before you arrived, Grant was telling me he'd just wound up a racketeering case that'd been a tricky one to solve."

Gib smiled sheepishly. "The perp made it a lot easier when he admitted on tape that he enjoyed getting one over on us."

I cocked my head in curiosity. "Oh?"

He shrugged. "We had our suspicions about a lobbyist representing foreign interests from a hostile country, working to bribe certain lawmakers to ease sanctions against that particular government. The lobbyist wasn't the sharpest tool in the box. I wore a wire and posed as the chief of staff to one of the targeted lawmakers, willing to represent and relay the details of the bribe, and we had this guy incriminating himself before happy hour was over."

"*You* went undercover?" I asked.

He looked humorously at me. "Yeah. Why does that surprise you, Dovey?"

A slight shiver tickled the hairs on the back of my neck. I loved the sound of Gib's naturally low but gravel-laden voice. It was similar in sound to Kevin Costner's, but whenever Gib said my name, the gravel disappeared and it became a soft utterance, not quite smooth, but still so sexy.

I drummed my fingernails against my water glass. "Undercover agents usually try to avoid standing out in a crowd, yes?"

"We do."

A smile spread along my lips. "You're not exactly someone I'd describe as blending in, Gib."

Ursula giggled. "Unless he's standing next to Brad Pitt, Chris Hemsworth, and Bradley Cooper."

I laughed too but Gib blushed, which only made him more adorable.

The bastard.

On the table between us was a small vase with a single daisy. "Should we order?" Gib asked, after clearing his throat and moving the vase out of the way so that he could pass us the menus sitting piled to the side, but the corner of one of the menus caught the vase and it tipped over, falling off the table. The three of us startled and Gib lunged for it, but I could tell he was too slow, and I waited to hear the crash of the glass on the floor. But then he straightened up with a shocked look on his face, and the vase firmly in the palm of his hand.

My eyes widened. *Ursula*, I mentally growled. She'd obviously caught the vase with a bit of her essence, placing it in Gib's hand. She shouldn't do that, of course, because Gib was an unbound. Using magic around him—and in a public setting no less—was dangerous. It could expose us as mystics, and that was a risk that was greatly frowned upon by upper management at SPL.

I narrowed my eyes at her, but she ignored me and quickly got back to pretending nothing was amiss by picking up her menu. "What're you in the mood for today, Dovey? The bisque or something more substantial?"

My gaze darted back to Gib, who was still blinking with surprise at the vase in his hand, no doubt wondering how in the world he'd caught it when he'd so clearly been slower than it on its way to the floor.

Still, it was now obvious that Ursula's magical reflex to save the vase was involuntary, and she was trying to cover it by acting normally.

I decided to play along and opened my own menu. "The bisque for sure, but maybe a sandwich too. I went for a ten-mile run this morning, so I'm famished."

"I knew you were a runner," Gib said, setting down the vase. I was relieved to see that he seemed to have gotten over his initial shock. I didn't know what he was chalking it up to, but I hoped he'd simply forget about it and mentally move on.

"Do you run?" Ursula asked him.

"Three times a week. I get bored doing only one form of fitness, so I mix it up with some cross-training and martial arts."

My friend smiled slyly at him and did her toggling finger routine at him. "It's working for you. Keep it up."

I bit my lip to hide my own smile. Gib had a beautiful body, and I only knew just how beautiful his physique was beneath those clothes because there had been an afternoon when we were on an investigation together and he'd jumped into a pool to save someone, then later had taken me home with him to change into some dry clothes. I'd gotten a full view of his chest, shoulders, and arms, which looked like they'd been cut from marble.

Our server arrived again with our iced teas and a basket of bread. She departed once we'd given her our orders.

I was surprised that Ursula had only asked for a small shrimp appetizer when she usually went for the bistro's fish tacos.

"If you'll excuse me for a moment," Ursula said, placing her napkin beside me and scooting out of the seat. "I need to visit the ladies' room. Back in a jiff!"

I glared daggers at the back of her head for leaving me alone with Gib. I had no idea how to explain myself to him. With Ursula there, he was unlikely to ask for that explanation, but now that she was conveniently away from the table, all bets were off.

"How've you been, Dovey?" he asked.

"I've been well, Gib. And you?"

He toggled his hand back and forth. "So-so."

I didn't know what to say to that, so I pivoted. "Can you believe this weather?"

He gazed with smoldering eyes at me. "I love the rain. It helps bring out the roses."

The way he looked at me I knew he wasn't referring to the flowers so much as he was referring to my attire.

I felt like I couldn't breathe when he looked at me like that. "You know, I think I also need to visit the ladies' room. Would you excuse me a moment?"

Before he could even answer I was out of the booth and hurrying to the back of the restaurant, ducking quickly into the restroom and expecting to find Ursula there, but the ladies' room was empty.

And I hadn't passed Ursula on my way here.

Which meant . . .

"I. Will. *Kill*. Her!"

Dashing out of the powder room I wound my way through the tables, being careful to keep to the rear of our table so that Gib wouldn't see me running for the door, which I reached just in time to see Ursula getting into her car across the street.

"Oh no you don't," I muttered, stepping forward to the curb and away from any pedestrian's earshot. Lifting my open palm to my lips while focusing my gaze on Ursula's car, I softly sang:

> *"For auto bound for sacred ground,*
> *Take a pause to look around*
> *Spin the wheel and take a turn*
> *Around the block for lesson learned."*

While I sang, I'd poured some of my essence into my palm, and after I'd uttered the final phrase, I blew gently on that essence and watched the small orb of green energy drift right out into traffic, where it smacked into Ursula's windshield with a satisfying *splat!*

Ursula startled at the noise, her head whipping in my direction, and I made sure to smile and wave at her as she passed by me, struggling to straighten the wheel while the car slowed down and turned the corner.

Crossing my arms I waited for her to reappear again, which she did only a few moments later. Expecting her to pull over to park in the same spot again, I was unprepared to see her sitting in the seat, wearing a furious look, her own arms crossed as the car moved past the open parking space, then past me, only to turn at the corner again.

"Uh-oh," I whispered. I may have put a little more essence into that spell than it called for.

Glancing at my watch a bit nervously, I decided to head back inside to Gib and wait for Ursula to rejoin us.

She would, of course . . .

Eventually.

"Everything okay?" he asked as I slid into the booth. I realized our food had already arrived, but he hadn't started in on his lunch, which made me feel bad.

"Yes, sorry. Everything's fine. Ursula had to take a call from a client. She'll be back with us shortly."

Gib lifted his fork once he saw that I'd settled into the booth. "What does Ursula do?"

I blinked. I'd never been asked that by an unbound before, and I had no idea what Ursula told them when they asked. "She's a therapist."

Gib's brow rose in surprise. "A therapist? What's her specialty?"

I swirled the bisque with my spoon. "Love," I said simply. It was true, after all.

Gib beamed that beautiful smile at me, and I felt my resolve to keep him at arm's length melt away. "I can see that," he said. "She's definitely been helping me out lately."

It was my turn to look surprised. "Helping you out? How exactly?"

His gaze dropped to his salad, poking at the bowtie pasta for a moment. "It's been a tough couple of weeks, Dovey."

My heart began to race. Gib looked so sad. Was he truly *this* upset that I'd seemingly lost interest? Was he far more into me than I'd suspected? As much as I was secretly into him? I didn't think I could handle knowing that.

He poked some more at his salad when he explained, "Last week was the third anniversary of my wife's passing. For whatever reason, it hit me harder this year than last. I thought I was doing okay, you know? Handling it. But then I wasn't, and since I knew you didn't want to hear from me, I reached out to Ursula, and she's been great. She's a good listener."

My heart slowed down and with it came the heavy weight of guilt. The poor man had needed a shoulder to lean on and I'd been cruel to him with my silence and distance routine. I reached out and laid my hand on his arm. "I'm so, so sorry, Gib. I had no idea."

His gaze traveled to my hand and there was a softness that spread over his features. The harsh lines of sadness smoothed out simply from knowing I cared. That gutted me.

"Of course you didn't, Dovey. How could you?"

"I feel terrible," I whispered. "I shouldn't have ghosted you. I should've explained my—"

"You didn't need to. You never need to with me. I get it." With a shrug he added, "There's no denying we had some chemistry, and I took your silence to mean that you weren't interested in pursuing anything romantic with me."

Oh God, how wrong he was, but I couldn't tell him that. "Truth," I said as gently as I could, adding a nod. "And I'm so sorry for that too."

His gaze continued to linger on my hand, and I swore he struggled to form his expression into one of ease and nonchalance. Lifting his eyes to mine again, he said, "You will always have a friend in me, Dovey Van Dalen. Even when you don't need it. I'll always be here for you."

I could feel the porcelain-thin wall of my heart begin to break. Once again, my eyes misted, and I blinked furiously to keep control of my emotions. "I love that," I said honestly. "It means the world to me, Gib. But getting close to you again . . ."

He didn't say anything as my voice trailed off; he simply allowed the unspoken to linger.

With a sigh I finally added, "It's complicated and I'm simply not in a place where I can start a romantic relationship."

"Hey," he said when I dropped my own gaze. "Like I said, you don't owe me an explanation. Whatever your reasoning . . . literally *whatever* your reasoning, is okay with me. I'm just happy to see you. I didn't know Ursula had invited you, so this was a nice surprise."

I closed my eyes and tried to get ahold of myself. Leave it to Gib to continue to say the exact right thing. I adored this man. I barely knew him, but I knew enough to know he was a sensitive, emotionally available, thoughtful soul. How could I resist getting closer to him?

Could I even *be* friends with him without risking my heart and my head? It was hard to think around him. Or maybe that was simply the effect of his cologne. I knew he wore Gio for men—an absolute favorite of mine with its strong notes of bergamot, sage, and patchouli. It was a sexy scent on its own, but on Gib it was elevated to something downright intoxicating. It made me want to drink him.

"Your being here was a surprise for me too," I told him when the silence between us became a bit too noticeable. Opening my eyes I took my hand away from his arm and plastered a smile on my face, then lifted my spoon again to tuck into my soup. "So tell me, what else is going on in your life?"

"Well, I'm thinking about getting a dog."

That surprised me. "A dog?"

"Yeah. I've been volunteering down at the animal shelter the past couple of weekends. They need volunteers willing to give the dogs a field trip away from the shelter for a day, so I usually head there and take a couple of the energetic ones out for a good run in the park.

"And there's this one pup that's got the best personality. He's part Rottweiler, part pit bull, so it's easy to see why he's at the shelter. Big boy with big energy, but a total love bug once you get to know him."

"What's his name?"

Gib pulled a face. "He came in as a stray, no name, no chip, so they're calling him Big Roy, which I hate. It makes him sound like a criminal, so I call him Moose and he seems to like it."

"What's stopping you from taking him home?"

Gib sighed. "There're days when I'm at work for sixteen to eighteen straight hours. If I'm on surveillance, it's not like I can leave to go walk my dog. But Moose needs a home, and I want to give him one."

"What about doggy day care?"

Gib chuckled. "Way ahead of you. I've already checked out every doggy day care within the Greater D.C. area. They've all got a six-month to a year waiting list. Now I'm looking into a dog walker, but even those are hard to come by."

"Wow, I didn't realize there was such a demand for dog day care."

Gib shrugged, chewing on the bite of his salad for a moment before commenting, and as I sat there across from him, I felt an easing of the tightness in my chest that'd been with me since I'd made the decision to keep my distance from him. I missed him so much and I hadn't realized how lovely it was simply to be in his company.

Maybe I could do this. Maybe we *could* be just friends.

"Ever since everyone who got a dog during the pandemic went back to work, pet sitters and doggy day care facilities have been in high demand. The market is limited because the rent for a large enough space to let the dogs play all day is excessive, so those places that're already established are probably going to continue to be the only places available until commercial rents comes down—which isn't likely anytime soon."

"Makes sense." And then a thought occurred to me. One of my neighbors three doors down from me had a young son of about fourteen, and he was such a sweet kid. He was always out feeding squirrels, rescuing small birds, and such. I wondered if he might be available for a dog walk before and after school.

Gib didn't live very far from me—perhaps only a few Metrobus stops away. "I might know someone," I told him.

"A dog walker?"

I smiled. He looked *so* hopeful just then. It was easy to see how much he'd already bonded with Moose. "Potentially. Let me make an inquiry and I'll let you know."

"That'd be great, Dovey. Thank you. Moose already feels like he's my dog, I just need to make sure I can give him the home he deserves."

Gib and I spent the rest of lunch chatting like old friends. It felt so natural to be in his company. Was it smart for me to rekindle a friendship with him?

No. Definitely not.

But was that going to stop me?

It didn't look like it.

We parted ways when Gib received a call that had him excusing himself for some kind of urgent matter at the Bureau. He apologized profusely for leaving so abruptly before dropping enough cash on the table to more than take care of all our lunches. And then he was gone.

I had Ursula's shrimp appetizer boxed up and put in an order of fish tacos to go, waiting until the to-go order arrived before I too left the table.

Heading out of the restaurant I looked around for Ursula's

car but didn't see it. She'd likely figured out a counter-spell and had headed home, her mischief for the day concluded.

I walked to Luna and got in, trying not to overthink such a wonderful lunch with an adorable man.

With a wistful sigh I started the engine, finding comfort as Luna hummed to life, then pointed her toward Ursula's address. I wasn't angry with my bestie per se, but she definitely needed a lecture lest she pull this stunt on me again.

Plus, there were fish tacos to deliver.

CHAPTER 3

"I was wondering when you'd get here," she said, greeting me at her door.

Holding up the bag with her boxed lunch, I replied, "Did you have a nice drive around the block?"

She giggled and snatched the bag from my hand. "You scamp! It took me *eleven* counter-spells to shake the effect, and I'm *still* not convinced that the next time I start my car I won't head around the block in an endless circle of left turns."

I breezed past her into her cozy home and plopped down on the supersoft sofa. "Serves you right, you meddling mystic."

She waved her hand dismissively. "Oh pish. The two of you, moping around like Romeo and Juliet, when what the both of you want is to simply be in each other's company. You were starting to depress even me!"

I sighed, rubbing my temples. In Ursula's presence I could allow the full gravity of the risks at hand to show in my countenance without fear. "Elric will murder him if he ever learns how attracted I am to Gib."

Ursula sat down next to me, unpacking her lunch onto the coffee table. "And you know this because . . . ?"

"Are you kidding?"

"No. Are *you*?"

"You *know* Elric, Ursula. He's killed for a whole lot less."

"And it's precisely because I *do* know Elric that I think you're overreacting, Dovey."

"Overreacting?!" I blinked rapidly, not knowing if I was more insulted or shocked by her lack of concern.

Elric Ostergaard is my binder, my mentor, my sometimes lover, and my friend. What he is *not* is forgiving. I'd never given him a reason to need to forgive me, but living within his orbit for nearly two hundred years had taught me that you never cross the most powerful mystic in the world without repercussions. I didn't have any fear of him hurting me—I innately knew he wouldn't—but hurting or killing Gib wasn't something he'd even think twice about if he suspected Gib was a competitor for my affections.

"Dovey," Ursula said calmly, clearly ignoring my insulted incredulity. "I have known Elric Ostergaard since at least the eleventh century, but more importantly, I've known him differently than you. Despite the rumors—spread by that hateful wife of his—he and I were never lovers. And we've been closer to friends than anything else. From the beginning we understood each other in a way others couldn't. It's because of that special bond between us that I can say that over the past thousand years or so, but especially in the past two hundred, Elric Ostergaard, the most feared mystic to ever live, has softened." I opened my mouth to protest, but Ursula cut me off. "I'm not saying he's turned into a cuddly koala, but he *is* more rational in his reactions than I've ever known him to be. And where *you're* concerned, he may be downright reasonable."

"That's a big if, though, my friend."

She shrugged. "Perhaps. But what's your alternative? To spend the next seventy years moping about and regretting not getting closer to someone who *could* be the love of your life?

"Honey, if you're willing to take a chance, you just might be truly happy with a man devoted only to you for a change."

Ursula was referring to the fact that Elric had never been monogamous—a condition I'd grudgingly accepted after the first several decades with him.

I sighed heavily. "If Gib were the love of my life, then I wouldn't have decades. I'd have maybe ten to fifteen years before my eternal youth became too obvious to ignore."

"Then bind him."

I shook my head vehemently. "No. I can't. I *won't*."

Ursula held one fish taco up to her mouth and asked, "Why not?" before taking a bite.

"Because it's unfair. Binding an unbound in general is unfair, given the fact that they have no idea what's about to happen to them or how their life will change."

She chewed thoughtfully for a moment before she said, "Then explain it to him and leave it to him to choose."

I shook my head again. "How do you fully explain all the repercussions that come with being bound? As a newly bound mystic, Elric would want him under *his* control, which means Gib would be required to quit the Bureau. And his longevity would eventually mean that he'd have to say goodbye to friends and family—forever. He'd have to move and maybe he wouldn't even be allowed to stay in the same city."

"Remind me again how long you've lived in your little house in Georgetown, Dovey?"

I rolled my eyes. She had me there. Theoretically. "My particular neighborhood turns over every five to ten years. No one has lived in any of the houses on my street longer than that, so hiding the fact that I'm not aging from my neighbors is easy, while Gib has lifelong connections to D.C. His father was up the food chain at the CIA."

"I thought Gib's father was deceased?"

"He is. But that's not the point!"

Ursula chewed thoughtfully, irritatingly unmoved by all my bluff and fluster. "Please tell me what your specific point is then," she said.

"Come on, Ursula, you *have* to admit we don't associate or befriend the unbound *for a reason.*"

"As a rule, mystics don't invite the unbound's scrutiny, and Elric frowns on any such alliance with an unbound," she said, dabbing at her mouth with a napkin.

"You're sugarcoating it, and you know full well that he does more than frowns. He all but forbids it."

"But don't you see how you're the exception, Dovey? Your very employment requires you to mingle with them. Retrieving trinkets from the unbound is in your literal job description."

"Mingling in their world is one thing, making long-term friendships and taking on unbound lovers are completely different."

"How do you know?"

My brow furrowed. "What do you mean, how do I know?"

Ursula folded her napkin and set it back in her lap. "Have you and Elric discussed this at length? Has he laid out the specific rules for you?"

I blinked at her again for several seconds. "Well . . . no. It's more of an understanding between us."

"Ahhh, an *understanding.* I see. No chance of misunderstanding that understanding then, is there?" She bounced her brows to emphasize the sarcasm, and I rolled my eyes again.

"Ursula, you've known Elric longer than me—"

"By eight hundred years, but who's counting?"

"—so, you have to admit, his relationship with me is different than with any of his other . . . women."

"True," she said, with eyes that were so filled with sympathy that it made me want to cry. "Elric loves you, Dovey, there's no question about it, but to allow him governance over your heart for the rest of your life when he's not granting you the same in return is unfair. Even by mystic standards."

"And when have you *ever* known Elric to be 'fair'?" I argued, using air quotes to emphasize the notion.

"Often," she replied defiantly. "He's been fair with me, and others who've proved themselves loyal—which you have also been—without question these past hundred and eighty years. If you'd simply *talk* to him, Dovey, I think you might be surprised."

I weighed that for a bit, imagining how that sort of conversation might go, but each time I ran the scenario through my mind, in the end I kept concluding that he'd forbid me ever to see Gib again and if I disobeyed that direct order, he'd kill Gib outright.

"It's too risky, Ursula. Not knowing how he'll react to the news that I've developed feelings for someone else—an unbound of all people—is as bad as knowing for certain that he'll be furious and jealous enough to kill Gib."

"Dovey." Ursula sighed. "You don't give Elric enough credit. I'm not saying that he wouldn't be jealous—of course he would be—but Grant is unbound, and as long as you agree *not* to bind him, then Elric, who is well over a thousand years old, and has a completely different perspective on the passing of time than most mystics, could surely allow you a brief dalliance here and there. All he has to do is wait for Grant to grow old enough for the two of you to end your relationship, either by you leaving him once he starts questioning why you're not getting older, or through the natural course of things as Grant gets old and eventually dies a mortal's death.

"From Elric's perspective, it would be the equivalent of you having a two-week tryst, and I can't imagine he'd deny you that after nearly two hundred years of devotion to him and him alone."

I stared at my folded hands, resting in my lap. The idea of Grant growing old and dying while I remained young was almost as bad as the thought of permanently walking away from him now. Both left me feeling bereft and deeply saddened.

"Starting to change your mind about binding him?" Ursula asked.

"No," I said quickly. "I'm not going to change my mind about that. I will not become his binder."

I won't! I mentally repeated.

But then another thought occurred to me, and it sent a jolt of alarm up my spine. What if Gib was in danger again and the only way to save him was to cast a spell of protection around him? Would that bind him?

I'd never bound anyone before, so I wasn't certain about the specifics. "Ursula?"

"Hmm?"

"How *does* one bind a mortal?"

"It takes a potent spell, and your essence must be filled with the intent of the binding."

"What makes the spell potent?"

"How much of your essence you're willing to part with to cast it," she said simply. "A binding spell for you might lay you out flat for a week, while the same spell from Elric would hardly elicit a yawn, which is the difference between the arguably most powerful mystic in the world and a fairly newcomer like you."

"So I can't accidentally bind Gib simply by using a little magic on him, right?"

"Doubtful. Highly doubtful, in fact. You'll gain more power the older you get and the more magic you wield, but I doubt you'd find it an easy thing to bind an unbound within Grant's lifetime. You could certainly do it, but it would take a toll on you."

The inner knot of worry that'd sat firmly between my shoulders ever since recognizing my feelings for Gib lessened a fraction. I offered Ursula a grateful smile. "That helps. Thank you."

"Of course! Now, tell me about your lunch. Did you stay and share a meal? Or bolt for the hills while I was touring the block a dozen times?"

I sat and chatted with Ursula for the next hour, and by the end of our visit I felt more in control of my feelings and less sad overall. Perhaps it was her assurance that should Elric discover I had feelings for an unbound, he wouldn't react the way my worst fears imagined. Or perhaps it was the relief that came with knowing I wouldn't accidentally bind Gib simply by trying to protect him against some unforeseen mystical threat.

Or perhaps it was the lingering effects of sharing a meal with the man I'd been thinking nonstop about the past several weeks. A release valve had been triggered, and I thought perhaps Gib and I might stay on friendly terms for a while.

I could handle being Gib's friend.

At least I thought I could.

By the time I headed home, the rain had stopped and a muggy haze clung to the air. After pulling onto my street, I spotted Mateo Gutierrez walking home from school.

Mateo was the fourteen-year-old young man I'd thought of as a possible dog walker for Gib, so I stopped at the curb and rolled down my window. "Hi, Mateo!" I called.

He startled a bit but then he looked over, seeing me inside Luna, and a big smile spread across his lips. "Hi, Miss Van Dalen!"

He came quickly over to stand next to the car and admire her. "Want a ride?" I asked.

His eyes lit up but then his expression sobered. "I gotta ask my mom, if that's okay?"

"Of course!"

I waited patiently while he retrieved his phone from his

pocket and sent off a text. A moment later the door to Mateo's house opened and Mrs. Gutierrez looked out, then waved at us. "Not too fast!" she called. I waved back to her and offered a thumbs-up while Mateo excitedly opened the passenger side door and hopped in. "Oh man!" he said, running his hand along the leather trim of the interior. "This is sick!"

"Sick is good, right?"

He nodded, the grin never lessening. "Yeah. How fast does it go?"

"I've personally never had her over a hundred and forty, but top speed is around a hundred and sixty-ish."

Mateo's jaw dropped. "You went *a hundred and forty* miles an hour in this thing?"

I put Luna into gear and pulled away from the curb. "I did."

I didn't tell Mateo that I'd been chasing after an unbound trying to abscond with the trinket of a mystic within Elric's territory who'd stupidly left his doors unlocked, but Luna had had no problem reaching that speed in seconds, overtaking the unbound, and bringing his car to an abrupt stop when it hit a line of garbage cans to avoid hitting me.

"Sick!" Mateo repeated.

Making a series of turns, I guided us out to a stretch of road with light traffic, and, using a bit of magic, was able to give us a clear line of roadway without fear of other drivers cutting us off. I got Luna up to ninety-five in four seconds and Mateo practically squealed with delight.

He was never in any danger—my magic protected us both— but I didn't want him to tell his mother that I'd driven too fast for her own comfort. Slowing the car quickly and once again going the speed of traffic, I made another turn to wind us back toward Mateo's house when I asked, "Hey, kiddo, do you want a job?"

"A job?" he repeated, his attention more focused on the illuminated dashboard than my question.

"Yeah. It's a small one, but it'd be some money in your pocket each week."

At last, he tore his eyes away from the dash. "What kind of a job?"

"A friend of mine is thinking about adopting a dog from the shelter—"

"Aww! I love dogs! I want one but Mom's not a fan. She doesn't think I'm responsible enough, but I am. I could take care of a dog, no problem!"

I grinned. It was like it was meant to be. "Well, then this job might be the perfect way to prove to her that you're ready. Like I said, my friend is thinking about adopting a dog from the shelter, but he's hesitant because his job sometimes requires him to work long hours, and he wouldn't be able to walk the dog and give him some company as often as he'd like to."

Mateo swiveled in his seat. "I could walk his dog!"

I laughed. I genuinely liked Mateo. He was a thin, gangly teen, small for his age, but his personality was oversized in the best way. He had boundless enthusiasm and such a fun, outgoing personality. It was impossible not to adore him. "You might have to walk him more than once a day, and he might also need you to feed him on occasion."

"I could do that!"

I giggled again. I could tell Mateo that he'd have to carry the dog uphill, barefoot in a snowstorm, and I had no doubt he'd still jump at it. "I know you can, my friend. But before we seal the deal, how about you ask your mom if it's okay, and if she's cool with it, then I'll introduce you to my friend?"

"Awesome! And she doesn't even have to pay me, Miss Van Dalen. I'll do it for free!"

I reached out and ruffled Mateo's hair. "You'll do no such thing! If this works out and you end up working for him, then you will demand a hundred dollars a week."

Mateo gasped. "A *hundred?!*"

"Yes. One hundred. Twenty dollars a day, and not a penny less."

I didn't know how much dog walkers charged in D.C., but twenty dollars a day to walk Moose, feed him, and keep him company for a bit seemed reasonable to me. Plus, Mateo was likely saving for college, and Gib came from a wealthy family where he was the sole heir, so I knew it wasn't an amount he was likely to even blink at.

"That seems like too much, though," Mateo said, and I could see the worry on his face, like he was afraid that asking for that amount would price him out of the opportunity.

"It's a bit more than walking the pooch, Mateo. You'd have to spend a little time with Moose every day. Maybe give him a bone to chew on for enrichment under your supervision, or re-inforce his training, and cuddle with him just to make sure he doesn't get lonely."

"Can I do my homework over at your friend's house?"

"You'll have to ask, but I think that'll be perfectly okay. Like I said, my friend is currently on the fence about bringing this pup home. If the two of you meet and strike up a deal, then I can't see why he wouldn't give this stray a good home and hire you to make sure Moose gets all the love and attention he deserves."

"What kind of a dog is it?"

"My understanding is that it's a cross between a Rottweiler and a pit bull, but super friendly."

"I love pit bulls," Mateo insisted. "They're really misunderstood. Everybody thinks they're dangerous, but they're great dogs."

"Agree a thousand percent," I told him with a firm nod.

Back in the early part of the twentieth century, when I'd first come to America, practically everyone who had small children had a pit bull. They were once known as America's babysitter, and they were absolutely beloved. It was only in the second half of the century that they were bred and trained for dog fighting—as cruel and inhumane a "sport" as I could imagine—and the breed that'd once been adored and prized above all others was given the reputation of being ferocious and unpredictable. What no one in the modern world seemed to understand was that pitties were bred to please their owners, and if an owner asked a pittie to fight, then the dog would obey without question, both to protect that owner and preserve the bond.

Pulling Luna over to the curb, I pointed to a town house and said, "This is where my friend lives. Would you like to see if he's home?"

"Yeah!" Mateo said, hopping out of the car before I could even stop him. We headed up the walk and climbed the steps together with Mateo bouncing on his toes while I knocked on the door. After a few moments of silence, it didn't seem like Gib was home. As we were turning back toward Luna, however, a familiar Range Rover pulled up right behind her.

"Dovey?" Gib said, getting out of the vehicle. For a moment I swore he looked distraught, but as he took in my companion, he forced a smile and nodded at Mateo.

"Hi, Gib. I'm sorry to show up unannounced—"

"You can show up here anytime, Dovey. It's always okay."

I smiled and continued. "This is Mateo. He might be interested in walking and feeding Moose if you decide to bring the pup home."

Instantly, Gib's expression brightened, and when he stopped in front of us, he stuck out his hand. "Mateo, I'm Grant, but my friends call me Gib. Glad to meet you."

Mateo shook Gib's hand. "Sir," he said formally. "I'd like to walk your dog if you get one."

"Is it okay with your parents?" Gib asked next—to my approving smile.

"I have to ask my mom. My dad'll go along with anything my mom says yes to, though."

"She'll probably want to meet me first, huh?" Gib asked next.

Mateo blushed. "Yeah, probably."

Gib reached into his back pocket, pulled out his wallet, and took out a business card. "Give her that, Mateo, and have her call me. If we can reach an agreement, I'll sign the adoption papers for Moose and bring him home in the next couple of days."

Mateo stared at the card, his eyes widening to saucer size. "*FBI?!* You're an FBI agent? For real?"

Gib grinned and held up a palm. "Guilty as charged."

"Oh man! Mom definitely won't say no now! My dad's the Executive Assistant Chief of the Metro D.C.P.D."

"Oh yeah? We work with those guys all the time. It's a well-run police department. You gotta be proud of your dad."

Mateo beamed and the pair chatted for a bit while I stood by, delighting in bringing the two together. Mr. and Mrs. Gutierrez were in the middle of a divorce, and even though it seemed amicable between them, I knew that it was breaking Mateo's heart. He adored his dad, who'd moved out of the family home just a month earlier. I was hoping that caring for Moose would be emotionally beneficial for both Gib *and* Mateo.

At last Gib said, "As for a daily rate, Mateo, would twenty dollars a day work for you?"

It was my turn to look surprised. That was the exact figure I'd told the young man to ask for. Mateo looked like he'd just been told he'd won the lottery. "*Yeah!*" he shouted. Then he cleared his throat and added, "Sorry. I mean, yes, sir. That would be awesome!"

At last, I motioned toward Luna and said, "I should get Mateo home before his mom starts to worry."

The pair looked at each other like they were both reluctant to say goodbye, but then Gib stuck out his hand again and said, "Talk soon?"

Mateo took it, pumping it enthusiastically. "Definitely!"

The teen then bounded over to Luna and hopped in while I started to take my leave of Gib as well. To my surprise, the second Mateo's back was to us, Gib's face fell back into that troubled expression I'd first glimpsed when he'd gotten out of the Range Rover.

"Gib? Everything okay with you?"

He shook his head. "No," he said softly. Then he nodded toward Mateo, currently putting on his seat belt. "Could you swing back by after you drop him off? I could use a friend, Dovey. If you're comfortable with that."

I didn't know what was troubling Gib, but I knew that it was something serious and even possibly sad. "Of course. Give me half an hour to get him home and change into something less . . ."

I looked down at myself and before I could add more, Gib said, "Red?"

I smiled. "Yes."

"You look great in that color, by the way."

I dropped my gaze again shyly. "Thank you. Still, I'm itching to get into some jeans and a T-shirt."

His hand came up to rest on my shoulder. "I'll see you in thirty."

Back at Mateo's house, he barely paused long enough after getting out of Luna to exclaim, "Thanks! Bye!" Then he raced up the steps, beyond excited to tell his mom all about his prospective new after-school job.

I waved at his mom, who was peeking out the window, then headed home to change into a pair of faded boyfriend jeans, a loose-fitting tank top with a cartoon likeness of Iris Apfel, a distressed jean jacket, and kitten-heel, cream-colored suede booties. With a quick glance in the mirror, I decided that I looked and felt far more comfortable.

Gib answered my knock wearing the same joggers he'd worn to lunch, but now in a dark navy T-shirt that hugged his muscled chest like a second skin. He'd also lost the suede boots he'd been wearing earlier and greeted me barefooted.

It was almost unfair how sexy this man was.

"Ordered some takeout. You hungry?" he asked, holding the door open for me.

I actually was. The bisque and half sandwich I'd eaten at lunch had been delicious but that ten miles I ran earlier was ramping up my body's need for calories.

Plus, it's a fact that most mystics have very high metabolisms. I'm no exception. Setting aside the large umbrella I'd brought in with me, I said, "I am hungry. What'd you order?"

He led the way into his kitchen, pulling out a stool for me at the counter. I liked Gib's kitchen. It fit his personality. "Italian," he said, pointing to two bags by the fridge. "I ordered from this family-owned place a few blocks over—"

"Cenzo's?" I interrupted. It was a favorite spot of mine.

He looked over his shoulder from where he stood in front of the to-go bags, his expression curious. "Yeah. I eat there at least twice a month. I love the place."

"Me too." I was surprised I'd never seen him there, but then Gib had only recently come back to the area. "I love their sweet pea agnolotti."

Gib grinned and blindly dug into the bag while maintaining eye contact with me. "Ta-da!" he said, producing a covered container of pasta.

"Get out."

"I took a guess that you'd like it."

"What'd you get?"

He set aside the agnolotti and took out another container. "The tortiglioni rosa."

I laughed and shook my head. "That's my second favorite."

"Huh," he said, staring at me with a twinkle in his eye.

"Huh," I repeated. And then I remembered. I could be Gib's friend, but I had to hold myself back from falling for him.

He portioned out our meals onto plates and brought them to the counter, setting mine down along with a knife, fork, and spoon before walking back toward the fridge. "White wine, okay?"

"Perfect."

I waited to eat until he'd poured us each a glass and sat down next to me. We tucked into our food for a minute or two before I said, "What had you looking so sad earlier, my friend?"

He wiped his mouth, chewed on the bite of food he'd just taken, and stared up at the ceiling. After a moment he said, "We lost a guy today."

"An agent?"

He nodded. "Bruce McNally. Great man. Hell of an agent, too."

"What happened?"

Gib shrugged one shoulder and poked at his dinner. "I don't know. Whatever it was, it's bad."

"What does that mean?"

"There's been no briefing yet, so I'm only going on the details that've been leaked from the techs working the scene, but according to them, Bruce died at home sometime between when his wife went to bed and early this morning. He'd been beaten to death. Lots of trauma to the body."

I winced. "That's terrible."

Gib's expression was pained. "Yeah."

"Is the wife a suspect?"

Gib shook his head, but the gesture was slighter than I expected. "We haven't ruled her out, but I don't think any of us believe she had anything to do with it."

"Any idea who murdered him then?"

He shook his head. "None. And that's the part that's got me a little wigged out, Dovey. Bruce worked low-level investigations. He was an accountant before he joined the Bureau, so he was the guy who'd follow the money and flag any irregularities for the field agents to investigate. As far as I know, he wasn't working anything high profile. Just a couple of suspected backroom deals between a ten-year junior-level congressman and a natural gas company."

"Maybe he found something neither of them wanted discovered."

"Of course he did. Like I said, Bruce was a hell of a good auditor, but by the time an investigation even gets to Bruce, it's too late for the suspects to do anything about it. The whistle's already been blown, and if anyone's going to get axed, it's gonna be the whistleblower, not the forensic accountant."

"Okay, then I'm back to asking, what about his wife? Maybe their marriage was on the rocks, or he was abusive, and she didn't want to deal with a messy divorce, so she murdered him and made it look like someone else did it."

Gib frowned and I could tell he was fighting the notion that Mrs. McNally had anything to do with her husband's death. "Bruce was a gentle giant. He was six-foot-five, while Maryanne—his wife—is five-foot nothing and the sweetest woman. They met in college, and I'd never seen them together and not holding hands. There's no way their solid relationship was fake. They adored each other."

"Robbery gone wrong?" I tried next.

At that suggestion, Gib seemed to stare off into space with a haunted expression. "See, that's just it: I talked directly to one of the photo techs who worked the site. She showed me the crime scene pics and, Dovey . . . none of it fits."

"What doesn't fit?"

Gib poked some more at his food. "The photo showed Bruce sitting in an easy chair, like he'd just fallen asleep, except for the fact that he was black and blue from head to toe, but there were no defensive wounds on his arms, no blood other than a bloody nose, and no sign of . . . and I mean *no* sign of a struggle. The place was immaculate. Nothing was missing or appeared tossed around. It's as if Bruce had been incapacitated, beaten to death with something that didn't break the skin but caused a lot of internal damage, then propped up in the easy chair without leaving any physical trace evidence behind. No fingerprints, fibers, hair, or foreign skin cells were found on him, but it seemed like every bone in his body had been broken.

"And remember, he was six-foot-five, Dovey, in the neighborhood of two hundred and forty to two hundred and sixty pounds. You don't bludgeon to death a guy that size without crashing into things, breaking furniture, getting blood on the carpet, and you don't move a man that size easily, either, especially if he's deadweight. If he was murdered somewhere else and brought back to his home to prop up in the easy chair, it would've taken two or three men to get that job done, and the motive for moving him *back* into the house doesn't make sense, either. Even though this happened overnight, someone could've easily spotted a couple of guys hauling a giant of a man back into his home." Gib shook his head slowly back and forth. "It's otherworldly."

A chill went up my spine. Maybe it was the way he'd said that last part, or maybe it was how he was describing the crime scene, but the thought did occur to me that none of the details about the agent's murder would've been unusual if the murderer was a mystic.

Mystics rarely get their hands dirty, preferring to handle the murder of an unbound by using magic that wouldn't make a mess or cause a scene that could be investigated and produce any clues.

But a mystic murdering an FBI agent in Elric's territory was tantamount to suicide. If Elric knew that a mystic had targeted anyone in law enforcement, he'd unleash his death squad, and Elric's death squad had a sterling reputation and a perfect track record cleaning up messes made by some wayward mystic having misadventures in the unbounds' world.

"What happens now?" I asked Gib, trying to set aside my initial alarm at the description of poor Bruce's murder.

He blew out a breath. "The agents assigned will work the scene."

"I take it you're not assigned?"

"No. They've put two senior agents on it, and these guys are good. One works in organized crime and the other works in tech, monitoring the dark web for illicit activity. Between them they might be able to ferret out a motive and a suspect or two."

I breathed a sigh of relief. I didn't want Gib anywhere near Bruce's case. I simply had a generally bad feeling about it.

A crack of thunder outside let us both know that Mother Nature wasn't finished hurling a few storms at the D.C. area today.

Gib turned his head toward the window. "Have you ever seen a spring this wet?"

"No." And I'd seen at least a hundred springs in the D.C. area.

"It's gonna be like this the rest of the week too."

I frowned. "Joy."

We were silent for a moment or two, and it seemed to me that Gib was working up the nerve to say something that made him uncomfortable. It was the expression on his face in those moments that told me he had something else on his mind. I waited him out and at last he said, "Dovey, something happened today at lunch. Something weird that I keep replaying in my mind, but can't explain . . ."

Oh no, I thought. *He's going to bring up the tipped-over vase and Ursula's little display of magic.*

Another crack of lightning flashed across the sky and at the same time there was a loud explosion, and the lights went out. Both Gib and I jumped.

He squeezed my hand reassuringly, the conversation momentarily paused when he got up to head to the front window and peer out into the darkness. "I think lightning hit a transformer."

I stood up from my chair and began to walk toward him at the window, when I heard him gasp then run to the door, throw it open, and dash outside. Then I heard him yell something I couldn't understand, and I too rushed to the door.

Peering out from the top stair of his town house, I saw Gib running as fast as he could toward the murky shape of someone hovering close to a downed and sparking electrical wire. *"Gib!"* I screamed. But he didn't stop.

I launched myself off the top step, blinking furiously into the pelting downpour. I chased after him, mindless of the storm. Whoever was hovering near the arcing downed power line seemed oblivious to the danger, and they were close enough to get zapped by it at any second. *Move, you fool!* I mentally commanded, but I wasn't close enough yet to cast a spell or throw out some essence to save the idiot.

Another few yards and I came to a stop, I was now fifty feet from the downed line, and Gib was about to reach the spot where the person was standing. I was within spell-casting distance, so, raising my hand, I threw out my essence, sending it to the power line as fast as I could. I felt a connection and then used my hand as an extension of my casted energy, gripping the power line like the head of a writhing snake, holding it away from both Gib and the pedestrian.

I was so focused on keeping the arcing line away from them, that I didn't see what happened next, but another bolt of lightning lit up the street, and there was Gib, standing where the pedestrian had been, but he was now completely alone.

CHAPTER 4

"*Gib!*" I yelled, trying to get my voice to rise above the wind and rain.

For a moment it looked like he hadn't heard me, and I literally had my hands full with the arcing line, gripped within my essence, fighting me with the powerful current surging through it.

At last, he seemed to realize that he was in danger too, just standing there near the line. He moved swiftly to the right, away from the danger, but he didn't come back my way. He continued to move down the street for a bit.

Yet another flash of lightning lit up the sky, illuminating the street, but only Gib was there. The pedestrian—whoever they'd been—was gone.

And about then I had the prickliest sensation. It creeped up my spine and raised the hair on the back of my neck. I was being watched. I just *knew* it.

Looking around, I was worried someone would see me struggling with what might appear to an unbound like an imaginary snake and follow that line of sight down to where the arcing head of the wire line was suspended in midair while its tail writhed and jumped.

It wouldn't take much to put two and two together. And if

that person had a phone and was recording this . . . well, *that* was bound to be trouble.

But as I swiveled my head right and left, I didn't see anyone, nor did I get a feel for what direction the sense of being watched was coming from. The even bigger problem in front of me, however, was how to deal with this electrical line so that it wouldn't put anyone else at risk until the utility company workmen could get out here and turn off the power to the junction box.

I blinked toward the area near where the wire connected to the pole and saw a large tree limb that I might be able to use. Lifting my hand, I made a motion to throw the wire over the limb, and it worked, thank God. I then caught the head with my essence again and looped it through itself, tying it into a makeshift knot, taking care to let the buzzing end of the wire dangle away from the tree itself—lest it catch it on fire—but high enough off the ground that it wouldn't strike someone walking nearby. Once I felt the downed wire was secure, I pulled my essence back, and not a moment too soon because when I looked up, I saw Gib turn and begin to run back toward me.

He paused only momentarily when he looked over at the line—now secured to the tree, and I saw him do a double take.

"It jumped and hung itself over the tree limb," I told him when he drew near. He stared at me with wide eyes. He then moved forward and took up my hand, before hurrying back through the rain to his town house, leading the way inside, both of us soaked to the skin.

"Did you see that?" he asked me, panting for breath.

"I did. Crazy, right?" I shook my arms to get some of the water off me, but I only managed to make a mess on Gib's floor. "Oh, goodness, so sorry, Gib. I'm making a mess."

"Don't even worry about it." Pointing to the staircase in front of us, he said, "Head upstairs to the master bath. There're fresh towels next to the shower and a pair of sweats you can change into in my closet. I'm going to call the power company and report the downed line."

The house was quite dark, which I wouldn't have minded at all if I were by myself. I could create light with the snap of my fingers, but I didn't dare risk it with Gib nearby. Staring around the dark interior, I couldn't remember or make out where I'd set my purse, which had my phone—a source of light—in it.

"Hang on," Gib said, moving to a table near the love seat. Fishing around in the drawer, he came up with what looked like a matchbook, then he moved to the mantel above the fireplace and lit one of the candles there. Bringing it back to me, he handed it off. "There're some more candles upstairs in my room. You can light as many as you'd like." Into my other hand he placed the matchbook, and I smiled gratefully before I hurried up the steps. I was soaked through and beginning to catch a chill.

Once upstairs I held the candle up to eye level and whispered a small incantation to make the flame much brighter—a trick from the old days before electricity was in every home. I found Gib's room easily enough at the far end of the hallway and wasn't surprised at all to discover it so artfully decorated with one wall covered in different hues of planks of wood, neatly stacked from floor to ceiling, which doubly served as a kind of headboard. On the king-sized bed were soft gray coverlets and navy blue pillows and shams.

The bed itself was made—with the sheets tucked in and the pillows fluffed. I appreciated that aspect to him. He was neat and disciplined—much like me.

Moving into the master bath, I closed the door and snapped my fingers, fully illuminating the space.

Inside the bath, there was no tub, but there was a walk-in shower with sand-colored tiles and monogrammed towels. Gib also had an array of colognes to one side of the double sink's granite counter, and I picked through the collection until I found the one scent that I particularly loved, holding it close to my nose and taking a good whiff.

I closed my eyes to savor the scent, but that was perhaps the wrong move, because I couldn't inhale the smell of him without thinking thoughts that were best left *un*thought.

A shiver pulled me to my senses, reminding me that I was cold and wet. With another snap of my fingers, I added heat to the light I'd created in the bathroom, and within moments the worst of the chill had left me.

Gib's closet was right off the bathroom, so there was no need to open the door and risk him seeing the bright light and warmth I'd created by magic. Shrugging out of my sopping wet clothes, I left them momentarily in a puddle on the floor, then wrapped myself in a bath towel. Stepping forward to the nicely sized closet, which was also as neat as the rest of his space, where most of his clothes were organized by season rather than color. I ran my hand over the perfectly folded sweaters, long-sleeved shirts, and stack of jeans in every color.

Then I paused for a moment of appreciation when I took in his shoe collection, which rivaled my own. And, as thrilling as it was to be in Gib's closet, admiring all the things we had in common, right down to our love of a gorgeous pair of shoes, it was also a moment to be cautious because Gib and I seemed to have so much in common that it was readily apparent we could easily become a thing.

I didn't need more reasons to feel connected to him. I needed to find fewer; but he was making it damn hard.

To the left of the closet entrance were a series of cubbies that housed his workout clothes. Joggers and tank tops mixed in with the occasional zippered jacket. I selected a black pair of joggers off the top of the stack, then an oversized sweatshirt he'd left on a hook next to the door.

The sweatshirt had clearly seen better days, and the lettering on the front was so faded I had a hard time making it out, finally seeing the lettering for "Wa-Hoo-Wa You-Vee-Ay!"

I knew from having lived in the area for over a hundred years that Wahoo was a moniker given to the baseball team of UVA by Washington and Lee University's baseball team when the schools had had a fiery rivalry. The W&L players taunted the UVA players by calling them a bunch of Wahoos. Over the years, the nickname stuck and somewhere along the way the tune to "Ta-Ra-Ra Boom-De-Ay" had been coopted by the Wahoos for their own version of "Wa-Hoo-Wa You-Vee-Ay!"

I smirked as I looked down at the sweatshirt, remembering once getting caught up in a winning game celebration at Gert's Mystic Bar back in 1923 with a bunch of frat UVA boys, raucously singing that chorus at the top of their lungs. The whole bar had joined in. Even Gert! It'd been an exceptionally fun afternoon.

After padding back to the puddle of my clothes on Gib's floor, I did my best to squeeze them all out, then wrapped them in a towel and made my way out of the bathroom, purposely dimming the light from the candle and extinguishing the heat before opening the door.

It was still dark in the bedroom but there were two large windows on the long wall next to the bed, and I could see the wind and rain were still going full tilt. More lightning and loud, reverberating thunder indicated this was a sizable storm system, still raging after half an hour.

I walked over to the window to peek out at Gib's backyard, which, like every other backyard this side of the Potomac, was quite small, and I was surprised to find what looked like the figure of a person, standing at the thin tree line that separated Gib's townhome from his neighbor's backyard.

The figure appeared to be dressed in something dark with a hood drawn up, and the more I squinted at the stranger, the more goose pimples lined my arms.

There was an energy coming off the stranger . . . an energy that felt mystic to me.

I couldn't tell if the figure was male or female, and certainly nothing in the way of identifiable features, other than it was creepy to see a lone stranger, standing in the rain, seemingly impervious to the raging storm all around them.

Their clothing flapped in the wind, but the hood remained in place and their sight line pointed directly at the kitchen window.

"Gib?" I called, keeping my eye on the stranger while my heart raced with the emergent danger. "*Gib?!*"

There was a pounding on the stairs and a moment later from the doorway I heard, "What's the matter? What's happened? Dovey, are you okay?"

Meanwhile, I stared down at the stranger who remained fixed in position below us, continuing to stare toward Gib's kitchen window.

And then, they lifted their chin. I could tell because the shadows from the fold in the hood revealed the pale skin of the person wearing it, but I couldn't make out any discernible features.

"There's someone out there," I whispered, finally looking over my shoulder at him.

He rushed to my side and peered out. "Where?"

"They're right—" I stopped midsentence. The stranger was gone. I'd looked away for maybe a few seconds—not long enough for an unbound to completely vanish from sight.

Which meant it'd been a mystic. It had to have been.

And if it was a mystic, then it had to have been one of Elric's spies. Which meant he'd been following up on me. Which meant that Gib was likely in terrible danger.

"Well, they're not there now," Gib said, still peering out at his backyard. "Maybe it was one of the neighbors trying to get a good look at the downed wire without getting too close."

My heart was pounding. That mystic could be an assassin, here to rid Elric of the competition, and what better time to rid himself of an unbound rival than during a raging storm? Elric would no doubt want to make Gib suffer for daring to step on the toes of the most powerful mystic in the world, and no one would hear Gib scream above the noise of the tempest outside.

"I called Pepco," he said, indicating the electric company. He was already turning away from the window, like the matter of the stranger was settled and nothing to be alarmed about. "There're downed wires all over the place and the crews are doing their best in this storm, but it could be a while before a crew gets here to get the lights back on. The fire department is sending a truck, though. They'll put up a perimeter of caution tape to keep people away from the wire's radius."

"That's a relief," I said, thinking quickly. There was no way I could leave Gib alone tonight. The second I headed home, he'd be as good as dead, but staying here also imposed a risk, because if Elric had sent someone merely to spy on Gib and not kill him, then my car parked out front overnight would be a certain sign that Elric had a rival to contend with.

And then an idea came to mind, and I didn't pause to over-think it. "Our dinners are probably cold."

"Yeah. Sorry, Dovey. I don't have any way of heating them up right now."

"Maybe power's still on at my place. I have to get home to Bits—my hedgehog—anyway, Gib."

He nodded, and even in the dark I could tell his shoulders sagged. "I'll wrap yours up for you, but are you sure you want to drive in this mess right now, Dovey? Tree limbs are cracking under the strain of this wind."

I reached for his hand. "Would you come with me?"

He looked down at our hands. "You want me to drive you?"

"No. What I mean is, would you come stay over at my place for the night? If I have power, then we could reheat our dinners and have some more wine."

Gib hesitated, and immediately I knew he didn't understand all the mixed signals I was throwing at him.

"I have a lovely guest bedroom. You'd be quite comfortable there. And enough hot water for us both to warm up with after getting soaked."

His gaze lifted to mine again. "Guest room, eh?"

I nodded even though what I really wanted to do was tangle myself in his arms and claim him for the night like a long-lost lover. I wanted to trace my finger along his lips before tasting them to see if the hint of wine remained. I wanted to feel his heat warm me from the inside out, and wind my fingers through his hair. I wanted him pressed against me, his weight on top of me, and I wanted to feel his strength claim me for his own.

I wanted all those things. And so. Much. More.

I cleared my throat and avoided looking directly at him. "It's got a very comfortable queen bed and plenty of cozy blankets. You'd sleep well, and I'd feel better knowing you weren't here alone in the dark with your cold dinner and no company to share such a troubling day."

Gib continued to hesitate, and I couldn't see his expression clearly, here in the dim light of his room, but I knew he was likely trying to search mine for any hint of hope that I might change my mind and return his amorous feelings for me. But I couldn't. Especially now that I was convinced Elric had sent someone to either spy on me and/or murder Gib. I had to keep my emotional distance for Gib's own good. And perhaps even mine.

"It would be nice to get a hot shower in, and warm up dinner," he said at last.

I let go of the small breath I'd been holding. "Perfect. I'll drive us to my place then bring you back here tomorrow."

"I should follow you in my Rover, shouldn't I?" he questioned.

I shook my head. "I hate driving in storms. I'll be a nervous wreck all the way home. Please come with me in my car and talk to me until we get there?"

"I could drive us in my car," he said next. "The Range Rover would handle this weather better than your Porsche."

"And leave Luna parked outside, exposed to the elements? I think not!" I said, adding a laugh and hoping he didn't continue to argue the point.

To my relief he chuckled too. "Okay, okay, Dovey. You win. Let me change out of these wet clothes and grab some pajama bottoms and I'll meet you downstairs."

"Perfect!" I said, hurrying away before he could change his mind.

After descending the stairs rapidly, I made quick work of repacking our dinners, all the while glancing furtively out the window, searching for any hint of the mystic I'd seen in the backyard earlier, but I could neither see them nor sense them.

And yet, I doubted they'd gone far.

Before Gib had a chance to head downstairs, I rushed to the front door to retrieve my umbrella, then located my handbag, which I'd set on the kitchen table, finally darting back to the kitchen to hover out of sight while I quickly infused my umbrella with a cloaking spell.

By using the umbrella to shield us from the rain, I could activate the cloaking spell, and if anyone looked on while Gib and I exited his town house, they'd only see me. For good measure, I closed all the blinds downstairs, making sure no one could peer in and see that his home was either occupied or empty.

Moving back to the front door, I was just in time to find Gib descending the stairs dressed in a similar sweatshirt and joggers to the ones I'd borrowed from him.

"Look at that," he said with a smile as he hopped down from the last stair to point at himself. "We're twins."

I pushed a laugh out of my lungs, but the truth was I was in a bit of a panic. I wanted to get him out of this house and home safe to my place as soon as possible. I knew I could protect him from there. Elric's wife, Petra, had sent an assassin or two my way over the decades, and I'd had to learn how to ward my home against any nefarious intrusions. She hadn't been able to launch a successful attack at me in three decades.

And even if the power was also out at my place, we'd still be protected. Warding spells didn't require electricity, so if I could convince Gib to stay, regardless of the power situation, he'd be safe. At least for the night. Tomorrow was another story, but I'd face that potential threat then.

"Let's go, you Wahoo," I said, taking his elbow and leading him to the door.

In the open doorway I popped open the umbrella, holding it over the two of us for a moment while we surveyed the distance between his door and my car.

"You sure you don't want to take my Range Rover?"

I leaned against him, hoping the intimate move might soften his resistance. "I can't leave Luna exposed like this, Gib. I have a garage at home, and she belongs under cover."

He nodded and we began to descend the stairs together.

The rain was still coming down hard as the storm raged on, but at least the lightning seemed to be moving away from our location, headed northeast. We made it to Luna without incident, getting only a spattering of raindrops on our clothes, and I was careful to wait until Gib was tucked into the passenger side before hustling around to the driver's side door. Chivalrously, he'd almost resisted getting in first, but I'd been quick to toss my wet clothes into the back seat and hover next to him until he got in. No way could I risk the mystic catching sight of him out of the protection of the umbrella.

Once I closed the door, I touched Luna's hood with my finger, pushing the same cloaking energy into her metal frame. To anyone looking, the interior of my car wouldn't be visible.

I then hustled around the trunk and got in, starting up Luna's engine and pulling away from the curb. I was forced to inch my way down the street because the rain started up again in earnest and the water battering the windshield was making it nearly impossible to see.

The wind was also problematic. Even though Luna has a low profile, I still struggled to keep her centered in the right lane. The wind kept pushing her over toward the curb.

The irony was that if Gib hadn't been in the car, I would've invented a spell to clear the windshield and navigate us safely home. I couldn't risk conjuring one up with him in the car, however, so I had to drive like an unbound—my least favorite way to drive.

Gib tugged on his seat belt. "Good thing you don't live far away, eh?"

I nodded even though my longing heart felt the opposite. Living so close to Gib and having to keep him at arm's length had been torture these past few weeks.

Luna's wiper blades were beating frantically, and I swore the rain was growing even worse.

Gib craned his neck to look up and out of the side window. "This storm is so weird! I swear it's made a U-turn and it's heading back over us again."

I shivered slightly as a chill traveled up my spine. In my experience, there's no such thing as "weird." There's only magic making things "weird" for the unbound.

A mystic was out there, manipulating the storm, and I was powerless to do anything about it with Gib in the car. I didn't even have any trinkets handy to distract him or make him forget he saw anything unusual if I cast a spell against the storm. I'd left my trusty silver dollar—a trinket I'd used on his memory before—at home.

With every second the storm seemed to intensify. Even with my hands locked on it, the steering wheel still shook uncontrollably, and the wind created a sheet of water against the windshield that completely obscured the view of the road.

"I can't see a thing!" Gib shouted, raising his voice above the hurtling rain.

A flash of lightning so bright that I winced flashed across the windshield at the same time a crack of thunder exploded right next to us.

"Pull over!" Gib yelled.

But I knew that if I did, we'd be sitting ducks. Our only hope was to continue forward, and I prayed that I didn't hit anything while I relied on the literal one second I had between the wiper blades toggling furiously back and forth, to glimpse the road and continue forward.

And then another sound rippled into the car from my side. A sound like the creaking of falling timber. Gib grabbed the wheel with his hand and pulled hard to the right. *"Look out!"*

I reacted by stomping on the gas, and we skidded sideways as the crackling sound of a tree descended overhead. It hit the pavement an inch or two behind Luna's taillights, and I continued to press down on the gas as I fought to wrestle the wheel from Gib's hand. "Please let go!"

He did, and I straightened out the car, darting around a large tree branch right before another flash lit up the windshield and *BOOM!* An explosion of earth erupted next to us on Gib's side of the car.

"We've gotta get off this street!" he yelled.

I couldn't agree more. Desperate to use a little magic for our own safety, I said, "Gib, I need you to lower your window and tell me if I'm going to hit anything!"

He'd get soaked to the skin again, and Luna's interior would definitely get wet, but I didn't know how else to make him look away from me while I cast a protective spell around the car.

To my immense relief he didn't even hesitate. He simply rolled down the window and craned his neck slightly to look up and out of the opening.

Rain pelted both of us, and I had to blink furiously to keep my vision clear, but somehow, I managed to gather my essence and whisper a spell.

> *"Storm that rages all around,*
> *Yield the way to give us ground,*
> *Light the path for us to take,*
> *Keep us safe for goodness' sake!"*

"What?" Gib shouted, still leaning his head halfway out the window.

I blew out a long breath after reciting the incantation and watched as my green, opaque essence floated away from me and took shape, wrapping itself around the car. "Nothing! Just sending up a prayer!"

Almost immediately the rain pelting the windshield lessened and I was able to see the road. Lightning flashed in front of us, illuminating the asphalt, but there was no thunderous boom for several seconds and it was muted like the lightning strike itself was several miles away.

The wind was still a problem, but somehow I managed to weave and dodge debris and downed tree limbs, and within a few minutes I was turning into my driveway. The house was dark but there were other houses on the block that appeared to still have their power on.

I pulled Luna all the way forward right up to the garage and breathed a sigh of relief when I hit the button for the garage door opener and it began to lift. "I've got power," I said to

Gib, pulling Luna forward again quickly then hitting the button to close the door behind us.

"Finally, some good luck," he replied, rolling up the passenger side window once we were safely inside the garage.

I glanced over at him at the same time he turned his head toward me, and I had to clamp a hand over my mouth to keep from laughing. His entire head and chest were dripping, and his hair was so wind-whipped and wet that he looked hilarious.

Gib adopted a goofy grin. "I look bad, huh?"

I shook my head but kept my hand over my mouth. The struggle to keep from laughing was real. There was a mischievous twinkle in Gib's eyes right before he crossed them. I lost it, erupting in laughter. Gib started snickering while also keeping his eyes firmly crossed, which only made me laugh harder.

And within moments, all the tension and worry that I'd felt on the drive from his place to mine evaporated. I realized once again how much I relished being in his company and how much I'd missed him.

A switch flipped inside my mind in that moment, and as I watched him finally uncross his eyes and laugh while squeezing my arm, I decided I was going to find a way to keep him in my life. That would mean having a very difficult conversation with Elric, but I had to try.

After all, his life was already in danger if that had in fact been one of Elric's spies outside Gib's home tonight. A mystic was responsible for the intensity of the storm following us back to my place, of that I was certain. Who'd sent that mystic was currently a mystery. It could've been Elric, or it could've been his jealous, petty, spiteful, hateful, conceited, narcissistic wretch of a wife, Petra, but I'd worry about pinning that down—and a few more colorful adjectives for her—later.

For now, Gib was safe and that's all I cared about. "Come on," I told him, still chuckling. "Let's get inside and throw that sweatshirt in the dryer."

We got out of the car and moved over to the side door, peering out the window to eye the storm and the twenty feet between the garage and the back door. "You ready?" Gib asked, opening my umbrella while I took out my house key.

I wiggled it. "Ready, Freddy."

He held the umbrella up and we sprinted to the back door. The wind whipped the rain all around us, further dampening my legs and soaking my feet, but we were moments away from the inner sanctuary of my home, so I didn't mind.

Still, it wasn't lost on me that the storm's intensity hadn't died down since arriving home.

At last, I got the back door open, and we scooted inside. I flipped on the overhead light and illuminated Bits, standing upright on his hind legs in the center of the kitchen table with a cherry from the fruit bowl clamped between his front paws.

"Hey there, little guy," Gib said, spotting the picklepuss. Turning to me, he asked, "Did he get out of his cage?"

My eyes widened just before I put my hand up to block the cherry that was lobbed at Gib's head. It bounced harmlessly off my palm and hit the floor.

Gib turned his gaze sharply back to Bits, who'd adopted what could only be interpreted as an insulted pout while he glared at my guest.

"Bits has free run of the place," I explained.

Gib's eyes roved from Bits to the cherry on the floor then back to the hedgehog, his mouth slightly agape. "Did he . . . did he *throw* that cherry at me?"

I laughed lightly. "He throws his food all the time. Don't take it personally." As Gib continued to stand there and stare in astonishment at Bits, and Bits continued to sit there and glare at Gib, I tried to distract them both by picking up the cherry, tossing it back onto the table, then taking Gib by the arm and leading him toward the guest room off the back of the kitchen.

He came along without protest, but he did say, "If I didn't know better, I'd swear your hedgehog was glaring at me and threw that cherry at my head on purpose like he understood what I'd said."

I forced myself to laugh lightly again. "Can you imagine if that were really the case? I'd have a magic hedgehog." Stopping in the doorway of the guest room, I flipped on the light and waved my arm toward the interior. "Here we are!"

I'd decorated my guest room in tones of desert taupe, white linens, a mahogany headboard, and accents of blush peach. I'd changed the décor in here at least a dozen times in the past hundred years, always switching it up to reflect the current decorating trends, but this particular version was perhaps my favorite.

Gib nodded. "Nice, Dovey. You've got great style."

I felt a blush tinge my cheeks before I quickly changed the subject. Pointing back toward the laundry room, I said, "There's a full bath next to the laundry room. I added the shower to the half bath and stacked the washer and dryer three years ago, to make it more convenient to shower after a run—"

"A wise investment. Savvy and beautiful," he complimented, winking at me.

I smiled, feeling that familiar blush touch my cheeks. "Thank you. Anyway, there's a fresh towel and washcloth above the toilet, and you can throw your sweatshirt in the dryer right next door in the laundry room and dry it while you take your shower."

"Perfect," Gib said, shrugging out of his sweatshirt, only to expose his exquisitely sculpted torso, abs, and arms, and my breath caught. Meanwhile he wadded up the garment and said, "This thing is soaked."

Backing up a step to resist the urge to run my fingers along the curved, smooth lines of his shoulders, I cleared my throat and pointed to the kitchen. "I'll heat up our dinners and head upstairs to change out of this sweatshirt, so you'll have something to wear while your other one is drying."

A slow, sly smile overtook Gib's lips. "I'm comfortable like this. Unless you're not?"

I cleared my throat and felt my cheeks redden even more. "As long as you're comfortable, I'm comfortable. Now, let me go take care of Bits and get what's left of our dinners warmed up."

I hustled out of the guest room to the kitchen without looking back. Gathering Bits into my hands (his quills never puncture my skin), I took him over to the counter and set him onto a favorite pillow of his. "Behave," I whispered sternly.

He wrinkled his nose and eyed the to-go containers on the opposite counter where Gib had put them when we came in the door. I knew immediately that he'd require a bribe for the courtesy of playing nice.

I sighed. "Fine. Give me a minute or two."

Before tending to the warming of our meals, and while Gib was taking his shower, I took several minutes to walk the house from room to room to strengthen the wards protecting my home. It's an easy enough exercise for a mystic, which merely involves reciting the five protective spells that cast a kind of magical force field around my house.

The spells are quite powerful. Elric had created the words to the warding spells when I'd first moved in, and then he'd taught the series of spells to me, forcing me to practice them until he was certain that I could conjure them easily. They were strong enough to fully protect me and any guests in my home from any nefarious mystics who might want to cause me trouble. As long as all the windows and doors were closed and locked, the house was practically impenetrable to any threatening mystical magic.

Once I'd warded the house, I futzed around in the kitchen for the next couple of minutes, hearing Gib now in the laundry room and the dryer start. "I folded the clothes from your dryer, Dovey," he called. I went still as a statue, embarrassed to my toes. I almost never leave clothes in the dryer to wrinkle, but apparently, Gib had caught me in a moment of distraction.

"Thank you!" I called back, shaking my head at myself.

From behind me, Gib asked, "Should I put these upstairs?"

Peeking over my shoulder I saw him, looking even more gorgeous in the soft yellow light of the kitchen while holding a stack of my folded clothes. The thoughtful beautiful bastard.

"Um, just set them in the living room and I'll sort them out later." I pushed what I hoped was an easy smile to my lips . . . like I had not a care in the world that a half-naked, breathtakingly beautiful man was standing there almost too desirable to be real.

He grinned, which took that sexy to the next level, and I tore my gaze away to focus on the remaining few seconds before the microwave beeped. He moved off to the living room and I doled out a portion of my pasta for Bits, then plated both of our meals onto my favorite china and set the meals down at the counter.

Gib joined me as I was putting out utensils and napkins next to the plates. "Wine?" I asked him.

He pulled out a barstool and nodded. "Please, but just one glass. Tomorrow's gonna be a long workday."

I took out a bottle of white from the fridge and two short wineglasses from the cabinet, bringing all of it over to the counter. He got up and pulled out the barstool for me, then lifted the bottle from my hand and began to pour for us. "Since you cooked dinner, I'm doing the dishes," he said with a wink.

"It's two plates, Gib. I think I can handle it."

He wagged his finger. "You cooked. I clean up. Them's the rules."

I couldn't keep from smiling. He had such an easy and affable manner about him. I genuinely liked this man. Too much.

Lifting his fork, he tucked into his reheated dinner before motioning with his elbow toward the window, where the storm was still raging outside. "That was an adventure."

I nodded, eyeing the storm outside nervously. We were safe in here from anyone trying to enter, of that I was certain, but I didn't like the fact that a mystic had clearly been set loose to cause me some havoc. I could take care of myself, but Gib was vulnerable. Which reminded me of something. Motioning to Gib's bare wrist, I asked, "Where's your watch?"

He twisted the top of his wrist toward himself. "The one my dad gave me?"

"Yes."

"At home. I must've forgotten to put it on after changing out of the wet clothes."

I focused on the food, but my thoughts were clouded with worry all over again. The watch we were referring to was now a trinket. Weeks earlier, I'd brought the exquisite, luxurious but otherwise ordinary timepiece to a trinket repairman named Arlo.

Arlo wasn't what we referred to as a "merlin"—a mystic so powerful they are able to enchant an unlimited number of trinkets with numerous levels of power—but Arlo had some merlin talents. He seemed to land somewhere between ordinary mystic and a merlin, which is what made him an excellent trinket repairman.

For a hefty price, I'd had Arlo turn Gib's heirloom into a protective trinket that would be activated the moment Gib was dealt a death curse. I'd intended for the watch to protect him from Elric, even though Arlo and I knew that Elric could hardly be put off by a simple trinket. If he wanted Gib dead, Gib would be dead. It was that simple. Which again, made me glance toward the window because I realized that if Elric *had* wanted Gib dead and had sent an assassin to get the job done, Gib *would* be dead right now and not having his reheated dinner with me. My presence likely would've made little difference in a targeted strike, which was a curious thing to consider.

"Hey, Dovey," Gib said, waving at me. "You okay?"

I started slightly as Gib's question pulled me out of my troubled thoughts. "I'm fine. It's just the storm is still so strong. I'm worried we might lose power here too."

"I'm surprised *anyone* under the blast of this storm still has power, especially with the way it's taking down trees. The one that almost fell on us had to be thirty feet tall. We're lucky to be alive—whoa!" Gib jumped, and for a moment I thought he'd been struck, but then I looked at his left arm and saw Bits peeking out from a spot next to Gib's plate. "What the . . . ?" he said, staring down at my quilled little troublemaker.

"Oh you little minx!" I snapped, getting off my stool to walk around and pick Bits up, knowing that my hands were safe from Bits's quills, but Gib was quite vulnerable to their prickly spikes. "I'm so sorry, Gib. He finds a way to get into trouble every chance he gets."

"I thought he was over there on the table." For emphasis, Gib pointed to the fruit bowl in the center of the table.

"He finds a way to scramble his way all over the place. Which is why I don't keep him in a cage. He's a master escape artist."

Bits eyed me like wasn't *that* the truth.

I frowned down at him, then forced a light laugh, hoping Gib didn't focus too much on the improbability of a hedgehog clambering down from a kitchen table, traveling across the kitchen floor to then scramble up onto the kitchen counter when there were clearly no footholds for the little scamp to accomplish such a feat.

"Let me just take him upstairs and tuck him into his snuggle. It's *well* past his bedtime."

Bits made a chuffing noise of protest, but I offered him a stern look and waved at Gib to continue with his meal. Hurrying out of the room, I carried my picklepuss up the stairs, whispering my irritation at him. "He's an *unbound*, Bitty. You *have* to behave around him!"

Bits looked completely unfazed by my admonishments, offering me up a yawn just to prove that I wasn't the boss of him.

Turning into my bedroom, I left the switch to the lamp on the bedside table off because there was enough light coming in from the hallway, and I tucked the little monster into his snuggle. "Now stay there," I ordered as he curled into a ball. One black eye peeked out at me along with part of his nose, waiting for me to leave. "No teleporting. Do you hear?" I whispered.

Bits's pink nose wriggled slightly before he tucked that away as well and I was left staring at the part of him that made up his butt. "You little scamp!" I giggled, tickling a few of his quills just to show him I wasn't really mad. "Now stay put."

I stood tall after tucking him in, but instead of leaving the room I headed to the window to peer out at the storm. Pulling the drape partially aside, my breath caught when I realized there was someone standing at the foot of my walkway dressed in a long cloak with a hood.

I knew immediately that it was the same mysterious soul who'd been standing outside Gib's house, and now I was one hundred percent certain that the stranger was a mystic. No unbound could've followed behind us all the way here. *We'd* barely made it.

As a chill took hold of my insides, I began to gather some of my essence, ready to do battle. Whoever was standing outside my house was a threat, and I'd defend my home and my guest to the bitter end if need be.

As I stood there preparing for battle, the hooded figure began to lift their head, like they could feel that I was up on the second floor, staring at them through the window.

I hadn't made a sound, and the room was too dark for them to see me at the window, and yet the face within the folds of the hood lifted until I knew they were staring right up at me, and in their hand something round glinted when a bolt of lightning flashed across the sky.

As much as I tried to see the menacing stranger in detail, the storm was raging too much for me to see anything clearly, and I was just about to head to my stash of trinkets in the closet downstairs when I felt a vibration of energy hit me so hard that I flew off my feet and began sailing through the air.

In the next moment, the world went dark.

CHAPTER 5

"Dovey," Gib said softly. "Dovey, can you hear me?"

My eyelids fluttered with the effort to open them.

"Dovey," Gib said again, more urgently this time. "Hey, come on, girl. Wake up. You're scaring me."

I tried again to open my eyes, but my lids felt like lead. And so did the rest of me. Whatever spell had hit me had packed a serious punch.

And then Gib's hand stroked my cheek and I could feel the warmth of his skin while I lay in his arms. He was close enough to kiss, and that sent my heart racing, helping to further clear the cobwebs and that leaden feeling. I finally managed to open my eyes.

"Hey there," he said, worry etched into the creases near his eyes, but there was also the flash of relief when I stared up at him, fully conscious now.

"Hi," I managed. My jaw felt tight, and my mouth was dry. I wondered how long I'd been out. "What . . . what happened?"

I knew exactly what'd happened, but I wanted to see what Gib thought had happened to me before I offered some kind of plausible excuse for him discovering me unconscious.

He helped to prop me up against him and wrapped his arms around me protectively. "I think you fainted."

I put a hand to my head. A throbbing headache was beginning to form, and I suspected it'd only get worse before it got better.

I've been hit with a lot of spells in my lifetime. You don't live two hundred years and not experience a few doozies, but this one . . . this one had knocked me out flat, and I hadn't even seen it coming. Whoever had cast it was one hell of a powerful mystic, that's for sure. That spell had cut through my wards like a knife through butter, and I was convinced that the only reason I was still alive was because I'd taken a moment to strengthen those wards while Gib was in the shower.

"I fainted?" I repeated, playing coy. It wouldn't do for him to suspect the real reason I'd been knocked on my keester.

"You say you ran ten miles this morning, right?" he asked in turn.

I nodded.

"I think you're dehydrated. Sit tight. I'll bring you some lemon-honey-salted water. It'll put those electrolytes back into your system."

Gib gently set me next to the bed and hustled back downstairs. I stood quickly and edged toward the window, gathering my essence in a ball of energy, ready to hurl it at any suspicious character who might still be hovering outside.

Peeking out of the corner of the window, however, I didn't see anyone. Whoever had come to zap me out of existence had disappeared, likely thinking the deed was done. One thing remained certain, however; if that mystic had cut through my wards so easily and zapped me into an unconscious state, he or she could just as easily kill Gib.

On tiptoe, I hurried to the landing next to the stairs, where there was a large half-circular window that would give me a clear view of the backyard. No mystic assassin stood there, either.

For now, the threat seemed to have moved on.

Hearing Gib's footsteps from the kitchen as he headed back in my direction, I hustled to my spot against the bed like I was still struggling to remain conscious when he appeared in the doorway and moved to my side. "Do you think you need a doctor?"

I took a long sip of the water, which was a perfectly balanced mixture of tangy, sweet, and salty. It was soothing and really helped with the dryness in my mouth. "No. I'm okay, Gib. Thank you. I think you're right. I'm simply dehydrated."

He was squinting with worry, and I could tell he was trying to decide whether to insist on a trip to the ER or to take my word for it that I was okay.

I laid a hand on his arm and smiled. "I promise. I'm fine."

"Feel like eating anything?"

My head was really starting to throb now, and I didn't want to do anything but try to sleep it off. "Not really."

"How else can I help?"

I couldn't let Gib out of my sight for the rest of the night. There were too many windows in this house, and the guest room faced the driveway, so he'd be an easy target downstairs while I still felt relatively safe up here if I kept out of sight.

Motioning over my shoulder, I said, "Help me onto the bed and stay with me for a while. We can watch an old movie or something."

It was Gib's turn to grin. "Or something."

I rolled my eyes but gave in to a chuckle. "You're a scoundrel."

"When I'm around you, my lesser angels take hold. Here, wrap your arm around my neck . . ."

I did as he instructed and in one fell swoop the man had me lifted into his arms as easily as if he'd picked up a pillow. Being cradled by him wasn't something I was quite prepared for, and

I could feel the heat creep up my neck and bloom onto my cheeks.

If he noticed his effect on me, he didn't let on; instead he moved around the bed and gently set me down. For a second or two his lips were mere inches away from mine and in that moment, I lost myself to his nearness, his warmth, his utterly intoxicating masculinity. My fingertips rose to his bottom lip and traced the smooth curve of them. They were the softest thing I'd ever touched. I heard his breath catch, and when I met his eyes, they were dark pools of desire, boring into mine.

How did I ever think I could resist him tonight? Or any night. Or . . . ever? The man was an addiction, and being this close to him only intensified the need.

The inches between our lips began to close. I tilted my head slightly in anticipation. I wanted to taste him. I wanted to feel his weight against me. I wanted to run my fingers along the planes and delicious curves of his back and shoulders. I wanted his arms to wrap around me, and I wanted him in a way that I didn't think I'd ever wanted Elric.

And for many, many years I had *wanted* Elric.

My lids began to close while the heat of his breath caressed my lips a moment before they would no doubt devour my own . . . and I wanted it to happen. I'd never desired anything more than I desired this moment, this tension, this build to an eventual release . . .

"Yeow!" Gib shouted, his body immediately rigid and lifting away from mine.

My palms smacked the bedcovers, alarm coursing through me. It was the mystic. Somehow they'd gotten into the house!

Gib shot back across the room, his arms raised, and pain etched onto his features. He grabbed at something behind him but immediately hissed again in pain and his palm came away bleeding. I raced toward him, a ball of essence gathered in my palm, ready to hurtle it toward whatever mystic had made it inside.

But then Gib twisted slightly, and I saw Bits holding on to Gib's shoulder, his quills pressing into the poor man's skin. "Dovey," he groaned through clenched teeth. "Can you get him off me, please?"

"Oh my God, *Bits!* Get off! Get off!" I commanded, holding out my palms so the little guy could easily detach himself into safe hands.

But the next thing I knew, Bits had disappeared from Gib's shoulder, only to reappear wrapped around his leg, those quills once again digging into Gib's skin.

Gib made a noise that is hard to describe—a sort of high-pitched yowl—and I knew my beloved little companion was doing this on purpose. Elric, after all, had been the one to gift Bits to me, so my picklepuss's loyalty was showing.

Still, I genuinely had to hand it to Gib. He didn't bat, hit, or punt Bits off himself, he merely held very, very still, hissing air between his teeth, waiting for me to pick the prickly pear off his leg.

I scooped Bits up as fast as I could and carried him back over to his snuggle. Setting him down I looked the little monster sternly in the eye and whispered, "One more move like that and I *will* lock you in the closet for the night!"

And I could too, with the right spell to prevent him from teleporting.

Bits made a chuffing noise, pawed at his snuggle, curled himself into a ball, and eyed me meanly from the one beady eye that stared out through his quills.

Turning quickly back to Gib, I hurried over to grab his hand and escort him into the master bath. "Here," I said, putting his palm under cool running water. The quills had dug in deep—on purpose, no doubt.

"Wow," Gib said as he watched the water turn pink. "I didn't realize his quills were so sharp. He's more porcupine than hedgehog."

I grimaced. "How's your leg?"

Gib looked down and I did too, only to see a few red dots appear on his pajamas. "He got me good."

"Oh God . . . I'm so sorry!" I didn't know what to do or say. Bits had never reacted to any guest like that. Then again, I'd never entertained a guest whom I was romantically interested in besides Elric.

"It's okay, Dovey. He's obviously protective of you. I can't blame him for that."

I stared into Gib's soft gray—nearly silver—eyes and felt my heart melt yet again. Damn him. He should be angry, or at least irritated with my naughty picklepuss; instead he seemed to hold no grudge, even admitting a kind of fondness for the creature.

"Oh trust me, I can still blame him," I said quietly. "He's definitely getting fewer treats from me tomorrow."

Gib laughed. "Listen, I heal up quick. It's no big deal." For emphasis he pulled his hand out of the water and used a tissue to mop it dry, then showed me his palm, and sure enough it had stopped bleeding. Only a few small red, swollen dots remained.

My brow furrowed. Gib *did* heal up quickly for an unbound. One of the trademarks of mystics is our ability to heal quickly from a wound, no matter how severe. In fact, a mortal wound for an unbound wasn't necessarily a mortal wound for a mystic. Of course we liked to speed up the process of healing by using a healing trinket. An injured mystic was a vulnerable mystic. I didn't have much in the way of healing trinkets here at the house. They're rare and expensive, and Elric had always given me access to any of the healing trinkets within his trinket vault, so I'd never felt the need to collect them.

I pulled Gib's palm toward me to inspect it again and run my fingers over the tender spots, just to make sure nothing looked too deep. "I'm sorry I don't have any antibacterial ointment on hand."

For good reason too. I had no need of the stuff. Mystics don't catch infections or suffer from disease.

"It's fine, Dovey. I promise," he said, closing his hand around mine. "Now, how about you head to bed, and I'll go downstairs, clean up the dishes, then turn in myself, eh?"

The thought of Gib downstairs near any of the windows sent my heart back to racing. Just because the mystic who'd zapped me earlier had gone from view didn't mean they'd gone away. They could be lurking nearby, simply waiting for the opportunity to send another strike through my wards.

"Leave the dishes," I told him, unwilling to release his hand. "I'll get them tomorrow. Stay with me up here for a while."

Gib arched a skeptical eyebrow as he shifted on his feet to look around me toward the bedroom, where I knew Bits was curled into a ball but still on guard duty. "You wouldn't happen to have any body armor handy, would you?"

I laughed. "We can put a pillow between us so that Bits won't think he needs to protect me."

Gib nodded. "Deal."

He and I propped ourselves up on pillows and watched *Six Days, Seven Nights*—a favorite of mine—and before the end of the movie, Gib's eyes had closed, and his breathing had deepened.

When I was certain he was asleep, I grabbed my phone and crept downstairs to the closet next to the staircase in the living room.

This was where I stashed my trinkets. The door wasn't simply warded, it was locked tight by a door handle and hinges that were themselves trinkets. Only my touch and a short incantation by me could open the door.

Once it was open, I left it ajar so that I could listen for any hint that Gib had woken up and was looking for me. Not hearing anything, I walked deeper into the trinket closet, using my phone for light—my headache made magically drumming up some light seem daunting—and then gazed at my neatly stacked trove of treasures with satisfaction.

I supposed that seeing the rows of small cubbies that held various sized and shaped boxes would bring the same kind of satisfaction and reassurance that an unbound would have if they kept bundles of cash and jewels in a secret vault within their home. Trinkets are both treasure and currency in my world, and having a cache close at hand always makes me feel safe and reassured.

Beginning my search through the boxes housed in the cubbies, I was on a quest for both a weapon and a specific trinket—a magnifying glass that Elric had given me sixty or seventy years earlier. I hadn't thought to use it in ages, and its power was only a level five, but essentially, when looking through the magnifying glass, I'd be able to spot the approximate location of a mystic, gathering their magic, ready to wield.

Going to a section of the cubby where I kept my weapons, I found a good option with a set of small push daggers from the early fifteenth century, specifically from the Aztecan rule of Itzcoatl. Designed to be used in hand-to-hand combat, under their enchantment, they were also quite suitable—even preferable— for throwing. In fact, during one particularly turbulent time between Petra and Elric, I'd once hit one of her assassins in both his right and left shoulders from a hundred yards away. The daggers were enchanted not only to hit their mark, they were also designed to seal themselves into an assailant's skin and bone, making them excruciating to extract, thus helping to deter further attack.

"Good times." I smirked as I spun the daggers expertly with my fingers, remembering their heft and the way their handle so perfectly fit my palm. I hadn't used them in at least fifty years, but they seemed like the best option at hand for the moment.

Tucking them into the pockets of Gib's joggers, I continued my quest for the magnifying glass.

A mystic's essence had to be quite powerful to be seen by the magnifying glass, and the trinket couldn't see through even the most basic of cloaking spells, but the mystic who'd attacked me so boldly while standing out in the middle of a raging storm hadn't tried to hide their presence at all. I was hoping the magnifying glass might be able to spot them if they'd changed course and were now hiding somewhere nearby.

If I could locate the mystic, I might be able to go on offense with the daggers and thwart any further attack. I didn't necessarily want to tangle further with this obvious enemy, but if the assassin mystic were still waiting for an opportunity to kill me, Gib, or both of us, I wouldn't hesitate to use lethal force in return if necessary.

Pointing the beam of my phone's flash to the corner where I thought I'd stored the magnifying glass, I pulled forward a box only to reveal a second box behind it, wrapped in a red ribbon.

Immediately, the hurtful memory of Valentine's Day came to mind. Just three months earlier I had taken great pains to spend a romantic evening with Elric, preparing a special meal for us, buying myself a gorgeous negligee, and adorning the whole house with rose petals and soft lighting. At the last minute, Elric had sent a messenger to my door, alerting me that he was canceling the evening as he had an urgent matter to attend to.

The low-level minion at my door had then awkwardly handed me the small box, wrapped in ribbons, and said, "From Elric," before he turned and hustled away.

The insensitivity of Elric's handling of the evening and my own crushed expectations had felt like a slap to the face.

Angrily, I'd gone back inside and immediately shoved the gift box into the back of the cubby, not at all curious about its contents, lest whatever token trinket he'd selected for me prove further disappointing.

Taking out the box now from the back of its cubby I set it to the side while I opened the first box, seeing the magnifying glass there and exhaling in relief. Then, with a glance over my shoulder toward the stairs, I listened for a moment, and after not hearing Gib up and about I decided to risk it by closing the closet door and pulling the cord to the overhead light to illuminate the space. I then sat down akimbo and stared at the ribbon wound around the Valentine's offering, which held the box closed.

With a sigh I tugged on the bow and the ribbon fluttered to my lap. Removing the lid, I found a blank note card and an adorable set of salt and pepper shakers.

The inside of the top of the box was marked with the logo for L'Objet—a company that specializes in whimsical accents for the home.

The shakers were glass, encased by fourteen-karat golden filigree of grapevines. When I took one of the shakers out, I realized it had a nice heft to it. Each shaker fit neatly in the palm of my hand, and they were exactly the sort of thing a mystic would make into a trinket.

Our kind simply love turning everyday objects into enchanted treasures.

The shaker I held had two small holes at the top, while the other had three. In Europe, the two-holed shaker is traditionally for salt, while in America, the two-holed shaker is typically for pepper. Americans love their sodium, after all. I tended to lean toward the American preference. I liked salt too.

Setting the shaker back inside the box, I sighed. "Dammit," I whispered. I loved them, as I loved almost all things from L'Objet, and I hadn't thanked Elric for the gift because I'd never opened it. I'd been too hurt by his last-minute canceling of our special night together.

It was far too late to thank him now—I couldn't very well reveal that I'd tossed his gift into the back of my trinket trove without even opening it. Gushing over them now would make me look a bit desperate, and I didn't want to add that on top of angling to keep an unbound FBI agent around as my . . . "friend."

Still, the trinkets might hold some magic that could help me thwart the current threat to my life and possibly Gib's, so I ran my finger around the rim of the pepper shaker, seeking that familiar buzz that all trinkets give off. Most unbounds aren't sensitive enough to pick up on it, but a mystic knows.

The thing is, though, there was no buzz coming from the shakers. Not even a little. With a furrowed brow I lifted the shaker to eye level and pushed some of my essence into it to see if I could awaken it.

My essence met cold metal. There was no "catch," as we like to call it—a term for the moment when our magical essence takes hold of the power locked within a trinket and we're able to harness the magic within.

Setting down the pepper shaker, I picked up the saltshaker and had the identical experience, as in . . . nothing. "Wow," I whispered. Elric hadn't even bothered to have the shakers infused with magic. He knew plenty of merlins—one or two were even on his payroll—so it shouldn't have been much trouble to give me *something* magical on Valentine's Day.

But he hadn't. These were just regular salt and pepper shakers, and although they were quite lovely—had I not been bound and a mystic, I'd have loved them—the hurt of that night just a few months earlier was still fresh and raw, and the petty side of me scowled anew at the added insult to injury. Every gift Elric had ever given me had been enchanted. In the 180 years I'd known him, he'd never given me a simple "thing." Even Bits was enchanted, so discovering that what I'd thought was a trinket wasn't really a trinket . . . well, it just stung.

Irritated, I stood and put the shakers back in the box then placed the lid on top. I even rewrapped the box with the bow, then shoved it back in its cubby, where it belonged. Bending to pick up the box with the magnifying glass in it, my eye landed on the blank note card on the floor. I lifted it up and studied it, seeing that it was embossed with Elric's initials and the crest he'd created for himself a thousand plus years before.

"You couldn't have even written a *Love, Elric?*" I grumbled.

With a scowl I turned off the light, exited the closet, and closed the door. Standing still for a contemplative moment, I tapped the blank note card against the magnifying glass's box a few times, while I tried to tamp down my hurt feelings, but it was no use. I'd need a friend to help me put it all into perspective, which is why I mentally planned to stop by Ursula's in the next day or so to show her Elric's Valentine's Day gift. I'd never told her that Elric hadn't shown up that night, so I'd have to come clean, but I needed her wise and guiding friendship to commiserate with over this added slight. I didn't like to think of myself as so ridiculously petty, but my feelings were my feelings and the whole thing bothered me deeply.

Shaking my head I tried to regain my focus—there were currently far more important matters at hand, and I'd best get to the mission that brought me to my trinket closet in the first place.

I set the blank note card inside my purse, intending to show Ursula later, then opened the box with the magical magnifying glass and held it up to eye level.

Pushing some essence into it, I felt the catch as my energy connected with the enchantment within. The clear glass of the lens fogged for just a few seconds but then cleared. It was ready for use. I moved the magnifying glass around the perimeter of my house also making sure to peek through blinds and drapes, staying out of view as I went.

The glass worked through walls, but only for a few yards, whereas it worked for much farther if I looked through it out a window.

I was waiting to see if a spot of warm yellow light appeared, indicating that magic was afoot. But the lens remained clear except for the spot where I'd seen the mystic right before they zapped me. That still held a bright glow of residual magic, indicating that the mystic was powerful indeed.

As I was moving the magnifying glass along the kitchen, I heard something clatter onto the roof. With a gasp, I lifted the trinket toward the ceiling, immediately noticing a warm dot of magic appear in the direction of my bedroom.

I sucked in another breath and raced to the stairs. The glow had been faint, but I'd seen it, so I dashed up to the second floor where, in the doorway of the master bedroom, stood Gib, palming my snow globe like he was prepared to use it as a weapon.

In a strained whisper he said, "Did you hear that?"

I nodded, glad I'd tucked the magnifying glass into the palm of my own hand as I'd ascended the stairs. "Yes. I was downstairs getting a glass of water." I felt a need to explain where I'd been when he was jolted awake.

He motioned to the roof. "Could be the storm."

We both looked up toward the ceiling and listened for a long moment in silence. I could feel the tension rippling through me. If the mystic had somehow gotten onto the roof, and was about to attack, I'd have to use my daggers, which would quite likely completely freak Gib out, but what choice did I have?

Fortunately, no sound other than the wind and the rain came to our ears, and just as I was about to release a sigh of relief, Gib said, "I should go check it out, Dovey."

I stepped forward to him. "No."

His brow furrowed in confusion, and he opened his mouth to reply when I gripped his arm and said, "It's too windy. If a branch fell on the roof, what's to say another won't fall on you?"

"I'll be okay," he insisted. "If your home has been damaged, then I should take a look."

"In. The. Morning." I refused to let go of his arm and stared hard into his eyes, willing him to listen. "Please, Gib? Don't go out there."

His shoulders relaxed and he smirked at me. "Fine. You win." He handed me the snow globe and I let go of him to accept it. "Don't know what I was gonna do with that." He chuckled. "I left my gun at home."

It was my turn to smirk. Lifting his hand in a motion that made his arm flex, I tapped his bicep and said, "No, you didn't. Your gun's right there."

He grinned, clearly pleased I was fawning over his physique.

"And you even brought a spare," I added, tapping his other bicep.

He laughed then wove both of those guns around me, pulling me close. I melted into him, and we stood like that for a long moment. I didn't ever want to let go.

"I missed you so damn much, you know," he said gruffly.

I inhaled the scent of him, closing my eyes. The man was intoxicating. "I do know."

He stroked the back of my head and kissed my forehead. I didn't dare lift my chin, because I knew we'd end up in bed together. This time without our clothes or the pillow divider.

Gib seemed to sense my reluctance to throw caution to the wind, and he backed away a step to take up my hand. Then he turned and led me back to the bedroom, only letting go of my hand when we stood at my side of the bed. "We should get some sleep," he said, turning away to round the bed to the other side of the pillow barrier.

I nodded, not trusting myself to speak, and got into bed. Not a word was spoken between us for the rest of the night.

I woke the next morning to the gray, bleak-looking sky. I love an occasional rainstorm—especially in the summer—but this spring had been ridiculously wet, and this current weather system was predicted to drop five to eight inches of rain on us over the course of the next three days.

It was depressing.

As I came more awake, I realized my hand was holding on to Gib's, partially hidden by the pillow barrier between us. I lifted my head slowly and came face-to-face with Gib's gorgeous silver-gray eyes.

"Mornin'," he said through a smirk.

I couldn't help smiling in return. "Morning."

"You talk in your sleep."

A jolt of alarm scurried up my spine. I didn't remember dreaming and I could only hope I didn't whisper a spell or something too noticeable. "Do I?"

He nodded. "Who's Eric?"

I had to focus hard on not allowing my eyes to widen. I knew I must've spoken Elric's name and Gib had interpreted it without the *l.*

"My boss." A half-truth was better than a complete lie, right?

"Is he mean to you?"

I sat up and stared at Gib curiously. "No. Never to me."

"Huh. Well, in your dream you were begging him to stop."

My heart pounded, but I plastered a placid look on my face. "Stop? I wonder what that was about."

Gib sat up as well to stretch and yawn. "Don't know. Not

my dream. But you seemed a little frantic about it. Kinda made me want to meet this Eric and tell him to back off."

I laughed, mostly because it was such a ridiculous notion . . . an unbound telling Elric to do *anything* was actually hilarious to think about.

Until it wasn't.

Elric wouldn't take kindly to someone like Gib showing him any form of disrespect. I had to pray that the two never, ever, *ever* met. "He's harmless," I lied. "I've worked for him for ages." At least that was the truth. "I wouldn't work for anyone else, in fact." Also true.

"Yeah, well—" Abruptly, Gib's phone rang from the side of the bed where he'd slept. Distracted, he twisted to search for it, finally finding it on the third ring. Pausing to look at the caller ID before he put the phone to his ear, he said, "Good morning, sir."

The way Gib had sat straighter right before answering the call told me that it was likely *his* boss on the phone. I was about to give him some privacy by heading downstairs to cook us both some eggs when I saw Gib's complexion pale and his eyes go wide. "Fell?" he said incredulously. "H-*how*, sir?"

I didn't know who fell or what that meant, only that it was something terrible given the look of shock on Gib's face. "Yes, sir. Text me the address. See you in twenty."

He hung up the phone and stared off into space for a long moment. I couldn't take the suspense. "Gib? Who fell?"

His gaze darted to me. "No one."

My brow furrowed and I was about to ask a follow-up question when Gib explained, "The call was about John Fell. My ASAC."

"Assistant Special Agent in Charge, correct?"

"Yeah," Gib said, that haunted, faraway look still in his eyes. "He's dead."

It was my turn to look incredulous. "*Another* agent at your Bureau has died?"

Gib nodded, his stare far away. In a haunted whisper he added, "He was murdered exactly like Bruce. John's husband found him, propped up on a barstool, laid out over the kitchen counter, bruised from head to toe and a mess of broken bones. No sign of forced entry, and no indications of a struggle."

I shuddered, even more convinced that a mystic was responsible for the deaths of these two men. But why? Why were these agents being targeted?

Gib pivoted and stood up from the bed to look around his feet like he expected his clothes to be there. When he realized he'd come upstairs wearing only his pajama bottoms, he said, "Dovey, I have to go. Like now. Can you drive me back to my place?"

I hurried out of bed too. I was still in Gib's joggers and his sweatshirt, and for a moment I didn't know if I should shrug out of them and change or simply get my keys. He made the decision for me by heading to the doorway toward the stairs, his legs moving rapidly.

Abandoning the thought of changing, I simply followed.

Passing through the kitchen I noticed the clock on the wall read five forty-five, which meant I'd gotten only a few hours of sleep the night before. I should've felt tired, but the adrenaline coursing through my veins was better than a strong cup of coffee.

Gib wasted no time hurrying to the laundry room to retrieve his sweatshirt and joggers. Not bothering to change other than to throw on his sweatshirt and shove his feet into his running shoes, he moved to the door and pulled it open.

Outside there was a steady drizzle, which made Gib pause only long enough to grab the umbrella from where he'd set it just inside the door and hand it to me. He didn't even wait for me to spring it open; he simply darted out into the rain on his way to the garage. The mounting sense of urgency quickening his movements sent me rushing to catch up with him after locking the door.

In short order we were pulling out of the garage, and it was then that I took note of all the damage the wind and water had done.

Broken and battered flora littered the entire area. From behind the wheel, I wove my way around the debris-littered streets until we came to the tree that'd nearly crashed down onto Luna's roof. It lay across the full width of the road, making it impassable.

For a moment I didn't know what route to take, but Gib solved that problem by opening his passenger-side door, saying, "We're close enough, Dovey, thanks. I can run to my house from here. Get yourself back home safely. I'll call you later."

With that, he jumped out of the car, shut the door and ran off, leaping the tree like a track star.

I watched him for a long minute, my windshield wipers steadily knocking back and forth, wishing I could go with him so I could see for myself what deadly mystic mischief might be afoot. Away from my side, Gib was vulnerable, and that worried me deeply.

On the short drive back to my house, I couldn't help but think about the details he'd given me regarding Agent McNally's death—specifically how it'd looked like the man had been beaten to death, yet he'd been found sitting in a chair in his living room with nothing else in the room disturbed while his wife was upstairs, none the wiser. And, from the brief description he'd given me about Agent Fell's death, it appeared the same method had been used.

I tried to think of a way for an unbound to commit a murder like that, and I couldn't imagine a method of murder committed by an unbound that would result in the catastrophic injuries of each man coupled with the neatness of the crime scenes at both agents' homes.

But a mystic could do something like that. Not easily, but it could certainly be done with the right trinket or the right spell . . .

By the time I made it back to my house, I'd made up my mind to investigate the circumstances of Agent Bruce Mc-Nally's death. I had to try to find out not only if my suspicion of a mystic murderer was correct, but *who* was killing these agents.

I didn't dare go near Gib's ASAC's crime scene—at least not yet. There'd be too many eyes there right now, and my five-foot-eight-inch-tall frame didn't exactly blend in with a crowd. And while I had a trinket or two that could allow me to go unnoticed to most observers, I couldn't risk Gib seeing through the enchantment and spotting me snooping around.

Once inside my kitchen again, I popped a bagel into the toaster, waited for it to toast, then lathered it with cream cheese and headed with my breakfast upstairs to shower and change before committing to some reconnaissance.

I didn't know where McNally lived, but I was betting I could find out. An FBI agent dying mysteriously was newsworthy. There'd be something online about it.

Bits came out of his snuggle long enough to sniff at my bagel, but he didn't try to steal a bite, opting to get a little more shut-eye. I couldn't blame him for being tired—it'd been an eventful night.

By eight a.m. I was back inside Luna and headed across town, weaving my way through both the aftermath of the ferocious storm, as well as the poor, wet-soaked work crews assigned to clear the roads.

My online search had revealed that Agent McNally had lived in Hyattsville, Maryland, just over the border from D.C.

He was survived by his wife of thirty-one years, Maryanne, and their three daughters, Jenny, Patricia, and Stephanie.

I suspected that, when I arrived, the whole family would be gathered, and I didn't quite know what my approach would be, but I'm pretty good on the fly so I wasn't overly worried about it.

I'd dressed in shades of charcoal and pinned my hair back while wearing little makeup and clear lip gloss. I didn't want to be especially memorable, and hoped the subdued look would give me a pass.

In my purse, I carried a few trinkets to help with that, but it could get tricky the more people were gathered at the murdered agent's home.

I arrived in the McNally neighborhood around eight thirty, and to my surprise, when I pulled up to the address listed for the family, there were only two cars in the driveway. "Maybe they've gathered someplace else," I mused. Which would make sense. Bruce had died in the home, after all, and it would be perfectly understandable if the last place his family wanted to be was at his murder scene.

And I had no doubt the living room where his body was discovered was *the* murder scene. By now I was somewhat convinced that a mystic had entered the McNally home and assassinated the agent while he sat in his chair. The who and why were questions I needed to answer.

Parking at the curb, I approached the front walkway, surprised when the door opened and out stepped a woman in her late fifties to early sixties. She was lugging a large black garbage bag, filled to the brim and obviously heavy the way she was struggling with it. I hurried to her aid.

"Can I help?" I asked, stepping up to her.

She startled slightly and looked up at me in surprise. "Yes," she said, breathlessly. "Yes, please."

I didn't make a point of studying her face, because that would've been rude, but the glimpse I got hardly showed a woman in mourning. Her eyes were clear, there were no tearstains on her cheeks, her hair was combed, and her attire was neat.

I hauled the garbage to the curb next to the mailbox and before letting go of it I looked over my shoulder to make sure that's where the woman wanted it. She nodded and for the first time I saw the strain on her face when she attempted a smile. "Thank you," she said.

I moved back over to her. "You're welcome. I heard about the tragedy that happened here yesterday. I'm so sorry."

Her hands came together, and she twisted the simple, gold wedding band on her left ring finger. "Thank you," she said softly. "Are you one of our new neighbors?"

For emphasis she motioned with her chin toward a duplex at the far end of the block. I looked there too before turning back to nod my head. "Yes, actually. We just moved in." Sticking out my hand, I added, "Sorry, I'm Debra Cox."

"Hi, Debra. I'm Maryanne McNally." We shook hands and then Maryanne made a wide, sweeping motion with her hand. "It's a nice neighborhood . . ." Her voice trailed off as if she'd just caught herself saying something ridiculous. "Other than what happened here, that is."

I put a hand on her shoulder. "Again, my sincerest condolences."

"Thank you," she said simply but added a heavy sigh. I had a feeling she wanted to talk to someone about what'd happened, but there didn't seem to be anyone at home other than herself.

"Are you here alone?" I asked.

She nodded. "I have three daughters. They all live on the West Coast. They'll be here later tonight. Yesterday's storm made air travel impossible."

"Ahhhh," I said knowingly. "Yes, that was a wicked mess, wasn't it?"

She let go of her ring to rub her hands on her thighs. "I should get back to work."

She motioned over her shoulder toward the door, and I smiled and made like I was about to let her get back to it when I pretended to think twice about it. "You know, we just lost my dad not long ago, and I remember my mom trying to be so brave for us kids. She went on a cleaning spree before immediately going on a cooking spree, taking care of the rest of the family while we were all in the throes of grief. It didn't occur to me until later that none of us had offered Mom some strength and support immediately following my dad's passing." I paused for a moment, looking meaningfully at Maryanne, and I saw her placid façade crumble and tears welled in her eyes. "That's the long way of asking, Maryanne, would you like to get a cup of coffee with me? I've been told I'm a good listener and I'd love to hear a little more about your husband."

She swallowed hard and cast her gaze downward, wringing her hands again. "Actually," she said in a watery whisper, "that would be really nice, Debra."

When her gaze lifted again, I smiled, relieved I hadn't had to use magical means to get her to agree to a talk. I pointed to my car just down from her house and said, "I parked at the curb last night. Too many cars in the new driveway."

"Ooo," she said, her brow lifting in surprise. "I've never ridden in a Porsche before."

I took up a conspiratorial tone. "Your first time is always the best."

"Let me just get my purse," she said. She darted inside for a moment then came out and we headed toward Luna. I told her all about how I'd named the car after the moon, and how much joy it'd brought me to be able to purchase her on my birthday.

"What birthday are you up to?" she asked when we were underway.

"Thirty-three," I said easily. I could pass for thirty-three, even though I hadn't seen that age in a hundred and sixty-seven years.

A bit later, we arrived at an interesting little coffee shop named Vigilante Coffee that looked like it'd been converted from an autobody repair shop. Luckily, there was no smell of oil or car fluid when we went inside. In fact, the fresh baked pastries and ground coffee filled the air with a welcoming and delicious fragrance.

Once at the register, I insisted on picking up the tab, which provoked Maryanne to order a small black coffee, and I wanted to hug this woman who was clearly so generous and thoughtful that she struggled to accept generosity in turn.

After she'd ordered, I then ordered two honey lavender lattes with extra foam and two honey-and-pistachio-cream-filled, flakey pastries, warmed up.

She blushed when we sat down, and I pushed one of my lattes toward her. "I've always wanted to try one of these," she said.

I took a sip of mine before sighing contentedly. "Heaven."

We talked about the abysmal weather until our pastries arrived, and I had to hand it to this coffee shop—their pastries were spectacular.

The unexpected excursion was having an effect on Maryanne. The tense line in her shoulders began to relax and the furrow between her brow was less pronounced.

"So tell me about your husband," I said, speaking gently. For someone who'd just lost her husband, the woman seemed remarkably held together, but I suspected that was because her daughters were soon to arrive, and she was putting on a brave front, refusing to give into the grief until she was sure they were okay.

"Bruce," she began with a sad sigh. "He was a good man. But he worked too much. He should've retired ten years ago, but he always said he couldn't think how he'd fill his days if he didn't have a job to go to."

"Not someone to take up golf in his golden years, eh?"

She shook her head. "He hated golf, and he refused to join my pickleball league. Bruce was an introvert, content to sit in front of his laptop and work while life passed him by."

"That must've been hard on you."

She shrugged. "Early on in our marriage, Debra, I realized I'd married a workaholic. I also knew that I loved him more than he loved me."

I winced. In the 180 years Elric and I had spent together, that was a truth I had also borne.

Maryanne took another sip of her latte before continuing. "I always wished for my husband to find something that could offer him a little joy and had hoped that our daughters would bring him a more balanced focus, but he never seemed to take to domestic life. I knew he loved me and the girls; he was sweet about displays of affection with all of us, but it always seemed to take effort. Like he had to remind himself to hold my hand or give his family a hug and a kiss now and again."

"Was that hard on your marriage? Or on you?"

She shook her head. "No. Not really. I knew who he was, what he was capable of, and I accepted that. I took what he could give and was grateful. Still, there were times when I wondered if Bruce might've been more content if he'd never married or had children. He simply lived and breathed work, work, and more work."

"What did Bruce do?"

Of course I knew, but I was curious to see if she'd tell me.

"He worked for the FBI," she said, looking me in the eye like she held a bit of resentment for the Bureau.

I feigned surprise. "He was an agent?"

She nodded. "For forty-two years. He was recruited right out of MIT, which is where I met him."

That surprised me, although it shouldn't have. "You went to MIT?"

"Yes. I had a long career as a software engineer and retired eight years ago. Unlike my husband, I couldn't wait to quit working. We'd needed two incomes to raise our daughters, putting them through private school and then supporting them all through college, but the second my youngest graduated with her master's in engineering, I was out."

"Your family sounds quite impressive, Maryanne."

Her chest lifted with pride. "All my girls are academically accomplished. My two oldest each have their doctorates, and my youngest may go back for her PhD at some point too."

"Losing their father so suddenly must've been a blow."

Maryanne's face fell and there was something that crept into her eyes that looked like fear. Genuine chilling fear. "They're expecting an explanation," she said softly.

I didn't reply. Sometimes, I find it's best to simply wait for the finished thought.

The technique worked. "My husband was murdered," she said, her voice quavering and unsteady.

I again feigned surprise. "*Murdered?* Oh, Maryanne, that's awful. What happened?"

To my further surprise, she reached out and clutched my hand, looking at me with imploring eyes. "You can't tell a soul, Debra."

"I won't."

"I'm only telling you because you live in the neighborhood, and I want you to be safe."

"Of course. I won't tell a soul."

I probably wouldn't keep that promise, but she'd never know it. "What happened?"

Maryanne inhaled a deep breath. "Two nights ago, I went up to bed at my usual time—nine thirty. Bruce was still at work in his office; at least, that's what I thought when I headed to bed. I wear hearing aids—my father was deaf as a doorknob—so I sleep like the dead while they charge overnight. I never once heard anything that seemed suspicious or like there was an intruder in the house—"

"*Was* there an intruder in the house?" I interrupted.

Maryanne cast her gaze at the tabletop, her eyes wide and unblinking. "I . . . I don't know. But there *must* have been. When I came downstairs the next morning, Bruce was slouched sideways in his favorite chair, and it was . . . it was like he was one giant bruise. He was literally purple. From head to toe."

I put a hand to my mouth, which again was more for dramatic effect than my genuine reaction. "Oh my God, Maryanne. That's terrible!"

Her gaze lifted to mine, and I could see how haunted and terrified she was. "The thing of it is, there was no sign other than Bruce's body that there'd been any kind of a struggle. And"—she paused to swallow hard while her eyes once again filled with tears—"when . . . when they took his body away, I overheard the medical examiner tell the Bureau director that he'd never seen anything like it. The M.E. said that he suspected that every bone in Bruce's body had been broken, and he'd died from massive trauma, but it hadn't been quick. It'd taken time. He'd likely felt almost every break." Maryanne gave in to a shudder, and tears leaked down her cheeks before she added, "He must've screamed, Debra, but I never heard him, and Bruce screaming *would've* been something that should've woken me up, even without my hearing aids."

A chill rippled along my skin. It was the two details together about Bruce not uttering any cries of pain and every bone in Bruce's body being broken that brought to mind a terrible and haunting memory.

Elric had taken great pains in our 180 years together to shield me from the violence that often came with his position. To survive well over a thousand years, and climb to the heights of power, he'd had to be ruthless both to his enemies and to those who betrayed him.

It was a side of him that I had relegated to a necessity. He had no choice but to thwart violence with even greater violence, but I'd never believed Elric a sadist. I'd always considered him a pragmatist.

And I'd understood that about him from the very beginning when I was nearly kidnapped by pirates that'd raided our vessel on our way from Amsterdam to London. That incident had occurred when I was a newly minted mystic of only a few months.

The pirates had been successful in killing some of the crew, but with Elric on board, they never stood a chance.

Once captured, the captain of the pirating band had been tied to the mast and forced to watch as Elric had personally dispatched his crew, one by one over three long, terrible days. He'd done it by coaxing the men to sit on a stool, without bindings or shackles, settling them into a false sense of security as he promised to negotiate their release if they cooperated. To a man they all sat down, and the moment they did, Elric cast his enchantment—a spell that proceeded to break every bone in their unbound body. In my mind I could still hear the snapping sounds of their bones breaking, one by one by one, while the unfortunate men sat completely frozen, unable to move, speak, or scream.

But their eyes had told the story of their pain. Their eyes, and the bloody tears leaking out of them, had let me know just how excruciating a death they had endured. Later, I would learn that the last bone Elric broke in the bodies of his enemies was the axis vertebrae—also known as the hangman's fracture.

He kept the men alive right up until that moment, working his way slowly up from their toes.

The spell he'd cast on them was known as the Crushing Curse, and I would also later learn that it took someone of *significant* power to wield it even once without the aid of a trinket. The fact that Elric had used it against twenty-three men over the course of three days was beyond extraordinary—even for one of the Seven—a collective of the most powerful mystics in the world, including his wife, Petra.

On that trip across the high seas, Elric had spared only one member of the pirate gang—the second-in-command. Instead of dispatching him, he'd forced him to watch the captain's death, then he'd bound the pirate with a spell, turning the man—Leonardo Vegete—into a mystic who, by the tenants of the binding, was loyal only to Elric.

Elric had then turned Leonardo into a diplomat, dispatching him to the courts of the other five most powerful mystics. (Elric and his wife, Petra, share a court, making six courts in total, but seven mystics—known collectively as "the Seven"— that rule over all mystics and territories in the world.)

Wherever Leonardo traveled both at home in the Court of Dobromila-Ostergaard or abroad to the other courts, the new mystic had repeatedly told the tale of Elric's execution of the pirates using the Crushing Curse. It was a story Elric encouraged Leonardo to spread far and wide, and one which helped to cement Elric's legend.

Not even Petra could've done what her husband did on that vessel, something he was sure to lord over her whenever she irritated him with her quest for dominance within their shared court.

As I sat in the coffee shop, listening to the details of Bruce's murder, I couldn't argue the fact that everything she was telling me certainly fit with the Crushing Curse, but I also couldn't fathom a scenario where Elric would want to kill an unbound with it. Wielding such a powerful spell required skill, and power, no matter who the victim was, and to my knowledge Elric only cast it when he wanted to make a very clear point, one that no doubt would've been lost to a bureau of unbounds. And yet, Bruce, a pencil pusher for the FBI of forty years, had been murdered by it or something very similar. Why?

And if Elric hadn't been the assasin, then who was powerful enough to wield that particular spell? It would've taxed Petra and stirred trouble for her with the unbound—something she was even more loathe to invite than Elric.

So if not either of them, then who?

"I'm sorry," Maryanne said, shaking me out of my troubled thoughts. "I didn't mean to scare you, Debra."

I forced a smile. Patting her hand, I said, "Please don't worry over it, Maryanne. I appreciate you telling me. Do you think your husband's murder had anything to do with him being an FBI agent?"

She wiped at a tear that had escaped down her cheek. "I don't think there's any doubt. I'm lucky, though, that no one suspected me. Bruce is . . . *was* a big man—six-five and two hundred and fifty pounds. I'm five-one and a hundred and fifteen pounds. No one thinks I could've done that to him, which is a relief because I'm struggling to handle the memory of seeing my husband like that. Being dragged into an interrogation by the FBI would be my undoing."

"And you said there was no sign of a struggle?" I wanted to be sure. Absolutely sure about the scene to rule, out an unbound as the murderer.

"None. It was like he was beamed up in a spaceship, murdered so violently that he was almost unrecognizable, then beamed back into his lounge chair without anyone disturbing a thing. All of our doors were still locked and there was no sign of a broken window anywhere in the house. Plus, we have one of those wireless doorbell cameras and an alarm on all the doors and windows. No one tripped the alarm or showed up on camera."

"Have you been staying at the house since this happened?"

Maryanne shook her head. "I'm staying at a hotel until the girls arrive and we figure out what to do. The only thing I know for sure is that I'm never sleeping in that house again. In fact, the only reason I was there today is because I'm trying to clean it up a bit for the Realtor that's coming by tomorrow morning. I'm going to put the house up for sale. I can't live there. Not after what happened."

"I understand," I said, and I did. I felt so sad for this poor woman. I didn't think the trauma of finding her husband murdered in her living room had quite caught up to her yet, but I had no doubt it would sometime soon. "Your daughters are on their way, though, right?"

"Yes. My oldest two daughters live in Southern California and the third lives in Oregon. They're all flying to San Francisco first to take the flight to D.C. together. I'm picking them up at Dulles at seven o'clock tonight, and we'll all stay in the hotel until the funeral on Saturday."

I reached out to lightly touch Maryanne's arm. "Can I simply say that you're handling this so very well, and I'm quite impressed with how composed you seem."

She gave a one-shouldered shrug. "What choice do I have? I've got to keep it together for the girls. I can fall apart later. For now, I just have to get through the next few days."

I motioned to our empty plates and cups. "Can I get you anything else before I take you back home, Maryanne?"

"No. Thank you. And thank you for listening. I don't have any family besides my girls, and this isn't something I want to talk about with my friends at pickleball. I appreciate bending your ear, Debra."

I stood up and held my hand out to her. I wanted to tell her that everything was going to be okay, to reassure her that nothing like this would ever touch her life again, but how could I make that claim when I didn't even know why her husband had been targeted?

By a mystic.

But why?

To answer that I knew what I had to do first, and I was absolutely dreading it.

CHAPTER 6

I rode the elevator up to the eighteenth floor at SPL Inc.—the corporation owned by one Elric Ostergaard.

SPL is all about mergers and acquisitions, meaning that its directive is to merge the powers of less powerful mystics under Elric's umbrella, while also seeking to acquire as many powerful trinkets as its coffers can hold.

Elric has seemingly bottomless coffers. The entire seventeenth floor of his fifty-thousand-square-foot building is just *one* of his many, many, many trinket depositories. I've been on the seventeenth floor numerous times and can attest to there being at least a hundred thousand trinkets there.

None of them are below a level four on a scale of one to fifteen. Well, in truth, a one to fourteen scale. No one, and I mean *no* living mystic, has ever glimpsed the one and only level fifteen. Collectively, all mystics accept this as fact because the level fifteen trinket—dubbed the Phoenix—would empower that mystic beyond any other living mystic in the world.

All powerful mystics have trinkets that can bring them back to life—and the rest of us have at least one or two healing trinkets that can heal us from significant injury or bring us back from the brink of death, but each time a trinket is used to revive or heal a mystic, the trinket's power decreases, sometimes significantly.

Trinkets with the power to bring life back to the dead are supremely coveted by the Seven. All six courts possess a sizable cache of trinkets that can heal any wound or bring a mystic back from the dead. The most famous of those trinkets can even do that after two or three *days*. (Elric supposedly has a trinket that can breathe life back into his corpse up to *thirteen* days after his death. I've never seen it, but the rumor persists that he possesses such a thing).

The Phoenix, however, differs from all the others. Supposedly, it can not only bring any mystic or mortal being back to life—no matter how severe the injury, and by that I mean it's rumored to be able to bring someone back from a pile of *ash*—it's capable of doing so eternally. One has only to hold it to be granted its healing powers, and no amount of use will—in theory—lessen its power.

A mystic who wields the Phoenix not only wouldn't fear death—any mystic swearing fealty to that mystic wouldn't have to fear it, either. The Phoenix could heal and/or bring back to life whole *armies* of mystics, making the ruler of those armies invincible.

If a mystic possessed the Phoenix, there would be only one court, one king or queen, and one truly immortal mystic. The quest to find the Phoenix is thousands of years old, but, so far, no mystic has discovered its whereabouts, which hasn't dampened enthusiasm for it one iota, but, if you ask me, the Phoenix is either eternally lost or never existed. Which again, in my opinion, is good because no one needs that kind of raw, unbridled power placed in any one mystic's hands for all eternity. True immortality breeds boredom, and boredom is *always* trouble.

Still, it wasn't a trinket I was concerned about at present: it was a spell. A specific death curse that could only be wielded by a mystic far above my skillset. Even though I've shown significant promise as a spellcaster, I'm still young by mystic standards and I don't have nearly the command over magic that other, far older mystics do. Well, except for Ursula. She's way up there in age, but she's told me she's never been interested in spellcasting, whereas I relish the challenge of its mastery. Casting a spell using words and essence alone without the aid of a trinket is a skill that takes hundreds and hundreds of years of practice, so I have a long road ahead of me, but it's still fun and I get a thrill when an improvised spell actually works.

The best spellcaster I've ever known is Elric. It's one part of the reason he's thought to be the most powerful mystic in the world; his massive cache of trinkets and his willingness to be as ruthless as necessary are the second and third parts of that reason. His power has yet to be challenged—if you come for the king, you better aim for the head—and none of the leaders of the other five courts has shown the confidence to try it. Plus, they'd not only have to battle Elric, Petra is bound in alliance to her husband—and he to her—so going up against them would be suicide.

As I watched the numbers on the elevator panel light up the higher it climbed, I pondered that, while I'd always been impressed with Elric's power, I'd never been afraid of him. Not even once.

Until now.

Ursula once said to me that true fear comes from the tangible awareness that someone else knows your vulnerabilities and isn't afraid to exploit them. I never gave her observation more than a passing thought, because it never occurred to me that Elric would ever exploit my vulnerabilities. But in the last few weeks—since meeting Gib—things had changed. Gib had become a vulnerability, and now that I was certain of the method used to murder one of his fellow agents, I wondered if that exploitation of my vulnerabilities had, in fact, begun and was taking shape in the form of a warning—directly to me.

Was Elric demonstrating how easily he could dispatch Gib by murdering other agents at his Bureau? Or was there something else at hand?

The elevator doors parted, and I stepped out to the magnificently appointed lobby. Elric has the most exquisite taste.

I hadn't made an appointment with him, and truth be told I didn't even know if Elric was in the building, but impulse had brought me to what I hoped was the source of an explanation. Once I knew why he'd killed Bruce McNally and John Fell, if in fact he had, I could formulate a plan of diplomacy that hopefully would appease Elric and keep Gib from meeting the same fate.

Hyacinth—Elric's assistant—was at her new post behind the reception desk, and she coldly eyed me as I approached.

There was no love lost between us. I'd liked and gotten along with her identical twin sister—Elric's former assistant, Sequoia—well enough, but Hyacinth had always struck me as more of a manipulative opportunist than her sister, who'd always seemed just opportunistic without all the calculation. Plus, Hyacinth appeared to be quite jealous of my position at SPL. I was the lone investigator working to retrieve trinkets that fell into unbound hands. It was a job that was coveted for its "cushy" duty, even though most of my peers didn't fully understand how tricky some of my assignments were; everyone at SPL considered dealing with the unbound an easy task indeed.

Sequoia had never appeared to covet my title, but her sister did. That much I knew. Hyacinth had never said as much directly to me, but the vibe definitely wafted off of her whenever we were in each other's company, which bothered me.

Not that I'd let that show. "Hello, Hyacinth," I said, keeping my tone as neutral as possible. "Is Elric in?"

She clicked her tongue and looked down at her tablet screen. "Do you have an appointment?"

"No. But I would like to see him."

"About . . . ?"

My brows arched. *That* was none of her damn business, and I was taken aback by the audacity of asking me such a question. If Elric knew she was asking *any* of his top-tier people the business they had with him, Hyacinth would likely get a "demotion." And by "demotion," I mean she'd be put on dragon-feeding duty—the job at SPL Inc. with the shortest life expectancy.

But then I realized that Hyacinth wouldn't be nearly this bold if Elric were anywhere within hearing distance, which meant he wasn't in the building or likely even in the city.

I eyed her knowingly before dipping my chin in a slight nod and taking a step away from her desk. "You shouldn't so easily show your hand, Hyacinth. I'll catch up to Elric when he's back."

She narrowed her eyes at me in a glare that I suppose was meant to send a ripple of fear down my spine, but it only made me scoff. Such petty games were wasted on me, and she should know better as it was well-known that I was Elric's favorite among the women he kept company with. After all, I was the only one in his entourage that Petra continually tried to assassinate.

Still, Elric's favor was something of a double-edged sword. He was somewhat open about it, which protected me as long as I was in his company, but the minute I was anywhere alone, I could be targeted by far more powerful mystics.

Like the one that'd tried to kill me last night.

Turning away from Hyacinth without another word, I headed back to the elevator. There was another mystic here at SPL who could help me understand some of what I suspected was going on—a source I trusted because she was Elric's lieutenant, which was a job *everyone* coveted for its power and prestige. Except me. Elric's lieutenant, Jacquelyn, kept him safe, and she'd never shown an ounce of jealousy toward me, which I fully appreciated.

After getting back inside the elevator, I took just a moment to look inside my handbag for a supply of chocolate bars I always carry, then, satisfied with my cache, I punched in a special code on the control panel and rode the elevator down to the fourteenth floor, which was also the fifteenth and sixteenth floors.

From the exterior of SPL's skyscraper, it's impossible to tell that three of the eighteen stories are combined into one gigantic space.

And they need to be, because this is the space where Jacquelyn keeps her dragons.

Before the elevator doors opened, I made sure to step all the way to the front corner, putting the space that housed the elevator panel between me and the elevator doors, while casting a spell to shield myself in a bubble of essence—just in case.

Good thing I took the extra precaution because the doors pinged open and immediately a huge ball of flame roared into the elevator car, leaving the entire space—save my little corner—completely charred.

"Hello, Brutellah!" I called. The guardian of the fourteenth to sixteenth floor is a twenty-foot-tall dragon with a grumpy demeanor and a territorial disposition. It'd taken me decades to win him over and I had a scar on my right hip from a burn he'd given me to prove that it hadn't been easy.

A low rumble echoed from the chamber. I dropped the essence bubble I'd encapsulated myself in and peeked around the corner. Brutellah's one good eye was narrowed in my direction; his massive snout and double row of needle-sharp teeth were exposed while he sniffed the air. "Hi," I said again, adding a little wave.

He snuffed dismissively, breathing out several rings of smoke into the hazy air.

"Is your mom around?" I asked him.

His lower lip twitched, and he sniffed again. Reaching into my handbag I dug around for a moment before bringing up a Twix bar.

King size.

Brutellah has a sweet tooth and Twix are his favorite. He opened his mouth slightly and I tossed the candy bar at him, wrapper and all.

He chomped on it for all of three seconds, sticking his forked tongue out to lick his leathery lips, then he swung that massive head toward a hallway leading off the central room.

"Her office?" I asked.

Brutellah answered me by lifting his head and stomping off to a massive (and I do mean *massive*) dog bed to curl himself into a ball and close his one good eye.

He sighed contentedly, allowing a plume of smoke to circle above his head, which I took to mean he was giving me a free pass to traverse the space without being turned to ash.

I walked quickly forward (lest he change his mind) and entered the long hallway. To the right and left of me were glass-fronted enclosures, and in each of these slept a dragon. All of them were of various shapes and sizes.

By far the most ferocious of the lot, however, is a blue dragon at the very end of the room named Priscilla. She's quite small by dragon standards, only eight feet tall at the shoulder, but she's fast as lightning and impossible to tame by anyone else but Jacquelyn. And even then, it's a tenuous relationship.

Priscilla can tear apart anything or anyone in a manner of seconds. She doesn't breathe fire, she spits acid, and as I passed her glass-walled enclosure, I noticed that, of all the dragons housed along this corridor, only Priscilla was awake, curled into a ball similarly to Brutellah, but both of her eyes were open and following my every move.

I was careful to avoid looking her directly in the eyes, lest I pique her interest. I walked warily by as I wasn't convinced her enclosure was secure—she is, after all, the cleverest of all of Jacquelyn's "pets" and she'd escaped at least a few times in her history here at SPL.

Elric put up with the deadly dragon's antics only because Jacquelyn was his most trusted advisor, most loyal ally, and one of his oldest friends, which is why he made her his lieutenant. All the courts had a leader backed up by a lieutenant—a secondary security measure should a rebellion or a battle be at hand. Elric and Jacquelyn had saved each other's lives many times over, and I believed he thought of her as a sister rather than simply part of his guard. The pair trusted each other, implicitly. Which is why I trusted her to help me find some answers.

Just as I was passing the last few feet of Priscilla's enclosure, I heard a loud *splat* next to me, causing me to jump.

Looking over my shoulder, I saw green slime against the glass, oozing its way downward, bubbling and sizzling as it went. Had the protective glass not been there, the slime—acid— would've taken my head off. My gaze drifted back to Priscilla, who was still in her bed, curled into a ball as if she hadn't moved a muscle since I passed on by, but her tail flicked like a pleased cat.

This time I didn't bother dropping my gaze. Instead, I eyed her intently and turned fully toward her to offer her a low bow. This was obviously an unexpected move as her head lifted off her front paws and she studied me for a long moment before settling her chin back down onto her paws, then she closed her eyes as if she were drifting off to sleep.

I didn't fool myself into thinking I'd won her over with my display of respect, but I did suspect that she'd been pleased by my overture. Only after her eyes were shut did I turn my back to her again and approach a closed door at the end of the corridor.

As I raised my hand to knock, I heard from beyond the door, "Just come in, Dovey."

Opening the door, I found Jacquelyn, seated at her massive white desk with an array of maps strewn about its surface and a magnifying glass in her hand.

"Good afternoon, Jacquelyn," I said, pushing a nervous smile to my lips.

"Dovey," she said warmly. "To what do I owe the pleasure?"

From a physical perspective, Jacquelyn is easy to underestimate. She's small in stature and slight of build with long black hair that's perpetually twisted into a French braid which snakes down the length of her back.

Her heart-shaped face and large green eyes give her a doll-like appearance but there's a cunning intelligence swimming in the pools of her irises that's easily recognizable if you're looking.

She is perpetually dressed in skintight leather attire of varying colors with the occasional decorative accent. Today she was dressed in a deep azure-blue leather jacket, matching leggings, and of course her signature dragon brooch secured to her jacket's left lapel.

The brooch's origins are a mystery to me, but its power isn't. At a level twelve it's arguably one of the most powerful trinkets in the world—and it needs to be as it gives Jacquelyn the power to tame dragons.

With it, not only can she convince them she's one of their own, but she can secure them inside the brooch to travel with her if need be. It's why she's so feared within the mystic world.

If Jacquelyn shows up at your door, it's a safe bet you're about to become a dragon's next snack.

One touch of her finger on the brooch and within seconds a dragon will emerge—seemingly teleported right out of the brooch. A second touch recalls the pet to carry back home, and the dragon is never the worse for wear having been shrunk twice to fit inside a brooch no bigger than 2.5 inches by 1 inch.

"I need to ask you something," I said. "And I'm hoping you'll answer."

"Why wouldn't I answer?"

"Because, as Elric's second, you might choose to protect him rather than be honest with me."

One perfectly sculpted eyebrow arched high onto Jacquelyn's forehead. "Ah," she said.

That was it. Just . . . "Ah."

Taking a deep breath for courage, I asked the question I feared the answer to but desperately needed to know. "Is SPL targeting FBI agents for assassination?"

The arched eyebrow plunged into a flat line, joining its twin on her now-furrowed brow. "Why would we concern ourselves with the unbound's federal investigators?"

I shrugged. "I don't know. Which is why I'm here, asking."

"Why aren't you asking Elric?"

I felt that Jacquelyn might purposefully be being vague. But it was hard to tell. She was a sly politician—you had to be if you were of any worthy rank at SPL. She might've simply been stalling to see where I was going with this, however.

So I put the cards on the table. "I believe FBI agents are dying by mystic means. Elric has always guarded against targeting the unbound's law enforcement, or targeting any unbound who might attract the attention of law enforcement. I'm wondering if there's been a change in policy that I haven't been made aware of."

"How do you know these agents are dying by mystic means?"

"It's not even that they're dying by mystic means, Jacquelyn; it's that they're specifically dying from the Crushing Curse."

The arched brow rose slowly back to full mast. "You're positive?"

"Fairly positive, yes."

"How many agents and when?" she asked, her eyes darting back and forth as if she were looking through a mental Rolodex.

"Two agents. One was assassinated two nights ago, then another was taken out last night."

"You saw the bodies?"

I shook my head. "No, but their injuries and the crime scene were both described to me. All bones in the body broken, no sign at all of any struggle, and at the time of their murders, each man had a spouse sleeping nearby, and neither spouse heard a thing."

Jacquelyn grunted and crossed her arms. "*Every* bone in the body broken?" she clarified. "But no compound fractures, and no cuts or abrasions on the skin, correct?"

"I haven't seen the bodies, but the way they were described to me by people who did is exactly that."

Jacquelyn rose from her seat and began to pace. She knew the gravity of what I was describing, and I suspected she knew that very, very few mystics had the power to invoke the Crushing Curse. The only mystic I knew who used it to dispatch his enemies was Elric, but surely Jacquelyn would be capable of wielding the curse.

She seemed to notice I was looking earnestly at her because she said, "It wasn't me."

"I didn't think it was."

"You think it was Elric?"

I shrugged. "I don't know, Jacquelyn. Truly. That's why I'm

here. I went upstairs to ask him about it, but I got the distinct impression he's not in the building."

She frowned. "Hyacinth," she hissed. "She needs to shut her trap!"

"I only figured it out because she has a tell. She didn't volunteer the information."

Jacquelyn eyed me intently. "What's the tell?"

"Her jealousy of me emboldens her. She wanted to know what my business was with Elric today."

Jacquelyn snorted. "Sequoia was far better at concealing her emotions. I told Elric not to bring Hyacinth on after Sequoia was . . . retired, but you know how he is."

"Keep your enemies close, and the sisters of those you . . . *retire* closer?"

"Exactly. Anyway, Elric is with Petra. She just got back from Europe and something's up. There's a debriefing."

It was my own brow's turn to arch. "And you're not there?"

"Petra's lieutenant and I don't get along. Elric was afraid he'd start something, and I'd turn him into dragon kibble."

I laughed but Jacquelyn didn't even crack a smile. She was serious. "He went *alone* to Petra's?"

She shook her head. "He's there with Solo."

Solo was an old, wizened mystic who'd once been a merlin, but whose powers had greatly diminished over time as happens to a few of them. He was also a trusted advisor to Elric and could still wield a spell or two. Elric was well protected.

"Do you think, Jacquelyn, that these assassinations could be Elric's doing?" I pressed.

The dragon tamer shook her head but added a shrug. "Not directly, at least."

That was telling. If it were Elric's doing, then he hadn't told his lieutenant—his most trusted advisor—and I couldn't fathom a reason for him to keep her out of the loop about something like this.

"There's more," I said, hoping I could trust her.

She came around the desk to lean back against it and crossed her arms. "Tell me."

"I believe a mystic stood outside my home last night, actively looking for a way to kill me."

"You believe *you're* a target?"

I nodded then shook my head, undecided. "I don't know. Maybe?"

Her eyes narrowed. "Why would *you* be a target, Dovey?"

I was entering very tricky territory here. I couldn't give Jacquelyn too much information about Gib, lest she report all that I said back to Elric, but I also couldn't ignore that there'd been a mystic creating a far more powerful storm for us to navigate last night between my home and his. And then the mystic who'd followed us had also knocked me unconscious. It was plausible that he or she had originally followed me from my home to Gib's, then back again when the storm picked up.

But to answer Jacquelyn's question, I said, "I sometimes work with the FBI on cases that overlap mine."

She appeared genuinely surprised. "You do?"

I nodded.

"You entangle yourself with the unbound FBI?" she pressed.

I nodded again and hoped she didn't ask me to elaborate further.

"And you're working a case with them now?"

"I wasn't, but now I feel like I have to. We can't have the unbound FBI looking too deeply into mystical malice. That's not good for anyone."

She nodded in agreement. "Someone could be doing this on purpose. To stir up trouble."

"Yes. That's my thought."

She stared at me for a long moment before nodding a second time. "I'll look into this, Dovey. For now, keep your guard up, stick close to the FBI agents you're working with, and keep us in the loop if any more agents are killed."

I felt a flood of relief. Jacquelyn would investigate on Elric's behalf, and while it didn't mean she'd discover who was murdering these agents, it did mean I had a powerful ally watching my back, which was at least *some* reassurance.

I offered Jacquelyn the same bow I'd performed in front of her blue dragon. I'm always willing to pay deference to those of superior power—with the notable exception of Petra. *She* gets nothing but my bland indifference.

Jacquelyn chuckled. "Now, now, no need for that."

I stood tall again but couldn't help noticing that she looked pleased. "Thank you. I'm grateful."

Still smiling, she made a shooing motion with her hand. "Get back to work, Dovey. And thank you for bringing this to me."

"Of course. Thank you for seeing me."

After walking out of Jacquelyn's office, I looked toward Priscilla's enclosure, finding her still wound in a tight circle, the end of her tail dancing ever so slightly, letting me know she was both awake and aware.

Pausing in front of a small window within the glass pane of her enclosure, I opened it and dropped a Twix bar into the interior of her pen. She deserved a sweet snack every bit as much as Brutellah. Besides Elric and Brutellah, Priscilla was one of the central reasons SPL had never been breached by enemy means. Her reputation preceded her and helped to keep the facility secure.

I waited a moment or two for the sapphire-blue dragon to pounce on the candy bar, but she was unmoved. Perhaps next time I'd bring steak.

In parting I also offered Brutellah my very last Twix bar, making a mental note to stop at the store on the way home to stock up again as one never knew when distracting a dragon with a sweet treat might be necessary.

Getting into the elevator to head back down to the parking lot, my hand hovered above the first floor button while I reconsidered that plan.

Deciding it might be nice to catch up with Elric's trinket guardian, I hit the button for the seventeenth floor instead.

When the doors opened again, I found all four feet eleven inches of Qin Shi standing with legs spread, knees bent, and arms raised in a defensive posture while a set of 3D gaming goggles hung comically over his eyes, all but obscuring his face.

I opened my mouth to announce myself when a bolt of energy flew at me, and I barely dodged it by dropping to all fours. The elevator absorbed the blow, taking it on the chin just like it'd taken Brutellah's fire, leaving the interior again looking worse for wear.

"Qin!" I shouted. "What the hell?"

Qin tugged on his goggles, and they dropped to his neck. He blinked several times, taking me and the open elevator in. "Oops. Sorry, Dovey. My bad."

I scowled at him, picking myself up off the floor to dust myself off. "You could kill someone like that, you know."

"Which is the point of this infuriating game. Still, I wasn't aiming at you."

"Who were you aiming at?"

"Some rapscallion called Darth Vader-Gator."

I stared at Qin's ancient, weathered, bent frame, dressed in a long robe and leather sandals. "Let me guess, your gaming handle is Yoda."

He cocked a finger gun at me and clicked his tongue. "Close. It's Yoddha but spelled like Buddha. Get it?"

"I do."

Qin offered an impressive impression of the *Star Wars* character's voice when he said, "Clever it is, would Gautama think. Sage warrior master, I am." For emphasis, the ancient one raised both fists above his head and flexed. It was like watching two walnuts emerge from sickly thin branches.

"Impressive," I told him. It cost me nothing to toss the old guy a bone.

Qin smiled for a second then grimaced and changed his pose to a side chest pump.

It was like watching a garden gnome struggling to pass gas.

I covered my mouth to hold back a belly laugh, but a flood of giggles escaped me. Qin rolled his eyes and stood straight again looking a bit offended.

Clearing my throat and pivoting quickly, I pointed to the goggles still around his neck and asked, "Who gave you gaming goggles?"

"Elric. Early Christmas present."

"It's May."

"Early Memorial Day present."

I shook my head but couldn't contain my smile. Motioning to the elevator, I said, "Well, maybe reconsider playing with them lest you take someone's head off next time."

Qin chuckled. "Dovey, you're more formidable than you realize. And you have excellent reflexes. I pity the fool who thinks they can get the drop on you."

"Thank you?" I said as a question. Qin didn't seem very apologetic for almost unaliving me, but then, that was perhaps to be expected from an ancient mystic. The older the mystic the less sentimental about the life and death of allies and friends they become.

Removing the goggles, Qin said, "You look like you didn't sleep very well."

"You're having a hard time containing all that charm today, huh?"

Qin laughed. "I calls 'em like I sees 'em!"

I smirked. "Well, I'll give you *some* credit. I actually didn't sleep well last night."

"Was it anxiety or fear that kept you up?"

Sometimes it's easy to forget just how inciteful the trinket guardian is.

"A bit of both."

"Who's got you anxious?"

"An unknown."

"Who's made you afraid?"

"The same. A mystic purposely strengthened the storm around me last evening while I was driving toward my house, and if I hadn't had my guard up, I'd be under a tree right now."

Qin pointed his trusty finger gun at me again. "See? Formidable with *excellent* reflexes!"

I rolled my eyes. "More like lucky, but that's beside the point. Do you have anything in that big, vast, well-stocked trinket vault that you'd be willing to part with to help an old friend?"

Qin tugged on his long silver beard, which trailed nearly to the floor. "What happened to the ring I loaned you?"

I frowned. "All the juice got used up in the battle for Pandora's Promise."

Qin nodded and grinned wide. "I heard about that. Lucky thing I put that on your finger, eh?"

I definitely deserved his "I told you so." He'd been right. And he'd saved my life and a few others' in the process when I'd gone up against a formidable foe named Lavender weeks earlier.

"I'm very grateful to you, Qin. And I can return the ring, although it's now just a dud."

He waved with nonchalance. "Keep it. It's pretty if nothing else. Come with me. We'll look through the inventory and see what might offset some of what's troubling you, Love-Dove."

It was my turn to grin. Qin was the only one who called me that, and never in front of anyone else. I suspected that not even Elric knew of his trinket guardian's special affection for me.

Qin led the way to a set of massive double doors made of bronze. He then placed his right hand on one of the doors, closed his eyes, and a moment later there were a series of clicks. He then took his hand off the door and used his index finger to push it open.

Smiling over his shoulder at me, he whistled a happy tune as he entered the trinket storage room, and I followed both in step and in accompanying whistle.

The guardian led me down the central corridor, lined on both sides with literally thousands of trinkets. While I followed, I tried to keep my gaze looking forward, but it was hard with so many sparkling, tempting trinkets on display, begging to be touched and activated, which made me think again about the ring that Qin had placed on my finger several weeks back, binding a spell to it that wouldn't allow me to take it off until after it'd defended me in a duel to the death. "Qin," I said as I walked slightly behind him.

"Yes?"

"I don't want another weapon. Just loan me something that'd be useful in a dangerous situation, if you've got something like that in here."

He scoffed. "We've got something like everything in here. Come along, Dovey. I know just the thing."

We got to the end of the central corridor and Qin turned left. He led me past three rows, finally turning left again. We traveled a little way before he stopped abruptly, as if startled. Something had caught his attention, and his head whipped to the left, his gaze searching a wood vanity. From the style and expert craftsmanship, I guessed it was a Lacroix, circa late eighteenth century, made from what looked like black walnut and kept in pristine condition. On top of the vanity was a pillow with a palm-sized, round indentation—absent of any trinket—and next to that was the dust outline of what looked like a hand mirror.

"Something wrong?" I asked as Qin simply stared at the vanity looking shocked.

In answer, Qin ran two fingers over the pillow that had obviously held a trinket and said, "The Casting Bead. It's gone."

"Casting Bead?"

Qin nodded and turned abruptly to me. "Did you take it?"

"Did I . . . ?" Was he kidding? "Qin, I've been with you the whole time. How could I have taken it?"

He nodded dully, his eyes far away, and for the first time since I'd known him, I saw real fear creep into his countenance. And that, in turn, scared the daylights out of me.

"The Casting Bead is missing," I said, trying to get him to focus on the problem.

His eyes focused again, briefly on me then on the pillow. "Yes."

"Did you loan it to someone?"

Qin Shi's voice was hollow when he replied, "I would never loan it to someone."

My arms lined with goose bumps and the hair at my nape stood up on end. Whatever the Casting Bead's purpose, it was obviously an incredibly dangerous trinket. "What does it look like, Qin?"

He turned up his palm and a bubble of turquoise essence appeared, which then morphed into a hologram for a round bead about the size of a squash ball, made of tiger's eye.

"What does it do?" I asked next, even though I thought I had a pretty good feeling about its purpose. Turns out I was wrong. Well, partly wrong from the standpoint that I wasn't worried enough about it being gone from Qin's watchful eye.

"It enhances a mystic's power tenfold," he said. "While in possession of the Bead, any mystic of any ability—even a novice—can whisper the words of the most powerful spells and have them take effect as if they were uttered by a mystic ten times as powerful. A novice could become a king with it."

My mind immediately pondered whether a mystic had used the Bead to cast the Crushing Curse, which meant the curse probably wasn't cast by Elric—he'd have no need of the Bead to whisper its incantation.

"Is there a chance someone gained access to this place when you weren't here?" I asked.

Qin shook his head, his complexion pale. "When I'm not here, the trinket vault and the elevator access to the lobby are on total lockdown. Only Elric can get in."

"Maybe Elric came down here, took it while you were away, and forgot to tell you."

A tiny spark of hope flickered across Qin's face, but it seemed fleeting.

What lay unspoken between us was the knowledge that, if something as dangerous as the Casting Bead had been stolen from Elric's treasure trove, Qin would pay the price, and the price was quite likely to be his life.

A long silence played out between us and then Qin looked around the area and another note of alarm went through him. "Dovey, you have to go."

"I . . . do?"

Qin began to push me away from the vanity and back toward the double bronze doors. "Yes. I need to take an inventory to see if anything else is missing. And you can't be here because if Elric didn't take the Casting Bead, then you're going to fall under suspicion."

"I . . . would?"

Events were unfolding far faster than I could keep up with. Elric would *never* suspect me of being a thief.

Would he?

I stopped resisting Qin's efforts to grant me a hasty exit and quickened my step toward the doors. "Are you going to call Elric and see if he's got the Bead?"

Qin stopped and stared at me with wide eyes. "No. Not yet. I need time in case it's not with him. I have to try to get it back."

"I'm assuming the Casting Bead has a comeback spell."

"It does. A powerful one. I just hope it's not with Elric when I call it back. If he's got it, he needs it and he'd be furious if it was taken off him."

"Do you want *me* to ask him if he has it?" I said at the same time Qin nearly shouted, "Don't tell Elric it's missing!"

I heard his plea above the sound of my own voice. "Of course, Qin. I won't ask him about it or tell him it's not in its assigned spot."

He looked the tiniest bit relieved. "Thank you, Dovey, oh, and . . ." His voice trailed off as he scanned one of the last shelves of trinkets right in front of the doors. "Here," he said, shoving a silver-and-gold money clip, in the shape of a pound sign—the symbol for the British pound note sterling—into my hand. "That'll come in handy."

With that he pushed me through the double doors and as I turned to ask, "What does it do?" he replied by slamming the double doors in my face.

I stood blinking at the reflective bronze surface for a solid minute. I felt terrible for Qin. I'd never in my life seen the man even rattled. He was perhaps the most laid-back mystic I'd ever known. So for him to be this shaken was beyond chilling, leaning hard toward terrifying.

And I couldn't say a word to anyone about it.

Heeding Qin's warning not to be anywhere near the trinket vault with the Bead missing, I shook myself from my troubled thoughts and hoofed it over to the elevators, pressing the button for the garage.

"No more pit stops," I whispered as the elevator descended. I planned to be far away from SPL until the Bead was found.

Little did I know I wouldn't even make it a day before I'd be right back here, facing the music.

CHAPTER 7

After leaving SPL, I stopped briefly at a convenience store located just down the street to purchase their entire inventory of king-sized Twix bars, then texted Ursula to see if she was free for a get-together. She texted back an emoji of a teapot and a chocolate chip cookie, which made me chuckle. Ursula's all about treating her guests to small comforts, especially when they're in need of some.

Sure enough, she greeted me at the door with a steaming cup of tea, and I couldn't help smirking while I sniffed it to make sure there wasn't any kind of magical potion simmering within the brew.

"Don't trust me?" she asked with a laugh.

I took a small sip. "Not for a second."

She chuckled again. "I hate to admit it, but that's probably wise."

"Liar. You don't hate it at all."

Her laughter filled the entryway and she ushered me all the way inside, motioning toward the sofa.

After sitting down I took another sip of the brew. It was delicious. "Is this a new blend?"

"It *is* a new blend!"

I hovered my nose over the rising steam. "I detect notes of

cardamon, ginger, cinnamon, and clove, plus a hint of . . . orange peel?"

Ursula smiled broadly. "On the dot, Dove."

I leaned back against the cushion, feeling worn-out. One glance at the coffee table, however, and I perked up. Pointing to the small wooden tray placed on the table, I asked, "*What are those?*"

"Pistachio brownies," she said with a grin. Ursula can *bring it* in the kitchen, but then, as a potions maestro, how else *would* her culinary skills be? "I didn't have time to make a fresh batch of chocolate chip cookies, but those I took out of the oven only twenty minutes ago, so they're still warm."

On the tray were four perfectly square chocolate brownies infused with chunks of nuts and halfway covered with a gooey glaze of pistachio cream. Also on the tray was a steaming teapot with two additional cups and saucers. I sucked in a breath as I realized that I might've just interrupted a planned tea party between Ursula and an unknown guest. "Are you expecting company?"

And just as I said that, Ursula's doorbell rang.

She smiled awkwardly. "I thought you knew and were merely joining us."

I cocked my head, staring at her in confusion. In turn, Ursula offered a slight shrug and got up to answer the door, only to reveal the world's sexiest FBI agent. "Ursula," Gib said warmly, giving her a brief hug. "Thanks for seeing me on short notice, I could really use a break today."

Ursula had her back to me, so I watched as she stepped to the side, revealing me on the couch staring shyly up at Gib. I knew he and Ursula were on friendly terms, but his appearance here was a shock. Then again, she *had* invited him to lunch, so, it shouldn't have taken me aback. What *was* surprising was the little tickle of jealousy I felt threading its way along my insides. I quickly reminded myself that Ursula was my best and dearest friend, whom I trusted implicitly, *and* she was madly in love with one of SPL's professional thieves—a muscular and devilishly handsome Australian with charm for days.

But why had Gib asked to meet up with Ursula? On short notice? Just like me?

That tickle of jealousy got a little bigger and a little more worrisome in those few seconds that Gib and I stared at each other, him caught off guard and me expectantly.

"Dovey," he said, quickly pushing a warm smile to his lips. "I didn't know you'd be here."

"Surprise," I said, inserting a forced chuckle. "I didn't know you'd be here, either." My gaze slid to Ursula, and I flattened my tone. "It's like déjà vu."

To her credit, Ursula's cheeks did pink up a hue. "I readily admit to taking matters into my own hands yesterday, but today's afternoon tea session with the two of you came together completely by chance. The both of you invited yourselves, apparently independently and at the same time."

My gaze slid back over to Gib, and I added an arched eyebrow. He smiled sweetly at me in a way that made my heart flutter. There was just something about the way he looked at me—a certain innocent but sincere charm that took over his countenance—and I knew then that I didn't have anything to be jealous about. He simply looked at me differently than he did Ursula.

Still, I did wonder why he'd come. I had a feeling it was about me, which made me especially curious.

"I bet you're wondering what I'm doing here," he said.

Was he . . . nervous?

"Not really," I said with a wave of my hand. There was no way I was going to look thirsty for his attention.

Ursula waved him in. "Well, *I'm* wondering. Perhaps you can come in, have some tea, and tell us about it."

Gib stepped forward, closing the door behind him, then

took up the chair across from the sofa. He eyed both the tea and the brownies hungrily. "Man, those look good. I go weak in the knees for brownies."

I made a mental note to ask Ursula for the recipe.

She pointed to the tray. "Pistachio."

Gib's eyes lit up and he reached for a brownie, setting it on one of the small china plates that Ursula had gathered for the occasion, before he also poured himself a cup of tea. "I have a sweet tooth."

I couldn't help but smile. "Me too."

Ursula raised her hand. "Me three."

We all chuckled. Inwardly, however, I wondered when Gib would get to the point.

He sighed. "It's been a hell of a day."

"You went to the crime scene?" I asked, meaning the murder scene of John Fell.

Ursula's head pivoted back and forth between me and Gib. "What crime scene?"

"An agent died," I told her.

She gasped. "An agent died?"

Gib took a bite out of the brownie, then held up two fingers.

"Peace?" she asked, staring at him in bewilderment.

"No," I said, laying a hand on her arm. "Two agents have died. Likely murdered." If it'd been just me and Ursula, I could've filled her in on my certainty that the men had both been victims of a mystic assassin, but Gib was here, and I couldn't very well just blurt that out. Instead, I added, "Gib said, when he told me about the first agent who died two nights ago, that every bone in the poor man's body had been broken, but there were no signs of a struggle, or forced entry to his home, or signs of defensive wounds. He'd simply been discovered slumped over in his chair."

Pointing to Gib, I added, "I'm assuming Agent Fell's crime scene was nearly exactly the same?"

Gib nodded grimly, his eyes unfocused as he stared at the

coffee table, no doubt recalling the details of his ASAC's murder.

Ursula's eyes grew wide as both shock and understanding dawned on her. I knew she'd recognize the Crushing Curse when she heard the details of the agents' demise. Swiveling her gaze from me over to Gib, she carefully asked, "The mafia?"

He had his hand in a relaxed fist, covering his mouth while he chewed, then took a sip of tea before he answered. "We don't know. Maybe. Both these agents were longtime veterans, so they've both worked organized crime cases in the past. Bruce, in particular, worked a lot of those cases, but at the Bureau, we were careful to keep his identity and job title a secret, exactly because we didn't want him targeted. People could've known he worked for the Bureau, but what he did for us was a closely guarded secret."

"Still," I said, deciding to push the organized crime theory along because I felt we mystics should be offering up *something* other than assassination through magical means. "The mafia has been known to get very creative with the way they take out their enemies, correct?"

"True," Gib said, wiping his fingers on a cocktail napkin. "But *these* murders seem to defy explanation. To figure out *who* did this, we need to figure out *how* they did it, and so far, none of us can come up with any kind of theory that would be physically possible. It's like these two agents were beamed up into a spaceship, beaten to death using some sort of other-worldly means, then teleported back to their respective living room and kitchen."

Ursula winked at him. "Your crowd would have more knowledge of an alien invasion than we would. Any truth to that theory?"

Gib scoffed and took up his teacup again. "Not a chance, which is to say that I still checked the police blotters in the area to see if any UAP sightings occurred—"

"UAP?" she interrupted.

"Unidentified Aerial Phenomenon. It's the new acronym for UFO."

"Ah," she said. "I guess I'm not up on all the new lingo."

"It can be a lot to keep up with," Gib told her. "Anyway, other than an influx of calls due to the storm, nothing UAPish got reported."

A brief silence followed before Ursula asked, "So what brings you by, Grant? Other than needing a break from this tragic mess at your Bureau?"

Gib blinked at her for a long moment, and it was obvious that, with me in the room, he was uncomfortable saying what he'd come here to tell her. I felt my cheeks heat while simultaneously watching his redden.

Luckily, we were saved by the bell when Gib's cell phone pinged with an incoming text. He quickly took the phone out of his pocket and stared at the screen, his expression crumpling into sadness and shock. Then he began swiping as if scrolling through pictures. "What the . . . hell?"

Ursula and I both sat forward. Obviously, the text he'd received was terrible news. Maybe even tragic. Reflexively, I crossed my fingers that it wasn't yet *another* agent murdered.

Abruptly, he stood up, and for a second, he looked almost lost. "I gotta go."

Ursula and I stood too. She laid a hand on her chest and said, "Is it another agent? Has another one been murdered?"

Gib nodded absently while he stared sightlessly ahead. "Yeah. Felicia Cartwright. Another senior agent. She's been on a medical leave of absence and was due to come back to the office today. A UPS delivery driver just discovered her alone, in her car, in her own driveway, and in exactly the same condition as Bruce and John." Gib tucked his phone away and shook his head like he was trying to clear it. Focusing on us again, he added, "Sorry to bail, but I really gotta go."

"Of course," Ursula said easily. "Don't give it a moment's thought, Grant."

He nodded at her then eyed me. "Can I call you later?"

"You may," I said, flooded with a mix of emotions. I was thrilled that he wanted to reach out to me later but also concerned for his safety. I realized that none of the agents so far seemed to have been murdered when they were in the direct company of someone else.

Gib was already turning away from me when I reached out to grab his hand. I didn't want him to go because I didn't know if he'd be next on the executioner's list. "Double up with one of the other agents, Gib. Please. And don't just call me when you get off work. Come over."

Out of the corner of my eye, I saw Ursula staring at me in surprise, and I suspected she'd adopt a smug smirk the second Gib was out the door.

"I will," he said, gazing at me sweetly, then squeezed my hand before he went to the door. There he paused ever so briefly to say, "Ursula, thank you for the tea and the brownies. I owe you lunch one of these days."

He then waved over his shoulder and left.

The second the door was closed, I pivoted to Ursula, wagging my finger at her and the smug smirk she was wearing. "Don't start."

"Don't start what? The 'I told you so's'?"

"Yes. Those. We have far more important matters to discuss."

The smirk vanished and she sat heavily back down on the sofa. "You mean like the fact that a mystic is murdering FBI agents?"

"Yes. That. Exactly that." I slumped down next to her, all my fatigue returning.

She looked pointedly at me. "Is it Elric?"

I shook my head. "I don't think so. I was at HQ before I came here, but he wasn't in."

"Is he at one of the other courts?"

"Yes, if you count Petra's court separately from Elric's."

She grunted. "I wish. He'd be able to fully commit to plotting against her if she dared to strike out on her own."

"Indeed, but it's never going to happen. Petra still thinks it'll work out between them."

Ursula scoffed. "It's been over a thousand years. The woman needs to *move on.*"

I held up a hand. "Preachin' to the choir, my friend."

Ursula was quiet for a moment before getting us back on topic. "It makes sense in a way that it *is* Elric, though. No mystic would *dare* stir up trouble in his territory by assassinating unbound FBI agents using the Crushing Curse. Unless it was Petra. Which might be why he's over at her court today."

"That makes more sense to me than Elric being the assassin."

"But why?" Ursula said next, and I could tell she wasn't asking me so much as she was simply giving voice to the conundrum of why Elric's wife would do something so stupid.

"How many IQ points have you removed from her?" I asked.

Ursula chuckled mirthlessly. "Not enough to bring her down to *that* level of dumb. Murdering unbound federal agents would stir up trouble for every mystic in the territory—including, and maybe most especially, her."

"Then who else?"

"Possibly the Flayer," she said, referring to Petra's lieutenant, known as Finn the Flayer.

"*He's* powerful enough to wield the spell?"

She pursed her lips. "From what I've heard? Definitely. The man has mad skills and a cache of powerful trinkets at his disposal. Rumor has it that the Flayer came back to life after being shot with one of the arrows from the Bow of Anubis."

"Whoa. That's one of the deadliest trinkets ever created. An arrow from that bow is supposed to end you, permanently."

"It would require quite the powerful healing trinket to come back from. It seems either Petra outfitted him with one or he had one on hand."

"Speaking of lieutenants, I met with Jacquelyn this morning. She's going to look into this mess, which means she didn't know about these unbound assassinations until I brought it up with her."

As I told her about my morning, I was on the fence about telling Ursula about the missing Casting Bead. I knew I could trust her with any secret I held, but in telling her about it, I could be involving her in a matter she was best kept out of. It was bad enough that I'd been in the trinket vault when Qin discovered it missing.

So instead I nodded toward the door. "I'm worried for him."

"With good reason. How do you plan to protect him?"

I took the next ten minutes to explain everything Gib and I had endured the night before, and as I spoke, Ursula's eyes simply stayed wide open. It was clear she was now worried for my safety too. "Dovey, you need to arm yourself. Today. Go see Qin Shi. Get a weapon. Something powerful. Very, very powerful."

I dug out the money clip that Qin had given me. "I got this from him a little while ago. . . ." I needed to be purposely vague here. "He said it would protect me."

She held out her hand and I dumped the money clip into her palm. As I watched, I saw her pump a little bit of light green essence into it, but she immediately scowled. "Why did he give you this? It's a level five—at best. Which won't kill a mystic even at the novice level if they come after you."

I took the clip back. "I told Qin I didn't want a weapon. I just needed something to protect me when trouble came looking."

Her frown deepened. "What's its enchantment?"

I tried to laugh lightly but it sounded forced. "I have no idea."

She held out her hand again and I placed the trinket into her palm. She pumped more essence into it and literally nothing happened. "Have you fallen out of favor with Qin Shi?"

"It's a dud?" I was shocked. Yes, Qin had been in a hurry to get me out of the trinket vault, but I thought he'd at least give me *something* helpful. "Maybe it'll give a warning if I'm in danger. Maybe that's why it's not doing anything right now."

She stared at me flatly. "Please be kidding me."

"Why would I be kidding you?"

"Because a level five trinket will never be enough to avoid the danger of a mystic on par with Petra, or the Flayer. You'll be dead before the thing even activates—*if* it activates."

I tucked the money clip back into my handbag. "Qin was distracted. He'd lost track of a trinket."

Realizing I'd just blurted out the secret, I slapped a hand over my mouth. How could I have been so foolish?!

Meanwhile, Ursula was blinking at me like I'd just spoken in some foreign language she wasn't familiar with. "Come again?"

With a resigned sigh, I said, "First, you have to promise me that you won't tell anyone else about what I'm about to say."

"That goes without saying, Dovey. Secrets between us remain between us."

"Thank you. I knew that, but Qin might be in big—*fireable*—trouble here, and I don't want to be the one responsible for any consequences that might come his way before he has a chance to fix it."

"Okay, now you're scaring me. What're we talking about here, Dovey?"

I sighed and tried to start at the beginning. "While Qin was leading me along in the trinket vault, on a quest to get me something appropriate, he discovered that a powerful trinket wasn't in its assigned spot and might be missing."

Again, Ursula blinked at me. "How is that possible?"

I shrugged. "No idea, but I'll bet Elric nabbed it and forgot to tell Qin about it."

"What was the trinket?"

"Something called the Casting Bead."

Ursula's jaw dropped. "Empress Wu Zetian's Casting Bead?!"

I'd never heard of the empress. "Maybe? Why?"

Ursula got up and began to pace. "There are certain trinkets within Elric's possession, Dovey, that he makes certain are *never* removed from SPL's property. They're considered so dangerous that even the mere *hint* of them not under lock and key would send ripples of unease throughout the six courts— including his, because Petra would have an absolute *fit* if one of them went missing. If *the* Casting Bead fell into the wrong hands, it could lead to war. At the very least it'd cause irreparable shifts in the balance of power across all six courts."

I felt the blood drain from my face. I'd had no idea the Casting Bead was dangerous enough to cause a mystic war. Certainly, I understood that it held immense power, but I didn't even consider the implications of its impact across the courts.

"What other super-dangerous trinkets beside the Casting Bead do you know about?" I was remembering Qin's frantic effort to get me out of his space so he could do a full inventory to see if anything else was missing.

"Besides the Bow of Anubis?" she asked in turn.

"We don't have to worry about the bow. Elric hangs that in his conference room."

She crossed her arms and stared at me. "It's been a while

since you've been to the conference room on the eighteenth floor, huh?"

"Um . . . maybe a few months. Why?"

"The Bow has been moved to a safer location. Sequoia took it out of the building one night, which is why she was . . . fired."

I gasped. I'd had no idea!

"Where is it now?"

"Rumor has it he had Jacquelyn store it under Priscilla's bed."

"He's hidden it under the blue dragon?"

"Yes. He's hidden a few baubles of significant value there, in fact."

I let out a sigh of relief. "Oh! Well, that *must* be what happened to the Bead! Elric must've moved it to the dragon floor for safekeeping."

But Ursula appeared skeptical. And worried. "Why would Elric move the Bead and not tell Qin?"

I shrugged. "Elric's a busy man. I'm sure he just forgot. That, or he's got it on his person and took it with him to Petra's this morning."

Ursula gazed at me like she was patiently waiting for me to get it, and it frustrated me that I didn't seem to be understanding the gravity of the situation.

"Elric," she said softly, "would *never* head to Petra's side of the fence with something as powerful as the Casting Bead, Dovey. It'd be too much of a risk—even for him. If she were somehow able to overpower him and obtain possession of it, who knows what havoc she'd wield with it?" Ursula paused to look meaningfully at me, and her eyes held a pinch of both worry and sorrow. "Or who she'd kill."

A sweat broke out across my brow. If Petra got her hands on the Casting Bead, she could easily kill me and head off any counter, retaliatory strikes from her husband. I added a shudder to the sweaty brow.

"Then he must have it hidden with the dragons," I concluded. The prospect of Elric not having complete control over such a powerful and potentially destructive trinket was too much to contemplate.

"Perhaps," Ursula finally conceded. "But remember that Elric is about as predictable as the winds of chaos."

I sighed. The very topic of Elric's predictability was irritating to me in the moment.

"What?" Ursula asked, reading my expression.

"There's something I didn't mention to you. Something about this past Valentine's Day . . ."

Her brow crinkled. "Valentine's Day? Dovey, you know that's my busiest day of the year. Every mystic in town puts in an order for a love potion. If something happened and I missed it, I'm so sorry."

"You didn't miss it, Ursula, and I know how busy that day is for you." Clearing my throat, I got to the point. "Do you remember anything about my plans to celebrate the night with Elric?"

"Of course. You were set on a very romantic evening in with him, if memory serves me correctly."

"Yes. Yes, I was. But it never happened."

Her crinkled brow furrowed. "It didn't? Why not?"

I sighed again and retrieved the blank note card from my handbag, feeling the shame of having created a fantasy about our love, when in fact the only thing he'd given me on that night was the casual cruelty of having my Valentine's gift be delivered by a low-ranking assistant. A gift that included an unsigned note and a set of regular salt and pepper shakers.

"As you know, Elric has always lavished me with delightful trinkets on Valentine's Day."

"Oh, I know. I'm still envious of that diamond bracelet that gives your hair such luster every time you wear it." She laughed.

I smiled. As it happened, I was wearing that very bracelet

today. "Well, this past Valentine's Day he canceled at the last minute. And he also had a messenger drop off the equivalent of a set of paperweights and this blank note card."

Unbidden tears formed in my eyes. It was so hard for me to admit this to my best friend. My shame bubbled to the surface—like I was the one that'd been so callous and thoughtless.

Ursula took the note card I handed to her, but before looking at it she squeezed my arm, reassuringly. Then her gaze dropped to the card, and she squinted, holding it closer to her eyes for a moment before she looked back at me and said, "Dovey, this isn't blank."

It was my turn to furrow my brow. "What're you seeing that I'm not?"

She held the note card up to face me; tapping the surface of it, she whispered, "Reveal what's hidden so we can see, what waits for us on the count of three . . . *en, to, tre*," she finished, pronouncing the numbers with a perfect Norwegian accent.

Instantly, lettering appeared on the note card. In swirling script it read,

> *Tortelduif,*
> *Apologies for tonight—a pressing matter I couldn't avoid. The gift is but a small token of my love. Take these with this card to the merlin Falcon the Wise and have him enchant them for you. He awaits your call.*
> *Love you, dove of my heart,*
> *E*

Fresh tears sprang to my eyes. I had no idea the message on the card was hidden, and when I thought about it, it made perfect sense. Elric would never have trusted a messenger to resist peeking at the personal note to me. If the messenger had known he was delivering a set of blanks for a merlin to enchant and all that was needed was to present that very note card, there's no telling what he could've sold the package for. Petra herself would pay a hefty price for them, in fact, and she'd also likely promptly put the messenger on her payroll, protecting him from Elric's wrathful revenge.

Ursula flipped the card around so that she could read it, and her gasp was audible. "Oh, Dovey, *this* is a *gift*! Falcon the Wise is one of the most powerful merlins in the world! To have a carte blanche trinket for his services is an exceptionally generous gesture."

I wiped my cheeks, my feelings tumbling like clothes in a dryer. I loved Elric. I did. And I was so moved by this, after feeling so hurt by what was now quite obviously a misunderstanding. I felt like a fool. "I haven't even thanked him," I said in a choked whisper.

"Did he notice?"

I took the note card from her outstretched hand, staring at the script in awe. "He didn't seem to. It was a week later before I saw him again, and by then I'd mostly tucked my hurt feelings away."

"What was the gift?"

"A set of glass and gold filigree salt and pepper shakers from L'Objet."

"Oh, I *love* that line. Their glassware is exquisite." For emphasis she pointed to the shelves of her built-in bookcase that displayed the many goblets and glasses she created her love potions in. At the near end was a whimsical set of prism martini glasses in shades of turquoise, green, orange, and purple.

"What should I have Falcon create for me?"

Ursula rolled her eyes, but she added a smile. "A weapon, of course. Or at least a proper defensive trinket to counteract any death curse lobbed at you." She then tapped her lip thoughtfully. "Actually, if he gave you *both* a salt and pepper shaker, then Falcon could create one of each."

I sighed. I somewhat hated that I had to take a perfectly good opportunity to have a set of trinkets turned into armor and a weapon when there were so many other playful and entertaining options to consider. But Ursula was right; both Gib and I might be in danger, and we'd need a proper defense to go up against whomever was powerful enough to inflict the Crushing Curse on the poor FBI agents, not to mention the mystic who'd zapped me into unconsciousness the night before.

I turned the card over to look at the back, but there was no script there. "How do I get in touch with Falcon the Wise?"

Ursula cupped my hand in hers. "Leave it to me. I'll get in touch and make an appointment for you, and we'll visit him together."

"Okay. Thank you, Ursula. That would be lovely. And I'll think of a way to thank Elric for the gift that won't seem like I've only just now opened it."

Ursula smiled. "Good luck with *that*." She was right, of course. Elric could spot a lie a mile away, and at any time he could simply ask me about my feelings and my binding spell would compel me to tell him about my guilt, then I'd have to explain it to him, and I dreaded that scenario.

My cell phone gave a sudden chirp, startling me. Reaching into my handbag, I lifted it out and looked at the screen. "Speak of the devil."

"Elric?" Ursula asked.

A chill went up my spine. "He's back at headquarters and wants to see me."

"Good. This is just what you want. A one-on-one meeting to ask him about the Crushing Curse being used against the FBI. Ask him if it was his directive and if he plans to target Grant."

I let my phone drop back into the opening of my handbag and turned to stare meaningfully at Ursula. "What if he intends to kill him?"

Ursula's lips pressed together thinly. "You have to tell him not to, Dovey. If this really is Elric's doing, then you've got to convince him to spare Grant."

"What if he wants to know why? He'll read my feelings! He'll know how I feel about Gib, and he'll kill him, Ursula! I know he will!" My voice cracked and I choked down a sob. I hadn't realized how terrified I was by the prospect of confronting Elric about Gib until I told Ursula my worst fear.

My friend reached out and took both of my hands in hers. "Dovey, I have known Elric longer than almost anyone. I have seen him at his worst. His most ruthless. His most deadly. And I have seen him at his best. His best has always been in the presence of your company. You soften him like no other mystic I know, and I have never known him to deny you. Trust this man with the truth. Trust his love and affection for you." She paused to tap the note card resting on my knee. "He loves you, Dovey, and even *he* could understand if your heart finally, after a hundred and eighty years together, would want for another."

My gaze fell and watched a few tears drop to the floor. I was so worried. So scared. I didn't want to be the cause of Gib's death. It would kill me to think I was responsible for any harm that came to him.

Ursula rubbed her thumb along the back of my hand. "He'll find out anyway, Dovey, so, as I see it, you have little choice in the matter."

I allowed Ursula's words to sink in for a moment. In the end, I realized she was right. I couldn't avoid this discussion, and if I did, and if Elric was responsible for the murders of these unbound agents, then Gib could well be next. If I didn't talk to Elric about my feelings for Gib, he might kill him all the same. "All right," I said with a nod. "I'll talk to him."

Ursula got up with me and walked me to the door. "You can do this," she encouraged, "and if things start to go sideways, reach out to me. Elric has been my friend for a long, long time. I'll do my best to make him see reason if you can't."

In a brief moment of weakness, I almost asked Ursula if she would go to HQ and meet Elric in my stead, but after thinking on it for another moment, I realized my longtime love and binder would lose all respect for me for pulling a move like that.

I hugged Ursula before leaving, hoping she understood how grateful I was for her sage advice and her steadfast friendship. I hoped she was right, and that Elric would be open to reason. As I walked toward Luna it seemed such a flimsy prayer to bet Gib's life on, but it was all I had.

CHAPTER 8

The rain had started up again, so I parked in the underground parking garage near the elevator, finding a slot easily for once. As I exited Luna and headed to the elevator I felt a sense of dread. I didn't know why Elric was summoning me, but given the gravity of the situation with the dead FBI agents, the mystic who'd staked out my home the night before, and/or the fact that Gib had stayed the night with me, I couldn't be certain that Elric didn't already know everything there was to know about what I'd been up to the last twenty-four hours. What awaited me could be trouble with a capital T.

There was also the possible disaster of the missing Casting Bead from the trinket vault. If it was indeed missing, and Qin had already confessed that fact to Elric, my binder's mood would be dark indeed, and a chat with him about my fee-fees wasn't likely to go well.

This was a thought that sent a tremor through me as I entered the elevator, because I hadn't considered it prior to driving over to HQ. And I only had eighteen floors to steel myself, because if I walked into Elric's office with even a hint of the terror coursing through me, he'd pick up on it and ask me why I was so afraid to see him, and my binding spell would force me to confess my fears—no matter his mood. If he were feeling dark and murderous before I even arrived, I gave Gib less than an hour to live once my tête-à-tête with Elric was done.

Closing my eyes and taking a deep breath to calm my frayed nerves, I waited until I couldn't hear my own heartbeat pounding away inside my rib cage before I pressed the up button for the eighteenth floor. The whole way up I continued to breathe deeply, with eyes closed, imagining the soft embrace of a seaside sunset, with lapping surf, seagulls' calls, and the whipping whisper of wind through the palm trees.

The technique worked better than expected and when I arrived at the eighteenth floor, I felt I had my nerves mostly under control.

Stepping out of the boxcar, I noticed there was only light afternoon traffic parading through the lobby. Hyacinth was at her station behind the reception desk, and now that I knew why her twin was no longer an employee, I approached the mystic warily. She glanced up and plastered a fake smile onto her face, which was quite a change from earlier and a sure sign that Elric was in residence. Still, she made certain to look at me with dead eyes lest I have any doubt about our chances of becoming besties.

"I have a meeting with Elric." I spoke firmly, like I owned the place.

She offered a slow blink and said, "He's expecting you."

She then waved her hand airily in the direction of his office before looking back down at her tablet, effectively dismissing me.

I rolled my eyes as I walked away. Still, she wasn't a battle I wanted to fight today.

Pausing in front of Elric's office door, I took one more deep breath, quieted my mind, stilled my emotions, and knocked.

The door handle turned and with a click the door gave way. Across the room I took in the man himself, sitting casually on the love seat, one leg crossed over the other and a glass of something dark and liquid held lazily in his hand.

Near his desk was a Louis Vuitton rolling duffel bag. The bag he typically traveled with.

"Torteleduif," he said with a smile.

I couldn't be certain, of course, as Elric was a master at hiding his feelings, but I swear I saw a flash of fatigue before he spoke. Fatigue was a rare expression on him, but then he'd spent much of the day with Petra, so it seemed fitting.

"Come in," he said gently.

Before moving, my gaze lingered on his luggage. I wondered where he was headed off to. "Europe," he said, reading my mind, then he waved his hand airily, sighed heavily and added, "Vostov has requested an audience. His court is always so dramatic."

I offered him a nod as I well understood the European Court was always the one either in trouble or making trouble, never giving Elric a moment of peace.

Knowing Elric likely had no time to waste, I drifted to the love seat opposite his and sat down, immediately realizing my mistake. I'd never not sat next to him when he'd summoned me. And I could tell he recognized the subtle shift.

"Elric," I said, matching his gentle tone. "How are you, my love?"

My binder's gaze shifted to the glass in his hand. Swirling the amber liquid, he asked, "Am I?"

"Are you what?"

His gaze snapped back to me. "Your love, Dovey? Am I still your love?"

A tingling sensation coursed along my skin. My binding spell would prevent me from telling him anything but the truth about how I felt about him. But this truth was easy for me to reveal because Elric *was* still my love. Right now, he just wasn't the only one. "Of course," I told him. "Of course."

He squinted at me for the briefest of moments before throwing back the entire contents of the glass. "I hear you were looking for me earlier."

I nodded. "I was. But first, I wanted to tell you that I'll be making a visit to Falcon the Wise sometime soon. I don't think I ever thanked you for your lovely gift."

He set his glass on the side table and eyed it like he was considering a refill. "A shame I couldn't have given it to you in person."

"I'm sure you had far more pressing matters to address that night. If I was wounded by your absence, I'm over it." And I was. "Anyway," I added, picking at a bit of lint on my slacks. "You wanted to see me?"

There was a brief pause, and I lifted my gaze back to his. There was a knowing look in his eyes, but I had no idea what he knew or from whom. "You first, Dovey."

I folded my hands in my lap and squared my shoulders. It was now or never. "I'm not sure if Jacquelyn has spoken to you yet, but I think we have a problem."

"Tell me."

"A mystic is assassinating FBI agents."

His brow furrowed and he sat forward. Clearly, Jacquelyn hadn't had the chance to brief him yet. "Tell me more."

"In the past two days, three agents have been murdered by mystic means."

"What spell or trinket was used?"

"The Crushing Curse," I told him, being sure not to blink as I said it. I wasn't outright accusing him, but we both knew the Crushing Curse was the preferred method he used to dispatch an enemy.

"You're certain?"

"Yes."

Elric tapped the arm of the love seat with his index finger. I had no idea what he might be thinking. Above all, Elric is a strategist. It unnerved me that I couldn't tell if the news I'd brought him came as a surprise or a confirmation.

My worry over the situation and my feelings for Gib pushed me to recklessly ask the next question. "Is this your work, Elric?"

His index finger stopped tapping and he eyed me keenly. "If it were, Dovey, would that upset you?"

Again, the tingling along my skin alerted me that I was about to tell Elric the truth. "Yes."

He nodded. "As I suspected." He then motioned casually with his hand. "The FBI agent you were seeing before."

Alarm hit my spine like an ice pick. "I wasn't *seeing* him, Elric. He was simply helping me with a case."

He smirked at me. "In the span of two minutes I've gone from 'my love' to 'Elric.' How quickly my rank falls whenever the attractive agent is mentioned."

Heat erupted onto my cheeks. I was a fool to think I could keep anything about my attraction to Gib from Elric. The man knew me better than I knew myself. Which made this meeting between us very, very dangerous, definitely for Gib and quite possibly for me.

"Your *rank* with me, Elric, has never wavered. You are my binder. My love. My adore, and for the past one hundred and eighty years, you've been my whole world. You know that."

He sighed as he looked at me, but another flash of emotion skittered across his eyes before it was gone. For just a moment he'd looked sad. "I do, my dove. But things have changed, have they not? You're seeing him romantically now, are you not?"

It was my turn to look sad. "There is a confession I'm bound to share."

Elric adopted a bemused smile. "I'm all ears."

I dropped my gaze to my lap again and struggled to keep my fingers from trembling. It was time to take Ursula's advice. What other choice did I have? "Special Agent Barlow and I *aren't* seeing each other. And we *haven't* been seeing each other. Our relationship has been professional. Somewhat."

"Somewhat?"

My gaze lifted and I forced myself to look Elric straight in the eye. "I like him, Elric."

A silence unfolded between us. I might describe it as uncomfortable, but the reality was more complicated. Nothing was said, but everything was revealed.

At last, he broke the silence. "What are you really saying, Dovey?"

I continued to hold his gaze, barely blinking as I repeated in a soft whisper, "I *like* him, Elric."

He considered me expectantly. "And . . . ?"

My limbs had begun to tremble. With these next words, I might be ending Gib's life, but there was no way to backpedal. No way to take back what I'd started to say. I inhaled a shuddering breath and said, "I *want* to start seeing him romantically."

Another lengthy silence played out between us. I simply continued to look at Elric, my lover, my mentor, my friend, and my binder, and I wasn't about to break that silence. I owed it to him to allow the next words uttered to be his.

"And how does he feel about you?" he said, casually getting up to fetch the decanter of his favorite brandy from the shelf next to his desk.

Before answering, I studied his posture, trying to determine his true mood. Was he angry? Indifferent? Or something in between? "I believe he would like to start seeing me as well."

Elric tipped the bottle, elegantly pouring out two fingers of amber liquid into the bottom of his glass. Replacing the stopper with a melodic clink of crystal on crystal, he held it in his hand as he turned to me and said, "For the better part of two centuries, Dovey Van Dalen, you have served me well. And you have been loyal like no other. Even when I broke your heart—other than that year you spent in Spain, you've never held it against me. How can I deny you your heart's desire now?"

Unbidden tears filled my eyes, one trailing down my cheek. It was the most meaningful thing Elric had ever said to me. To know he'd seen my love for him. My acceptance of who he was. And my willingness to follow him to hell and back. It simply meant the world to me.

"Do you really mean that?" I managed in a choked whisper.

Elric set down the decanter and walked to my love seat. Sitting down next to me, he emitted a heavy sigh. Taking my hand in his, he said, "Yes. Of course I do."

My lower lip trembled, and tears fell. I willed myself not to give into a sob of relief, and all I could do was mouth, *Thank you.*

He nodded. "You may have your tryst, but I have some rules." I nodded eagerly. "Rule number one: I cannot be seen as someone cuckolded by his mistress."

My eyes widened, and I swallowed hard. That hadn't even been a consideration of mine, and I mentally chastised myself for not considering how my seeing an unbound would look to other mystics within the court. "Of . . . of course, Elric. Of course you're right."

"You will need to leave here in tears," he continued, nodding toward the door. "You will need to walk out of this office begging me to take you back."

I continued to stare at him with widened, watery eyes. "I understand." And in that moment, I did. The full gravity was hitting me in real time, making my insides feel leaden and heavy. Elric wasn't going to make me perform a breakup scene simply to save himself any embarrassment. He was publicly ending our relationship in a way that brokered little chance for reconciliation. And that stung in a way I wasn't prepared for when I'd entered his office.

He reached up gently and used his thumb to wipe away a tear. "Rule number two," he said. "You are *never* to bind him, Dovey."

"I have no such plans."

"I believe you, but there may be a time when you will want to extend your romance with this man. And I'm telling you, he must remain mortal. Even if it will break your heart, you must leave him unbound."

What Elric wasn't saying was that, as far as he was concerned, I could have my tryst, but I could only have it for a relatively short length of time. As soon as Gib began to age, and notice that I wasn't, I'd have to end things. There would be no way to broker more time with him. These were Elric's terms, and I could take them or leave them.

"He will remain unbound, Elric," I vowed.

"You may not ask anyone else to bind him, either," he insisted, and I knew he was thinking of Ursula, because Ursula would bind Gib for me in a heartbeat.

"I won't. I promise you; I won't bind him or ask anyone else to."

He nodded, apparently satisfied. "Rule number three: you will not reveal to this unbound agent any aspect of our world. The last thing we need is an unbound FBI investigator, poking around in mystic business, or curious about his mystic girlfriend and with an inquisitiveness to learn more."

My brow furrowed. That was an odd demand, but my head was spinning with all the sudden changes happening between us, so I dared not question it. Instead, I nodded, showing him I understood.

"Do you accept these terms?"

"I do."

"And I do not have to remind you of the penalty I would be forced to exact if I was disobeyed."

My heart slammed against my chest as his words shot adrenaline through my veins. Elric had never threatened me. And because of our nearly two centuries together as lovers and the closest of confidants, I did not take that statement as a threat against me. But it was clearly a threat against Gib. Elric would take Gib's life in a heartbeat if I disobeyed his rules.

"You don't need to remind me," I assured him. "I understand completely."

Elric nodded and his expression softened into something I had only very rarely seen. He looked sad. And as he reached up to cup my cheek, I couldn't help the flow of tears and quivering lip as my own emotions got the best of me. I couldn't know for certain, but this felt like something had broken between us. Something that had been my everything for most of my life. "I love you, Elric Ostergaard," I whispered.

"I know you do," was his only reply.

He then lifted his hand away from my cheek and nodded toward the door. Helping me to my feet, he escorted me to the exit before wrapping me in his arms and hugging me tightly. He then pulled away slightly to lean over my shoulder and loudly say, "We're done! My decision is final!"

The boom of his voice startled me, and I sucked in a breath, but I quickly recovered, looked up at him with wet cheeks, adding my shuddering voice to his chorus. "No! Please! You don't mean that!"

"It's over, Dovey! Don't make a scene!"

A sob escaped me. Very little of that was performative. "*Please*, Elric! I'm begging you! Don't do this! I love you!"

Eric released me, kissed me lightly on the lips, then took a full step back. Reaching around me, he grabbed the door handle and yanked it open. "*Leave*. Now."

I shuffled backward through the open door, my hands pressed together as if in prayer. "I'll do anything! Just don't send me away!"

Behind me in the lobby you could hear a pin drop. Even the minimal traffic walking by had come to a full stop.

The look on Elric's face was one I had seen him wear thousands of times before. It was an expression of disdain and disappointment, and it killed my soul to have it aimed at me. "I will send word of your next assignment. Until then, stay away from HQ." With that Elric slammed the door in my face.

I crumpled to the floor, curling up next to the door, openly weeping for several moments. Cognitively, I knew we were putting on quite the performance, so why did it all feel so real?

Sniffling loudly, I finally worked my way to my feet. Traffic in the lobby was now much thicker. It seemed the entire eighteenth floor had come out to witness my humiliation. And I knew that news of our breakup would go viral within the mystic world before I even left the building.

Keeping my head down I scrambled through the crowd and rushed toward the elevator. My trembling fingers found the button and I pressed it incessantly until the doors opened. Barely waiting for the two passengers to exit, I leapt forward, repeatedly stabbing the button for the parking garage.

I lifted my gaze only as the doors closed, seeing an entire lobby chock-full of astonished faces . . . with one notable exception. Hyacinth stared back at me, wearing a smile that was ear to ear.

Once the elevator reached the garage, I rushed out of the boxcar. I had to admit, all the tumbling and turbulent emotions pouring out of me felt entirely too real. I had loved Elric for 180 years. I had loved him like no other, with my body, heart, mind, and soul. And it wasn't lost on me that he had let me go without resistance. Not a single protest. He simply laid down a few rules that wouldn't besmirch his reputation and helped me to the exit.

And I couldn't quite reconcile that. Mostly because it wasn't what I'd been expecting. I'd been expecting something of a battle; not a physical one of course, but some back and forth that would help me to convince him that what I wanted mattered. Before I'd even entered the elevator from the garage, I hadn't even considered that we'd break up as succinctly as we had. I don't quite know what I'd expected the outcome to be. I know what I'd hoped, but I don't think I'd spent much time considering a scenario where our romance wasn't simply set aside for a spell; it was *over*.

It was now my understanding, given the look in his eyes and the very public breakup that he'd requested, we were in fact over . . . for good. At some point in the future, long after Gib was but a pleasant memory, we might spend some time as lovers again, but we'd never again be seen as a couple. I knew that in my soul.

And that's what was causing me to continue to tremble and cry, well after there were no witnesses to see it. The end of Elric as my *partner* had arrived, and it was hitting me like a ton of bricks right in the solar plexus.

I scrambled into Luna and simply wept for at least an hour. When I finally managed to make my way out of the parking garage, I found myself driving aimlessly. I had no intention of going anywhere, but the simple fact of powering the car forward began to make me feel a little better, and before I knew it, I was back at Ursula's.

Her door opened before I even got out of the car, a worried look on her face, and when she saw me up close, she threw her arms around me and hugged me while I sobbed into her shoulder. My breakup with Elric felt like a death, and it was hitting me so hard that I began to question why I was doing it.

We sat together on Ursula's sofa, and I told her everything over another cup of tea. This time a different special blend that took away the sharp edge of my heartbreak, leaving me feeling calmer if also a bit numb.

"I don't even know why I'm being so dramatic," I said, wiping a lone tear from my cheek.

She squeezed my hand. "I would've worried had you shown up here and not been devastated. You love him, Dovey. Discovering that you also have feelings for Grant doesn't negate that. And it doesn't help that Elric is your binder, either. Protégés always have more intense feelings for their binders than for other mystics. Sometimes, when the binder proves himself or herself benevolent, those feelings grow into love, and when that binder has been cruel, those feelings can form hate. It's a special trick that comes with being able to cast a first spell around an unbound. It helps us to make wise choices both in who we choose and how we treat them afterward."

"He's been nothing but good to me all these years, Ursula. Am I doing the right thing? Should I *actually* beg him to take me back?"

"By the gods, Dovey! Don't even go there. Elric Ostergaard doesn't do pity, and he will *not* pity you if you go crawling back. You will only permanently disappoint him, and he may *never* show you kindness again.

"No," she continued, "the deed is done and now you must grieve and move forward. You and Grant will make a wonderful couple, and it could be ten to fifteen years before he realizes you're not aging as you should. A decade and a half ain't nothin'. Trust me. I've lived well over a hundred of them and the few I took an unbound as a lover were the most magical."

I smirked, then sighed heavily and sipped some more tea. "I didn't mention the Casting Bead to Elric."

"Qin Shi will be most grateful for that. If he lives long enough to thank you for it."

I studied Ursula's face, looking for a hint of humor, but there was little to be seen. "Would Elric really execute Qin for the missing trinket?"

"He would. You haven't known Elric like the rest of us have, Dovey. He's always been nothing but sweet love and devotion with you, but for the rest of us . . . let's just say there isn't a mystic within his court that he doesn't consider disposable."

"Then we have to do something for Qin Shi," I insisted. "I love that little gnome. I'd be devastated if he were executed."

"If you want to help Qin Shi, then don't mention the Casting Bead to Elric or any other mystic. Now, or ever. Allow Qin to retrieve the trinket on his own. He's incredibly powerful in his own right. And crafty. He'd have to be to survive this long as Elric's trinket master."

"Should we . . . I offer to help Qin Shi track it down?"

"Again, *no*. You'll only call attention to the matter. Best to pretend you think nothing's amiss. Let Qin do his job." Ursula seemed to think of something and added, "Speaking of mystics doing their job, I contacted Falcon the Wise. He can see us tonight at ten p.m."

I lifted my wrist to look at my watch. It was already close to five. "I should get home then. I've got to give Bits his dinner, wash my face, and freshen myself up. It wouldn't do to present myself with puffy eyes and red cheeks to a merlin."

"It wouldn't," she agreed. Standing tall and offering me a hand up, she said, "Go home, Dovey. Take care of that little beasty and freshen up, then come straight back. I'll whip up some dinner for us and we can hang until it's time to see the merlin."

I took her hand, got to my feet, ready to leave when a thought occurred to me and I plopped right back down on the sofa again. "Now what?" Ursula asked.

"Gib. I can't leave him on his own, and if we won't be meeting the merlin until ten; we likely won't be back until . . . when?"

"Well after midnight. He'll make us wait for the trinkets to be enchanted. It shouldn't take too long, depending on what you'd like him to create for you."

I put a hand up to cover my eyes. "I totally forgot to think of what I want them to do!"

Ursula reached down and took firm hold of my wrist, pulling my hand away so she could look at me keenly and say, "Go home. Take care of Bits. Call Gib, tell him you're working a case that requires surveillance, but you'd still like him to come over and hang out at your place until you get back, which should be sometime around ten."

My brow furrowed. "That's when we'll be meeting the merlin."

"It is. You'll text him when we arrive at Falcon's estate and let him know that the surveillance is running later than expected, but you should be able to head his way within the hour, then, keep extending the time it's taking until we're *actually* able to leave. That way, he'll be safely warded inside your home until you get back. Just leave him a key to your house inside your garage and give him the garage code so he can get it and let himself in. Make sure to also tell him to lock the doors and keep the windows closed as you heard there was a break-in down the street right after the storm."

I smiled. "That is a great plan, my friend."

"Of course it is. Now get outta here so I can prep our dinner!" Getting to my feet again, I headed to the door while Ursula turned toward her kitchen. I paused at the door to say over my shoulder, "Thank you, my friend."

"Anytime. And don't forget those salt and pepper shakers. We can't show up empty-handed, and if we did, it's doubtful Falcon would allow you to go back home and retrieve them. He'd take it as a personal insult that you arrived without something for him to enchant."

"On it," I said, hurrying to Luna and jumping inside, ready to get home, take care of business then come back again.

It was still drizzling when I made it home. I parked Luna in the garage and moved the spare key I kept on a top shelf under one of the many empty flowerpots I kept there over to an empty shelf next to the bay door. Gib should be able to find it, no problem.

Then I hustled out of the garage and over to the back door. When I inserted my key into the lock, however, it wouldn't turn. I used some muscle to try and twist the key, but it was like the door was wedged shut. I glanced at the drizzle from under the cover of the porch's roof and considered that the damp was making the old wood of the door expand. I probably could've used a little magic to get the lock to turn and the door open, but I honestly didn't have it in me. I felt exhausted and all I wanted to do was get inside, take care of Bits, retrieve Elric's Valentine's Day gift, freshen up, and get back to Ursula's. I figured I could relax for three hours or so before we met the merlin.

So, I abandoned the back porch, retraced my steps to the driveway, and went around to the front door. Heading up the steps I inserted my key hoping this door wasn't also wedged shut, and to my relief the lock turned easily. I made my way inside, coming up short when I realized there was someone in my living room, sitting casually in my favorite wing chair.

"Hello, Dovey," the lieutenant said.

I froze. Finn the Flayer was in my living room, and one only gets a visit from the Flayer if he's the last person you're about to see.

I'd only ever seen him from afar, but he cut quite the figure. Dressed head to toe in black, he was six-foot-six if he was an inch, black hair, gorgeous hazel eyes, a delicate nose and a square jaw. And while I didn't know a lot about Petra's lieutenant, I knew enough to know that his reputation and resulting nickname were well earned.

My keys dropped to the floor with a loud clang. My mouth

fell open too, but no words or screams came out. In fact, for a long moment, it was all I could do to suck in a ragged breath. Finally, in a voice as soft as a whisper, I asked, "Why now?"

"You've fallen out of favor," Finn said, inspecting his nails like he had not a care in the world.

My heart was thundering against the wall of my chest like a caged animal, staring death in the face and frantic for a way out. "Which is why I'll repeat, Lieutenant, why *now?*"

Finn shrugged nonchalantly. "Petra's had a hundred and eighty years to stew about your very public affair with her husband."

I blinked and shook my head at the absurdity. "*She's* the one that has a son out of wedlock! And she doesn't even *like* Elric!"

"This is true. But she likes you even less, Dovey."

"She won't get away with this without repercussions," I insisted. My mind was a flurry of neurons firing, desperately trying to find a way out of this certain death moment. The weight of realizing that I'd risked everything and lost someone I dearly loved in order to explore a relationship with someone I was immensely attracted to only to come home and be assassinated felt like the grossest injustice I could think of. "He could even kill *you*, Flayer."

Finn looked up at me with half-lidded eyes. "He could try."

I scoffed at him. Of all the absurdity unfolding in this moment, that statement was perhaps the *most* absurd. Elric was the most powerful mystic on earth. No one could challenge him and survive, and the only reason Petra herself was still alive was because he was bound by the contract of their marriage vows, which was a binding that wouldn't allow him to kill her.

Movement across the room caught my eye, and, with horror, my gaze settled on Bits emerging from the fabric snuggle he used as his downstairs bed, which sat atop my desk. My sweet picklepuss appeared sleepy, adorable, and oh so vulnerable.

More tears filled my eyes. I was so tired of crying. This day had been filled with such loss, and I couldn't take it. Ignoring Finn for a moment I rushed over to Bits, lifted him into my arms, and carefully snuggled him against my chest. He made a squeaky noise that brought even more tears.

Glancing over my shoulder, I looked at Finn and said, "Don't kill him. You'll do what you'll do to me, but don't kill *him*."

Finn's expression was unreadable, and we spent a long moment in silence broken only when he asked, "What's his name?"

The question took me by surprise. I thought about not answering because I didn't know the level of his brutality. If he killed Bits in front of me before killing me, it would be unspeakably cruel. The mere thought of it had me holding Bits even closer. I'd protect him with my body and hope it was enough to see him through whatever death curse the Flayer was about to throw at me. "His name is Bits," I said when the silent moment lingered into awkwardness. "He was a gift to me from Elric." Maybe tying Bits to Elric would get my hedgehog's life spared.

"He's a cute little guy, I'll give him that."

I continued to hold Bits protectively, suddenly undecided if I should try to settle him back in his bed before facing the music or use my body to shield him from harm any way I could. If Finn assassinated me with a death curse, would any living creature nearby also be slain?

Petra's lieutenant pushed himself to his feet and came to stand in front of me. I was a trembling mess, and I didn't know what to do with Bits. I didn't know how to protect him from the assassin. And I never wanted more to know how Bits teleported himself from place to place so that I might command him to do so right now.

But it seemed, instead of feeling my fear and fleeing the scene, Bits snuggled closer and squeaked again. I knew he sensed the danger in the room, but he was unwilling to leave me.

Finn raised a hand, and I flinched. "Easy, easy," he said, placing an index finger on Bits's quills. I shook my head hard and I badly wanted to slap the Flayer's hand away. He was going to kill my sweet picklepuss. "Please, Flayer. Please, please, don't kill him in front of me. Don't let that be the last thing I know!"

My breathing was coming so hard I thought I might pass out, but then I realized that Finn was not casting a death curse. He was petting Bits, sweetly, almost playfully.

Was this part of his method? Did he like to play with his victims before he killed them?

And then his eyes found mine and a small smile pushed at the corners of his lips. "Petra sent me here to look for vulnerabilities in your wards, and, if I found any, to take care of business."

I merely blinked at him, and a pregnant pause played out between us. "Annnnd . . . ?"

"*And*, when I report back to Petra, I will tell her that your house is impenetrable. I found no vulnerabilities. But you should know that I gained easy access to this house, Dovey Van Dalen."

My mind seemed almost incapable of taking in what he was saying. Was he sparing me? Would Finn the Flayer not follow through on an assassination order?

Another long silence played out between us, and it finally occurred to me that Finn was waiting for me to ask the obvious question. "Where am I vulnerable?"

"The window in your back bedroom, off the laundry room. You left it open a crack, and your wards were easily penetrable there. Now that you're out from underneath Elric's protection you'll need to ward this house with every precautionary measure at your disposal, and keep all doors and windows shut tight."

And with one last stroke atop Bit's head, Finn the Flayer— arguably one of the most feared mystics in existence—turned away and walked to the door. Without looking back he opened it, stepped out into the rain, and promptly disappeared.

I fell to my knees gasping for air. It seemed I was slow to pick up on a lot of things that had occurred today. The full impact of my new status as Eric's ex was only now starting to hit home. I was as vulnerable in that moment as I'd ever been in my entire life. It was a sobering notion when I realized I could no longer live life even remotely as carefree as I had been. I'd never appreciated the full context of Elric's protection.

Without it I might as well paint a bull's-eye on my back.

CHAPTER 9

I spent much of the next hour both trying to calm my nerves and, after firmly shutting and locking the window that Gib had no doubt opened a crack in the guest bedroom, I warded the house again from top to bottom.

If I wasn't exhausted before, I was definitely feeling it now.

For his part, Bits ate his dinner then teleported himself into every room I moved into while I casted more warding spells. During that hour, Gib called, and I put him on speaker as I checked the windows in my own bedroom. "How's the investigation going?" I asked after saying hello.

"Not good. It's going to be a long night, Dovey. I won't be able to stop by. We're going over the forensic evidence hair by hair, looking for anything that can point us in a direction."

I picked up the phone and took it off speaker. "So, you'll be working all night?" Gib might be much safer at work among his colleagues than alone in his house or even my house.

"Definitely. If I need to catch a few winks, there're a couple of sofas in the office. We've already decided to take turns once the fatigue really kicks in."

I exhaled a sigh of relief. He'd be there all night. I didn't have to worry about him being alone and vulnerable.

"What're you up to?" he asked next.

Just in case he *did* get let off work earlier than expected and came over here to see me, I said, "I've got a case I'm working that requires a bit of surveillance."

"Oh yeah?"

"Suspected cheating husband. He's fond of his personal assistant. Maybe a little too fond, according to his wife."

"Be careful, Dovey. Cheating husbands can turn angry and violent when they're caught in the act."

"I'll be fine." One glance at my watch told me I was running behind schedule. "I'll let you get back to work, Gib. And if you can't knock off early and come by—and that invite is still open, by the way—then maybe we could try getting together tomorrow night?"

"I'd like that," he said. I felt that flutter of desire and happiness twirl around my abdomen.

After finishing warding my master bath, I headed downstairs again, finding Bits next to the front door, looking up at me expectantly. "Bitty, I can't tonight. Ursula and I have to go see a merlin about a trinket, and we'll be out late."

Carrying him over to his favorite snuggle on my desk, I placed him gently within its folds, then fussed about making sure I had the shakers, my handbag with a trinket or two that were good in a pinch, and my umbrella. Walking to the back door again, I found Bits perched on the small table where I kept my keys and the mail, once more looking up at me expectantly.

I paused to heavily sigh at him, which bothered him not in the least. If I attempted to put him back in his snuggle, he'd no doubt show up in my handbag on the way over to Ursula's. When Bits wanted to go with me, the easier version was always to give in and take him along.

Moving back to my desk, I grabbed the snuggle, traded my clutch for the larger handbag I'd taken to HQ that morning before tucking the snuggle inside and heading back to get Bits. But when I got to the back door, he was no longer on the table. "Bitty?" I called, searching around the kitchen.

Maybe I'd gotten it wrong, and he didn't want to go along. Maybe he was simply playing a game to see if I'd give in.

"Bitty?" I tried again, scanning the room. There was no sign of him. I growled low and muttered, "I don't have time for your games, you wicked little picklepuss!"

Grabbing my keys and patting my handbag to quadruple check that I'd transferred the shakers to the larger bag along with my wallet, I unlocked the door and stepped out into the drizzling, chilly night.

I'd changed into a thick black sweater with a cowl-neck, skinny jeans, and knee-length leather boots. I'd also tied my hair up into a loose ponytail. It was a relief to see that, when getting myself together earlier, my eyes weren't nearly as puffy from the afternoon's pity party.

Hurrying to the garage, I stepped inside, patted Luna on her roof, and climbed into the driver's seat, settling my handbag on the passenger seat . . . where it moved.

The movement was slight, but I'd seen it. Reflexively, I gathered a bundle of defensive essence into the palm of my hand. Weeks earlier, I'd battled a serpent who'd slithered underneath a pile of trinkets, unseen until it decided to show its fifteen-foot length and head the size of a dinner plate, so I was understandably still flinchy about any random object moving on its own.

The handbag fell over. I held my breath, ready to hurl the essence and scramble from the car, but then a small black nose appeared from the opening, and it twitched while it sniffed the air.

"You. Little. Beast!" I scolded, letting go of the breath I'd been holding.

The nose disappeared and the handbag jiggled as Bits

worked his way into the snuggle still inside the bag. While he was working his way into a more comfortable position, a noise echoed up from the bottom of the bag that sounded very much like a cash register ringing up a sale. A sort of *cha-ching* sound that was faint, and pleasant to the ears. Curiously, I peeked into the bag, thinking my phone must've made the noise, but Bits's butt was blocking my view of the bottom of the bag, and he seemed annoyed that I was invading his privacy, because he chuffed irritably when I began to poke around his sides, searching for my phone. Another *cha-ching* sounded and now I was convinced my phone was emitting some strange noise. Maybe I'd accidentally changed the text alert to chime to the sound of a cash register?

"I'll look at that later," I muttered. Wasting time on something that didn't matter right now wasn't on the agenda.

Starting the car, I hit the garage door opener. Looking back at my handbag, I once again addressed Bits. "Hey, you little picklepuss, no getting into trouble at Ursula's. The last time you were over there you broke three of her goblets and I don't have it in me tonight to repair them, Bitty."

The handbag didn't move, which meant . . . nothing, really. My hedgehog might behave, or he might not. He did his own thing and got away with it every time, but I had never stopped believing I'd someday be able to order him around and he'd obey.

Putting the car in reverse, I glanced in the rearview mirror and saw the same cloaked and hooded figure I'd seen from last night taking up the whole mirror, standing right behind my car. In the darkness, I couldn't make out any features, but I knew it was the same mystic.

When they began to raise their hand, revealing a palm-sized trinket that twinkled in the light from the garage, I knew I was seconds away from death.

Again.

Without even thinking, I stomped on the gas and Luna rocketed backward. The move caught the mystic by surprise and there was a loud *whack* against the trunk as he or she flew up onto the roof of the car, tumbling down the right side and out of my view.

I continued to stomp on the gas, because I knew I wasn't lucky enough to have killed the mystic, so I had to hope that I'd at least severely injured them. Bolting down the drive, I spun the wheel the second we hit the pavement of the street, then immediately pulled on the gearshift and stomped on the gas again, praying I didn't hit any car coming or going down the street.

Behind me someone honked, but my focus was getting us out of there as fast as possible. It was several seconds before I dared glance back in my rearview mirror again, and it didn't appear that anyone was behind me.

Still, I wove in and out of traffic all the way to Ursula's, constantly checking to see if we were being followed, but if I had a tail, I didn't spot it.

Once I got to Ursula's block, I drove around it twice before I was certain no cars behind me were following. At last, I pulled into her driveway, right behind her car. Then I grabbed my handbag and bolted for the front door.

My best friend answered the frantic pounding on her door quickly, thank God.

"What's happened?" she asked, ushering me inside.

I was a trembling mess but managed to tell her about the mystic at my garage door and the ensuing race to get here. "I'm so sorry, Ursula, I know I probably shouldn't have come here with an assassin on my tail, but I have Bits with me, and I couldn't think of anywhere safe. Elric forbad me from showing up at HQ so soon after our public breakup and—"

"Shhh, Dovey," she said, putting gentle hands on my shoulders. "Stop. Of course you should've come here. Go sit on the sofa and keep that little scamp away from my goblets while I put the wards up and retrieve a trinket to hide your car."

I did as she asked and parked myself on her sofa while watching her hurry about, setting up her protective wards at every door and window, not even overlooking the fireplace. Then she hurried to her spare bedroom to retrieve a thick set of gold bangle bracelets and a brass-handled stamp about three inches by two inches. Slipping bangles onto both her wrists before opening the door, she said, "Be right back," and left me.

I got up and moved to the storm door to watch my best friend trot to Luna and performatively stamp her hood. Leaving the stamp on the hood, she stepped away and made a circular motion with her hand. I saw an orb of her energy zip from her palm to the stamp, and in the blink of an eye, Luna was gone.

I gasped in awe at the neat trick, a bubble of envy rising to the surface. Mystics often struggle to control their lust for another mystic's trinkets. Most of us are thieves at heart, and had Ursula not been my *best* friend, I might've worked out a few ways to relieve her of it.

It's an impulse that's hard to control—as a group we're materialistic to an unseemly degree by unbound standards. Trinkets don't represent just power, prestige, and wealth, they're also tied to our longevity. Our very lives depend on gathering as many as we can to ourselves. Feeling that familiar lust for another mystic's trinket, however, was a good reminder to keep my new trinkets well under wraps once the Falcon enchanted them.

I still hadn't made up my mind what kind of magic I wanted them to produce, but I was currently leaning toward an invisibility option.

I got out of the way when Ursula came back to the door. She

moved inside, locked the storm door, then bolted and chained the front door and finally warded it to firmly secure us inside.

Luring me to the sofa again, she pointed to the cushion next to my handbag, which seemed a little less bulgy, and only after I took my seat again did she head to the kitchen. I heard the clink of china and utensils, and a moment later she returned with two steaming plates of food. Setting one down in front of me, she commanded, "Eat."

I was still jittery after the adrenaline rush, but the food looked and smelled delicious.

The fare was a combination of roasted sweet potatoes, butternut squash, and brussels sprouts, all tossed with a cranberry glaze and topped with crumbled goat cheese, dried cranberries, and candied pecans.

I took one bite and moaned. It was exactly the comfort food I needed. While we tucked into our dinner, Ursula asked, "This mystic that tried to kill you tonight . . . Was there any hint to their identity?"

"No. But it's the same cloaked figure that was outside my window last night—the one that zapped me from the street. Although . . . it could've been one of Petra's minions. Her lieutenant was waiting for me this afternoon when I got home, and my God, is that man gorgeous. If he weren't so terrifying, I'd probably make him my friend for the eye candy factor alone."

Ursula dropped her fork and it clanged on the side of her plate all while she stared at me with wide, disbelieving eyes. "The *Flayer* paid you *a visit?*"

"He did. I discovered him in my living room, sitting in my favorite wing chair like he owned the place."

"*How* are you still alive?"

I shrugged. "I think he took pity on me."

Ursula shook her head. "The Flayer isn't known for taking pity on *anyone*, Dovey."

I shrugged again. "What can I say, Ursula? After my breakup with Elric went mystic viral, Petra heard about it and ordered him to look for a weak point in my wards. He found one in the guest bedroom because Gib had left the window open a crack. The Flayer told me that Petra wanted me dead. I begged him not to kill Bits, then he gave the picklepuss a little pat on the head and left."

"Incredible," she said. "Is it possible he changed his mind and came back to finish the deed?"

My own mind flashed back to the blur of the mystic in Luna's rearview mirror, and something hit me full force. "No. It wasn't him. It was someone else. Someone much more dangerous."

"More dangerous than the Flayer? That could only be Petra. Maybe she decided to take matters into her own hands."

"I don't think so. I'm certain this mystic was holding the Casting Bead when he or she was about to kill me. I swear I saw it in their hand."

Ursula set her fork down and her complexion went white. In a haunting tone she said, "So the Bead really did make its way out of Elric's trinket vault."

"It seems so."

"Dovey, this is very, very bad. It's bad for Qin Shi, bad for you, and possibly bad for the rest of us, *including* Elric."

I rubbed my temples. The stress of the last two days was beginning to wear on me. "Maybe Elric *gave* it to someone."

"Elric would *never* give another mystic the Casting Bead. And he would never send someone *else* to kill you, even if you'd fallen out of favor enough to warrant it. And even then, I can't imagine him sending an assassin for you. I truly believe you're the only mystic Elric has ever loved, and before you came along, I didn't think he was capable of any kind of love at all. He adores you enough to allow you a tryst, after all. What other mystic would allow their bound lover that excess?"

I shook my head. I didn't know. "We have to warn Qin Shi."

"We do indeed. And we need to do it before we meet with the Falcon. Finish your dinner—you'll need fuel for the night ahead—and then we'll head to HQ."

"I'm not allowed to enter the building," I reminded her, tucking into my meal once again.

"Then we'll put you in disguise."

I cocked a skeptical eyebrow at her, but didn't argue.

Forty-five minutes later, Ursula came to rest her car in a slot near the elevator in the underground garage at SPL.

As she did so, I once again pulled down her vanity mirror to stare in awe at the face in the reflection. My dark blond hair was now raven colored, my blue eyes were brown, my heart-shaped face was squarer, and my skin tone was just a tad fairer.

Centuries ago, Ursula had been a spy for Elric. She'd traveled to the other five courts and went mostly unnoticed because of a special trinket in the shape of a necklace with a lion's-head medallion that allowed her to craft her own visage. She could look like anyone; all she had to do was push a little essence into the medallion and imagine what she wanted to look like, and voilà! Depending on how much essence she pushed into the medallion, she could be someone else for hours and hours.

I now wore the necklace and with her help I'd shaped a completely different identity for myself. It was a remarkable transformation.

"I sooo want this trinket," I said softly, after we'd gotten out of the car and approached the elevator.

Ursula chuckled and pressed the button to call the elevator. "You know I love you, but that would only happen over my dead body. That trinket is one of the best I've got, and I use it often."

My brows arched. "Oh? And who might you be spying on of late?"

Ursula cleared her throat and focused on the lit numbers above the double doors as they displayed the boxcar's descent. "Almost there," she said, pointing up.

The bangles on her wrist slipped down her forearm, capturing my attention.

I tapped one with my fingernail. "Offense or defense?"

She smiled wryly. "A little of both. They act as slingshots, capturing a volley of power and tossing it back at an attacker. They're a trinket of last resort, though."

"They sound fantastic," I told her, that bubble of envy rising again. "Why are they a last resort?"

"They require an immense amount of essence to activate. A more powerful mystic might not feel the toll, but they've bled me nearly dry before. A powerful enough foe could kill me in a sustained battle."

"Let's hope it doesn't come to that," I muttered, reaching to tuck the edges of Bits's snuggle around him as he snoozed at the bottom of my handbag, and my fingers rubbed against an unfamiliar object. Rooting around I pulled up the trinket Qin had given me when he forced me to make a hasty exit earlier in the day.

"Ahh, the dud," Ursula said. "You should ask Qin why he sent you off with something completely worthless today when you were at your most vulnerable."

I studied the money clip, suddenly remembering the *cha-ching* sound that'd been coming from the bottom of my purse when I'd been in the garage. Had this trinket made that sound? "I'll ask him about it," I said, turning the trinket over in my palm.

Ursula tapped my elbow and pointed to the elevator where the doors had just parted. "Shall we go up, total stranger?"

We got into the elevator, and I grinned when I thought about the medallion around my neck. I suspected Ursula had been spying on Dex. She had it bad for that man.

A minute or two later, we'd made it up to the seventeenth floor and stepped out into the vestibule only to find Qin at his desk fussing over its messy array of trinkets, his gaming goggles, papers, and pink message slips of likely unreturned calls that'd no doubt been delivered daily by Hyacinth.

Qin looked up when the doors parted. "Hello, Ursula," he said, nodding at her. "Dovey," he added, nodding to me.

My eyes widened. "How'd you know it was me?"

He shrugged. "Who else would it be?"

I smiled at first, but then I took in the hauntedly worried look in his eyes and the way his hands were trembling. I immediately understood that he didn't know where the Casting Bead was, nor who'd stolen it.

"We're here with some news about the Casting Bead, Qin," I said quickly.

His gaze became laser focused. "Speak to me."

"There's a mystic out for my blood—"

"Petra," he interrupted with a nod. "I'm guessing she's sent her lieutenant, the Flayer, to handle you?"

I wasn't necessarily surprised that Qin knew that Petra had it out for me now that Elric and I were over. The trinket guardian was tapped into the mystic gossip tree just as much as anyone around here.

"No," I said, shaking my head. "I mean, I'm not speaking about the Flayer. I'm talking about the other assassin who was out for my blood *before* Elric and I split up. The one I came to you about when I was looking for a protection trinket."

Qin tugged on his long beard. "I'm listening."

"Tonight, he or she tried to ambush me. I barely got away."

"I'm glad you did, Dovey, but what does this have to do with the Bead?"

"They were holding it right before I made my escape."

Qin left his chair and came around to stand in front of me.

The man is an inch below five feet, and I towered over him, but that meant nothing. Qin could handle himself against just about anyone. Well, save Elric, of course. "Describe them," he demanded.

"The best that I can do, Qin, is tell you that this assassin dresses in a hooded, gray cloak, and works to keep his or her identity hidden."

Qin nodded. "A cloak, eh? Goin' old-school."

"It didn't seem out of place with all the rain. It's not much different than a regular rain poncho."

"Thank you for this information, Dovey," he said, then he looked pensive. "Um . . . you didn't tell Elric about the missing Bead before you two broke up, did you?"

I shook my head and Ursula said, "If she had, Qin, do you think you'd still be here?"

He shrugged. "Here as the Trinket Guardian? No. Here as in alive? Also . . . no."

"Which is why I plan to tell no one," I assured him. "Well, save Ursula, but we both know she can keep a secret."

Acting as Elric's spy for literally centuries, Ursula had long ago proved that secrets were safe with her.

Still, she placed a gentle hand on his shoulder. "I won't say a word about it, old friend."

Qin blew out a relieved breath. "Buys me a little more time."

"Elric's gone to Europe," I told him. "He might be there long enough for you to retrieve the Bead."

Qin crossed his fingers with a grimace. "I did a thorough inventory and, from what I can tell, the only other thing the thief took was a hand mirror."

"What was its purpose?" Ursula asked.

Qin shrugged. "It's a storage trinket and a pretty good hiding place if you want to hide something quickly."

Ursula cocked her head curiously. "What can it hold?"

"You name it. Anything, really. The mirror was once used by Eleanor of Aquitaine to imprison her enemies. They starved to death suspended in the mirror, leaving behind a pile of bones. Elric acquired it shortly after Eleanor's son, King Richard, died, and she needed a new identity to hide her mysticism. It took both Elric and me to clean up what she left behind—once you're in the mirror, you need a mystic to let you back out— and what a mess!"

I smiled as he made a face at the memory. "Eleanor had lots of enemies, eh?"

He *t*sked. "Duh-zens."

Curious, I couldn't help but ask, "She's still alive?"

"Yep. Currently an actor off in La-La Land—an Academy Award winner a few times over, in fact. *Very* good with dialects, wink, wink."

My brow shot up. I thought I knew who she might be and wanted to see if I was right. "Is it—"

"It is," he answered before I could say her name aloud. "That mystic is *thirsty* for attention."

We all laughed. "What would the thief want with the mirror?" Ursula asked him, getting us back on track.

"I'm assuming he or she is using it to hide the Casting Bead because every time I try the Bead's comeback spell, it won't work."

That was an interesting twist I hadn't thought of. "The mirror is impervious to comeback spells?"

Qin nodded at me. "It's why it makes such a good hiding place. Any thief would kill for it."

"It seems one already has," Ursula said. Then she elbowed me and said, "Show him the dud."

Rooting around in my handbag again, I pulled up the money clip and showed it to Qin. "Whatever this is supposed to do, it doesn't," I told him.

Qin cocked his head. "Did you wake it up?"

I pointed to Ursula. "She put some essence into it and nada. Nothing happened."

He frowned and held out his hand. I put the money clip into his open palm and watched him pour some aqua essence into the clip. "Bah," he said. "I feel the catch. It's working fine."

He handed the clip back to me, and Ursula and I traded looks. "Maybe it would help if you explained what it's supposed to do," she said to him.

In answer, he looked at me. "You said the assassin was waiting outside your garage tonight, right?"

I nodded.

"Did you hear a chime before you opened the garage door?"

"Oh! I did! It sounded like a cash register ringing up a sale."

"Exactly. You didn't want a weapon, so I gave you a warning trinket."

I frowned. "Well, then, it doesn't work consistently, because there was no chime when I walked through my front door to find Petra's lieutenant in my living room, waiting to *kill* me, Qin Shi."

He rolled his eyes. "If the chime didn't sound, then you were in no real danger."

"Did you not hear me? Petra sent him to *unalive* me!"

Qin eyed me shrewdly. "And have you been *unalived?*"

I blinked. "Well, no. But only because the lieutenant took pity on me."

He and Ursula eyed each other and chuckled. "The Flayer doesn't do pity, Dovey," Qin said, mirroring Ursula's observations from earlier. "He never intended to assassinate you. He probably just wanted you to know that he could if he was in the mood, and you'd better watch your back." For emphasis, Qin pointed to the money clip still in my hand. "Maybe by keeping that around, eh?"

My grip closed around the clip before I tucked it safely back inside my handbag. "Thank you. I'll do that."

Ursula glanced at her watch. "We should go. We've got a merlin to meet. Maybe he can craft you something to keep you safer than a chiming trinket until Qin retrieves the Casting Bead and Petra gets bored of trying to have you axed. She'll eventually move on to bigger fish. Someone's always on that woman's hit list."

"You're going to see a merlin?" Qin asked as we were turning to leave.

"Yes. A gift from Elric," I said over my shoulder.

A sly smile quirked at the corner of Qin's mouth. "I knew he couldn't stay mad at you."

"A gift from Valentine's Day," I clarified.

The smile faltered. "Ah," he said. "Which merlin?"

"The Falcon," Ursula told him, moving into the elevator as the doors parted.

I joined Ursula and once I'd turned around to face front again, I noticed how Qin's brows had shot up in surprise.

"The Falcon?!" he said with a note of alarm, just as the doors began to close. "Dovey, you *must* remember—"

The doors shut, blocking out the rest of Qin Shi's warning.

I put a hand on the doors, essence already tingling my fingertips as I tried to get them to open again, but it was too late, the elevator had begun its descent. Frankly, I should've known better; the elevators at SPL resist attempts to control them magically by anyone other than Elric, Jacquelyn, and Qin Shi. It was a first line of defense amongst many at SPL.

Turning to Ursula I tried not to sound too freaked out when I asked, "Must remember what? What was he about to say?"

She shrugged. "No idea. Did Elric mention to use caution when approaching the merlin?"

I thought back to our conversation earlier that day. "No. He didn't. And I told him I was going to see the Falcon sometime soon. If there was anything to fear or to be warned about, you'd think he would've told me, right?"

Ursula bit her lip. "One would hope."

I gulped. "Can this day get any *more* terrifying?"

She put her hand on my arm to calm me. "So far, your track record for getting out of life-threatening situations is one hundred percent, Dovey. Whatever the warning was about, we'll face it. Together."

The elevator reached the garage, and the doors parted. Ursula stepped out but I held back. "I think we should go back up and ask Qin what he was going to tell us."

She wavered for a moment before looking anxiously at her watch. "Dovey, we don't have time. And we cannot be late for the Falcon. It would be seen as a grave insult."

"Dammit," I muttered, following her out into the garage. Qin Shi didn't have a cell phone, so I couldn't send him a text, and he didn't have an office phone, either. To get him a message and receive a response you'd quickly need a carrier pigeon.

Not kidding. The man was *old*-school.

Getting back into Ursula's car (a Mercedes S-Class—elegant and stylish just like the woman herself), I checked on Bits, who was still snuggled in the bottom of my purse, curled into a ball with only his twitching nose exposed. Carefully, I took out the box with the shakers that were about to be enchanted.

"How's the minx?" my friend asked.

"Snoring. I don't know why he insisted on coming, but with so many assassins lurking around my home, I'm not unhappy about it."

"Better safe than sorry."

"Truth."

Opening the lid of the shaker set box, I showed Ursula, and she smiled while reaching over to touch the filigree ornamentation on them both. "These are lovely. They'll make wonderful trinkets."

"Agreed." I sighed. They were the perfect blanks to use for enchantment.

Some trinkets can be so unwieldy for their purpose. It did no good to enchant a piano to bring you good luck if you couldn't take it with you into the outside world.

After starting her car, Ursula drove us out of the garage toward the street. "I think you should stay with me for the time being, Dovey."

"You have no idea how tempting that offer is, my friend, but I can't."

"Why not?"

"Two reasons: the first is that there's no way I'd risk your life trying to save mine. The second is Gib."

"I understand the first—and wholeheartedly disagree—but not the second."

"Someone, probably the same mystic who stole the Casting Bead and is trying to kill me for unknown reasons, is murdering FBI agents, which means Gib's in as much danger as I am. The only way I can protect both of us is to keep him close when he'd otherwise be alone, which means inviting him to my place and setting my wards to lock us in."

"What if he opens another window?" she asked. Ursula is ever the pragmatist.

"That's a no-brainer. I'll enchant them to only open on my command."

There was a pause as I thought about other ways to ensure our safety, then I said, "I've got two shakers. I can ask the Falcon to enchant one to protect me and the other to protect Gib. It'd be unusual to create a trinket for an unbound, but we've seen it before. The Egg was created to protect the Tsarina."

One of the most famous merlins in the world was also one of the most famous jewelers in the world. Peter Carl Fabergé created an enchanted trinket in the shape of an Easter egg specifically to protect the Tsarina, but the Egg was stolen by another mystic named Grigori Rasputin, who'd used it to save his own hide several times over. The Egg, along with Rasputin, had disappeared shortly before the entire Russian Imperial Romanov family was executed by the Bolsheviks in 1918. The Egg was top of my mind because I'd recently learned Elric had acquired it.

"About choosing your trinkets' purpose..." Ursula said, sounding pensive.

"Yes?"

"I didn't want to bring you down after such a difficult day by telling you this, but I have a bit of history with the Falcon—"

"You do?"

Ursula reached over to tap the medallion around my neck. "He crafted that for me."

I quickly bent my neck forward to unclasp the chain, removing the medallion and feeling the tingling sensation of the disguise enchantment fall away from me. I then leaned over to reclasp the necklace around Ursula's neck, being mindful not to interfere with her driving. "And you were saying?" I asked when she didn't continue the discussion.

"There are some rules you should be aware of for this appointment."

"Rules? What kind of rules?"

"For starters, you're not allowed to specifically dictate what kind or the power level of a trinket he makes you."

"What does that mean?"

She glanced over at me. "The specific purpose of the enchantment must be his idea, and he will assign the power level to fulfill that task. If you mention a choice you'd prefer, you're likely to get the opposite, a trinket of low power and of little value both to you and the mystic marketplace."

I stared incredulously at her. "But the *whole* purpose of this appointment is to come away with something that'll protect me from those who're trying to kill me, and for that I need a powerful trinket on a level seven or eight, *at least.*"

"Agreed, but, Dovey, you can't *directly ask* for that. You've got to be more subtle. It has to be delicate. He crafted this medallion for me after the brief suggestion by his mentor that I required a powerful trinket for my espionage assignments. Back then, if I'd have had a say in its design, I would've requested a trinket to render me invisible. But now, looking back, I can see that being invisible would've been problematic. As you know, the courts' castles and fortresses could be quite crowded, and avoiding touching another mystic while moving around them was next to impossible. A mystic concealing themselves with invisibility would've been quickly detected—and dealt with. Wearing a disguise, however, I could float through the courts in a visage that didn't raise alarms. More than a dozen times I went disguised as a serving wench. The medallion's enchantment was a much better choice for me."

"Okay, so can I be vague? Can I suggest a trinket that will simply keep me, and anyone else in close proximity, safe from an assassin's intentions?"

"I think that would be risky. The Falcon is quite temperamental, and remember, his title is *wise.* If he thinks for one second that you're trying to influence his creative genius, he'll quickly dispatch your efforts by providing a trinket you'd find worthless.

"What I'm hoping for is that he'll engage us in conversation, and ask you about your profession—what you do for Elric to be specific, and in explaining your unique role at SPL, you can casually mention that your work often invites the envy of mystics who'd think nothing of permanently removing you from the payroll in hopes of sliding into such a cushy assignment."

"So . . . we have to go in there and wait for him to *ask?*"

"Yes."

I shook my head. The way my luck was running today, the merlin was unlikely to do that, and he'd probably send me home with a trinket to change the polish on my nails without needing to sit through a manicure. "Ursula, how can this be? He could send me home with a set of trinkets I have no use for!" I didn't know why I was arguing with *her.* She had little say in the matter.

She turned again to look pointedly at me. "I'm sorry, my friend, but we simply cannot overplay your hand. We've got to tread carefully and hope for the best."

My brain raced to find a solution, and it couldn't land on anything solid, which was likely because I was on the verge of panic. I'd been so relieved when Ursula helped to reveal the message on the card. I'd thought of it like a golden ticket to the chocolate factory.

Some merlins could create trinkets all the way up to level nine or ten with significant longevity, and while I'd heard of Falcon the Wise, I didn't know how powerful he was likely to be. Still, the fact that Elric had retained him for at least the last five hundred years suggested he was quite powerful indeed.

From what Ursula was telling me, if I tried to use my looks or some charm on the Falcon to manipulate an outcome, he was likely to spot that a mile away. Mystics, by nature, are both materialistic and manipulative, not to mention self-involved and narcissistic. We mostly can't help it. Our entire lives often depend on our looks and the value of *things,* and if we're to survive our first hundred years, experience will teach us to lean hard into our charms and manipulative coercions, which might work on some of the dumber mystics, but it certainly wouldn't work on a merlin.

Merlins are constantly bombarded by those tactics, so they learn quickly to spot them and put up buffers. Most merlins are quite secluded creatures. Access to their power is often too tempting for the general mystic population, and no merlin wants to end up a slave.

Since this was the first time in nearly two hundred years that Elric had allowed me to meet his merlin, my guess was that he respected the Falcon's privacy and protected it fiercely.

I settled into a pensive mood, saying nothing as Ursula drove, and I didn't realize until I glanced at the clock on the dash that we'd left HQ sometime after nine o'clock—which explained Ursula's focused attention on casting soft spells at traffic lights and surrounding traffic, allowing us to zip out of the city, heading west.

She continued on the highway for forty-five minutes until exiting and eventually pulling onto a dark street without street-lights, street signs, or any homes in sight. I wondered where we actually were.

"It's creepy here," I whispered, eyeing the dark landscape, which gave off a distinctly foreboding vibe. "His wards?"

Ursula nodded. "The Falcon doesn't allow himself to be disturbed. Without an appointment, we'd be far too unnerved to turn onto this street."

I squinted into the distance. "I don't see any hint of a home or a building. Are you sure we made the right turn?"

"Give it a minute," was her only reply.

We continued on in silence for a good while when there was a sudden flash followed by a loud crack of thunder. The gloomy skies decided to dump even *more* rain onto the already-soaked countryside, and Ursula was forced to put her windshield wipers on full speed. Even then, we could barely see the road. I tried to help by casting the same spell I'd used on my own wipers last night during that storm, but when I tried to form some essence, only a tiny bubble appeared in my palm. "What the . . . ?" I said, staring at my open hand.

"Magic won't work out here," Ursula said. "It's part of the merlin's wards."

My brow shot up. Falcon the Wise was powerful indeed to extend wards so far out from his home—however far down this road *that* was. I still couldn't make out anything that looked like a man-made structure. All around us were trees and forest.

"Should we pull over until this deluge passes?" I asked, having to raise my voice to be heard above the din.

"Can't," she said, leaning forward to hover over the steering wheel. "We'll be late."

I glanced nervously at the clock. It was three minutes to ten.

I squinted again into the distance and still couldn't make out any semblance of a home or a structure. Lifting my phone, I thought to site our location, but my phone showed zero bars. It was effectively a glass and plastic brick out here.

"It's two minutes to!" I said, my nerves shot by the arduous, grueling, and somewhat terrifying day. We couldn't be late, I knew that. It was a hard and fast rule for any meeting with a powerful mystic.

In the nearly two centuries that I'd formally worked for Elric, I had never, *ever* been late. Not out of fear, but out of respect, and, even then, I was aware of the unspoken rule that if you were ever running late for a meeting with the world's most powerful mystic, you'd better keep on running because there would be consequences that were likely to be . . . uncomfortable.

"I'm aware!" Ursula replied when I pointed to the clock on the dash. Another flash of lightning was so bright that I winced, and the accompanying clap of thunder sounded like a plane crash, the roar tumbling over and over on itself, rattling the interior of the car.

"There!" Ursula shouted as the last of the lightning flash winked out.

It took my eyes a moment, but then I too could see a large, foreboding structure in the distance.

Mindless of the storm, Ursula increased her speed for the rest of the quarter-mile drive.

As we pulled into the circular drive of what appeared to be a *massive* structure, I shuddered. The place looked like Dracula's castle, and not anyplace one might want to be in the middle of a raging storm.

I glanced at the clock. It was ten o'clock, and I had no idea how many seconds into our appointment time it already was. Ursula threw the car into park, we each grabbed our things then scrambled out of the car, mindless of the sheet of rain coming down on us when we sprinted to the front door, which was under a stone archway, offering us a bit of shelter. I raised my hand to knock, my heart pounding as hard as the rain, but before my knuckles could land on the wood door, it creaked open to reveal a circular foyer, lit only by candlelight from a smattering of wall sconces.

As we stood stock-still, daring not to cross the threshold, a bright flash from behind us caused us both to jump. Thunder roared so loudly that we followed that jump by reflexively taking several steps inside.

The door slammed closed behind us, and we each heard the crank of a bolt sliding into place.

My breath was coming in short, rapid pants, and I glanced at Ursula, who slid over to rub shoulders with me and stare forward, her eyes filled with alarm.

"We're locked in," she whispered.

From inside my purse came the sound of that cash register and no sooner had it chimed than a low, rumbling growl echoed loudly from one of the hallways off the foyer.

The money clip chimed again—and I swore it did so more urgently.

Another growl echoed out to us, followed by the soft plop of a padded footfall.

Ursula and I stared at each other in fear.

There was something in here with us.

Something big . . . and possibly hungry.

CHAPTER 10

Instinctively, Ursula and I both gathered orbs of essence within our palms, and I was relieved to see that my magic seemed to work inside the merlin's home, within the confines of his wards.

I hadn't even *considered* bringing a weapon, and I knew that Ursula hadn't, either. One never greeted a merlin with a weapon, lest one wanted to be quickly snuffed out.

The growl rumbled out into the foyer again, this time sounding closer. "I think it's coming from the hallway on the left," I whispered.

She nodded, her gaze focused on the same hallway I'd been looking toward.

"What's our plan?" I asked.

"If it comes for us, we throw every ounce of essence at it and run."

"Run *where*?" I whispered, motioning with my chin over her shoulder. "We're locked in."

Another growl drowned out any response she might've given, which meant whatever beast was making it was closer still.

"Pick a hallway," she told me after the rumble that somewhat mimicked the thunder outside went quiet again.

My eyes darted about the place, frantically searching for options. "There has to be some kind of a weapon we can use around here."

Ursula opened her mouth to speak but stopped short and her eyes grew wide. I turned my head slowly to where she was staring and saw a monstrous animal begin to emerge from the hall.

The beast was at least as tall as me at the shoulders, its head as large as a polar bear, but its fur was as black as night. Its head was somewhat doglike, but its body was more like a bear. I had no idea what it was and didn't much care other than to consider how hungry it looked and how fast it might be able to run.

"A beariena," Ursula said shakily. "I've only seen a few of them before. Quite rare."

"Dangerous?" I asked, hoping for a herbivore.

"Deadly."

I gulped.

The beariena lifted its snout and sniffed the air. I wondered if it could smell fear because the two of us were simply ensconced in it.

"Should we run?" I whispered as it took another slow, lumbering step toward us.

"We'll never make it out of the room, Dovey."

"So, what do we do?"

She shook her head, simply lifting her palms where the orbs of essence were still gathered. Tossing orbs of essence at a violent, threating beast like the bearina was a last line of defense for a mystic. A much better tactic would've been to have a trinket enchanted as either a protective shield or a battle weapon, and the *most* preferable option was to have both. We had neither, and Ursula's bangles would've been worthless against the beast because it wouldn't need to hurl magic at us. It'd just need to close the distance and give us a nibble.

I thought about the twin push daggers I'd left at home. Such a stupid decision in hindsight given the gravity of our current situation. Bringing a weapon to the home of a merlin might be suicide, but at the moment, we appeared to be dead either way.

Raising my palms as well, I stared pointedly at the space to the right and left of the beariena's nose. I'd aim both orbs at its eyes, hoping to blind it, and was about to tell Ursula to do the same when there was a wiggle from my handbag and a moment later Bits, wound into a tight ball of quills, appeared at the foot of the beariena.

I gasped, and heard Ursula do the same. "*Bits!*" I cried, as my little picklepuss uncurled himself and stood on his hind legs to sniff up toward the beast.

The thought bulleting through my mind was that my little beloved was sacrificing himself so that we could get away, but I would never abandon him and could only hope that when the beariena struck, Bits would manage to teleport himself out of the way.

But then something incredible happened. The beariena lowered its snout and sniffed at Bits, who sniffed back, and then the beast nudged Bits playfully with its nose.

Bits fell backward into a ball and rolled a foot or two, then popped out of the ball to stand on his hind legs again as if he'd just performed a trick and was giving a little "ta-da" flare at the end.

The beariena did something even more incredible. It began to chuff in a sound that could only be laughter. Heck, even its mouth turned up into a smile.

"What the . . . ?" I whispered, watching Bits curl himself into a ball, roll forward again, and uncurl himself right under the beariena's nose. Again, the beast nudged Bits playfully, and my sweet hedgehog repeated his trick.

"Do they . . . do they *know* each other?" Ursula whispered.

I was about to tell her no when we heard someone say, "Of course they do."

The voice had come from right behind us, and we both whirled around to see a tall, lean man with a gray beard that reached nearly to the floor and long silver hair ending at his shoulders staring back at us. He was draped in a black tunic with matching leggings and pointed soft-soled black leather shoes. He also held a staff as tall as himself that was gnarled and worn smooth, ending in a round nob at the top, beset with rubies and diamonds.

If I hadn't known better, I'd have sworn it was Merlin himself making his presence known.

It was Ursula who recovered herself first. "Falcon the Wise," she said, bending at the waist in a formal bow. "So nice to see you again."

I followed suit and muttered a greeting, but to be honest, I was still quite thrown by everything unfolding in front of us, and I was equally unnerved to show the beariena my back.

When I straightened up, I was even *more* shocked to see Bits cuddled against the merlin's chest while the merlin gently pet the top of my picklepuss's head.

And then, in a flash, I understood. "*You* enchanted him."

The Falcon laughed. "I did indeed, Dovey Van Dalen. Elric rescued the baby hedgehog from the clutches of a housecat decades ago, and brought him here, asking me to save and enchant him for his new love, a new protégée he'd won in a game of chance."

Elric had never told me Bits's origin story, and my heart panged at the thought of such a sweet gesture. I'd had no idea that Elric had *rescued* Bits and saved him from certain death.

I bowed again and said, "Then I thank you from my heart, Falcon the Wise." Straightening up again, I added, "Bits is my little beloved, and my constant companion. I adore him."

The Falcon beamed a smile at me and there was something in his eyes, something that suggested he approved not just of my comment about Bits, but me as well. Stroking Bits's quills, he asked, "What have you brought me?"

I blinked in a moment of confusion, and then I remembered the shakers, which I'd frantically tucked into my purse right before bolting from the car. Reaching into my handbag, I withdrew the box and held it out to him. He traded Bits for the box, and I cuddled my picklepuss the same way the merlin had.

The Falcon took the box and looked at the lid, smiling as if he recognized the brand. "I know what these are," he sang. Opening the lid, however, he seemed a bit surprised. "Oh, a different version. I like these better, actually."

I didn't know what he meant by that—but then it occurred to me that L'Objet produced at least a few different styles of salt and pepper shakers, and they did make for perfect little trinkets.

Looking back at me, he said, "I expected to see you months ago, Dovey. What's taken you so long?"

Heat seared my cheeks as I fearfully wondered if I'd inadvertently offended him. "I . . . I was waiting until I had an urgent need for something powerful, Falcon."

He nodded like he accepted my explanation. "You need a powerful trinket for . . . ?"

Ursula's warning bulleted its way into my mind. A sideways glance at her showed me I was wise to be cautious. His question was a bit of a trap, but I thought I knew a way around it.

With another demure nod, I said, "I'll leave their actual purpose up to you, Merlin. All I can tell you is that my position is coveted by more than a few enemies, and . . ." I didn't know if I should mention the most current threats stalking me.

"And?" he prodded.

I stole another glance at Ursula. She dipped her chin once to let me know I should continue. "And I'm being targeted for assassination by an unknown thief who's stollen a powerful and deadly trinket they intend to use to end my life, making the use of whatever fabulous treasure you create for me likely short-lived."

His smile turned somewhat smug. He seemed to approve of the carefully chosen wording. "You are as clever as Elric suggested," he said. "I shall enchant you the perfect pair of trinkets, Dovey. Please, enjoy some refreshments while I work."

Pointing to an area behind us, Ursula and I both turned and gasped anew to discover a small table with two chairs, beautiful candlesticks aglow with brightly lit candles, an assortment of fruits and cheeses, and two glasses of white wine set in front of the chairs.

Missing from the area was the beariena, which helped me relax for the first time since entering the merlin's home. I glanced at Ursula, and she smiled. We'd passed the test. As one we turned back toward the Falcon, but he'd vanished.

"Wow," I said. "He's amazing."

"Indeed," she agreed. She then waved toward the fare set out for us. "Shall we?"

Bits, who'd been curled into the crook of my arm, disappeared, only to reappear on the table, waddling hungrily toward a slice of pear. I chuckled and looped my newly freed arm through Ursula's. "We shall!"

Falcon the Wise proved just how powerful he was by reappearing only two hours later with my newly enchanted trinkets.

The merlin had even discarded the box the shakers had come in, swapping it out for a gleaming, polished wood box with a hinged lid. He held it open, presenting me with the shakers nestled in a velvet cushion, and immediately I realized that he'd even filled the shakers with both salt and pepper, and the salt gleamed like tiny pink diamonds while the pepper appeared to sparkle like black diamonds.

"Here you are, Dovey," he said.

I was so overcome by their beauty that my eyes misted, and I accepted the gifts with another deep bow, doing my best to show him my gratitude and the deference he deserved. "Thank you, Falcon."

Standing tall again I saw that he was looking at me expectantly, so I took out the saltshaker and pushed a bit of essence into it, immediately feeling the catch as my magic met with the trinket's and they melded into one.

The catch was powerful enough to tell me that the newly enchanted shakers were at *least* a level eight but probably closer to a level nine. Tears sprang to my eyes with the generosity of both the merlin and Elric. Level nines are considered nearly priceless in the mystic world, and I was truly humbled by the gift.

The magic of the trinket guided my hand as I wrapped my palm around it and raised it like a ball being readied to throw. I had no idea what the trinket actually did, but it lit up my energy like a Christmas tree and I felt a touch invincible with it in my palm. "What does it do?" I asked, my hand still raised high.

Falcon the Wise took several steps away from me and raised his own palms, where swirling orbs of dark blue essence spun. The glow his essence gave off was astonishing. It lit the entire room with sapphire light. "This," he said, and launched both orbs directly at me.

Before I could even think, my arm flung the shaker toward the merlin. Time seemed to slow down while I watched the trinket on a collision course with the merlin's energy and, reflexively, I braced for impact.

The trinket and pair of orbs collided just as the merlin spun his hands in a circle, and the resulting explosion that should have thrown everyone in the room hard enough to slam against the walls became fully contained within a large, nearly transparent sphere of energy. And even though there was no physical shockwave to affect us, there was a spectacular light show. The explosion continued for several seconds, reverberating off the walls of the clear sphere until, at last, it winked out.

The instant it did, I felt the warm thrumming energy of the

trinket back in my palm. Lifting my hand and turning it over, I gazed at the shaker in wonder. There wasn't a scratch on it, and it hummed with energy as if it'd never been discharged at all.

But then I noticed that my own energy had fallen a notch, as if the trinket had taken a small toll on me. The difference was subtle, but there.

"Wow," I said, breathlessly, staring in wonder at my new treasure. "This is incredible."

The Falcon twisted a ring on his middle finger, and I saw that it was glowing. No doubt that'd been the trinket that'd created the sphere that contained the explosion. I could only imagine how powerful that ring must've been to have contained the energy given off of a level nine trinket.

The merlin appeared pleased with my reaction. Motioning to the box I still held in my other hand, he said, "The other shaker is to be used only in case of extreme emergency."

I set the first shaker back on its velvet cushion and took out the pepper shaker. Pushing a little essence into it, simply to feel its power, I was shocked again to discover that it was equally as powerful as its twin. "What does it do?" I asked, wondering if another dramatic test was in order.

"It summons the best defense at hand for your situation, but mind you," the merlin warned, "whomever or whatever it summons will be powerless to refuse, and once you are properly defended, there may be a favor or a debt owed."

"Ah," I said, hoping my expression still appeared grateful.

Glancing at Ursula for reassurance, I found her slowly nodding, like that condition was to be expected. "Don't ring the bell unless you're willing to pay the toll."

"Hence why it's to be used only in the most extreme emergency," the merlin agreed. "When there's no one left to save you, that might do the trick."

Very carefully I pulled my essence back from the trinket lest

I accidentally trigger it, as I didn't think I was in extreme danger right now, but who knew with a beariena around.

"Noted," I said. "Thank you for both your talent and your wisdom, Falcon. You have served me perfectly."

"Of course I have," he said, rocking back on his heels, as smug as one could be.

I closed the lid of the box and moved back over to the chair at the table to set them carefully back in my handbag, while the merlin's attention suddenly turned to Ursula. "I have a gift for you as well, Potion Master."

I glanced up to see Ursula take a step back in surprise, and her long lashes fluttered while she blinked nervously at him. "You do?"

"Indeed," he said, holding out his curled hand toward her.

Hesitantly, she raised her palm, and sure enough, the Falcon dropped into her hand two gold rings, each crowned with an ancient-looking gold coin, slightly smaller than a penny. "Oh my," she said, her hand trembling a bit while she eyed the trinkets.

I understood her apprehension. There was no telling what the merlin would ask for in return. If he had anything inappropriate in mind, I knew that it would put Ursula in the very dangerous situation of refusing a merlin's gift, which was insult indeed.

Looking up at him, she said, "These are truly exquisite, Falcon. Too exquisite a gift for someone of my mediocre talent. I fear these would be wasted on me."

I swallowed hard. How he reacted to those words would likely determine how Ursula left this place—either on her own power, or draped over my shoulder, headed to the nearest burial site.

"Nonsense, my beauty. They were crafted specifically for you and the lover of your choosing."

I could tell that Ursula's nervousness was ratcheting up. We were in more danger right now than when the beariena had shown up.

Hoping to give her a bit more time to think about how to get out of accepting the merlin's "gift," I got up from the table and moved over to her, peeking over her shoulder, admiring the gold bands, before asking, "Falcon, what do these beautiful trinkets do?"

"They bind the hearts together," he said simply, but with a manipulative sparkle in his eye. "I have learned, through very discreet sources, that the potion master is on the losing end of unrequited love."

Ursula and I both uttered a small gasp, but neither of us said another word.

Into the shocked silence the merlin added, "Those will command the heart of anyone you choose, Ursula Göransdotter. Be it a king . . . or a *thief,* if you each wear a ring, he will love only you. And, as long as your chosen bears the ring, you'll know *exactly* where to find him."

Standing shoulder to shoulder with my best friend, I could literally feel the tremor that rippled through her, and I couldn't fault her for it. Falcon the Wise should've been called Falcon the Shrewd. It was clear he had enchanted the trinket specifically for her and the man she was madly in love with, and I doubted she could refuse the merlin's gift—with any flattering prose—a second time and live long enough to make it to the door.

As if to emphasize the point, behind us there was a chuffing sound and the pad of large paws. The beariena was back in the foyer.

Ursula glanced sideways at me before she straightened her back and bowed to the merlin, closing her fist around the rings. When she straightened, she said, "Your trinket mastery has no equal, Merlin. I shall accept your gift with gratitude, and ask if I might return the favor in kind? A love potion specially crafted for you, perhaps?"

A shrewd smile turned almost sinister. He had every intention of exacting a price for the trinket, and I shuddered to think what kind of potion Ursula would have to craft that would satisfy his desire.

"A lovely gesture," he said, thoroughly pleased with himself. He'd clearly outsmarted us, and I felt a wave of guilt for ever allowing Ursula to take up booking my appointment and driving us here. It should've been me and me alone if only to avoid such a predicament. "I will endeavor to call upon you in the future, Potion Master. For now, enjoy the rest of this lovely evening, and safe travels home."

In a sweeping gesture he motioned toward the door and we both bowed yet one more time then hurried forward. His voice rang out one final time, stopping us in our tracks. "Mystics," he called. Ursula and I glanced over our shoulders, and he said, "Make *sure* to cast your comeback spells before you leave my property. It will give the trinkets' return an extra bit of power. You wouldn't want to lose track of those rings, Ursula. Or your trinkets, Dovey."

It wasn't lost on me that he'd mentioned the rings he'd given Ursula first and referred to my shakers simply as trinkets. He wanted to make sure she didn't come back to him with an excuse that the rings had been stolen, and the deal was off. I wasn't looking at her, but I guessed she'd gone a bit pale.

"Yes, Falcon," she answered weakly.

"Of course. Thank you, Falcon," I said.

He waved casually and I heard the bolt sliding. Turning my attention to the door, I watched it swing open on its own, revealing that the storm outside had calmed to a steady rain.

We hustled to Ursula's car and climbed in, shaking some of the wet off ourselves before I took the trinket box from my purse, removed the lid, and stared down at the shakers.

"How good are you at comeback spells?" I asked Ursula. Personally, I was fairly adept at them, but I was finding my nerves rattled so exhaustingly that my brain was having trouble thinking.

"Probably as good as yours," she said.

She looked rattled too.

"What're you going to do?" I asked her.

When she eyed me curiously, I pointed to her fist, where the rings were still clutched. She huffed out a hollow laugh. "I have no idea." Then she pointed at me. "Let's work on the wording of your comeback spells first, then mine so we can get the hell out of here. The merlin won't tolerate us on his property for long."

I nodded and focused my attention on the beautiful trinkets. They each looked so much more sparkly than when I'd brought them to the merlin. It was as if the gold had been shined to its most gleaming.

Selecting the saltshaker, but without pouring any essence into the trinket yet, I said, "Okay, how about this:

"Shaker filled with salt of rose,
Entwined with vines of gleaming gold,
Heed my sound and clear command,
Come to nestle in my hand."

"That's perfect," Ursula said.

I smiled, gathered my essence, and pushed it into the shaker while repeating the spell. Sparkles of bright green fluttered about the shaker, letting me know it was now doubly enchanted.

Ursula reached over and lifted the shaker, quickly tucking it into her pocket. "Call it back," she ordered.

I repeated the spell and within a second the saltshaker was once again in the palm of my hand. I grinned with pride.

"Now do the other one," she said, wagging her finger at the pepper shaker.

I settled the saltshaker back onto its cushion and lifted out its twin.

Feeling more confident, I gathered my essence, pushed it into the shaker, and sang:

> *"Shaker filled with spice like night,*
> *Entwined with vines of golden light,*
> *Heed my sound and clear command,*
> *Come back to my outstretched hand."*

The pepper shaker glimmered with sparks of green, just like the saltshaker had after being enchanted with its comeback spell.

Again, Ursula snatched the trinket away and tucked it into her jacket pocket. "Call it back," she ordered bossily.

I repeated the spell, and the trinket appeared in my left hand, which was odd, because the saltshaker had come back to my right hand.

"If you want them to come back to you together, you'll need both hands," Ursula said when I pointed out the oddity.

"Makes sense. Okay, now your turn."

Ursula looked forward and her brow furrowed in concentration. I could see her lips moving as she put together the words for her enchantment. After just a few moments she seemed to nod to herself, then she opened her palm, revealing the rings, and encircled them with a bubble of essence. Then she sang:

> *"Rings for lovers sealed in fate,*
> *Claim your partner, claim your mate,*
> *Hear my call to bring you near,*
> *Come back to my essence sphere."*

The orb of essence surrounding the rings lit up like tiny fireworks and then winked out.

"Oooo, I love that, Ursula," I told her, complimenting the wording of her spell.

She grinned. "Thank you."

I then held out my hand and Ursula dropped the rings into my open palm. In turn, I put them in the box with my shakers and closed the lid. "Okay, go."

She created an orb of her essence in the palm of her hand and recited the comeback spell, and the moment she finished, the rings appeared in her palm.

Instead of appearing happy at their return, however, she looked troubled.

"Hey," I said. "You okay?"

She shook her head slightly. "Fine. I'm fine. Can you hand me my handbag? I want to put these away."

I twisted in my seat and nabbed her handbag from the back, lifting it out for her. She dropped the rings inside and I put her bag in the back footwell then turned to face front again, offering her a reassuring smile.

She nodded, but she still looked so troubled.

"Wanna talk about it?"

She shook her head again, her eyes moving to the merlin's front door, then reached over her left shoulder to grab her seat belt and said, "Buckle up, kiddo. We can talk more about the rings once we're off the Falcon's property." She then started the car while I buckled in and we set off, circling the drive before gaining the road again. Neither of us spoke until we'd made it off the unlit road and were headed toward the freeway.

I was the first to break the silence. "I'm sorry about the rings, Ursula. The Falcon's entrapping you is all my fault. I should've come here alone."

She sighed heavily. "Please don't shoulder any guilt over

this, Dovey. The Falcon would've found some way to lure me into a trap. No doubt he's been planning to corner me like that for some time."

"What could he want from you that he couldn't enchant in a trinket? I mean, you're clearly the best at your craft, but, Ursula, . . . he's a *merlin.* What couldn't he create on his own that would accomplish the deed he's got in mind for any potion he commands you to make."

Ursula's posture was stiff, the tension clear in the way both her hands gripped the steering wheel. It was obvious there was something about the exchange back at the estate that I was missing.

"Ursula?" I asked when she didn't respond.

She bit her lip. "I have knowledge of certain potions that would be lethal," she whispered. I could barely hear her above the thrumming of the rain.

"I know," I assured her. "No potion master would be considered a master if they didn't know how to poison an enemy."

"It's more than that, Dovey."

"How so?"

To my surprise, Ursula pulled off onto the shoulder of the highway and put the car in park. She stared miserably out into the dark, dreary night. "It's complicated."

"How so?" I repeated, turning fully toward her, unnerved by her haunted expression.

Before answering me, Ursula muttered an incantation, and I felt the pulse of power surround her Mercedes. I knew intuitively that she'd just wrapped our conversation in a dome of silence.

Turning to me, she said, "What I'm about to tell you, you must *never* repeat. Promise me."

Without hesitation I held out my hand to her. She clasped it and I said, "I vow to keep your secret, Ursula Göransdotter."

There was a tingling along my skin and then a warmth formed

in my fingertips, traveled through my palm, along my arm, across my shoulders and rapidly gained speed as it fluttered throughout my body, finally ebbing with a residual pleasant feeling that made my mind buzz.

Ursula and I had just formed a magically bonded pact. I could no more reveal her secret than I could breathe without air.

She pushed a small, sad smile to her lips, the worry overshadowing any attempt at reassurance.

"Centuries ago," she began, "during the Mystic Wars, I was given a trinket by the great merlin Adolpho the Imperial. Adolpho and I had both pledged fealty to Elric, and we were often paired together on our spying assignments.

"Adolpho's apprentice at the time was the Falcon, and it was the Falcon who created the medallion for me at Adolpho's request."

Ursula paused to drift her fingers over the golden lion's head at her throat.

I said nothing, but nodded, showing her that I was listening to her every word.

"Adolpho," she continued, "had been my lover for decades, throughout the darkest days of the Mystic Wars we had each other. I loved him and I believe he felt the same, but the tide was beginning to turn against our side, and Elric and Petra's forces along with the other courts of the time were strained nearly to the breaking point against the forces of the Pharo.

"On the eve of the Battle of the Rhine, Adolpho came to me and offered me a new trinket he'd created just for me. The trinket he gave me was a golden ring topped with a golden coin."

My eyes widened. She was describing the rings the Falcon had just given her.

"He told me that its creation had drained almost all of his energy, and he needed to go to his hideout for a bit to rest."

"A merlin was drained in the creation of a single trinket?" I asked. It was my understanding that merlins had a near-boundless resource of energy to pull from to create their treasures.

Ursula's lips flattened into a thin line while her eyes stared off into the distance where whatever she remembered of that time was obviously painful. "A merlin can be drained if the trinket they're creating is powerful enough. This trinket was Adolpho's magnum opus. And it never should've been created."

I'd heard of Adolpho. I'd also heard he did not survive the Mystic Wars.

"The day after he gave me the trinket, when he arrived at his hideout, he was ambushed by the Pharo's forces and immediately executed by the Pharo's High Priestess, Clepsydra."

I lay a hand on Ursula's arm. The sadness in her expression was difficult to witness, but her story also offered me some insight as to why she hated Petra so intensely. Clepsydra had been granted quarter by Petra after the High Priestess's capture, and Petra had eventually promoted her to her most trusted advisor.

"Adolpho hadn't told me the trinket's specific purpose," Ursula continued. "He'd merely told me that it would help me on my missions if I should ever find myself behind enemy lines. I was so angry after hearing of his execution that I purposely used the medallion to infiltrate the Pharo's territory, and then emptied my essence into the trinket Adolpho had gifted me. I was wholly unprepared for the insight it offered."

"What insight?" I asked when she didn't continue.

Her gaze found mine. "It showed me the recipe to poison each and every member of the reigning courts, and all of their subjects. With it, I could focus on any mystic and the formula for their demise would magically appear in my mind's eye.

"Each mystic's formula is different, you see. When given access to their own life-saving trinkets, most poisonous potions don't work on the more powerful among us.

"But these potions would. Eventually at least. With these formulas, there is no antidote. All I had to do was gain access to my target, infuse a bit of my essence into the ring, follow the formula that appeared in my mind's eye, then slip the poison into their food or drink. It would be harmless to their poison-testers, but permanently lethal to the mystic. And if the doomed mystic managed to come back from the dead, the poison would immediately reactivate itself until the poor soul had gone through the power of every trinket that could bring them back to life. Once the poison formula got into their system, it would never leave."

My jaw dropped. A power like that could get Ursula killed by any mystic who knew of it. Even Elric wouldn't spare Ursula's life if he knew she'd been exposed to a trinket like that. A mystic who knew how to completely end you was a permanent threat. Someone to be eliminated at all costs, regardless of their previous loyalty.

"My God . . . Ursula . . ." I whispered.

"Exactly," she said, nodding her head. "Possessing the trinket was a death sentence, but also the only thing that could possibly save me. I could use it to barter a trade—my life for the vanquishing of that mystic's enemies."

"Who knows of the trinket's existence?"

She swallowed hard. "Me. Now you. And given the similarity of the Falcon's gift to the ring that Adolpho gave me, I'm convinced he knew too."

"Have you ever used it?"

Her expression turned hard. "I've used it only once, and the time that I did, it reshaped the world order."

I felt the color drain from my face. "Who did you target?"

She inhaled deeply. "Mystic history will tell you that the Pharo died on the battlefield in a final match against Elric, Petra, and members of the other allied courts. In truth, he died an agonizingly painful death the evening before, coming back to life a dozen times before his available trinkets had been drained. No one but his most loyal attendants knew of the timing of his demise, and all of them were eventually executed.

"On the day of the final battle, his generals propped him up on his throne at the highest overlook to make it appear like he was still in command of his forces. He wasn't, of course, which was the main reason the Pharo's forces lost."

I shook my head. Elric had long been credited with delivering the Pharo's death. After capturing Clepsydra, he'd used her bow—the Bow of Anubis—to fire the lethal arrow into the Pharo's chest.

To learn that the Pharo was already dead when the arrow struck him was a shock, and I wondered if Elric even knew he'd shot the Pharo's corpse.

"If everyone who knew the Pharo had been poisoned was executed, how could anyone know that you were responsible?"

Ursula stared hard at her hands, which were trembling slightly. "If the Falcon crafted a medallion for me that could completely disguise me, who's to say he didn't craft one for himself?"

I gasped. "You think he was nearby when you poisoned the Pharo?"

She shrugged but added the smallest nod too.

"What disguise did you use to infiltrate the Pharo's inner circle?"

"I began with the guise of an unbound slave then methodically killed and took over the identities of other unbound attendants until I made it to his Great Royal Wife—his queen. She was dead and her body hidden two days before the Pharo summoned her to his bed. Lucky me, he enjoyed several goblets of wine before coitus. Unlucky him, I was the one disguised as his queen, and I was also the one who poured and offered him a full goblet of wine, laced with a specially crafted poison, making sure he drank every drop."

"Ursula . . ." I whispered on an incredulous sigh. To know that she'd held such a pivotal role in the shaping of the current mystic power structure was nearly too much to take in. "If the Falcon knows you possess this trinket, why not just steal it from you?"

"Because I destroyed it the night Elric and Petra's forces won the war. I couldn't risk it being discovered or I might've been one of the thousands executed that night too."

I shook my head, trying to follow the facts because I was again unclear why she looked so fearful.

"Then, that's a problem solved, right? The Falcon can't ask you for a potion you can't create now that the trinket has been destroyed."

She stared sadly at me. "I wore it all throughout the battle, Dovey, watching it quite closely, observing every powerful mystic engaged in battle as the recipes for their demise flittered across my mind. As you well know, I'm famous for remembering every potion I've ever crafted. It's part of what sets me apart as a potion master. And even though I haven't ever crafted a potion to kill the remaining mystics who now head the courts, I still know how to kill each and every one of them."

The color once again drained from my face, and the shock hit me so hard, it left me lightheaded. "Even Petra?" I asked.

"Yes."

I gulped. "And . . . Elric?"

She simply nodded.

To my knowledge, no other mystic in the world knew how to deliver a death blow to Elric. He was too well insulated. Too well protected by both loyal mystic and trinket alike. Ursula was one of the most trusted members of his court. He would never, ever suspect her of being disloyal to him, and I had zero doubt that she'd ever willingly craft a potion that could kill him.

But the key word was *willingly*.

A merlin with the Falcon's powers could bind her to such a task, and I wondered if he already had. "You can't use the new trinkets," I said quickly, referring to the rings he'd gifted her.

"Of course I can't. I can't even *think* about using them, my friend. I've still accepted them, however, which is bad enough. I don't need to further entrap myself by using them."

"Good. That's good." I added a fervent nod.

"Elric shall not die by my hand, Dovey," she said, reaching for my hand again, ready to make the pact with me. I suddenly realized it was a way to protect herself. Making a pact with me would prevent her from creating the potion that could kill Elric.

I sighed in relief and wrapped my fingers around hers, clasping them tightly.

"I solemnly vow—" she began.

She never got the opportunity to finish. A chime echoed from my handbag, parked at my side, only a second or two before the front of Ursula's car exploded like it'd been hit by a bomb, causing my head to whiplash and slam against the dashboard. In an instant, my world went dark.

CHAPTER 11

Someone was screaming.

And my skin was very hot. Far too hot. On-fire hot.

With a jolt I came to and stared in confusion at the hood of the car, which I could make out through the shattered glass of the windshield.

The car was on fire. The leather of my boots was starting to smoke. I was about to be engulfed in flames. Frantically, I looked around, forcing myself to get my bearings, but my motor skills were slow to respond, and I was so, so dizzy. It was as if my body was numb to the panic my mind was experiencing.

I fumbled around for the door handle, realizing belatedly that there was none, because there was no door.

I was also distracted by the sounds of the screams, which made it even harder to think.

"Stop . . . screaming," I mumbled.

And then it hit me. No one was screaming; a siren was approaching. Not quick enough to save me from the flames, however, so I worked hard to focus on the action at hand. I tried to unhook myself from the seat belt, but it was jammed in the lock.

I closed my eyes as flames licked at the leather of my boots, burning through my jeans and blistering the skin on my shins. Placing my fingers on the buckle, I pushed what little essence I could into it and muttered,

"Lock that holds me belted fast,
Let go your hold upon the clasp."

The buckle opened and the seat belt came free, zipping away from my body to fall out of the frame of the car.

I rolled out onto the wet grass. The stinging pain of the flames burning my flesh was briefly extinguished.

"Bits!" I cried out, but it came out like a whisper. Panic coursed through me, sharpening my focus. I searched for him frantically even though the world was spinning. Closing my eyes I put more voice into it. *"Bits!"*

I felt the soft tickle of quills next to my arm. Opening my eyes again, I found his head, peeking out of my handbag, which was, miraculously, right next to me on the grass, lying on its side and looking no worse for wear.

I blinked at Bits and the purse he was halfway out of. My handbag hadn't been there next to me when I rolled onto the grass, had it?

"Thank God," I whispered, swallowing hard against the dizziness, and putting a hand on the handbag to make sure it was real. It was. Inching my fingers inside it, I grazed Bits' quills, then felt the smooth wood of the trinket box that housed my newly enchanted shakers. "Thank all the gods," I groaned, laying my head down on my outstretched arm.

Then I remembered Ursula and I willed myself to look up, turning my gaze toward the car again, but it was completely engulfed in flames.

The siren sounded so close and so loud now—it was impossible to think!

I couldn't seem to manage more than to simply lay there on my stomach, mere feet from the burning car. I knew I needed to get farther away from it, but it seemed all I could do to stay conscious right now.

And Ursula! Was she still inside the burning wreck? *"Ursula!"* I cried out. She didn't call out in return.

My head wobbled as I looked up at the burning car; the heat from the flames was starting to singe my face. Reaching deep for any show of strength I could muster, I struck an arm out and crawled forward a foot. Dragging my handbag with me, I repeated the gesture until I'd gained several more feet.

"Ursula!" I cried, crawling forward, desperate to hear her voice somewhere on the other side of the car. But there was no sign, sight, or sound of her, and I wanted to weep with worry that she might still be in that car. And if she was, she was beyond saving, even by mystic means.

The grass around me lit up with the pulsing red and white colors of a strobe light, and the siren finally cut off. A few moments later, an unbound paramedic reached my side. I tried to push up from the grass, but he laid a hand on my shoulder. "Easy, easy there, ma'am. I need you to lie still."

"No," I told him, shaking my head. "Ursula. Where's Ursula?!"

"There was someone else in the car?" he asked.

"Yes! Please. Please check to see!"

The paramedic didn't leave me. Instead, he called over his shoulder and two firemen dashed to the burning car, carrying fire extinguishers.

They sprayed the interior, but the flames were too strong. "Please," I whispered as my eyes filled with tears. "Please save her."

"Ma'am," the man attending me said firmly. "They're gonna help your friend, but I need you to lie still while I check you over, okay?"

My head sank to rest on my arm again. "You can't help me," I muttered. Unbound medicine is all but lost on mystics.

"What?" he asked, leaning toward me.

I closed my eyes, suddenly unable to keep them open. "Nothing," I muttered, and then blacked out again.

I came to in the emergency room, finding myself lying on my back, wearing a neck brace and an oxygen mask.

The oxygen was cool as it entered my lungs. It helped to clear my muddled thoughts. Maybe I'd been wrong about the unbound's modern-day medicine. After all, I hadn't seen a physician in all of my two hundred years.

With effort, I sat up and looked around.

"Whoa, whoa, whoa!" a doctor in blue scrubs and a white lab coat said. He put his hands on my shoulders and gently but firmly pushed me back to the cushion. I didn't have the energy to fight him.

"Where's Ursula?" I demanded. Had the firemen gotten her out of the car? Was she alive? I couldn't remember anything past my eyes closing on the soaked grass.

"Who?" he asked me.

"*Ursula!*" I practically shouted, knowing my voice was muffled by the mask. I reached up to pull it away when he caught my hand and kept it from the task. "Ma'am, you've been in an accident. You're at Inova Loudoun Hospital."

He said that like I should know where I was geographically. I didn't. "The other woman in the car with me," I told him. "Where is she?"

His brow furrowed. "No one else was brought in."

I sighed in exasperation. The unbound were so unhelpful. "How long have I been here? Are they still looking for her? She isn't *dead,* is she?!"

There were beeping sounds near my right shoulder, and I realized they were keeping in tune with my racing heart.

"Hey, now, easy, easy," he said in a soft, slow tone. I wondered if all medical professionals spoke like that to frantic patients. It was beyond annoying. "I'll try and get some information if you'll promise me to lie still until we take you upstairs for a CT scan."

I merely blinked at him. "I'm fine. I don't need a scan."

I knew I wasn't *actually* "fine," but I also knew that my thoughts were flowing through my brain much more readily, which meant any concussion or brain injury I might've sustained was already rapidly healing. If I didn't need to know about Ursula, I would've already been fighting him off and asking to be discharged.

"You sustained a head wound," he said, pointing to my forehead. I raised a free hand to my forehead and felt the bandage there. "It's standard procedure to order a CT when patients come in with a head trauma."

I glowered at him. He wasn't going to let me out of it. "Fine," I relented. "But can you give me my handbag? I want to call a family member."

He went around the bed to reach under it and bring out a bin. My handbag was in it along with my ruined clothes, which were tightly wrapped in a plastic bag. Belatedly, I looked down at myself and realized I was wearing the world's ugliest hospital gown, and my shins were covered in a thick layer of Vaseline and gauze, while ugly green-and-blue grippy socks covered my feet.

Little did they know that none of their efforts on my behalf were necessary.

Grabbing the bag out of the bin, I pulled it open to look inside. Bits was nowhere to be seen, which only made my heart race a little until I remembered that he could teleport himself back home with ease, and I shouldn't worry.

Probably thinking I was alarmed about the jostled contents of my purse, the resident said, "We tried to find some ID, but you don't seem to be carrying any. We'll need your personal information for the intake forms, though."

I smiled tightly at him. "No problem." I wasn't about to offer up my personal info or fill out any forms. The moment his back was turned, I'd disappear from his life entirely.

The young resident placed a hand over mine, as if to reassure me that I'd be okay. "Make your call. An orderly will be here in a bit to take you upstairs for that scan."

"Thank you, Doctor . . ."

"Layoe," he said.

"Dr. Layoe. Thank you. And could you please pull the curtain so that I have a little privacy?"

He backed away and reached up for the large green curtain. "Of course. Sit tight for now and try to relax."

With that he pulled the curtain, and I wasted no time sitting up and pulling the mask off my head. A small wave of dizziness hit me, but nothing that threatened to sink me back into unconsciousness.

Looking down past the ugly gown to my arm, I saw that I was also sporting an IV hooked up to a fluid bag hanging on a rack next to the bed.

Pulling that out was going to be tricky. While on a case for a missing trinket, I'd once followed the trail of an unbound to the hospital. He'd developed appendicitis, and when he saw me coming, he yanked out his IV, thinking he could run. Blood had sprayed everywhere as the equalized pressure of his vein was released, and the place had resembled a very grizzly crime scene.

He didn't get very far before he saw the mess he was making and fainted to the floor. I'd gotten that trinket back without any further hassle.

Easing the tape from my arm, I clamped my palm over the IV needle, pressed some essence into the area, and whispered,

"Needle blocking blood's due course,
Come away with careful force,
Seal the path on your way out,
Closing off this open route."

The needle began to slide out from under my skin and a moment later it fell into my lap, leaking only a bit of saline. Still, I kept my hand clamped on the puncture wound until I felt calm enough to peek at it. Easing the pressure off slowly, I breathed a sigh of relief when the wound appeared sealed shut.

"That worked."

Reaching quickly for my handbag, I pulled it open and found Bits, staring up at me, his little nose twitching. "Oh, you're back! Thank God," I said, reaching down to stroke his belly. He made his happy, squeaky-toy sound and I smiled. "We gotta keep it down, Bitty. Stay hidden for me for a minute, okay?"

He curled into a tight ball, as if that made him invisible. It was so cute I wanted to laugh, but I didn't have time for giggles.

"Sit tight, Bits," I told my sweet boy, then turned on the gurney cushion and dangled my legs over the side. "Mama's gonna break us out of here."

Fishing through a zippered pouch in the side of the handbag, I pulled up a silk satchel of various trinkets I kept on hand for those occasions when I found myself fully immersed in the unbound world and in need of walking among them unnoticed.

The satchel held a silver dollar—perfect for extracting information from an unassuming unbound who wouldn't remember ever even speaking to me afterward; a metal jack from the child's game that allowed me to enter rooms and nose about unseen by any passersby; a large paper clip that was newly acquired and allowed me to access any computer without the need for passwords or permission; a sterling silver toothpick that allowed me to pick any lock; and a simple gold band that had probably once been a wedding band, but which was now enchanted to allow me to walk among the unbound without being noticed—even if I were naked, which, in this gown, I practically was.

Slipping the gold band onto my thumb—it was too large to stay put on any other finger—I pushed a touch of essence into it and grabbed my bag of clothes, my handbag, and snuck out of the curtained area.

I then paused for a moment to see if anyone noticed my sudden appearance, but no one even looked in my direction.

"Good." I sighed. The unbound required very little magic to fool them. A trait I rather liked.

Moving swiftly away from the bay of beds, I walked toward a closed door that had a sign suggesting only E.D. employees were allowed to enter. Placing my ear to the door, I heard no one on the other side, so I tried the handle, which, as expected, was locked.

Using my handy silver toothpick, and with no unbound the wiser, I unlocked the door and slipped inside.

I entered a locker room and today, unlike the day before, was my lucky day because above the lockers, stacked in neat piles, were blue scrubs, masks, and scrub caps.

"Bingo."

After finding a size that would fit me, I changed, then dug around in my clothes' bag, only to pull out my knee-length boots that were now completely useless as they had suffered the worst of the fire before I was able to throw myself out of the burning car.

"Damn," I muttered, looking around for another option. I didn't relish the idea of leaving the hospital in my bare feet, but I'd do what I had to to get me and Ursula out of here—assuming she *was* in fact here.

My gaze was suddenly pulled toward movement at my feet, and I looked down to see Bits perched on his hind legs as if trying to get my attention. Once he saw that I'd discovered him, he wrapped himself into his trademark ball and rolled forward to one of the lockers. Stopping just short of bumping into it, he uncurled himself, stood up on his hind legs again, and wiggled his nose at me.

I didn't even hesitate. Moving quickly to the locker, I used my toothpick again on the padlock and it easily gave way. Opening it, I saw that there was a pair of fur-lined clogs perched on a shelf at eye level.

Taking one off the shelf, I slipped my foot into it, discovering it felt like it was made for me. "Thank you, picklepuss," I said, grinning down at him. "You're a gem."

Picking him up I put him gently back inside my handbag then got the other shoe off the shelf and, because we mystics simply can't help our kleptomaniac tendencies, I also took the soft, gray cardigan hanging on a hook inside the locker. I was about to turn away when a small wave of guilt washed over me. Rooting around in my handbag again I unzipped an interior pouch and pulled out a couple of hundreds. I didn't know how much the shoes and sweater had set back the healthcare worker who used this locker, but I figured two hundred dollars should cover it.

I then left the room immediately after setting the hundreds where the shoes had been and closing the locker back up and reattaching the lock. Back in the hallway with my features obscured by the face mask I'd snatched on my way out of the locker room door, I scanned the area without seeing any sign of Ursula in any of the emergency bays lining the semicircular room of the emergency department. Still, I had to be thorough, so I approached the desk in the center, removed the gold ring, and gained the attention of a woman with short white hair, a pleasant expression, and smiley-faced patterned scrubs.

"Can I help you?" she asked, her eyes darting around my chest, no doubt searching for an ID badge.

I looked down at myself, making a show of patting my chest. "Oops, sorry. Forgot to wear my lanyard again." I then rummaged around in my handbag. "Where did that thing go?" I muttered, retrieving my hand from the bag while holding the silver dollar trinket and a bit of loose change. Reading her name tag that read *Molly Donahue, R.N.*, I said, "Would you hold this a sec, Molly? I swear, someday I'm going to organize this purse!"

She took the coins, and I went back to rummaging, sneaking a peek after a few seconds and seeing her expression turn blank.

Taking back the coins from her open palm, I said, "I'd like you to check your tablet and tell me if an Ursula Göransdotter was brought in by ambulance."

The nurse lifted her tablet and began to tap at it while repeating, "You'd like me to see if Ursula Göransdotter has come into the E.D."

I nodded, knowing that she didn't really need the encouragement. She'd do whatever I asked for the next few minutes and remember not a bit of the exchange.

She stopped typing and her eyes roved over the screen. "No one by that name has come into the E.D. recently. Or . . . ever."

A tickle of panic washed over me. Was Ursula still out at the crash site? Had she died? "Now check to see if there are any incoming victims of the car accident from where I—I mean, from an accident where a woman with burns to her shins and a head wound was brought in."

The nurse's brow furrowed, and I knew I was risking snapping her out of my spell with such a detailed request. If she couldn't perform the task I assigned her, she'd snap back to consciousness.

She began to type again, and I took that as a good sign. "Looks like that Jane Doe with the burns to her legs was the only victim from that crash. No one else has been routed here."

Again, I was stumped because not only was Ursula not here, neither was the driver and possible passengers from the car that'd hit us. And in my mind, I reasoned that a car had hit us head-on while going the wrong way down the expressway. I couldn't remember any details of another car, but I barely remembered managing to crawl out of Ursula's burning Mercedes. My focus in the immediate moments after coming to at the crash site had been to get myself to safety, then make sure Bits was safe before begging the firefighter to help Ursula, who I thought was still in the car. Shortly after that, I'd lost consciousness again.

"Two more questions," I told her, dreading asking the first. "Where is the morgue, and who can I ask for more specifics about that car crash?"

"The morgue is directly across the building from us," she said, waving to the corridor leading deeper into the hospital, "and you can ask Pete Ortez about the crash. He's the paramedic that brought Jane Doe in, and he's grabbing dinner with Nurse Sadie McMasters, his girlfriend, in the cafeteria."

Wow. This unbound was *helpful!* "Perfect, thank you, Molly." I turned away and then whipped back, hoping the spell hadn't lost its hold on her yet. "Which way to the cafeteria?"

"It's in the same direction as the morgue but it's off the first corridor on your right. Follow either corridor to the end and you'll reach either the morgue or the cafeteria."

"Excellent. Thank you."

I left the nurse quickly as there was less of a far-off look in her eyes and I could see that the spell was definitely starting to wear off.

Moving out of the E.D., I heard a male voice call out, "Hey! Where's my patient?!" and I knew that must be about me.

I turned toward the cafeteria first, hoping the paramedic who'd brought me in would have more information about the crash site and where Ursula might be if she hadn't been brought here.

I found the couple at a corner table, and I was relieved to see they were right in the middle of their meals.

Making sure the mask was still obscuring my features, I approached the table and said, "Nurse McMasters?"

"Yes?" she asked, looking up at me with impossibly blue eyes and a perky nose, while soft blond hair framed her lovely face.

"Hi. Sorry to bother you, I'm one of the new orderlies. Nurse Donahue needs you upstairs. STAT. Something about giving a patient the wrong dose . . ."

Sadie pulled a small black pager out of its clip at her waste and eyed the little screen with irritation. "Then why didn't she page me?"

I simply shrugged.

"Grrr," she growled, while she got to her feet and prepared to hurry off. Looking at her boyfriend, she said, "I'll be right back."

"Gotcha," he called to her as she trotted off. And then he seemed to notice that I was still hovering over the table. "What's up?" he asked, and his eyes searched the front of my scrubs for my hospital ID, so I pulled the same shtick with pretending to have forgotten to don my ID badge, digging through my handbag to then lay the silver dollar in his outstretched palm.

Taking a seat when his expression went blank, I said, "What can you tell me about the accident that you just finished a call on."

"The one off 659?"

I nodded because I hadn't been paying attention to what expressway Ursula had been taking to the Falcon's estate. I'd simply known we were driving northwest, deeper into Virginia.

"Bad scene," Pete told me, his tone flat. "Lucky vic, though. She was found next to the burning car she'd been driving in. My boys got the fire out while I tended to the vic. Brought her in an hour ago. Some second degree burns on her lower extremities, a laceration on her forehead, a few other cuts and bruises, but she should walk out on her own power by tomorrow morning. As long as the CT comes back okay."

"What about the other victims?"

Pete's forehead wrinkled. "No other victims. Front of the car was all smashed up, but whoever hit her car managed to drive away from the scene, which is weird."

"Explain 'weird'?"

"From the damage to the front end of that car, I'd say whoever hit her was going seventy to eighty. There's no way that vehicle should've been drivable after that, and whoever *was* driving it should've been dead. The only thing that could've come away from that kind of a crash is a tank."

A cold, prickly tendril of alarm traveled up my spine. "Is anyone still on the scene?"

"Probably. The state troopers really hate it when a hit-and-run gets away with it, but they'll have to have some luck with this one."

"Why do you say that?"

Pete picked up his phone, which had been resting on the table, and wiggled it. "My captain says they can't find a single car part, piece of trim, or trail of leaking auto fluid to identify the other car involved. It's like that Mercedes was hit by a ghost car, or something."

The chill at the back of my spine spread, fanning out across my shoulders and curling itself firmly into my chest.

No unbound had hit us. A mystic had been responsible for the accident.

And Ursula was missing.

Closing my eyes to bring back the memory of waking up in that flaming car, working to get the seat belt buckle to release, I realized that the driver's side had been empty. Ursula hadn't been next to me. I would've seen her when I was fumbling with the seat belt.

My mind reached for other details: the fire that was more on my side of the vehicle than hers, my door gone but hers . . . open.

Yes, I was certain I'd caught a glimpse of the door open. And even though I remembered that the windshield had been shattered, Ursula had been buckled in when we began our drive away from the Falcon's estate. I was certain she hadn't been ejected because I distinctly remember her telling me to buckle up right before she snapped the buckle on her seat belt and started the car. When we pulled off onto the shoulder, neither one of us had unbuckled our seat belts.

So Ursula had somehow made it out of the car, but whether that was on her own power or via someone else's was the mystery of the night.

My attention went back to Pete when he shifted slightly in his seat. He was coming back to full consciousness.

"You'll remember nothing of this conversation," I told him.

"I'll remember nothing of this conversation," he repeated.

I got up and left him, moving quickly toward the morgue now. I didn't think Ursula was there, but I had to make certain.

Arriving at the clearly marked double doors, I waited for two orderlies pushing a gurney loaded with a fully sheet-draped body to make its way through them first before I followed behind at a discreet distance.

The body in question was much too large to be Ursula, and the two men guiding it along the corridor had just passed me when the orderly on the left stopped their progress after looking intently at an X-ray he'd been distractedly holding up to the light. "Hey, Gunner," he said, holding out the X-ray to his partner. "Take a look."

"What is it?" Gunner asked, taking the X-ray and turning it up to the overhead light.

While Gunner was looking, the first orderly said, "Crazy, right? I've seen some weird *X-Files'* level stuff in my day, but never anything *that* freaky."

Gunner whistled as he looked at the image. "I see what you mean. Does the rest of him look like this?"

The first orderly nodded. "Yep. Every single bone in this guy's body's broken, but the weird part is that there's not a scratch on him."

Standing a few feet away from them, I stiffened.

Gunner lifted the sheet, which I could now see covered a body bag. He reached over to tug at the zipper and have a peek inside. "He didn't bleed out?" he asked as he peered in at the corpse.

The first orderly picked up a file that'd been resting on the body's legs and opened it. "According to the doc's notes, there was massive internal hemorrhaging, and some blood loss through the nasal cavity, but other than that, not a single derma cell was ripped open or cut. And from what Doc Katz told me before she checked out for the night, this guy's just like three *other* bodies the feds have on ice in D.C."

"Get outta here," Gunner said, lifting his gaze with a disbelieving scowl.

The first orderly held up his hand. "Hand to God, brother. Hand to God."

"Car wreck and a lot of air bags?" Gunner asked, zipping up the body bag.

"Nope. That's the really weird part. Katz was recording the autopsy, so I got to listen while I was organizing the mess the day shift left us, and I heard her say that this guy was found lying in his bed, still in his pajamas. No sign of foul play, either."

"Come on, man, you're pullin' my leg," Gunner said with a nervous laugh. "That's impossible."

The first orderly held up his hand solemnly for a second time. "I swear to you, Gun. I'm not lying. The doc couldn't figure it out, either. I mean, he looks like someone took a bat to him, you know? But, like she said, you can't break *every* bone in a body without cutting some skin or making a big messy crime scene, and yet, here we are." For emphasis, he waved his hand along the body.

Gunner blew out an exasperated breath. "You're givin' me the creeps, bro."

The first orderly leaned over the body, cupping the side of his mouth conspiratorially. "I think it's aliens."

Gunner chuckled and it wasn't nearly as nervous. "Here we go. You and your UAPs or UFOs, or discs in the sky!"

"No, I'm tellin' you, Gun! It's the only thing that makes sense! It's aliens getting their revenge for Area 54!"

Gunner waved dismissively at his partner and continued to chuckle. "Yeah, yeah, whatever."

The first orderly laughed too, but then his cell phone beeped and he removed it from the clip at his waist to look at the display, all hint of humor vanishing. "No. Freaking. Way."

"What?" Gunner asked, beginning to move the gurney along again. Neither man had given even the smallest hint of being aware of my presence.

"There's another body comin' in. Just like this one."

The gurney stopped for a second time, one orderly staring at the other, both wearing matching shocked expressions.

"Jessie, come on, man. Stop it, okay? You're overplaying it."

Jessie turned his cell phone screen around so that Gunner could see. "My roommate's a cop. He was at the scene and took pictures. See? Exactly the same."

Gunner squinted at the screen, hissing out a breath. "Not *exactly* the same."

Jessie scowled at him and flipped the cell back to himself. "Cuz it's a woman?"

"Yeah. And she don't look dressed in her pj's. She looks dead by the side of the road. That's a hit-and-run, man."

The first orderly shook his head, clearly irritated. Whipping the screen around again—which was too far away for me to see—he said, "Then explain where all the blood is. How do you get hit by a car and not have any open wounds leaking lots of blood?"

Gunner pointed to the phone. "It's raining, man! The rain washed it away!"

Jessie shook his head again and clipped the phone back to his waist. "Not according to my roommate, brother. He says she was still warm when they found her off Highway 659. She died maybe an hour or two ago. No ID, either. Just lyin' by the side of the road, like she was dumped there."

I stopped listening as I moved away along the wall, leaning hard against it. "Ursula," I whispered while my mind began to scream and scream.

CHAPTER 12

Perched on the wide sill of a window, I waited numbly for the ambulance to arrive at the back door to the morgue. No one questioned me as they passed by; they simply went about their business.

The morgue orderlies, Gunner and Jessie, appeared shortly after the ambulance stopped under the archway leading out from the back entrance. They helped lower a gurney from the bay and push it inside.

She lay within a black body bag, her form taking on something non-human, like a lumpy garment bag.

Tears had been leaking down my cheeks ever since overhearing the two men talk about her impending arrival. I felt a wild assortment of emotions: profound loss, fear, rage, and even something hovering around the edges of all that, like the Falcon's sphere when it'd contained the explosion. Something that provided the same protection from the overwhelming onslaught of emotions that threatened to send me into an emotional abyss.

There was no one I could call. I doubted I could even reach Elric in Europe, as, when he's out of the country, all of his calls and texts get routed through Hyacinth. And even if my call to him did get through, I didn't think he would risk losing the illusion of his very public anger and rejection of me.

And I couldn't call Qin because there was no way *to* call him that also wasn't routed through Hyacinth—and again, I didn't have a carrier pigeon handy.

Reaching out to Jacquelyn was also risky because her loyalty was first, last, and always to Elric. Diplomatically speaking, talking to me right now was akin to taking a side for team Dovey, and no way would she risk that.

I also couldn't call Gib, as much as I wanted to. I couldn't have him see Ursula and identify her. He'd want to know how she—and possibly me—was mixed up in all this, and those were answers that I couldn't give him because of my promise to Elric.

I knew he and his team would soon hear of the woman found on the highway with similar catastrophic injuries to the Bureau agents. The FBI would definitely want to take a close look at her, which is why I *had* to get in to see my best friend's body alone. I needed to use some magic to alter her appearance so that Gib wouldn't find out it was her. What I was hoping for was that she was still wearing her medallion, which was the method I could use to alter her appearance. I had no idea if it'd work on a dead body, but I felt I had to try.

As for what'd happened to her when she suddenly disappeared from our lives, I'd have to come up with something else for him to believe. Something less tragic, like Ursula had decided at long last to run away to Australia with her one true love, Dex . . .

I shot forward to sit straight up. "Dex!"

Not only could I call him, I *should* call him. Even though his feelings for his thieving partner, Esmé, were more than his feelings for Ursula, he'd still mourn her loss and wonder what happened if she disappeared.

Plus, he might be able to help me identify who the mystic responsible for all this was. A mystic I would find a way to kill, given the level of rage swirling among all the other emotions inside the pit of my stomach right now.

My hands were shaking when I pulled my phone out of my handbag, and I thanked the powers that be that I had Dex's number stored in my contacts list, something I'd done almost randomly a few weeks earlier after he'd saved me from certain death.

He answered on the first ring. "Dovey," he said curtly. "What's happened?"

His response to my call threw me a bit. "How do you know something's wrong?"

"Why else would you be calling me?"

"Fair point."

"What's going on?"

I bit my lip and tears welled in my eyes. "I think . . . I think Ursula is . . . has been . . ." My voice felt trapped behind a sob, and I couldn't get the words out.

"Drop me a pin and I'll come to you. Sit tight. I'm on my way."

In the background I heard the loud rumble of an engine. Dex drives a souped-up Mustang. I knew he'd be here as quickly as he could.

I spent most of the time waiting for Dex pacing the hallway. I'd gotten rid of the mask and scrub cap; no one from the emergency department would be looking for me in the morgue, so I felt safe exposing my face. I still wore the gray cardigan, but it was similar to any other gray cardigan, and unlikely to call attention to me.

Dex arrived at half past two, breezing through the doors to gather me in a hug and squeeze tightly. Letting me go, he stared down at me with a heavy, sad expression, and I swore he looked on the verge of tears himself. "What happened to her?" he asked, his voice choked with emotion.

I told him the long story of having gone to see Falcon the Wise, but I didn't tell him the details of the trinkets we'd come away with. Dex, after all, was a professional thief, and as much as I liked him, I still wouldn't trust him around trinkets as valuable as the ones in my handbag.

"Why were you parked on the side of the road?" he asked when I got to that part.

"I'm working a case, and Ursula and I were discussing our next moves," I said, offering him a lie for why we'd really pulled over.

"What kind of case?"

"A mystic is murdering FBI agents in the same way I believe he murdered Ursula."

Dex flinched. "Two questions: How do you know it's a he? And, if these agents were hit by a car, how do you know it was a mystic behind the wheel?"

"One, I don't, and two, Ursula and the agents weren't hit by a car. They were on the receiving end of the Crushing Curse."

Dex's eyes widened and his mouth formed an *O*. "The Crushing Curse?" he asked after a shocked pause.

I nodded, which elicited a shudder from the big, brawny man. "That's Elric's specialty," he said. "He had a go at Esmé with it and she barely survived."

It was my turn to widen my eyes. "*How* did she?"

"She had something to trade for her life and Elric took the deal."

"Lucky her."

"Lucky us," he corrected. "Tell me more about this case with the dead FBI agents."

I spent the next several minutes filling Dex in on everything that I knew about the Bureau agents who'd been murdered by the Crushing Curse.

He grunted at times and nodded along as I spoke, then, when I was finished, he eyed me keenly and asked, "Do you think your lover killed Ursula?"

"No and no."

"A double no?"

"Correct. No and no."

"How can you be sure?"

"For one, he's in Europe right now and two . . . I just know he didn't, Dex. You have to trust me on that."

He wiped his face with both hands. He looked tired and I noticed for the first time that there was a new, long scorch mark fully healed on his forearm. I pointed to it. "Dragon?"

He nodded. "I remember not to feed the trolls but always forget not to feed the dragons."

"Yikes."

"I'll say. Getting back to Ursula, you saw her murdered?"

"No." I explained further, bringing Dex fully up to speed about what'd happened in the minutes after the crash and here at the hospital when I came to. When I'd finished, the heavy sag to his broad shoulders lifted a bit. "What you're saying is that you haven't seen her body, then, right?"

"No, but . . . who else could it be, Dex? The two orderlies that brought her in mentioned that a woman with the same injuries as the recently murdered FBI agent was found on the side of the same highway where we were parked when we got hit."

"Who hit you?" he asked, and I realized I hadn't made it clear that the accident was also likely caused by a mystic.

"I have no idea, but I'd lay odds that it was the same mystic who killed Ursula."

"If it is her."

"Yes. But if it isn't her in that morgue, then *where* is she?"

"Let's start by making sure that it's not her and go from there."

"And if it *is* her?" I asked, my voice breaking again.

"Then we hunt down the bastard that killed her and deliver

some justice." For emphasis, Dex curled his hand into a fist and the look in his eyes was indeed lethal. "Where is the murdered woman from the highway now?"

I pointed to the directory on the wall. "She was wheeled to the third floor for an X-ray and CT scan, which I'm assuming is for the medical examiner. She hasn't been wheeled back down yet."

He made a sweeping motion. "After you, Dove."

I led Dex to the elevators, and we rode it three floors up in silence. It felt like we were both bracing for the worst. Following the signs and arrows for X-ray, I held out the hand wearing the gold band on my thumb to Dex and said, "The ring is a cloaking trinket. The unbound won't notice us. Hold my hand and I'll pump a little more juice into it."

He grabbed my hand, and we carried on. We came across the bodies of both the woman and the FBI agent almost by accident. The two gurneys each loaded with a body bag were parked in a side hallway off the main entrance to the imaging department, the white sheets removed from covering the black body bags where they were housed.

"There," I whispered to Dex, pointing to them.

He seemed to stumble slightly when he saw the gurney with the smaller form inside the body bag. I let him go ahead of me and he stood over it for a long moment, his lips pressed hard together, and his fists clenched. At last, he reached toward the top of the bag and unzipped it several inches.

From where I was standing, I couldn't see inside, but the reaction on Dex's face told me it was bad.

My lip began to quiver. It was her. One look at his face and I knew it. I put my hand up to cover my mouth, trying to hold back the sob as Dex pulled the zipper down several more inches and reached inside the bag.

Lifting a massively bruised arm and clearly broken hand, he

pulled it free from the bag, then bent to peer at the side of Ursula's torso.

I was about to turn away, overcome with emotion, when he said, "It's not her, Dovey."

I gasped, swiping at the tears that were leaking down my face. "What? You're sure?"

"Positive. This poor lass doesn't bear a single tattoo. Ursula has three."

I gaped at him. "She *does*?"

His mouth quirked upward a bit. "Her binder marked her. That was a thing back in the day. Also, this one's hair is too long and, I'd wager, she's four or five inches too tall."

"So . . . who's in the body bag?"

Dex stepped back to consider the woman's head. I didn't know what her body looked like after having gone through such an extreme form of torture and death, and, frankly, I didn't want to know. I had enough haunting images to fuel centuries of bad dreams.

"It's hard to say for sure, but I'd wager it's Tove Kalla."

I gasped again. Tove had been something of a rival of mine. She was one of Elric's *other* women. She favored him far more than he favored her, however, and I'd never felt more than a twinge of jealousy toward her, but still, the fact that she was dead and how she'd been assassinated sent a very, *very* cold shiver up my spine.

I'd heard a rumor a few months back that Elric had grown weary of Tove's incessant requests for his attentions. He'd been giving her the cold shoulder of late, if the gossip was true.

Had she pushed his patience to the boiling point? And if she had . . . and he did this to her . . . could I be next? Was Elric shedding some of the women in his intimate entourage?

In the entirety of the one hundred and eighty years of our relationship, and after witnessing firsthand Elric's power to vanquish those who displeased or betrayed him, I had perhaps naively thought that I was forever insulated from the threat of his violence because I loved him, and he loved me. I knew about the other women he kept company with, but I also knew I was his favorite.

I could no longer claim that to be the case, which, by extension, meant I was no longer insulated from the threat of his violence.

I began to tremble as Dex rezipped up the body bag.

"Dove?" he asked when he again looked toward me. "You all right?"

I shook my head. "No, Dex. I'm not."

He walked to me and wrapped me in a hug. I felt myself melt into him—not romantically, I wasn't attracted to Dex, and I doubted he was attracted to me—but right now I needed a steadying gesture, and that hug did me a world of good.

"Thank you," I said when he loosened his grip, and I stepped back. "I needed that."

He grinned. "Reassuring hugs are available anytime, Dovey, day or night."

"We have to find Ursula."

"We do," he agreed. "Come on. I'll drive. Shouldn't be too hard to find the site where you two were ambushed."

Dex began to walk away, and I was about to follow him when my attention went to the other body on the gurney next to Tove. I moved to it. The body bag was unzipped down to the victim's neck and the sight of his face was difficult to take in. The man was black and blue from head to toe, his face had fallen in on itself, his lips peeled back exposing broken and shattered teeth.

His face was the only source of blood that I could see. It had leaked out of his nose, his mouth, his eyes, and his ears, but I saw no cuts or abrasions and hadn't expected to see them, either.

Dex walked back to me to have a look over my shoulder. He grunted when he took in the sight. "Hell of a way to go, eh?"

"Horrific," I agreed, swallowing hard. I could imagine some truly terrible ways to be executed. This was among the worst.

It was also still unclear why he'd been targeted. Another agent in Gib's office picked off by one of our own. I couldn't fathom the agenda. It seemed so counterproductive.

"Why would a mystic target the FBI?"

"Only one reason mystics target the unbound, Dovey. For power."

"Power? How would murdering these men gain a *mystic* power?"

"Assuming the one doing the murdering isn't Elric or Petra—and I doubt it is—then picking off FBI agents one by one is bound to bring the Dobromila-Ostergaard court nothing but trouble. My guess is that the unbound agents investigating these executions will eventually conclude that their brethren were rendered unconscious, then hauled to a decompression chamber and locked in until all their bones were broken."

Gib hadn't mentioned that as a working theory, but then I'd only spoken briefly to him about the case since it started.

"The puzzle for the Bureau," Dex continued, "is going to be how the agents were taken out of their homes, crushed to death, then delivered back to their homes without anyone else knowing and no signs of a struggle at the site where the body was discovered.

"It'll be the thing that gets them to dig deeper, especially since its their own being targeted. Eventually, a clue or two will lead them back to us and the fragile veil holding our world secret will start to come down. *None* of the Seven want that. And because it's all happening in the Court of Dobromila-

Ostergaard, it could bring plenty of challenges from the other five courts."

"Then you don't think it's Petra behind this. She wouldn't hesitate to cause Elric trouble."

"True, and Petra's certainly capable of it, but if there's one thing Petra isn't, it's suicidal. She wouldn't invite this level of trouble to Elric while she remains his partner in power."

"Then one of the leaders from the other five courts is responsible," I said.

He nodded. "That'd be my guess. I doubt they'd come here personally, but every court has a lieutenant powerful enough to wield the Crushing Curse."

"So why kill Tove?" I asked, trying to work the puzzle out.

Dex glanced over at her body on the gurney. "No idea, love. No idea. But, as she was one of Elric's women, I'd be careful if I were you."

"Trust me, I'm already doing my level best to shore up my defenses. It's Ursula I'm worried about. She works for Elric, and they've been loyal to each other for a thousand years. She could've been taken by whoever's doing this. We need to find her before she ends up like . . ." I pointed toward the gurneys.

"Come on," Dex said. "Let's get to the ambush site. Maybe there's a clue we can follow from there."

Dex drove and it only took us ten minutes to reach the site where Ursula and I were ambushed, which was obvious given the charred asphalt and burnt grass.

What was left of Ursula's car had been towed away. Luckily, there were no investigators left at the scene either.

Traffic was light, given the hour at nearly three a.m., and Dex parked his Mustang on the shoulder of the highway. We got out of the car, and I saw him subtly lay his watch on the hood. I understood why when an approaching car moved over

234 / VICTORIA LAURIE

two whole lanes, giving us a wide birth, and then another car followed suit.

He didn't even have to put on his hazard lights with that handy trinket.

We walked around the site, using our phones' flashlights to see in the dark while we kicked at bits of wreckage that hadn't been picked up by the authorities after the crash. Ursula's bumper lay a few yards from the charred outline of where her car had been.

Dex moved toward the bumper and squatted down, shining the light from his phone onto it. "Let me guess," he said. "You didn't see approaching headlights right before you two were hit."

"We didn't." I had recalled those moments over and over again, remembering Ursula and me, hands clasped together and her about to utter a binding promise. There'd been no warning other than a chime from my money clip at the bottom of my purse, but no time to react to the warning. No lights, no movement, no sound of an oncoming car. Just *boom!*

"This pattern," Dex said, turning the bumper toward me so that I could see that it had a centrally placed crater, causing the rest of the front bumper to crumple in toward the middle. "That's consistent with a magical strike. Whoever delivered it was quite powerful."

"Crushing Curse powerful?"

"Definitely," he said, standing tall again and wiping his hands on his jeans. "Hang on. I think I've got a trinket in the car that could help."

I waited while he trotted off toward his Mustang, then watched him rummage around in the back seat before coming up with a trinket shaped like a palm-sized golden frog. He brought that back to where he'd just been squatting and set the frog down on the front bumper of the Mercedes. He then hovered his hand over it and a moment later the frog made a small leap all on its own.

"Oh goodness," I said. "I wasn't expecting that."

Dex grinned. "It'll retrace the trajectory of the death blow. Works just like one of those laser pointers the unbound detectives use, but Froggy here is more fun." He added a hint of a grin and I felt a little of the heaviness I'd been carrying the last several hours ease.

Dex and I began to follow the hopping trinket, and to my surprise the frog didn't head toward the highway, it leaped toward the woods.

Dex glanced at me, motioning with his chin toward the frog. "Now that's curious."

"It is."

He and I continued to stride forward, keeping sight of the frog, which wasn't hard. The gleaming little guy had quite the hippity-hop.

It got a bit trickier in the woods, but we still managed, mostly because what had looked like a thick cluster of trees was in reality pretty thin. Still, the trees and brush had all but obfuscated a road that ran along the highway but was tucked out of sight.

Here the frog stopped for a moment before choosing a direction, finally coming to a full stop once it'd crossed the road.

Dex and I moved to where the frog had stopped. With a bolt of surprise, I realized that we were looking over the side of a bluff, at the bottom of which was a large, stone structure.

A structure that even in the dark I recognized.

"The merlin," I whispered.

"Eh?" Dex asked.

I turned to him. "Falcon the Wise has kidnapped Ursula."

Dex stared at me for a long moment. "Why?" he finally asked.

"Because he wants to use her."

"For what?"

I turned back to the estate, shuddering at the thought of what Ursula must be going through right now.

"For what, Dove? What does he want to use her for?"

I didn't take my gaze off the fortress the Falcon hid within. "Murder, Dex. He wants to use her as his personal assassin."

"Come on," he said, bending to pick up his trinket. "We'll need to break her out of there."

I caught him by the arm. "He's got a beareina."

That stopped him. He looked down at me. "Crikey, Dovey, you buried the lead. We're going to need a different trinket to deal with one of those."

"Have you got one handy?"

He nodded. "Used one on a dragon a week or two ago. I still got dinged"—he paused to hold up the scar on his arm—"but at least I wasn't dinner."

"Petra sent a dragon after you?"

He shook his head. "No. And I can't give any more details than that. You know how Elric wants his thieves to stay mum."

"I'm aware."

We began to trot back toward the Mustang when I swore something glinted in the distance off the light coming from Dex's phone.

I paused and squinted in that direction, aiming my phone's light toward the thing.

Dex stopped a few feet later to look over his shoulder. "What?"

I pointed to where a small mound lay in the grass. It could've been the dark playing tricks on me, but whatever was over there didn't look natural.

Dex came back to where I stood and added his phone's beam of light to mine.

In the additional light we clearly saw a human form, lying in the grass, partially covered by a cloak.

I sucked in a breath when I realized it was a body. "The assassin?" I guessed.

Dex's stance went rigid. I started forward and it was Dex's turn to grab my arm. When I looked up at him, he held a finger to his lips and shook his head. "Could be a trap," he whispered.

"Or not," I replied. Either way, we couldn't simply walk away. We had to see who it was.

Stay here, he mouthed. Then he turned away and trotted back up the hill toward his car.

When he left me standing there, I also realized how vulnerable I was, standing here alone and defenseless.

Not quite defenseless, I thought. Rooting through my handbag and around Bitty's quills, I laid my fingers on the box with my new trinkets. Freeing it from my handbag, I opened the lid, trying to decide which shaker to use, when I felt Bits scramble inside my handbag as if he'd just woken up in a panic.

I looked down only to see he'd crawled to the handbag's opening, then he promptly launched himself into the grass.

Panic gripped me, and in a hissy whisper I called, *"Bits!"*

But he paid me no heed. Instead, he began to scramble through the grass. "No, no, no, no, no!" I whispered, chasing after him. "Bits! *Bits!*" I called as loudly as I dared.

He continued to run in a zigzag pattern through the wet grass, well on his way toward the cloaked figure. I raced after him, pausing only to grab one of the shakers out of the box. I didn't care which one at this point. I was ready to call for help just as much as I felt I might need to arm myself.

"Dovey!" I heard Dex call from just up the hill. I guess we'd dispensed with whispers.

"It's Bits! Dex, he's gotten away from me!"

"What's a Bits?" he asked, after he'd raced to close the distance between us.

"My hedgehog!" I replied, pointing to where the little minx was hopping along over the slick grass in a mad dash to keep ahead of us. In that moment I realized that he hadn't simply teleported himself to his destination, which clearly seemed like it was the cloaked figure on the ground. It was as if he was begging us to follow him.

And I should mention that my picklepuss doesn't like to scramble over wet ground. He likes to stay indoors to lounge. And eat. And sleep. Preferably in that order several times over throughout the day.

"Maybe get him a leash," Dex grumbled as he bent low to snatch up Bits, but my picklepuss darted to the side, avoiding Dex's clutches.

"It wouldn't do any good," I told him, barely missing when Bits's evasive move brought him closer to me. "He can just teleport himself out of it."

Dex came to a sudden stop, and I did too, mostly because Bits had arrived at the cloaked figure and was now scrambling up on top of the motionless form.

"He's enchanted?" Dex said next to me while keeping wary eyes on the body lying in the grass.

"Yes," was all I could manage, my focus now entirely on my hedgehog and the cloaked figure.

Bits had almost crested the shoulders of the hidden form, and when he got there, he turned back toward me and lifted himself onto his hind legs, making small squeaking sounds of distress.

I moved forward the last few feet and bent cautiously down, and that's when I saw the mystic's arm. It was badly burned, but what really drew my attention was the mystic's wrist, around which was wrapped a set of charred bangles.

"*No!*" I cried, pulling back the hood of the cloak to reveal a tangled mess of blond hair. "Ursula!"

Dex was squatting down next to me in a hot second. Carefully, he turned Ursula over. She let out a sharp cry and her eyes fluttered. With mounting horror, I took in her broken form, which literally *was* broken.

Her obviously broken nose, swollen cheekbones, and bruised brow told me many of the bones in her face were shattered. Dex eased her onto her back and bloodstained tears leaked out of the corners of her eyes.

Carefully removing the cloak off her, I could see her left arm lay at an odd angle, and her left hand was swollen so badly that it looked more like a paw. What's more, the bangles on her left wrist were charred and frail, as if they'd taken on far more of the battle than the bangles on her right wrist.

Somewhere in the back of my mind, I remembered that Ursula, though ambidextrous, favors her left hand over her right.

Her breathing was ragged and liquid; she seemed to gurgle more than she breathed. "Oh, Ursula," I said, my voice quivering with despair. "What's happened to you?"

Dex lay a hand at the side of her cheek, the fear and worry written all over his face. "We have to get her to the car."

I looked her broken form up and down. "You can't move her, Dex. Not like this! You'll break her even more."

A sound came from Ursula, like she was trying to speak. I looked down at her to see her lips moving, but whatever she was trying to say, it was inaudible. "Shhhh, honey, shhhh," I said, wanting to touch her in reassurance, but there didn't seem to be anywhere on her body that would tolerate even the lightest touch.

"We don't have a choice," Dex insisted. Then he got to his feet, turned back toward his car, and sprinted away, yelling over his shoulder, "Stay with her. I'll be right back!"

I watched him race up the embankment, and at my side I felt Bits clamber up onto my thigh, then he hopped into my handbag, which I'd dropped next to me. When I looked down again, I saw his butt wiggle into the opening. I waited only as long as it took for him to make it inside before I hooked my arm through the handle, prepared to help Dex get Ursula up the hill and into his car.

When I focused again on her, I suddenly realized the gurgling of her ragged breathing had stopped, and her swollen eyes stared up unseeing. . . . She was gone.

CHAPTER 13

"Nooooo!" I screamed, taking Ursula into my arms and clutching her limp and lifeless body. "No, no, no, no, no!"

Burying my face in her tangled, wet hair, I let out a sob. "No, Ursula, no! Please, please don't leave me!"

She was so cold against me, and there were no sounds to indicate she was still breathing.

I held her close, rocking with her, overcome with my own heartbreak. "Why?" I whispered wetly as tears streamed down my cheeks. *"Why?!"*

There was the roar of an engine coming to life and a moment later we were lit by bright lights. I didn't let go of my best friend, I simply continued to rock with her back and forth, tears melding with the rain that had dampened her hair.

I heard the car come close, then stop and idle before a car door opened and footsteps approached.

"What's happened?" Dex asked. His hand touched my shoulder, but I didn't have the will to look up at him or let go of Ursula. "Dovey," he said. "Let me see."

It was like I couldn't get my limbs to cooperate, because when he gently tried to pull Ursula out of my arms, I screamed out my bereaved agony and kept my grip on her tight. Shaking my head, I refused to let him take her from me. There wasn't anything he could do anyway.

"Dovey, *please* let go!" he insisted, and his pull on my shoulder was much stronger now.

With another sob I loosened my grip, and she fell away from me into Dex's arms. "Come on," he said. "I have a trinket in the car!"

He lifted Ursula like a rag doll and carried her the short distance to the car. I was still on my knees, keening forward, unable to get to my feet and follow him. Finding her broken and barely alive had given me a ray of hope that she could be saved. I'd been completely unprepared for her quick and sudden death thereafter.

"Dovey!" Dex yelled. "We've got to go! Come on!"

My arms were wrapped around my torso and my forehead rested just above the ground. I had known Ursula for nearly two hundred years. She had always shown me kindness and we had become especially close these past hundred years. Because she'd lived over a thousand years, her longevity had convinced me that she'd be around for at least a thousand more. To think that she wouldn't be there to walk them with me was more than I could bear.

It wasn't like back at the hospital, when I only suspected she was dead. Now I *knew* it, and it'd happened right in front of me. I didn't know how I'd survive losing her and Elric all in one week.

"She's not dead!" Dex yelled at me. "She's got a heartbeat!"

I gasped and looked up, my breathing still coming in heavy sobs. He stood next to the rear passenger seat, waving frantically for me to join him.

Gasping for breath I scrambled to my feet and clawed my way over to the car. "Let me see her!"

He stepped in front of me and dangled his car keys. "You need to drive. I've got her breathing and her heart beating, but she's not stable. The trinket I used is almost out of juice, but it can keep her alive until we get to my place. I've got a healing trinket at the warehouse that's a level eight. It should bring her fully back to us."

I was stunned by the admission. A level eight trinket would be coveted no matter what magic it could perform, but a level eight trinket that *healed* was perhaps worth even more than my shakers.

Many trinkets could offer some healing support, but none of them lasted very long. The higher the level of power, however, the longer the trinket could remain effective and the quicker it would heal you.

Elric likely had several healing trinkets of that level—and higher—but he'd be pressed to share one without being owed a significant favor, and Ursula wasn't a powerful enough mystic to warrant such an expense.

And now that I was on the outs with him, I wondered if he'd spare one even for me.

But Dex was willing to use his on Ursula, and he was willing to confess to me that he had such a trinket. Such generosity and trust was all but absent in the mystic world, so it stunned me when he spoke those words.

I pointed to his keys. "You should drive!"

He shook his head. "The trinket I'm using on her now needs my constant essence, Dovey. I'll navigate you from the back seat."

I looked in the open door of the car where Dex had laid Ursula carefully down. She was on her back, still looking lifeless. I wiped at my tears, my vision blurred. "You're sure she's breathing?"

He grabbed me by the shoulders and pushed his face into mine to garner all my attention. "Yes, now let's go!"

I nodded numbly then hurried around the car and got in. I waited for Dex to carefully lift Ursula's head and shoulders into his lap, then offer me a thumbs-up.

I backed the car up and turned carefully, making sure there was no oncoming traffic—there wasn't—then got on the highway and pushed the speed all the way to Dex's place.

We arrived around four a.m. without incident, but I'd checked the rearview mirror a hundred times, searching for signs that Ursula was still with us.

At his instruction, I drove the Mustang to the west corner of the three-story warehouse where Dex and Esmé lived. Ursula had told me that Esmé had won the warehouse in a poker game a few years back, and since then she and Dex had completely renovated it, turning it into a training facility, home, and fortress for themselves. When we pulled up, I wondered what his partner would think when we brought Ursula inside.

I'd never been here, but I thought Ursula had once or twice when Esmé was away.

"Park right here," Dex instructed as I rounded the corner into an alley.

Once the car was in park, Dex jumped out, turning briefly to say, "I'll be back in a jiff," then he dashed to the garage bay door just off the alley.

I turned in my seat, staring after him in confusion. I'd thought that we'd get Ursula inside right away so that Dex could use his trinket on her, and was wondering why he'd left us both behind, but it was too late to call out to him. He was already ducking under the garage door that'd begun to lift after he'd punched in the code on the panel mounted to the wall.

Worriedly, I glanced at Ursula in the back seat. She lay motionless, her back to me and her face and torso turned toward the back cushion.

"Ursula," I whispered. I didn't know what trinket Dex had used to get her breathing again. I'd truly thought she'd died, and, in my grief, I hadn't thought to check for a pulse. I reached out and touched her shoulder, which was bare since her sweater had fallen away slightly.

She wasn't just cold to the touch; she was cold through and through. My heart began to hammer against my rib cage. "No," I whispered, desperately. "Ursula!" I said, squeezing her shoulder to see if I got a pain response. There was none.

Had she died on the way here and Dex hadn't noticed? He'd said her heart was still beating, but if that were the case, why was she so cold and stiff to the touch?

I pulled my hand back and turned around in my seat, ready to reach for the door handle, when Dex reappeared from the garage. He was holding a bundle and fiddling with something in his hand. The moment he opened the rear door of the car I said, "I think she's gone, Dex! I think she's really gone!"

His expression seemed stricken, and he didn't reply. Instead, he got into the car, and something wriggled under his arm. Sure enough, out from under it popped the head of a copper-colored puppy.

I jumped. "What the . . . ?!"

Dex muttered, "Sorry, Dove, Esmé's not home, and I can't leave the pup all alone. She'll get into trouble."

My jaw dropped. I watched him put Ursula's head in his lap, then set the pup down right on top of her chest.

Dex looked at me and I stared in horror at him, then at the pup, then at Ursula . . . who drew in a ragged breath and moaned.

"What are you doing?!" I yelled at Dex, waving at the puppy. "Get her off Ursula's chest!"

"Sorry!" he said, quickly lifting up the pup, who yawned and blinked her sleepy emerald-green eyes at me.

My focus went immediately back to Ursula as Dex settled the pup on his lap, right next to my best friend's head. I wanted to slap him for being so clumsy with the puppy around my mortally wounded best friend. "Where's the trinket?" I demanded.

"Right here," he said. Reaching almost lazily into his coat pocket, he pulled up a white, palm-sized crystal. Closing his eyes I saw him push a bit of his essence into it and it began to emit a soft, yellow glow.

He tucked the trinket into Ursula's palm, then glanced back at me. "We should get her home, Dove."

I simply stared at him for a long moment. Why was he acting so weird? "What's wrong with taking her inside until she's well enough for travel?"

"Like I said, Esmé's not home *right now* but she will be soon, and I can't let her find you two inside."

I felt a wave of anger flood my bloodstream. "Are you *kidding* me, Dex?"

He took a deep breath, seemed ready to give me a long explanation, then thought better of it and said, "I can't. It'll cause trouble."

Turning in my seat I ground my teeth together and made a U-turn, heading out of the alley. In my heart, I knew I wasn't really angry at Dex for not allowing us inside his place—he was right. Bringing Ursula to the home that he shared with his partner was messed up, even though it was a life-or-death situation. I was angry that Dex clearly cared about Ursula, but not enough to risk his relationship with Esmé. If my friend hadn't been so severely injured, I would've had many words with him about needing to pick a woman, for God's sake, and set the other one free.

We drove in silence all the way to Ursula's house. I parked at the curb, unsure where my invisible car ended in the driveway. I didn't want to risk hitting it and injuring Ursula even more. I then got out and hurried around the other side to help Dex with Ursula.

His puppy jumped out of the car ahead of him and headed to the grass to tinkle, while I held the door open for Dex so that he could carefully get Ursula out of the car.

When he emerged with her I was shocked at the difference in her appearance. The swelling in her face had gone down enough to render her recognizable, and even though she still seemed to be in pain, it didn't appear to be more than she could bear.

"Ursula," I said, putting a hand to her cheek. "Thank the gods. I thought I'd lost you."

As I pressed my palm to her face, I felt the warmth of her skin. She still appeared to have many broken bones, but she no longer seemed mortally wounded.

After Dex made it all the way out of the car with Ursula, I shut his car door and looked toward the house. "I don't have her house key with me," I told him. "And I don't think the house key on her key ring survived the fire." Ursula's home was warded, so there was no way we were getting inside. We'd have to go to my place and I wanted to scream with frustration at all the delays in giving my friend the rest she needed to heal.

"Dovey," Dex said, gaining my attention. "Her house key is in my back pocket." He then turned his hip toward me, and I fished it out, honestly surprised that she had given him a spare. We then moved up to the front door, the puppy scrambling after us.

I got us inside and Dex set Ursula on the sofa, again placing her head in his lap, stroking back her hair and patting the cushion for the puppy to climb up next to them.

I glared at him. I doubted Ursula wanted a dog on her furniture, but she was too out of it to complain. Dex pointedly ignored my disapproval and moved the sleepy puppy into the crook of Ursula's arm, where she wriggled free and jumped to the floor to begin sniffing around.

"Ember," Dex said, patting the couch. "Come here, love. Jump up and cuddle with my friend."

But Ember ignored him and continued to sniff about. "Ember," Dex said again. "Come to Daddy, honey."

"Leave her," I said, suddenly feeling weary to my bones.

Dex gave another few pats to the cushion on the couch. "Come here, pup-pup."

"What is with you and that dog?" I demanded.

He glanced up at me, and there was something in his eyes. Something almost desperate, and it gave me pause.

At that moment, however, Bits appeared on the floor next to the puppy, gaining her attention, and I gasped. "Bits! No!"

I was more afraid of Bits hurting Ember than Ember hurting Bits, but before I could reach to grab him up, he did the oddest thing: he hopped about in front of the puppy as if he was trying to get her to play.

She wagged her long red tail and sniffed at him, and then she hopped a few times too. Before I knew it, or could do anything about it, Bits and Ember were racing around the living room, and then Bits simply vanished.

My head whipped around, looking for the spot where he'd teleported to, and so did the puppy's.

There was a squeak from the couch, and I looked over to see Bits waddling up Ursula's torso, nestling down in the crook of her arm, his quills laid flat so as not to prick her.

I bit my lip, hoping she didn't startle, or that his weight— slight though it might be—wasn't too much for her healing body. She was still in bad shape, after all. I was about to reach for him when the puppy scrambled up onto the couch as well, carefully worming her way along Ursula's side to tuck in next to Bits.

"We should settle the two rugrats in the other room," I told Dex, fully expecting him to agree.

Instead, he leaned back against the cushion and said, "They're quiet now. Let's let everyone rest for what's left of the night and we can let the trinket do its work for Ursula."

I sighed, giving up the battle, and headed to one of the chairs facing the sofa. Taking off the wet cardigan I still wore and trading it for a blanket set on the back of the chair next to the one I stood in front of, I wrapped it around me then turned and sank down into the chair cushion, feeling exhausted to my marrow. Closing my eyes, I was asleep within seconds.

I woke to a brightness at the back of my eyelids. Squinting, I opened them to look around the room.

Ursula lay on the sofa, partially covered by an afghan, sleeping peacefully. I could still see some bruising along her arms, but her breathing was smooth, regular, and gurgle-free.

The trinket that Dex had brought along to heal her was gone . . . as was he and his puppy.

I started to get up, thinking he might be in the kitchen, when I realized that Bits was tucked into my lap, curled into a ball and snoring softly.

Carefully, I moved him to my arms, then pivoted to lay him back in the chair. I then headed to the kitchen to make some coffee.

I started the kettle and got down Ursula's ancient French press, scooped some coarsely ground coffee beans into it, and then went out the back door, around the house to where I thought Luna was. I found her after I bumped my shin, then felt my way along her to the door and opened it, and that's when I realized that bumping my shin hadn't rocked me with pain. My shins had sustained second-degree burns, which I knew I'd easily recover from, but in no way should my skin have healed so fast.

Putting my hand on Luna to steady myself, I bent down to

pull up the pant leg of my mud-stained scrubs and have a look at the damage. My bandages were still intact, but dirty, so I unwound them starting with the right shin. Once I got it almost off, I put a hand to my mouth when I realized that my shin had completely healed; there was no sign of a burn of any kind.

"What the . . . ?" I muttered, pivoting to rest my rear against Luna and undo the other bandage, revealing that the other shin was equally healed and unmarred. And then my hand went to my forehead where I'd slammed it against the dashboard. I'd had a deep cut along my left brow and the E.D. doctor had medically glued it closed before I'd come to. I felt the bandage still covering the wound and peeled it away. The skin underneath was completely smooth and seemed unmarred to my touch.

My gaze then drifted upward as my thoughts tumbled. For the first time, I took note of the weather. It was a partly cloudy day and a bit chilly but the rain had finally stopped.

Had Dex given his crystal trinket to me while I slept? If so, I wished he hadn't. Ursula had needed all the juice it could give her. A car approached from down the street. and I quickly stood tall. I couldn't very well be seen leaning against an invisible car.

After the car had passed, I opened Luna's door and clambered inside, shutting the door quickly, lest only my lower half be exposed. Reaching into the back seat, I grabbed my gym bag, which had a pair of clean yoga pants and a light sweatshirt that I could change into.

Then I headed out of the car and retraced my steps to Ursula's back door, moving inside. The water was boiling, and I turned off the burner, removing the kettle to let it cool a bit. French press coffee is best brewed below boiling point.

Changing into my leisurewear in the kitchen, I picked up the borrowed scrubs from where I'd dropped them to the floor and tossed them into the trash. They were stained beyond saving anyway, so it's not like they'd be of use to anyone else. Pushing them down I felt a sharp sting on my palm and hissed at the pain. Pulling my hand back I saw that I'd cut myself, and I saw after nudging aside the scrubs, saw that Ursula had tossed a broken wine bottle into the bin.

I ran the cut under some water, wrapped it in a paper towel, and put some pressure on it. Once it'd stopped bleeding, I poured the hot water into the French press, waiting the three minutes for it to brew, and finally got down a mug from the cabinet.

Coming back into the living room with my coffee mug, I saw that Bits was still in his spot on the chair. He hadn't moved a muscle, which was a little unusual for him. If I got up in the morning, no matter how tired he was, he usually met me in the kitchen.

I walked over to him and stroked the quills on his back, and as I did so, the paper towel on my palm fell away. I eyed it in annoyance but couldn't resist continuing to stroke Bits for a moment. Then I left him to his slumber and reached for the paper towel, ready to rewrap my palm.

Taking a seat in the chair next to the one where Bits slept, I set down the coffee mug and turned my palm over to inspect the cut.

But it wasn't there.

In fact, it was as if my skin had never even been sliced open there at all. "What the . . . ?" I repeated. What was going on?

My fingers went to my throat to see if maybe Dex had put a healing trinket around my neck, but it was bare, as were my fingers and wrists.

I'd completely changed out of the scrubs, so I wasn't even wearing the same clothes as I had overnight when the sudden burst of healing had happened, which meant that there couldn't have been a healing trinket in a pocket. My gaze went to the cardigan I'd draped on the chair next to me, and I reached over to fish around in the pockets but came up with only a wrapped butterscotch candy.

I looked again at my palm. I had definitely had the cut when I'd walked from the kitchen to the living room; I remembered still feeling the sting . . .

Until I'd stopped to pet Bits. I'd been focused on him and not on the pain throbbing in my palm, and after I'd touched him, the throbbing had stopped.

My brow furrowed and I looked at him anew. "It couldn't be," I whispered. "He *couldn't* suddenly be a healing trinket."

But Bits *was* enchanted. And the merlin *had* held him when we'd arrived at the estate last night. Had Falcon the Wise enchanted my picklepuss with more magic without my knowing?

I got up again and went back to the kitchen, carefully getting out a piece of the broken bottle from the trash. I used one sharp point to slice my finger, hissing a little, then I walked back to Bits and stroked him again along his quills while staring at my finger, and before my eyes the cut closed and a moment later was completely healed over.

"By the gods," I whispered, staring down at him with my thoughts in a tumble. Bits could heal.

He could *heal!*

I blinked as my mind raced to consider this new magical power. I studied him carefully for a long moment and it dawned on me how deep his slumber was. I had obviously taxed him with my burned shins, then my sliced palm and finger. I suddenly felt bad for testing him. I should've let him sleep.

Moving him into my lap, I stared at him for a long, long time, thinking through this latest development.

Bits could heal. Given the quickness of the healing of my palm and finger, not to mention that there was no trace of a scar on my legs, he was *at least* a level eight or nine . . . maybe even a ten on the trinket power scale.

Any mystic that knew about him would covet such a magical creature.

Even, I suspected, Elric.

I shuddered. If Elric needed a member or members of his court healed, of course he'd use Bits. And what that would do to my picklepuss over time, I had no doubt, would be catastrophic to his system.

I also remembered how Bits had scrambled up to snuggle against Ursula last night. Had his power also lent itself to her healing?

I can tell no one about Bits's new power, I thought.

My gaze went to Ursula.

Not even her.

I got up again, carefully scooping my picklepuss up with me, and retrieved my handbag. After arranging his snuggle into a nest at the bottom of the handbag, I gently placed him inside.

He hadn't even twitched as I tucked him in. I then moved to the guest room and put my handbag on the bed against the pillow. If Bits's power extended to healing anyone in the room, I couldn't let his energy extend to Ursula. I didn't know what his limits were, and I wasn't about to risk him harm, even though I knew Ursula wasn't fully healed yet.

"She'll heal all right," I told myself. "She's already more than halfway there."

I left Bits and moved back to the living room, only to find Ursula awake and propped up on a pillow against the arm of the sofa.

"Hi," she said in a hoarse whisper.

I stopped in my tracks and felt tears well. "My friend, it is *so* good to see you. Even if you do look like a drunken sailor after a binge."

Her smile was faint, but it was there. "That good, eh?"

"You wish." I chuckled.

Her smile grew. "Is that coffee?"

I brought her the mug I'd left on the side table. "Freshly brewed. It should be the perfect temp by now."

She took the mug, and her fingers trembled ever so slightly. My eyes pinched with worry, but there was the hint of a smile on her lips right before she took a sip.

"How did we get back here?" she asked, lowering the mug.

"What do you remember?"

"Nothing after dying."

My eyes widened. "You remember *dying?*"

She closed her eyes, wincing slightly. The memory clearly haunted her. "I do. I remember looking up at you, sitting next to me, after Dex left my side, and I could feel myself going, and I thought that it was good he wasn't there to see me pass on, but I felt so bad for you."

Tears once again filled my eyes. "Losing you was the worst thing that's ever happened to me."

"Sorry, Dovey."

I swallowed hard. "Don't do it again."

She smiled again, wider this time, and it filled my heart with gratitude to see her able to do so.

"You weren't dead, though. Dex said you had a heartbeat, and he had an emergency healing trinket in the car that kept you alive until he got his level eight from his warehouse."

She blinked at me. "He took me to the warehouse? The one he shares with Esmé?"

"Yes."

"Was she there?"

"He said she wasn't, but she'd be back, and he didn't let us inside. He just ducked in, got his trinket—and his dog—and came back to the car ordering me to drive us here."

"He brought his puppy?"

"Yeah. She's adorable. She slept right next to you while the trinket did its work."

Ursula put a hand to her head then wormed her way up using her elbows to a more seated position.

"Does your head hurt?"

"No," she said. "I'm just trying to take it all in."

I left her for a moment to head back to the kitchen for a mug of coffee for myself, somewhat surprised that I didn't really need it. I should've been exhausted, but I felt oddly rejuvenated. "Bits," I muttered. It had to be his healing energy that'd given me such a boost.

"Did you say something?"

I jumped. Ursula was up and standing in the doorway. "Not really. I was just thinking I need to get Bits some breakfast."

Ursula made a waving motion toward the refrigerator. "Plenty of cut-up fruit in there. And I have some dry cereal in the cupboard."

"Perfect, thank you."

"Would you hand me the cream?" she asked when I opened the door to the fridge.

I handed her the cream, then took out the container of fruit and got down two bowls and a small plate. I cut up a few pieces into smaller chunks and put them on the plate. Then I spooned much of the rest of the fruit into the two bowls before heading back to the living room, where Ursula was once again sitting on the sofa. Handing her one of the bowls, I said, "Be right back."

I then set the plate of fruit on the nightstand next to the bed in the guest room. Bits would have no problem making it out of the handbag to the fruit, but I didn't want to wake him to try to get him to eat. Intuitively, I knew he needed sleep more than sustenance right now.

Making my way back to Ursula, I took my seat on the chair opposite her, rested my elbows on my knees, and said, "Tell me what happened."

"What do you remember?" she asked in turn.

"Getting hit head-on by what I thought was another car, managing to free myself from your burning car, then waking up in the hospital."

Her eyes widened. "The unbound took you to a hospital? They must have been surprised by your vital signs."

"My resting heart rate is usually in the mid-forties, so yeah, I'm pretty sure they were surprised."

"Were you terribly injured? I remember the fire."

I shook my head, because I didn't want her to ask to see the burns on my legs. "Not a scratch. It must've been the airbags and the paramedics found me in the grass near the car."

"Good," she said. Then, with a sigh, she began to tell me what'd happened while I was unconscious. "We got clobbered by a mystic. She was insanely powerful, Dovey—"

"*She?*"

"Yes. It was a female. I've never seen her before, so I don't know her name, but I could describe her."

"Please do."

"Do you remember last year when I went to Spain and found myself standing next to that famous actress at the Museo Reina Sofia?"

I shook my head. I had no idea who she was referring to. "Did you tell me this story?"

Ursula sighed and rubbed her forehead. All her bones were healed, but I could tell she was still suffering a bit. "I thought I had. She and I were standing in front of *Mujer en Azul*, and she quipped that it looked a bit like her, and I laughed because she had no idea Pablo had painted me during my brunette phase."

"You mean Picasso's painting of *The Woman in Blue*?" I asked, using the English translation of his famous portrait.

She pointed at me with her other hand. "Bingo."

Ursula had been one of Pablo Picasso's many lovers. And among his favorite muses. He'd adored both her company and painting her, but with his style, who could ever recognize it was Ursula Goransdotter in the portrait?

"I don't remember a story about an encounter with an actress in Spain."

Ursula shrugged. "I'm not feeling very sharp this morning. Maybe I forgot to tell you about it."

I nodded. I still had no idea who this mystic looked like. "Do you know what would help?"

"What?"

"Do you know what would help?"

"What?"

"If you simply gave me . . . ya know . . . even just a general description of what she looks like."

Ursula sighed. "Black hair. Olive skin. Feminine features. Brown eyes. And tall—like you. Probably Spanish. Gorgeous if she weren't such a bitch."

I smirked. "You got a good look at her in the dark?"

"Unfortunately, yes. The light exploding from the bangles as she attacked me lit up her face. I doubt I'll ever forget it."

"She sounds terrifying."

"She is. And, you should know, she was coming for you, not me."

I felt a prickle of fear at the back of my neck. "How do you know?"

"I was still conscious after the car got hit, and I saw her approach from the woods. She had eyes only for you, Dovey, and I could tell she carried a weapon."

"The Casting Bead?"

"Possibly."

"Did you see it?"

"No. It was hidden in the folds of her cloak."

That sparked another question I had. "How did you end up wrapped in her cloak, anyway?"

"I'm getting to that part. As I was saying, to me it was obvious she was coming for you. I barely got out of the car and in front of her when she struck, and had it not been for the bangles, you—and I—might not have survived. Pushing her with my defenses away from the car and down the hill, we battled for what felt like eternity..." Her voice trailed off as she stared without seeing, recalling the terrible fight.

"And then, Ursula?"

She shook her head and focused on me again. "Every curse she sent at me, I was able to deflect, but the bangle on my left wrist took most of the pummeling. It weakened until it all but disintegrated on my forearm, and I couldn't hold off her ensuing blows. She was *relentless.*"

I put a hand up to cover my open mouth. What Ursula had endured to try and protect me—it was an incredible act of courage and love.

"She finally knocked me flat," Ursula continued. "And I couldn't gain my feet. Then she walked right up to me and launched the Crushing Curse. I felt my bones begin to break, one by one..."

Again, Ursula's voice trailed off as her eyes pinched closed. The memory of it must've been so difficult to share with me.

"I've never felt such pain, Dovey," she whispered. "She only backed off when the unbound first responders were getting close, and by then, I was quite nearly dead anyway.

"She threw her cloak over me to conceal me from their eyes, thinking I'd die if not discovered. Then, I believe, mostly because you're still alive, she must've left the scene."

I shook my head feeling both shocked and afraid. "How did she know where to find us?"

Ursula shrugged. "I've no idea. But my guess is that she somehow followed us from the Falcon's estate. The road leading away from his estate and back to the highway is one long curve. I was so focused on getting us to your appointment on time, that I never paid attention to who might be following us."

Perhaps Ursula hadn't checked for tails, but I had. I'd kept a close, vigilant eye on the side mirror to make sure we *weren't* followed, and there'd been no one behind us once we turned on to the road leading to the estate.

"What if she was already at the estate at the same time we were?" I asked.

"Meaning?"

"Do you think the Falcon is involved with her?"

Ursula slowly shook her head. "Doubtful for two reasons: One, he didn't seem to realize that you and Elric are no longer together, which makes me think he hadn't heard about your public breakup yet. And if he assumed you two are still a couple, he'd be betraying Elric by allowing an assassin to have a go at you only minutes after you left his property.

"Second, if he was working with this assassin, why give you such a powerful set of defensive trinkets? You made it clear that you're under constant threat. If he were working with the mystic trying to kill you, he would've enchanted the shakers to do something trivial. He could've enchanted the shakers to make any food you prepare taste amazing—"

"The food I prepare already tastes amazing," I quipped.

"—or enchanted them to make your garden grow even in winter. My point is that the Falcon would've made sure to leave you vulnerable, but he didn't do that. He crafted for you trinkets that, by my guess, approach a level nine. He wouldn't have wasted his energy on you if he were in on the plot for your demise."

I nodded. "Both fair points, not to mention the merlin had just struck what he assumes is a bargain with you over something he obviously covets. If he knew you could also be killed in an ambush, he would've let you leave without a pair of trinkets of your own."

Ursula sat upright and winced. "The rings!" she gasped, patting the pockets of her jeans. "What did I do with them, Dovey? Did I put them in my handbag before we left the estate?"

I grimaced, remembering that she had put them into her bag for safekeeping, and I'd tucked it into the back of her car for her.

While my handbag had survived the car fire, I doubted Ursula's had. The rings could be anywhere. "Your comeback spell," I told her. "Remember? We gave our new trinkets a comeback enchantment."

Ursula was rattled, blinking rapidly while she sat back against the pillows again. "I can't remember the spell!" she said in a panic.

I closed my eyes for a moment, then recited it for her.

> *"Rings for lovers sealed in fate,*
> *Claim your partner, claim your mate,*
> *Hear my call to bring you near,*
> *Come back to—"*

"My essence sphere," she finished. "Yes, I remember now. Thank you, Dovey."

Ursula held out her palm and formed an orb of light green essence. She then recited the spell and almost instantly the rings appeared, looking a bit charred but otherwise intact. "Oh my," she said, staring at them, the black soot coming off in her palm. "I suppose from the look of these, my Prada bag has bit the dust."

"We'll get you another one," I promised. "And, with a little elbow grease, those'll be easy enough to clean up."

She smirked. "Elbow grease is for mystics who haven't discovered the miracle of cleaning trinkets. I have a steel wool pad in my kitchen that I simply wave at the countertops, and they turn immediately sparkling clean."

My mouth quirked. "Where can I get one of those?"

She sighed. "When I'm back to full strength, we'll enchant one for you, but I think we should get back to discussing this mystic who's out for your blood and shed quite a bit of mine."

"Of course. Sorry. Did she say anything to you?"

Ursula nodded. "She asked me where your new trinkets were."

My brow furrowed. "My new trinkets? Is she talking about the two shakers?"

"I believe so."

"How would she even know about them? The Falcon just created them, and we've already established that it's unlikely she was there."

"I don't know, Dovey. I don't know why she's targeting you, and I don't know how she found us, and I don't know how she knows about your shakers, or how she survived round after round of slingshot blows."

"She's got the Casting Bead," I said, simply knowing it.

"Yes, probably she does. It's the only explanation that fits."

I looked at Ursula meaningfully. "Thank the gods you survived."

"You can thank Dex for that. I truly don't know how I did make it through."

"I would've thanked him if he'd stuck around this morning. He crept out while we were sleeping. And he took his healing trinket with him, which is a shame because you look like you could use another dose of it."

"Yes, for sure. I still feel battered and bruised, but I don't think any broken bones remain."

I stood tall. What Ursula needed was rest and some food. And I needed to get Bits home and check in with Gib. It was nearly eight a.m. and if he'd worked through the night, he'd be exhausted.

"Are you leaving?" Ursula asked me.

I moved over to her and stroked her hair, which was still matted and caked in mud. "I'm going to draw you a bath, and while you're having a soak, I'm going to take Bits home and tuck him in for a nice long nap. It was an eventful night for him, and he's exhausted. After that, I'm going to check in on Gib, and *then* I'm going to come back here and make you a proper meal."

She smiled faintly. "I could use a bath. And some food. I know it's morning, but pasta would be lovely."

"I make a mean Parmesan garlic linguini," I told her. "Give me an hour or so and I'll be back."

She nodded but then scanned the living area like she was looking for something. "What do you need?" I asked. I didn't want Ursula to move more than she absolutely had to.

"My computer. I have to order a new phone, new car, and new handbag. STAT."

I grinned, having little doubt all three items would show up at her door within the day. Ursula's home didn't reflect her vast wealth. She made a killing on the love potions and Elric paid her handsomely. With money always comes speed.

But then a troubling thought occurred to me. "The authorities will be able to identify your car through the license plate or VIN number. They might show up here."

"No, they'll show up to Ms. Angelica Aguado's residence, and of course she won't be home when they arrive," she said, with a chuckle. "Our aliases always fool the unbound."

I cocked my head at her cleverness. Luna had been registered under my name and address. Perhaps I'd need to amend that. . . .

Getting to my feet, I said, "Your laptop is in the spare bedroom. I saw it when I settled Bits in there. I'll get it and bring it to you, then—bath time."

After drawing Ursula a bath and gathering Bits, I took the

stamp off Luna's hood, tucking it away should I need to conceal her later, and got on the road.

When I arrived at my house, I was shocked to discover Gib sitting on my front porch, leaning back with his head against the door. I paused in the driveway to speak to him, but he appeared to be fast asleep.

I would've thought it amusing if there weren't a mystic assassin intent on killing me and any FBI agent she came across.

Which is when it struck me that my attempted murder, Tove's murder, and the murder of those FBI agents were all somehow connected—but to what? What was it that we all had in common?

Tove and I had both been romantically involved with Elric, but what did that have to do with the murder of the agents? How did this all tie together?

"Gib," I called from the car. He didn't move.

"Gib!"

He still didn't move.

"Grant Issac Barlow!"

Nothing. He didn't even flinch.

"Oh . . . no. No, no, no, no, no!"

Throwing Luna into park, I leapt out, racing around her hood to dash toward my porch. *"Gib!"* I cried. He'd been murdered. Here. On my front porch. The assassin had gotten to him before I'd come home.

I got to his side and sank to my knees, reaching both hands toward his face, desperate to find him not yet gone. A sob rose from my chest, and I didn't even try to quell it. Tears welled and spilled over onto my cheeks.

My fingers touched his skin, which was cold. "Please, please, please open your eyes!"

And he did. Suddenly, and abruptly, his lids flew open, and he jumped. And I did too; nearly losing my balance and tumbling backward down my front steps, I flailed out with my arm and Gib caught me, pulling me back toward him. "Hey, whoa there, Dovey," he said.

I regained my balance and felt my cheeks flush with heat. Embarrassed, I stood tall and looked down at him. "I called to you."

He blinked, let go of my arm, and rubbed his eyes. I saw the dark circles there, the exhaustion. I wondered if he'd gotten any sleep at all in the last thirty-six hours. "Sorry. I was out cold."

I crossed my arms, unsure why I was angry. My emotions were all over the place.

He stared dully up at me. "We need to talk."

Uh-oh, I thought. His tone was dead serious. I swallowed hard and asked, "About what?"

He leaned his head against the door again. "Let's head inside."

"Fine. Sure. Come around back."

I had no idea what Gib wanted to say to me, but there was a hint of something . . . Irritation? Anger? I couldn't quite place it.

Trying to get my emotions under control, I kept my back to him as I retreated to Luna, got in, and parked her in the garage. I then grabbed my handbag with the still-sleeping Bits and my shaker trinkets, and met Gib at the back door. "Whatever you want to talk about sounds serious," I said, fiddling with the keys to find my house key.

He didn't reply, and that *really* set my nerves on edge. Something had happened. Something between yesterday when we last spoke and this morning.

Did he believe I was out all night with a lover? Was that why he seemed so upset with me?

And if he thought that, how could I convince him I hadn't been and not tell him where I'd actually been?

As I turned the key and pushed on the door he said, "I know where you were last night, Dovey."

I froze midway through the entryway. Looking over my shoulder at him, I tried to play coy. "You know where I was?"

"Yeah."

His expression was hard. Cold. Absent of any warmth. And it truly made me inwardly shudder.

Leading the way into the kitchen, I put my handbag on the table and crossed my arms, defensively. "I was at Ursula's."

He'd stopped at the counter to also cross his arms before he pushed a hard breath out through his nose in disbelief. "No. No you weren't."

Technically, he was mostly right; we didn't get to Ursula's until about four in the morning, but how would he know that?

"Why do you think that?" I asked him.

"It's not what I think, it's what I know."

"I don't much like being interrogated . . . or spied on, Gib."

Instead of replying, he held up a tablet that I hadn't noticed he'd brought inside with him. After tapping at the screen, he turned it toward me. There was a video playing . . . it was CCTV footage of yours truly with Dex, walking toward two gurneys, each hosting a body bag parked just outside the imaging department.

The footage was from the hospital, and there was no mistaking that it was me in the video. The pixel count was very good.

"I can explain—" I began. Gib cut me off.

"Who's the guy?"

I blinked at him, my mind momentarily going blank. And then I looked more carefully at his hunched stance, the circles under his eyes, and the drawn look to his complexion. The poor man was exhausted. Probably also a little jealous. And cranky.

I uncrossed my arms and abandoned my defensive stance. "He's a colleague."

266 / VICTORIA LAURIE

"A colleague."

"Yes."

"From your firm?"

"Yes."

"I thought you owned your own P.I. firm."

"I did. Now I don't. Now I work for a larger firm."

Gib made a rolling motion with his hand, looking for more detail.

I dodged the request and went with, "We're investigating a murder."

"Whose?"

I pointed to his tablet, hoping he wouldn't pester me for details I couldn't give him. Tove didn't mingle with the unbound. If Gib went looking for her, he'd find nothing, which would raise even more suspicion.

"The woman in the body bag?" he said after I motioned to the tablet. I nodded. "What's her name and address?"

"That's confidential."

Gib sighed. "Dovey, come on. This woman was murdered the same way the guy in the other body bag was killed—he happened to be another FBI agent—and his murder is raising *big* alarm bells, so I *need* her name, address, and the name and address of your"—Gib paused to form air quotes—"*colleague.*"

"I'm sorry I can't help you. I'm under a strict NDA."

Another sigh followed. "That's not an answer I can take back to my office."

"Why do you have to take any answer back to your office?"

"You're kidding, right?"

"No."

"Dovey . . ." He sighed, pinching the bridge of his nose. "The guy in the other body bag was my SAC. His death marks the fourth of the top-tier people in my Bureau. The SAC, ASAC, Bruce McNally, and Felicia Cartwright. These are the managerial agents, the ones with the most seniority, experience, and power. Someone is systematically murdering the people at the top of the FBI's power structure, and those of us investigating don't know how it's happening, and we also don't know who's next, but every single agent in D.C. is freaking out right now. And that includes me!"

"Gib, I don't know what I can tell you—"

He cut me off again, thumping his tablet in a display of impatience. "When our agents got to the morgue, they found an empty body bag next to that of my SAC. The write-up on the chart accompanying her bag along with the X-rays taken in the Imaging Department at the hospital show that every bone in her body was broken, just like his, just like the other four agents.

"It's as if my superiors are being taken to a decompression chamber and crushed from the inside out, and since those things cost about ten million dollars, we don't have the first clue about where to even start looking."

My brow shot up. Dex was right about what the FBI would conclude was happening to these murdered agents. It was the only explanation they could fathom.

"She's listed as a Jane Doe; no ID found on her or near her," Gib continued, "and the photo taken of her face at the scene is so distorted from the trauma she sustained that there's no way to get a facial recognition match, so if you know who she is, Dovey, I'm not kidding, *I* need to know!"

I'd never seen Gib like this. He seemed almost panicked. I completely understood where he was coming from, and knew that a lot of his impatient, interrogative attitude was born from exhaustion.

Pointing to a chair at my kitchen counter, I said, "Sit. Let me make you some tea and we can talk, okay?"

Gib shook his head and stared down at the floor. "They're looking for you."

My skin prickled with alarm. "Who's *they*?"

"The rest of my team."

"Did you tell them where to find me?"

"No."

"Do they know who I am?"

He lifted his gaze to mine. "No."

I hesitated a moment before asking my next question. "Are you going to tell them?"

His brow furrowed. "Of course not. I told the new acting SAC that I had a source who might know something, otherwise I'd be back at the office, pretending I was trying to find you or your partner."

"I'm sorry I've put you in a tough spot," I told him.

He shrugged and let out a long sigh. "It's not really *you*, Dovey. It's this case. And now I'm working under my archnemesis, which is opening up old wounds—"

I cocked an eyebrow. "Archnemesis?"

Gib sighed like he was carrying the weight of the world. "Atticus Hearst. From the Baltimore Bureau. He and I went to college and the Academy together. At one point we were best friends."

"He chose to become an agent too?"

Gib nodded. "Anything I did, Atticus wanted to do better. That included joining the FBI. I thought we had a friendly rivalry. I can be just as competitive, and for a long time I thought Atticus was only pushing me to be my best. But then . . ."

Gib's voice trailed off and his eyes were more than simply weary. They were sad. And hurt.

I motioned again to the chairs at the counter, and he shuffled to one, pulled it out, and sat down. I wanted to ask him what'd happened between him and Atticus, but I felt it was more important for him to tell me when he was ready.

So I busied myself by making us both some tea. While it was brewing, I threw together a simple turkey, lettuce, tomato, and

Swiss cheese sandwich for Gib and set it in front of him. I doubted he'd eaten much the last few days. He gobbled it down while I put all the sandwich fixings back in the fridge, then poured the tea and set a cup on the counter for him.

"Thank you," he muttered, taking a sip and the last bite of his sandwich.

"Of course."

I went around the counter and sat down in the seat next to his and sipped out of my own cup, as if I quite enjoyed the silence. Inwardly, I was impatient as hell, but you'd never be able to tell by the placid look I'd plastered on my face. It worked.

"Like I said, I thought Atticus was my friend. I thought I could trust him. I couldn't."

I turned toward Gib. He was still dancing around the heart of what he wanted to share, so I reached out and squeezed his hand to reassure him, while also withholding the urge to ask him directly what'd happened.

"Julia—Jules—and I met at a college football game," he said softly, refusing to meet my gaze but holding on to my hand. "She was a cheerleader for the opposing team—UF, and I was a running back for UVA." He smiled slightly, and I felt a tiny twinge of jealousy, but quickly tamped it down. "Swear to God, it was love at first sight. For both of us. We started dating, which I didn't think would work because she was in Florida and I was here, but she had a trust fund that she said she'd never be able to see the bottom of, so she chartered a plane every weekend to fly to me until she transferred to my school her junior year and we moved in together immediately.

"We were inseparable from then on. She was a gorgeous woman. We even did some modeling together and had a great time traveling around Europe. Jules would've been happy to live forever like that, but I needed a purpose. So we came back here, I reconnected with Atticus, told him I was thinking about joining the FBI, and just like that he applied too. He and I were accepted into the same class at the Academy, and from day one it was a competition for the top score in every course, every exercise, every interview and interrogation. He pushed me and I pushed him, always to be the best of the best.

"When we graduated, our scores differed by only two percentage points, and the Bureau assigned us to the same field office in Baltimore because, as they put it, 'Why break up a great team?'"

Gib was silent again for a moment, his face a flash of emotions, from contempt, to regret, to remorse, to guilt.

He took another sip of tea and continued. "Jules never liked Atticus. He'd come over to watch a game and she'd leave to run errands or hang out with her girlfriends. I asked her all the time what it was about him she didn't like, and she would always just say that he wasn't my friend, and he wasn't a nice guy. And he was cold to her in return. I thought they really disliked each other. . . ."

Gib didn't continue, but I could guess where this was going. "Until?"

He shook his head, as if to clear his mind of a painful memory. "Until I found out they were having an affair. She was taking a shower one morning and I was slow to get up. The stomach flu was going around at work, and I felt like crap. Her phone chimed and I glanced at it. It was a text from Atticus. He wanted to know if I was gone yet so he could come over. That was the only part I could read, but I knew her security code, so I punched it in and read the rest of the text along with all the other ones. They'd been having an affair for months, and I'd had no idea."

He went silent again, staring down at the countertop, reliving that moment of shock and betrayal.

I squeezed his hand. "Gib, I'm so sorry." What else could I

say? I knew the agony of a lover taking another lover. It was among the most emotionally painful things to endure.

He shrugged, looking like he was doing his level best to get ahold of his feelings. "Yeah, anyway, I wanted to work things out. I could forgive her. Not him, I'll never forgive him, but she said she needed her space and some time alone . . . and then she died, and the point was moot."

I waited again in silence to see if he'd say more, but he was lost to the terrible memories of that time, so it was up to me to draw him out.

"How did she die?"

He swallowed hard, then again; he seemed almost on the verge of tears and his voice did quaver when he began to speak. "Atticus, the asshole, claimed their affair wasn't true. That Jules made it up, but I *saw* their text exchange, so he was an idiot to think I'd believe him. Then we got into it. . . ."

"Physically?"

He nodded. "Like I said, we're evenly matched in just about everything so neither of us came away the winner. After that, I put in for a transfer to the D.C. Bureau, and he gave me a wide berth, which was smart, 'cause we might've gotten into it again.

"We had to hide the fact that we'd gotten into it the first time—the brass won't tolerate physical altercations amongst their agents—so we just hid our hatred and carried on, both of us waiting for my transfer to come through. But then, one night, we were both assigned a stakeout in a bad part of the city. We'd been keeping tabs on what we thought might've been a radicalized group of homegrown terrorists who were planning something big."

"What kind of big?"

"Blowing up a stadium or shooting up a mall kind of big. This was just after Thanksgiving; the holiday shopping season was in full swing, so lots of soft targets around.

"Anyway, Atticus and I are on the stakeout together, and we

had eyes on these guys, gathering video, when Jules shows up next to my car."

"She *what*?"

Gib shook his head ruefully. "She'd put an AirTag in the back seat of my SUV without me knowing about it. She thought maybe I was lying about being on a stakeout. She thought maybe I was having an affair to get back at her."

"That's a wild leap."

"Jules was beautiful, but she was also insecure. I think that's how Atticus got her into bed. He played on her insecurity and manipulated her into doing something she wouldn't normally have done."

"So what happened?"

Gib put his head in his hands. "Chaos."

Again, I waited him out. The trauma of whatever had happened to his wife was evident in his posture. He all but crumpled in on himself.

"Her showing up next to my car and yelling at me caused the terrorists' watchman to flag our car. I knew how dangerous the area was, especially at that time of night, and Jules was putting all of us in the crosshairs, so I got out of the vehicle, grabbed her by the arm, and was hustling her back to her car when all hell broke loose."

I got up when Gib paused to look at the bottom of his empty teacup, and went to the cabinet to get him a glass and some water. After setting that in front of him, he took a long sip, then continued.

"The terrorists started shooting at us, and Jules and I were caught between my car and hers. I'd left Atticus back in mine, so he was alone, taking on heavy fire. I pulled off my vest and threw it at Jules, yelled at her to put it on and stay down while I tried to get to Atticus. I was returning fire, moving back down the street when I got hit at the top of my right hip and I went down. Jules ran to me, helped me up, but then she took one in the gut, and it sent her flying. Took her right off her feet."

"Oh no," I whispered. I'd no idea he'd been through something so harrowing and terrible.

"I crawled to her—I thought she was dead; the bullet hit her midabdomen, just under the bottom of the vest, and I knew it was bad. I managed to pick her up, and that's when I saw a door next to us. I tried the handle, and it opened."

Gib was staring at the countertop, wearing the hint of a sardonic smile and shaking his head. "At the time, to find the door open like that seemed like some kind of miracle. What a joke. Anyway, I got her inside and propped her up against a pylon. I told her to keep pressure on her wound, and that I'd be back for her as soon as I could. She looked so scared. I begged her not to die. And then . . . I left her."

He'd paused yet again, his eyes haunted by the memory. "When I made it back outside, the gunmen were still firing and it seemed like Atticus was still returning fire, which was a good sign. It meant he was alive. My one thought was that I had to make it to the car so we could get Jules to a hospital. My plan was to drive it around the block and get into the warehouse from the opposite side. All the warehouses in that part of Baltimore have two entrances—east and west—which meant that there was a good chance my plan would work as long as I could get into the building from that side too.

"So I run for the car, firing the whole time, and my clip runs out. My spare is in the vehicle, so I just run for it. I make it to within about ten feet of my rear bumper when I see the reverse lights come on. I thought that Atticus had seen me, and was gonna back up to let me in, but he punched the gas and blew right past me without even stopping, leaving me completely exposed."

My mouth fell open in awe. The fact that he was sitting here, telling me this story, was its own miracle. Without his vest or cover, I had no idea how he'd made it out of that situation.

Gib continued. "Lucky me, there was a dumpster just a few feet away and I dove behind, then used it for cover while I crouched my way up the alley, which is when I saw Jules's car again, and realized it was close enough for me to make it.

"I didn't hesitate to overthink it, I just bolted for it and took one in my left thigh. I went down, and the adrenaline helped me get back up. Somehow, by the grace of God, I managed to make it to her car. She hadn't locked the door, and she'd left the keys in the well between the front seats, so I got the car started and was about to back up the same way Atticus had when one of the gunmen blew out the windshield."

"Oh my God," I whispered, my fingers at my lips. "Gib, *how* did you ever survive?"

"To this day, I have no idea. I got hit for a third time, under my collarbone. That one was through and through, with not a whole lot of damage, but, Jesus, did it hurt! That bullet, though, saved my life. The shot made me slam down across the seat to avoid getting hit again, and using the engine block for cover, I threw the gearshift into reverse, knowing I'd have to drive blind back down the street. Just before punching the gas pedal, though, I realized the gunfire had stopped. Like it had literally just come to a sudden and abrupt hault."

My brow furrowed. "Why?"

Instead of answering me, Gib continued with the story. "For a couple of seconds, I thought they'd stopped firing to see if I'd pop up so they could get a clear shot, so I used my phone's video app like a mirror, avoiding getting my head blown off, and on the screen I saw these guys running as fast as they could move back toward the building they'd come out of. My brain was too slow to figure it out . . . until it did."

"What happened?"

"We knew the terrorist cell was storing explosives, and we

thought they were in the building we were staking out. But they weren't in there. They were in the building where I'd just hid my wife, and rather than let their inventory fall into fed hands, these sons of bitches blew it up remotely."

I covered my face with my hands. "Oh, Gib," I whispered. I wanted to wrap him in my arms. Now I understood the heaviness whenever he referred to Julia. He no doubt blamed himself, and it was killing him.

When next he spoke, his voice broke with emotion. "The blast blew my car all the way across the street. If I hadn't been leaning down on the seat, it would've taken my head off. Inside the building, part of the second story collapsed onto the first and the fire was hot enough to give you blisters twenty feet away. And as for my wife . . ." His gaze fell to his hands in his lap, and I didn't think I'd ever seen someone so emotionally gutted. His voice wavered again when he said, "The pylon I'd leaned her against sheltered her body from the blast, but not the fire. She died instantly."

Now I did get up and hugged him from the side. "I'm so, so sorry."

His hands came up to cover my arms and we held on to each other like that for a long time. I finally knew the full story of how Gib's wife had perished, and I almost wished I didn't. It was painful to witness a man take on the blame of events and circumstances he had no control over.

At last, he let his hands fall away and I let him go. "I hate this case, Dovey."

"I can understand why."

"I'm now reporting to the guy who's just as responsible for my wife's death as I am."

"Why wasn't Atticus held accountable for abandoning you in the middle of a gunfight?"

"My word against his. Not that it would've mattered much. Atticus was always cozy with the brass. He's manipulative in a way that sometimes catches me off guard. Somehow, he managed to worm his way into becoming the head of my office."

"Has he spoken to you directly? Did he ever offer an apology for his abhorrent behavior?"

Gib barked out a laugh in disgust. "He didn't even send flowers to her funeral. No condolences, no apologies, no empathy."

"Pathological narcissist," I said. I was quite familiar with the personality type as most mystics are guilty of it. It's almost a requirement for long-term survival.

"Atticus is going to demand I give up my source if I don't come back with something, Dovey. I won't, but he could suspend me for it."

"Fine," I said, suddenly feeling bold. "Let's go meet this son of a bitch."

CHAPTER 14

It took me only twenty minutes to shower and change. I blushed with embarrassment when I took in my appearance in my upstairs bathroom mirror before stepping into the shower. My hair was a mess and there was still a hint of soot on my cheeks and neck, and dirt on my forearms.

I spent most of the first fifteen of those twenty minutes in the shower, scrubbing myself clean, then I took advantage of a handy little trinket I keep in my medicine cabinet that can instantly dry my hair and give it a lustrous shine. After taking only an additional four minutes to dab on a little makeup and select a pair of black slacks, leather booties, and a camel, cowl-neck sweater with wide bell cuffs, I was about to go back downstairs when I saw Bits curled into the snuggle on my nightstand. I stroked his quills, told him I loved him, then headed out.

"Ready?" Gib asked when I walked into the kitchen.

"Ready."

Once outside, I went straight to his Range Rover and hopped in, making like that was the plan all along. Thankfully, he didn't argue, and we got underway.

I didn't want to drive separately because I didn't trust that I could keep him safe on the road if I was trailing behind him. Who knew where this murderous mystic was at the moment?

On the way to the Bureau, I ordered Ursula a delivery of two slices of avocado tartine from *Maman* on Wisconsin Ave. It wasn't her requested pasta, but it was a favorite of hers, and the best I could do to provide her some nourishment at this hour well before lunch when the option to return to her place and cook for her had vanished. I tried calling her to let her know about the change of plans, but the call went straight to voicemail. Her new phone, it appeared, hadn't yet arrived.

I figured she'd know the food was from me when the delivery showed up at her door with her favorite dish. Hopefully, I could make quick work of this interview and get back to her soon.

Not much was said between Gib and me on the way over to his office, which was good because I was trying to formulate a plan. I had to give the agents *some* information while withholding most of the important mystic-related details. In other words, I'd have to thread this needle carefully.

Gib parked in the underground garage, and I allowed him to get out first so that I could discreetly retrieve the salt and pepper shakers from my handbag, and tuck them into the doorwell, leaving them behind before entering the building.

I knew we'd have to go through security, and I didn't want the shakers inspected and possibly confiscated, plus, I knew I could recall them with my comeback spell anytime if I needed to.

After entering the building, we did indeed have to clear security, and I was granted a visitor's badge after signing in on the register. Then Gib escorted me to the elevator and we rode it to the fourth floor. When the doors opened, we stepped out into a busy, bustling office. The tension was palpable, and understandable. Four senior-level agents murdered and not a single clue to point them in any direction . . . except for one that I might offer.

"Atticus is going to come at you like a freight train," Gib said, leading me through the maze of cubicles and personnel.

"Don't let him intimidate you. Just give him the information about the woman found along the highway, and who you work for, et cetera, et cetera."

I nodded. "Got it."

I wasn't about to be intimidated by an unbound, but I didn't want to show Gib that confidence because an unbound *would* be intimidated in my situation.

Gib led me to a closed door, which he opened, revealing a conference room with chairs at an oval table that would seat eight to ten people. There was an abstract art piece on the wall that I rather liked, and a soothing latte paint color to the walls. The table was a dark espresso, and the chairs were cream leather, which gave the room a professional flair without seeming drab.

I moved over to the far side of the table, and Gib joined me. As an afterthought he turned and asked, "Sorry, can I get you some coffee?"

"No, thank you, Gib. I'm fine."

A moment later the door opened and in came a group of four agents, three men and one woman. The last man through the door was the most striking—he was Gib's height, equally fit, but with jet-black hair, fair skin, and startlingly bright blue eyes. His lashes were long, which made them pop. His face was square, his nose thin, and a dimple on his upper lip and high cheekbones helped to accentuate his handsomeness.

He sat down next to the only female agent, who was quite pretty, and I sharpened my gaze on the pair. The chemistry of attraction between them was subtle, but there.

Also present from the female agent was a scrutinous cast to her gaze as she took me in. There was an instant acrimony in her eyes that, truth be told, caught me a little off guard. I managed to offer her a winning smile all the same.

But I withheld such pleasant non-spoken greetings for Atticus. I hated him on sight for what he'd done to Gib, so I allowed my smile to disappear altogether when I switched my gaze to him.

He regarded me with a hint of interest, but managed to mask it almost immediately, replacing it with a cool detachment that I found rather ubiquitous among most of the unbounds in law enforcement.

Except for Gib.

"Dovey Van Dalen," Atticus said, opening a folder, presumably one that'd been quickly put together about me, me, me, me, me.

I wasn't nervous. They'd find nothing of any substance. To the unbound, on paper I'm a thirty-three-year-old woman from Georgetown with perfect credit and a paid-off home valued at well over a million-five.

No doubt, they'd also discovered that I'm a fully licensed P.I. who pays my taxes and doesn't have so much as a speeding ticket on record—thanks, of course, to a handy little trinket that got me out of every speeding infraction, including even the most earnest traffic cops trying to make their end-of-the-month quotas.

Atticus turned a few pages in my file, then closed the folder and looked at me with a bemused, smug smile that told me he was every bit the asshole Gib had said he was. "You've been quite the busy beaver, haven't you?"

I didn't respond verbally. I merely cocked an eyebrow.

Atticus continued to look at me like, *Aren't you cute?* And I continued to look at him like, *You are wasting my time—asshole!*

This went on for a bit until Gib lost patience and said, "Atticus, she's a busy woman who came here voluntarily. Ask her your questions so she can get on with her day."

Atticus cut sinister eyes to Gib, and he *clearly* didn't like being addressed by his first name, let alone told how to conduct this interview. "I'd remember who's in charge here, *Agent* Barlow. It's either 'sir' or 'Agent Hearst,' capisce?"

Gib held up his palms. "Yes, sir," he said, but his tone was hardly apologetic.

I personally marveled at his restraint. Had my closest friend betrayed me like Atticus had betrayed Gib, I doubt I would've been able to withhold some form of violence in the moment.

Meanwhile, the female agent who'd come in with Hearst smiled like a crocodile at the rebuke Gib had taken.

I disliked her immensely.

After glaring for an extra few seconds at Gib, Hearst turned his attention back to me. "First, I'd like to know who you work for."

"I'm a subcontractor for an organization that would like to remain anonymous."

Hearst tapped an impatient index finger on the table. "We could find out, you know."

"If that were true, you'd have the name already and wouldn't need to ask."

"Why the secrecy?"

"I could ask you fellas the same thing, and if you took my question seriously, you'd tell me that discretion and secrecy were imperative components to conducting an investigation. The same holds true for my contractor."

More tapping of Hearst's index finger followed. Then, "Who was the woman?"

"What woman?" I was being difficult on purpose, and not simply because there were certain things about this case that the FBI couldn't and shouldn't know. I was being difficult because I enjoyed making Hearst look like a fool.

He opened the folder to withdraw a photo of me and Dex, hovering over the body of Tove. "This woman."

"Angelica Aguado."

Another long silence and more tap, tap, tap of that impatient finger. I'd lay odds he liked to waggle it when he thought someone was being naughty.

"Care to elaborate?" Hearst all but barked.

I folded my hands on top of the table. "No."

Angelica Aguado is a catchall name the female mystics in Elric's employ give to law enforcement anytime one of us finds ourselves unlucky enough to be questioned by the authorities. Angelica's name provides very little information but will show a slightly unfocused driver's license photo that always fit the Spanish origins of the name.

Within the system, Angelica's last known address is a house owned by SPL, which is always kept in pristine condition, lest the authorities drop by.

To my knowledge, they had in fact done such a thing a time or two whenever a female mystic's body was discovered before Elric's team could get to her. I had no doubt that Elric's minions had gotten wind of Tove's murder, and two of his trusted team had been dispatched to the morgue at the hospital to retrieve her body.

Elric almost never allowed an autopsy to be performed on one of his mystics. There'd be too many questions asked by an M.E. about the mystic's physiology. Like too many perfections of the individual's organs to be believed.

"Do you have an address?" the female agent asked. I noticed she'd been taking notes while Hearst had asked most of the questions.

"I'm not certain of the street or the number, but I do know she rented a home in Hollindale."

"Family?" the woman asked next.

I shrugged. If the unbound went digging, Angelica Aguado would appear to have no living relatives.

"How did you find out about her murder?" Hearst asked next.

"Through my employer."

He pointed to Dex in the photo on the table. "He your employer?"

"Colleague."

"We'd like to talk to him."

"He will, regrettably, have to pass on the opportunity to spend time with you, Agent Hearst."

"All the same, we need his name."

I offered him a hard smile. "And *I* will, regrettably, pass on the opportunity to provide it to you."

His jaw bunched and I braced for what I anticipated would be his loud rebuke, but he surprised me when he shrugged one shoulder and said, "Fine. We'll track him down one way or another."

Good luck, I thought. Mystics are very guarded about their identity—the vast majority of us don't exist in the public record, and none among us are more guarded about their identity than professional thieves, like Dex.

Hearst would have better luck finding Jimmy Hoffa.

The SAC moved on to another question. "What do you know about the victim's relationship with the FBI?"

"Nothing."

"Nothing?"

"That's correct."

"What *do* you know about the victim, then?"

"Very little, and what I do know about her, other than her name and vaguely where she lives, I'm not at liberty to share with you."

He stared hard at me. "Your reluctance to answer my questions is throwing a whole lot of suspicion on you, Ms. Van Dalen."

"I've answered every question to the full limit of my authority, Atticus," I answered softly. It was the perfect pitch to let him know that I didn't recognize his authority, nor respect him enough to use his title.

He flushed with anger. "We can keep you here under suspicion of murder, you know."

"Without evidence?"

284 / VICTORIA LAURIE

He pointed again to the photo. "Tampering with a body seems like a pretty good reason to me."

"I never touched Ms. Aguado, nor was I the one to open her body bag. If you decide to bring a charge or even an accusation suggesting anything different, my lawyer will have me out of here within fifteen minutes, and good luck *ever* getting a single piece of additional testimony from me or any other subcontractor of my employer."

Hearst's gaze cut to Gib like he was responsible for my recalcitrance, so I turned to Gib and said, "I told you I had nothing to offer you, Agent Barlow, and yet you insisted on pulling me in here to waste all of our time."

Gib's eyes widened for the briefest moment, and then he seemed to catch on. "Is this all the information you're willing to offer at this time, Ms. Van Dalen?"

"It is. I know nothing more about who murdered Angelica. I've literally only been on this case less than twelve hours."

"Where's her body?" Hearst barked, calling our attention back to him.

"I've no idea."

"Did you and your colleague take it?"

"Of course not. That would be in violation of the rules under which my P.I. license was issued. I wouldn't jeopardize my employment any more than *you* would."

He crossed his arms and glared some more at me. "I think you did. I think you and your *colleague* removed her body before we had a chance to examine it."

"Ah," I said, mimicking his posture by crossing my own arms. "And the video evidence of this is . . . where now?"

His lips pressed into a thin line. He didn't elaborate, but I knew that the first thing Elric's cleaners had done when they went to pick up the body was to disable all the unbound's surveillance cameras, as it required a relatively simple spell.

"I'm also quite certain that the hospital's exterior CCTV

cameras captured my colleague and I driving away with nary a corpse thrown over our shoulders." I spoke softly, adding a confident smile to really drive the point home.

Hearst glared at me. He had nothing. Nothing but questions I wasn't about to answer.

"How was Ms. Aguado murdered?" he asked next. Interesting that he'd gone straight to murder and hadn't used the term *killed*. It meant he already knew there could be no other explanation for her demise other than homicide.

"I'm guessing you already know that, but from what my colleague and I could determine, she was crushed to death from the inside out." It was the only scenario these unbound were likely to believe.

Hearst dropped his arms and leaned in over the table to eye me intently. *"How?"*

I shrugged then mimicked him by leaning in toward him as well. "My colleague and I have concluded that someone jerry-rigged a decompression or hyperbaric chamber to apply enough pressure to break so many bones in her body that it caused extreme exsanguination within the body cavity itself, and damaged most—if not all—of her vital organs."

He sat back again. "And you got all that from your colleague's one-minute observation of her body?"

"Yes."

"You're a medical expert?"

"Agent Hearst, a body that looks like it's literally been to the scrapyard and had a run through the car crusher without managing to break the skin . . . what else *can* you conclude?"

Another long silence played out between us, and I took the opportunity to glance impatiently at my watch.

"How do you two know each other?" Hearst asked next, breaking the silence by switching topics and pointing back and forth between me and Gib.

Gib opened his mouth to answer, but I beat him to it. "I

provided him with some intel I'd collected on the Ariti family murders several weeks ago."

I knew that Hearst was unlikely to be more than vaguely familiar with the case, given he'd come from the Baltimore Bureau.

That index finger went back to tapping. "What intel?"

"I'd come across some information that suggested there was an international prescription drug ring involved in the deaths of several members of the Ariti family, and I passed that information along to Agent Barlow."

"That still doesn't explain how you two first came to know each other."

I smiled demurely. "My neighbor's son walks Agent Barlow's dog."

I didn't elaborate more than that. I'd let Hearst draw his own conclusions, and so what if Gib didn't *yet* have a dog. He would soon enough so that if Hearst ever checked into it, I wouldn't be accused of lying to a federal agent.

Out of patience, Hearst grabbed the photo on the table and slapped it back inside the file. He got up and announced, "We're done here." Then he headed to the door and barked, "Barlow. My office. In ten minutes or you're suspended."

He then whipped open the door and stomped off with his female lackey and the other two agents trailing behind.

When we were alone again, I put a hand on Gib's arm and said, "Go face the music. I'm sorry I couldn't be more helpful. My contract with this client has a strict NDA, and it'd ruin me to break it."

"I understand. At least we have the name of this civilian casualty. We'll dig to see if there's any connection back to us."

There wouldn't be, but I wasn't about to dissuade Gib from going down a distracting rabbit hole while I hunted for the mystic causing so much harm.

"Give me a few minutes with Atticus and I'll take you home."

"No need. I'll call an Uber."

"You sure?"

"Yes."

I needed to hustle if I was going to stay one step ahead of the feds. At least I'd bought myself some time. No doubt they'd be investigating Angelica Aguado for the rest of the day, if not into tomorrow. Which reminded me . . .

"Come over later so you can get a good meal and a solid night's sleep, Gib. You're pale and you look almost dead on your feet."

He stood and I did too. "Me? Look who's talking. You must've been up all night working this case, too."

"I got in some naptime between four a.m. and eight. I'm good."

He rubbed his bloodshot eyes. "Maybe I should stay home tonight, Dovey. I doubt I'll be much company."

A ripple of fear snaked along my spine. There was no way I was going to allow Gib to be alone to face this murderous mystic anytime soon. Wrapping my arms loosely around his neck, I thought I'd sweeten the deal. "I'll make you some homemade gnocchi with a butter sage sauce and maple candied walnuts."

He appeared surprised that I was being so forward, but he quickly got over it. Sliding his own arms around my waist, he replied, "Tempting. What's for dessert?"

I wore the hint of a smile and stroked the back of his head, looking deep into his gray-silver eyes, hoping he'd infer some romantic interest into it. Inwardly, however, I was still a bit conflicted about the abrupt ending to my relationship with Elric. There was also the fact that Gib was exhausted, so I mentally vowed to lure him over with a promise of intimacy and good food, then use one of Ursula's sleep potions that I had on hand to send him off to dreamland.

The smile worked. "What time's dinner?" he asked with his own knowing grin.

"The second you come through my door. Text me when you leave here, okay?"

"I will," he promised.

We parted at the door, and I headed back the way we'd come. I was almost to the elevator when I nearly bumped into Agent Hearst. He stepped in front of me, which caught me off guard, and then he leaned forward to get into my personal space and whispered in my ear, "We're watching you, Dovey Van Dalen."

I stiffened. His use of the present tense "We're watching you" and not "We'll *be* watching you" was like a confession. It made me think he'd known about my existence before today, which was probably a lot to infer over a simple encounter, but there was something . . . something more to this insufferable man that I couldn't quite put my finger on.

Something familiar. Sinister. Powerful.

And that was troubling indeed.

Still, I squared my shoulders, moved to my right, and stepped around him. "Knock yourself out, *Aaaaticusssss.*"

I made sure to hiss his name as I left him behind. *He's just an arrogant unbound,* I told myself. *He's no threat to me.*

The thought that wouldn't leave me, however, was that I couldn't say the same for Gib. His former best friend meant to ruin him, and I wasn't certain Gib was aware of the threat Hearst posed to his career, and maybe even his life.

I got to the elevator and refused to look back to see if Hearst was still watching me, but I hoped he'd moved on. When the doors parted, there stood the female agent who'd been in the meeting with us, and there was something that struck me when I saw her and took her appearance in fully this time.

She had black hair tied back into a tight bun.

Olive skin.

Oval-shaped face.

Full lips.

Dark brown eyes.

Very pretty.

And there was a youthfulness to her complexion, giving her an ageless appearance.

Judging her height as she stared levelly back at me, I put her at five-seven or five-seven and a half, only a touch shorter than me as we were both wearing three-inch heels. And there was an athletic stance to her posture and a sense of confident knowing in her eyes that one only rarely saw in the unbound.

She held herself and looked like . . . a mystic.

CHAPTER 15

As she exited the elevator, the agent smiled a crocodile's grin, flashing lots of teeth and narrowed eyes. "Tootles," she whispered, brushing my shoulder as she passed me by. When her shoulder touched mine, there was an unmistakable ripple of current that passed between us. Reflexively, I gathered some essence into the palms of my hands.

Turning so as not to leave my back exposed, I heard her laugh; then she disappeared around a corner.

Every synapse in me seemed to be firing at once. She fit the description Ursula had given me of the murderous mystic to a T. Belatedly, I thought to confirm her identity by snapping her photo and showing it to Ursula. Fumbling to retrieve my phone from the pocket of my handbag, I hurried down the hallway toward where the agent had gone.

When I rounded the corner, however, the hallway was empty. It was a long corridor that ended at a set of windows, and there was no way she could've made it all the way to the end in the time it took me to follow her.

She'd vanished.

I trotted down the hall, wondering if she'd popped into an office, but the only door within the corridor was the one for the stairs. I opened it and leaned into the stairwell, listening. There were no sounds of footsteps on stairs.

Blinking through my memory of her attire—charcoal suit, light blue blouse, and patent leather heels—I knew there was no way her trip down the stairs would be silent. Pulling myself back into the corridor, I continued down the hall all the way to the windows, and at the intersection I looked right and left. This section was buzzing with activity. Personnel were bustling back and forth, oblivious to me at the center point between them.

Holding up my phone I texted Gib.

What's the name of the female agent that came in with Hearst?

If I could get her name, I might be able to find a photo of her online. It was a long shot, but it was better than walking up to her, shoving my phone in her face and snapping her photo. If she were a mystic, I doubted my phone would survive the encounter. Hell, if she were *the* mystic targeting us, *I* wasn't likely to survive the encounter.

I waited for his reply and tapped my foot impatiently. After several minutes, it was obvious he was in with Hearst and couldn't respond.

Undeterred, I retraced my steps, holding my phone so that I could discreetly snap a photo at any time, hopefully without anyone being the wiser.

I also *had* to get Gib out of here. If that woman was the murdering mystic, he was in very real danger.

"Can I help you?" a man wearing a shield on his belt asked me. He looked pointedly at my visitor badge on the lanyard around my neck.

"I'm looking for Agent Barlow. I believe he's in with the new SAC. We just had an interview and I forgot a detail that could be critical to the case they're working on."

The man—a youngish-looking agent with close-cropped hair, broad shoulders, and dark skin, waved toward a hallway to our left. "I'll take you."

"Thank you. That would be most kind."

He put a hand on his chest. "Agent Art Williams."

I mimicked his gesture. "Dovey Van Dalen."

"That's a pretty name," he said as we got underway. "Were your ancestors Dutch?"

"They were." I failed to mention that I was also from Denmark, but I'd lived here for over a century. Perhaps there'd be time to chitchat with the friendly agent some other time.

Williams paused in front of a closed door. There were raised voices on the other side. He grimaced, eyed me apologetically, and wrapped his knuckle against the door.

The yelling stopped abruptly. "What?!" Hearst shouted. Clearly, he didn't appreciate the interruption.

Williams opened the door and poked his head inside. "Dovey Van Dalen would like to share an additional detail with Agent Barlow."

A sort of stunned silence followed. "Send her in."

I readied my phone and when Williams turned to the side to let me pass, I hit pay dirt when I saw that the female agent was in the office with Gib and Hearst.

I began to put my phone away, discreetly snapping a photo of her as I did so. I'd show that to Ursula the first chance I got.

"I just remembered something that I can share with you about Angelica that won't compromise my nondisclosure."

Gib's eyes had widened with surprise. "Lay it on me."

"Angelica had a great-aunt who lived in town. I'm not sure if the aunt is still alive, but if she's not, then perhaps a cousin might be able to fill in some of the details of Angelica's life."

"Name?" Gib asked, grabbing a pen and a blank note from the stack on Hearst's desk.

"The aunt's name was Lutecia Aguado. I believe her daughter goes by her married name. Ursula Göransdotter."

Gib had started scribbling the names I spoke but paused when I mentioned Ursula. He covered the pause well, however, but something quite suspicious happened in that moment too. The female agent uttered a small, but distinct puff of disbelief, and when I looked at her, I could see the disdainful recognition in her eyes. She knew who Ursula was, and perhaps more importantly, she knew *what* Ursula was.

And because of her *You're kidding me* expression, I now knew for certain that she was a mystic.

Which meant that at least three out of the four of us were in mortal danger right there in that room, but only two of us knew it.

Trying to remain calm, I said, "Agent Barlow, on your way to check out my lead, would you drop me off at my office? I could call an Uber, but why should I shoulder the expense when you're the one who insisted on bringing me here?"

I needed to get Gib out of this office immediately, and demanding he take me back home seemed like a good way to get him out of the building.

"Of course," he said, while also turning to Hearst, who scowled but nodded. "Go. But bring me back something or don't come back until you do."

I couldn't usher Gib out of there fast enough. He came willingly if a bit sluggishly. He moved like he was asleep on his feet. We didn't speak until we were in the elevator headed to the parking garage.

"What was—" he began.

"Not here," I said sharply.

He clamped his mouth shut and we continued to ride the elevator down in silence. Once we were in the parking garage, I followed along next to him, back to his Range Rover, and hopped in. "We have to go to Ursula's," I said, buckling the seatbelt while he did the same from the driver's seat.

"Care to explain?"

"Not here, not now, Gib. I will, but just not anywhere near this building."

"Got it."

He started the engine, and we wound our way up the ramp to the street, turning right and moving in the general direction of Ursula's house.

While Gib drove, I checked the sideview mirror continuously, often looking over my shoulder for any hint of a tail.

As we pulled to a stop at a traffic light, I suddenly remembered something. "Did you hold on to the pen from Atticus's desk?"

Gib smirked. "I did. I'll tell him later that I forgot I was holding on to it and give it back to him, but for now I like the thought of him being aggravated that it's gone. Atticus loves his fancy pens."

I stiffened in alarm. Pens and keys are two of the most popular choices for trinket enchantments, with old coins and jewelry coming in a close third and fourth, but pens, specifically, are so popular because they're small, easily hidden, and can have the convenience of still retaining their general purpose as a writing instrument while also easily imbued with some essence to wake up their enchantment.

I had several pen trinkets, in fact. One that I was even carrying in my handbag, which kept would-be pickpockets and muggers from even being tempted to snatch the contents.

"Show it to me," I demanded.

He looked at me with a furrowed brow. "Sure." Leaning sideways he plucked it from his jacket pocket and handed it over. The moment it was in my hand I pointed through the windshield at the now green traffic light and said, "Green means go."

Gib turned his attention back to the road, and as he did so I was just about to push a bit of my essence into the pen to see if I could feel a catch if the thing was enchanted, when the pen literally vanished from my fingertips.

I sucked in a breath.

"What's wrong?" Gib asked, his attention back at me. He then lowered his gaze to my empty hand. "Did you drop it?"

"Yes," I said, trying to regain my composure. The pen had been imbued with a comeback spell, which—if Gib was correct and that was Hearst's pen—meant that not only was the female agent a mystic, but Atticus was likely one too.

To cover for the now-missing pen, I said, "I can look for it as soon as we get to Ursula's. It rolled under the seat."

Gib yawned and his eyes blinked dully. I should've offered to drive. "Don't sweat it, Dovey. I can always tell Atticus I lost it. It's not like he can fire me for it. For that, he'll come up with some other trumped-up infraction."

"The woman who was in the interrogation room with us . . ."

"She's our new ASAC," Gib said with a hint of disdain. "Assistant Special Agent in Charge Elisabetta Stoia."

Italian, I thought. One of the six courts was in Rome—the Court of Louis Vostov. Which was the same court that had sent a diplomat to the Court of Dobromila-Ostergaard several weeks earlier for a summit that Elric and Petra had hosted.

That diplomat, Nicodemus Kallis, had foolishly lost a powerful and deadly trinket that I'd ultimately tracked down, and didn't return. Which meant that Kallis was either dead—as the trinket had belonged to Vostov . . . or Kallis had gone rogue and had come back for revenge.

"Stoia came with Atticus," Gib continued. "And he passed up two other agents to put her as his second-in-command. Her promotion is causing a lot of anger on top of the anger already circulating around our office. Our guys are being systematically picked off, one by one, and no one knows why or how, and I don't know that I'm buying the whole decompression chamber theory, especially when we can't find a single trace of forced entry or a crime scene that looks like a crime scene should."

My knee was bouncing while my mind raced. I was listening

to Gib but not paying him my full attention. He hardly noticed.

"My brothers and sisters at the Bureau are chosen because they're cool under pressure, but between you and me, Dovey, we're all starting to spin out."

"No doubt," I replied flatly.

"So, is this Angelica Aguado a real person?" he asked me next.

My focus snapped back to Gib. "She is." I had to keep up the ruse to keep him out of trouble. Meddling in the murder of a former lover to Elric was likely to irritate him, so having Gib chase the fictional Angelica was a far safer avenue for him.

Gib cut me a sideways glance. "Angelica's a real person but you don't know her address."

"Sorry. I don't. It was something I was going to track down before you and your team got involved."

He grunted. "I'll drop you at Ursula's and then head home for a catnap. I can barely keep my eyes open and if I don't get some shut-eye soon, I'll nod off while I'm at the wheel."

I rubbed his shoulder. We were on the expressway just a mile from the exit; otherwise I would've demanded that he pull over and allow me to take it from there.

Ursula's home was just a few turns later, and we made it without incident or an obvious tail, as I'd continued my surveillance in the sideview mirror.

"Come inside," I told him when he parked at the curb.

He grimaced. "I gotta get home, Dove. I'm a zombie right now."

"Which is why you shouldn't be driving. Come in and take a nap on the sofa. Ursula would love to have you."

"I doubt that," he said with a chuckle. "I can make it home, I promise."

I touched his arm and smiled. "Of course. Thank you for the ride."

"Anytime."

I rummaged around in my handbag for a moment, pretending to look for my phone. "Now where did I put my phone?"

Gib looked over the console between us. "Did you have it with you when we left the Bureau?"

"I think so. Hey, would you hold this loose change for me for a second?"

Gib held out his palm and I placed the coins and my silver dollar trinket into it. I waited just a moment and his gaze went blank.

"You're going to come inside with me to Ursula's," I said.

"I'm going to come inside with you to Ursula's."

"And you're going to ask if it's okay to take a nap on her sofa."

"I'm going to ask if it's okay to take a nap on her sofa."

"And you won't remember anything about this conversation with me."

"I won't remember anything about this conversation with you."

I smiled and patted his back. "Good boy."

Gib gave himself a pat on the shoulder. "I'm a good boy."

I giggled and did my best to squelch it. Then I took back my change and waited for his expression to lose the blank stare. It took a few moments but he finally blinked at me, nodded to Ursula's front door, and said, "I'm gonna walk up with you, if that's okay?"

"Of course."

Gib opened his door. "I want to ask Ursula if I can take a nap on her sofa."

I grabbed the box with the two shakers in the well of the passenger side door, tucking them into my handbag before getting out and rounding the truck to Gib's side. "I think a nap is a marvelous idea."

Ursula opened the door before we were even to it. "Hello, you two," she said warmly.

"Hello, Ursula. I want to ask you if I can take a nap on your sofa."

Ursula's gaze cut sharply to me, and I winked to let her know that Gib was under a touch of magical influence.

"Of course, dear," she said. "Come right this way."

He followed dutifully behind her, giving himself another pat to his shoulder, and said, "I'm a good boy."

She bit her lip to keep from laughing and glanced back at me with wide eyes.

I grimaced and shrugged my shoulders.

Meanwhile, Gib wasted no time heading to her sofa, where he began to fluff up a throw pillow.

"Ursula, do you have any tea to help Gib sleep?" I asked.

She beamed at me. "The water is already hot, Dovey. I'm sure I can get him something to help him rest."

She disappeared into the kitchen and Gib stopped fluffing the pillows to look over at me. "I don't think I'll need it. I'll be out like a light in just a sec."

Ursula reappeared with a steaming cup of tea. "Nonsense. Sometimes it's when we're most exhausted that sleep eludes us. Sip on this, Gib, and your sleep will be restful and deep."

But he shook his head no. "I can't stay longer than an hour. If that knocks me out, I'll have a hard time waking up and being functional."

She grinned at him. "I will wake you in exactly one hour and I've got the perfect antidote to the sleepy effects of this tea. It'll perk you right up!"

Reluctantly, he took the mug from her and sipped it, nodding his head at the taste. "That's good. And not too hot, either." Eagerly, he downed the rest of the brew and set the teacup aside, then he blinked twice and began to slide down sideways onto the cushion, his eyes closed even before his head met the throw pillow, and his face went slack just a few seconds later.

Ursula and I watched him for a beat or two, making sure he was out cold. "That should keep him down for six to ten hours," she said.

"Perfect. Now, sit with me for a second. I need you to look at something."

We moved over to the two chairs opposite the sofa, and I got out my phone. Pulling the photo of Elisabetta Stoia up onto the screen, I leaned over and showed it to her. "That's the mystic that attacked you last night, right?"

Ursula's brow knit together, and she looked closely at the image. "No, Dovey. That's not her."

I blinked. "What? Ursula, take another look. She fits your description *perfectly*."

"No. No she doesn't. I said the mystic from last night looked Spanish. This woman looks Italian. And the shape of the face is all wrong. This woman's face is oval; the mystic who attacked us had a square-shaped face. Plus, this woman's not nearly as beautiful."

I turned the phone and the photo back to myself, wondering if perhaps the image was fuzzy or out of focus, but it was clear as day. "She was wearing her cloak, though, right? And it was dark out. Maybe her features were distorted because of all that."

Ursula regarded me patiently. "Dovey, you're forgetting that I've been an artist for over seven hundred years. Artists notice details most others don't. Facial shape, eye shape and color, lip line, nose shape, chin shape, forehead—these are all things we notice in detail, even when we're not planning to paint them."

I frowned and tapped the phone. "She's a mystic, Ursula. I'm sure of it."

My friend nodded like she was taking my word for it. "I don't know her. Or even recognize her. Does she work for SPL?"

"No. She's a fed."

"A fed? What does that mean?"

"She works for the FBI. She's Gib's boss."

Ursula's jaw fell open and she simply stared at me for a long moment. "You're sure she's one of us?"

"I am."

The way Elisabetta's shoulder had rubbed against mine at the elevator had caused a current of energy between us, and the pen from Hearst's desk being called back via a comeback spell, I felt, sealed the deal. At least one, if not both of them, was a mystic, and if only one of them was one of us, then I was laying money on Elisabetta. Meanwhile, Hearst could be a mystic, or he could merely be how Elisabetta was infiltrating the unbounds' federal investigative establishment.

"Why would a mystic become an FBI agent?" Ursula asked me.

"I don't know, but I suspect she's a spy."

"Spy? From where?"

"If I had to guess, I'd say she's from Vostov's court."

Understanding bloomed in Ursula's expression. "Kallis!"

I nodded. "Yes. Either he's still alive and orchestrating this whole thing for revenge against me for sending him packing back to his court without Pandora's Promise, or he's been executed and Vostov is orchestrating this whole disaster to cause trouble for the Court of Dobromila-Ostergaard to get back at Elric for the loss of his trinket."

Ursula shook her head. "Those damn Pandora's trinkets always invite trouble wherever they land." And then she eyed me keenly. "You know who might know for certain what's afoot, though?"

I took a guess. "Gert?"

She grinned. "Yes. She might be able to identify this mystic at the Bureau for you."

Gert was the owner of a favorite mystic watering hole named

Gert's Mystic Bar. She served incredible food, heavily poured cocktails, and terrible coffee. She also heard everything and knew everyone, so she was always a great resource for ferreting out information for those of us who came looking for it.

"She'll want a trinket for the trouble," I said. Gert was indeed a great resource, but she didn't work for free.

"What do you have on you?"

I rummaged around in my handbag, but all I had of any value were the trinkets the Falcon had created, my silver dollar, and the pen that kept would-be thieves out of my purse and a few other odds and ends that helped keep me out of trouble. "Nothing I'm willing to trade," I admitted.

"Anything at home in your trinket room?"

I pursed my lips, thinking through my inventory. The problem was that I'm quite attached to my trinkets. I have a decent collection and hated to part with anything that Gert would find valuable, which was the key. She wouldn't take any old trinket in exchange for information that came loaded with mystic danger. She'd want something good.

And then I had an idea: "I don't have any trinkets that I'd be willing to trade or that she might have use for, but I *do* know where there might be a supply to pick through."

"Where's that?"

"Lavender's crypt."

Ursula's expression turned doubtful. "The one with the serpent?"

Several weeks earlier, Ursula, Gert, and I had tricked a thief named Lavender into giving up the location of her trinket cache—her family crypt in a cemetery not far from Gert's bar. I'd gone there to retrieve a trinket she'd stolen from a friend, and I'd barely made it out alive. But circumstances since then had changed considerably. . . .

Still, when I thought about reentering the place, I shuddered involuntarily. Ursula noticed.

"The serpent is dead," I said, hoping to give myself some courage by reminding myself that I'd made it out alive and the serpent hadn't.

Ursula frowned. "I think it's unwise, Dovey. Lavender could well have moved her cache after discovering you'd raided the place and killed her pet, or worse, she could've set traps for you should you think of going back."

"I don't think she had the time to move all of her trinkets, Ursula, and again, the threat within the crypt was neutralized. There might still be some useful or even valuable trinkets in there."

I was trying to sound confident, but the truth was I hated the thought of heading back to that crypt. It'd imprinted a trauma on my mind, but I needed something to offer Gert that wouldn't cost me one of my cherished trinkets at home.

Ursula, however, placed a hand on my arm, like she was hoping I'd reconsider.

"I'll be careful," I promised her.

She frowned and got up, headed to her coatrack in the corner. "I'm coming with you."

I hurried to my feet and stepped in front of her. "Not a chance, girlfriend. You're still healing, and Gib needs a babysitter. If he wakes up and finds us both gone, he'll leave here either to look for us or to head home for more sleep, and he *can't* be left in an unwarded home, Ursula. It's far too dangerous given the circumstances."

She sighed. "I still don't like it."

I put a hand on her shoulder. "I know, my friend. But I'll be fine. Plus, don't you have a car and a phone yet to be delivered?" I hadn't seen either since arriving back here.

She glanced at the clock on the wall. "The car's on its way from the dealership right now. The phone should be here by three thirty."

"See? You can't leave. You need to sign for both deliveries."

She sighed and turned away, heading toward the kitchen. "If the crypt is locked, you'll need something to get in." From there, I heard a drawer open and the sounds of rummaging, then she reappeared holding an iron skeleton key.

"Thank you," I said, accepting it. My own silver toothpick lockpick was in my handbag, but I never pass up an opportunity to play with a new trinket.

Ursula nodded, but she continued to grimace like she was fighting the urge to argue some more about my going it alone.

"I'll be fine," I said to her again, as much as for Ursula's reassurance as for mine. I then went to the key fob that Gib had dropped on the floor next to the sofa and picked it up. "I'm taking his Rover. Luna's still at home, and this way he won't easily be able to leave should he wake up. *Don't* let him take your car if it arrives and he comes to and wants to leave."

"If he proves difficult, there's always more sleeping potion," she said casually.

I pushed a smile onto my face, hugged her, then I pointed to the coatrack where her leather coat hung and asked, "Can I borrow that? There's a chill in the air."

"Of course you can, but be careful with it. Marlon Brando gave that to me."

I chuckled. "Of course he did." I took the coat, waved at her, and left. The worried expression on Ursula's face stayed with me well after I'd gotten underway.

As I drove, I glanced nervously at the darkening sky. This eternal rain was simply insufferable! I hadn't had a moment to check the forecast, but it was obvious there was yet another storm brewing and that my route to the cemetery seemed to be heading directly into the storm.

"Great," I muttered. I didn't have my magic umbrella with me, and glancing around the front seat of Gib's Range Rover, he didn't have an umbrella, either.

The first drops of rain started just as I pulled onto the cemetery grounds. I was bound to get wet again, and I grumbled at myself for not checking my trusty snow globe to see if there was more rain on the way, but I'd been in a hurry to shower, change, and head with Gib over to the FBI field office. Still, all I'd had to do was peek at it and I would've known to bring my umbrella.

I parked and stared up at the rain now battering the windshield. I could wait out the worst of the rain in the warmth and comfort of the cab, but I didn't think I had time on my side. I had to get to the bottom of this case—soon.

Taking a deep breath for courage, I opened the door and hustled up a steep hill. A flashback to vaulting myself off the top of this same hill just a few weeks before sent another involuntary shudder trilling along my spine. "Just get in, pick through what's left, and get out," I muttered.

The rainfall was certainly intensifying when I crested the hill, and at the bottom on the other side I could just make out Lavender's family crypt.

Most of it was buried into the side of a hill, and the last time I was here I'd accessed it not from the chained iron gate at its entrance, but by digging my way in through the side of the hill using a simple earth mover's spell.

The hole I'd created had been filled back in, and I wasn't especially in the mood to worm my way through the mud into the crypt again, so I opted to try the locked gate using Ursula's key, hoping for a different outcome than last time when I couldn't get through Lavender's wards.

Making my way there I paused at the entrance to look around. On the way over, I'd kept my eye on the rearview mirror to make sure I wasn't being followed, but given the dark atmosphere and all cars on the road keeping their lights on, it was impossible to be certain I hadn't.

Getting into the crypt quickly was necessary—given my vulnerability.

I had the two shakers tucked into Ursula's right coat pocket, so I felt fairly well protected, but thinking back to the state of Ursula's broken body and the destroyed bangle bracelet trinkets that'd kept her an inch from death, I was less confident than I normally would've been.

I felt like, up until early this morning when Dex and I had discovered Ursula in such terrible condition, I'd severely underestimated the power of the Casting Bead. It was no wonder that Qin Shi was so anxious to get it back.

Squinting through the rain currently soaking my hair and shoes, I pulled on the large metal lock that held the crypt closed. It was rusted and ancient, so I wondered if it might not be so hard a lock to pick after all.

Taking out the skeleton key Ursula had loaned me, I pushed some essence into it, feeling that familiar catch, then I inserted it into the lock on the gate.

At first glance, the key would've appeared far too small for the large keyhole, but as I inserted it, I could feel it begin to twist the gears. With a little effort, I was able to turn the key a full half circle and get the lock to open.

"That wasn't so bad," I whispered. Then I pocketed the trinket and took the lock off the latch. Pausing to look all around in case another mystic had snuck up on me, I pulled open the gate only when I was sure nothing was amiss or anyone was nearby.

The gate swung reluctantly, groaning on its hinges. Beyond it was an iron door.

Gathering some essence, I lobbed an orb at the door to check for a ward, but my orb bounced harmlessly off the metal and came back to my palm.

"No longer warded," I said, which was probably to be expected.

I reached for the handle, gripping it tightly, and pulled as hard as I could. The door budged maybe an inch. "Ugh," I growled.

Backing up I thought for a moment, gathering the words for a quick remedy, then filled the air around my mouth with some of my essence, placed a hand on the iron door and sang,

"Iron guard to hide who died
Slide this way and step aside
Grant my entry to inside
Heed this spell as you abide."

The door began to slowly, slowly groan open.

I sighed and grumbled to myself impatiently. "Well, what'd you expect, Dovey? Not my best spell. Should've added a verse for speed."

A flash of lightning skittered across the headstones and a few moments later there was an accompanying crack of thunder. The rain turned to a pelting assault and the wind whipped the branches and budding leaves on nearby trees.

I pulled the collar up on Ursula's coat, trying to shield myself from the torrent until the crypt door finally opened enough to let me through.

Stepping into the crypt felt like stepping back into a bad dream. I'd turned on my phone's flashlight for light, and almost everything about this damp, miserable place jangled my nerves. I'd lived three different deaths in this tomb, and I wondered what I'd been thinking coming back here.

But that was the trauma talking. I could get through this if I could just calm my nerves for a moment. The sooner I found something to offer Gert, the sooner I could get the hell out of here and never look back.

Closing my eyes I took three deep, calming breaths, then opened them again and got on with it.

The bare dirt floor of the crypt was littered with a thick blanket of trinkets, in some places at least ankle deep, which wasn't quite as deep as the layer had been several weeks ago when I'd first made my way here.

Still, as I'd suspected, a good portion of Lavender's trinket cache had been removed. I had no doubt that she'd discovered her treasure hoard had been poked through, and before even coming after me, she'd hurriedly moved most of the good stuff out.

However, I also suspected that there were still some worthy treasures here. While Lavender was known for being an adept thief, she had terrible organizational skills. There was bound to be something here that would suit my purposes.

I began to shuffle my feet along the floor, sifting through the trinkets with my eyes, alert for anything that looked interesting. I got excited when I came across an old brass cross—brass is a terrific conductor for enchantment, and plenty of metal crosses get turned into trinkets.

But when I lifted the cross and pushed some essence into it, the only thing that happened was that it emitted a terrible, loud sound, like a foghorn.

"Ack!" I yelled, dropping the thing. It continued to wail away, however, so I rushed to the crypt door and yanked it closed, lest someone outside be alerted by the sound and head this way to investigate it. I didn't *think* there was anyone else at the cemetery during this storm, but I didn't know that, and I couldn't be too careful.

Finally, the noise from the cross faded and the crypt was once again quiet, but my heart was busy trying to pound its way out of my chest. *I gotta be a little more careful*, I thought to myself.

Then I went back to shuffling around the cache.

Right about then my feet kicked to the surface a small silver object that seemed like it might hold promise.

I couldn't bring Gert something obvious, nothing too large and obnoxious, but something small that she could hide among the bottles, glasses, and other items that lined the back of her bar. Anything too large was impractical and tempting to any professional thief visiting her bar.

Most mystics who tried to steal from Gert found out quickly why they should *never* try to steal from Gert, but she didn't need the headache of policing her trinkets during a busy happy hour.

Bending over, I picked up the object and held it to the light. It was roughly two inches tall and an inch or so wide, in the shape of a coopered barrel with a screw-off top. Untwisting the top, I looked inside and saw a small, slightly rusted metal plate with raised knobs lining the surface. "Ooo, a nutmeg grinder! I haven't seen one of these in ages."

I've enjoyed cooking and baking for myself for at least the last hundred and fifty years, and I once had a nutmeg grinder very similar to this one, but mine had been gold and it'd been a favorite trinket of mine for many years, having the power to trick the unbound into giving up all the things they felt guilty about, before I'd lost it on the way home from a case in the early 1940s.

Or, more likely, before a pickpocketing thief had lifted it from my purse.

The fond nostalgia for that trinket made me consider keeping this one, but I had to know what it did first. With just a bit of my essence I coaxed the trinket to life and . . . absolutely nothing happened.

"Dud," I muttered. Still, I might be able to get Arlo to enchant it with a similar power to my old one. Or I'd simply take it home and use it to grind fresh nutmeg; the find was still a prize in my book.

I put the grinder in my pocket and continued to sort through the mess, but there didn't seem to be much here that I thought would suit my purposes, and I was nearly at the end of my shuffling trinkets around. Lavender, it appeared, had removed all of the good stuff.

With hands on my hips, I turned in a circle, just to make sure I'd picked my way through everything littering the ground, when my gaze landed on something that glinted off the light of my phone.

The glint wasn't coming from the floor, however. It was coming from the back of the crypt, where Lavender's ancestors were interred.

On a triple row of bunks lay the skeletons of her long-deceased family, and something on the middle bunk was catching the light from my phone, glinting ruby red back at me.

I moved closer and saw that one of the skeletons who was wearing the slowly disintegrating period clothing from perhaps the late 1800s was also wearing a ruby ring of at least ten carats. Maybe more. The gemstone was just massive, and given the way my phone's flash glinted off it, it was very good—if not exquisite—quality. An unbound would literally kill for such a treasure.

Normally, I don't condone grave robbing, but desperate times called for desperate measures. Even though I doubted highly that the ring was enchanted, Gert would covet it, and I wondered why Lavender had left it behind.

The only thing I could think of was that she forgot one of her relatives was wearing it.

"That's why it pays to be thorough, you wretched thief," I muttered.

Turning sideways to get more of a reach, I stretched my arm across the skeleton of Lavender's mother, or grandmother, or aunt, or whatever, and felt around for the ring.

My fingers landed on something brittle and thin. I didn't know what it was, but when I put some pressure on it, I felt it crumble under my fingertips.

Curious, I pulled my hand back, holding on to a bit of the thing, and saw that it was an eggshell. *Weird*, I thought. *What would a bird be doing nesting in here?*

Maybe there was a crevice in the wall of the crypt that allowed a bird to make a nest and raise some young. It was damp, chilly, and smelled a bit fetid in here, but at least the tomb was protected from the worst of the elements, which a mama bird might think was a good enough trade-off.

Tossing aside the bit of shell, I bent to eye the ring again, and adjusted my angle turning sideways, reaching as far as I could, and pawed at the air. My hand finally landed on the bony finger and I smiled while I inched my own fingertips along the hand, locating the ring, and sliding it easily free.

As I was pulling it off the skeleton, however, something under the bony hand . . . *slithered.*

I froze, my blood turning cold. My mind began to put two and two together and I realized . . .

Birds aren't the only creatures to lay eggs.

Snakes—*serpents*—lay them too.

CHAPTER 16

*H*isssssssssss . . . came the first warning.

Hisssssss . . . Hissssssss . . . came the second and third. All from different parts of the crypt.

Frozen in fear but trembling all the same, I stood as still as I could manage, waiting to either feel the bite of poisonous fangs, or the slither of reptilian skin across my feet.

Without moving my head, I looked down at the ground, and sure enough the pile of trinkets to my left undulated like a layer of trash floating on an ocean current.

My mind spun, desperately trying to come up with a plan, but there were at least three deadly serpents in this tomb, and only one way out.

My eyes roved the chamber, looking for something—*anything*—that I could use to fight my way out of here. My shaker trinkets were in my pocket, and I'd have to reach for, then touch them to push some essence into them and wake them up, which meant I had to move.

I was about to do that when movement at eye level made me slide my gaze to my left. A serpent that resembled its mother in markings, if not in size, slithered down from the top bunk to the middle one and eyed me menacingly from the head of the skeleton I was currently robbing.

Its tongue darted out, fluttering toward me, as if it could taste my fear. If it could, then it was probably feasting on the absolute terror wafting off me.

Think, Dovey! Think!

But I couldn't. I couldn't think of a plan to get me out of here alive. I'd felt the sting of the hatchling's mother as her venom had rippled into my central nervous system, not once, but *twice*, and it was perhaps the closest I've ever come to a death you don't come back from.

The only thing that'd saved me was a trinket long since used up, and even if it hadn't been, I didn't know that I could've saved myself from three of these vipers.

The serpent that flicked its tongue at me had a head as large as my hand, and its body was well over six feet long—smaller than its mother by more than half, yes, but still more than capable of killing yours truly without much effort.

And its hatchling nest mates were somewhere slithering about, sight unseen.

Holding on to the bauble in my palm, I acted reflexively, without even thinking really. I pushed a panicked dose of my essence into the ring and to my utter shock I felt it catch.

Power flowed through the ring, emanating outward toward the skeletal remains on the bunk. The flow of red-tinged energy then radiated along the skeleton and, to my astonished eyes, seeped into the bones themselves, causing them all a sudden jerk.

If I was terrified before, it was nothing compared to how I felt when the skeleton jerked again and sat up.

Reflexively, the serpent on the bunk struck the skeleton, and the skeleton reacted by grabbing the serpent and wringing its neck in one horrifying, stomach-turning move. Meanwhile I continued to stand stock-still, watching with eyes wide and mouth agape, a scream caught in the back of my throat.

The ring was a necromancer. A trinket so powerful that only a few have been known to exist, and all of those are kept under very tight security within the vaults of the heads of the six courts.

Outside of those vaults, necromancing trinkets are illegal. Merlins are forbidden from creating them, and a mystic caught with one out in the world was typically executed on the spot, yet somehow, Lavender, a lowly thief who'd worked for no court, had obtained one.

But none of that mattered in the moment. I'd triggered the power of the ring, having no idea how to control it.

It turned out I didn't really need to.

Lavender's ancestor twisted her eyeless skull toward me, and in another move that was nearly too quick to catch, her hand shot out toward my throat.

I had no time to react let alone think as those bony fingers came right for me. Squeezing my eyes closed, waiting for the moment she'd crush my windpipe, I felt the whip of air by my cheek, the bump of something long and leathery sliding over my shoulder, and the second sickening crackle of a serpent's neck being broken.

Opening one eye I saw the limp remains of the second serpent dangling from the skeleton's hands. She dropped it onto the ground, where it landed on the scattered trinkets with a tinkling sound, then she nimbly hopped off the bunk, moving in a jerking, nightmarish way, and bolted for the corner to my right. Diving headfirst onto the layer of trinkets, she wrestled with something kicking and squirming against her, then she rolled onto her back and twisted the head of the final serpent clutched in her hands.

Throwing it off, she stood, and I saw that she'd lost the lower part of her jaw in the tussle. She then stared at me, and without her lower jaw she appeared to be caught in a mocking expression, as if she were gleefully deciding which way to kill me.

Slowly, slowly, I pulled my hand back from where it'd hung suspended in the air, clutching the ring that'd been placed on her finger for safekeeping, and opened my palm to show her that I was now the possessor of the power that'd called her to life—or, if not *life,* then at least animation.

Her skull tilted slightly, as if she were looking at the ruby ring in my palm, and a moment later a sort of chuffing noise echoed around the chamber.

It took me a moment to realize it was the sound of a skeleton laughing.

And I didn't quite understand the joke, until movement to my right caused me to turn my head sharply, only to see the skeleton that'd rested above her bunk sit up and twist to dangle his feet over the side, where they toggled back and forth right in front of my face.

My gaze traveled up the femurs to the torso and skull of the skeleton looking down at me, and it too began to chuff, adding to the growing cacophony of monstrous sounds within the chamber when more of Lavender's dead ancestors that'd been placed at the back of the crypt sat up and turned their empty-socket attention to me.

For the first time I realized that I was in even more danger now than I'd been in when the three serpents were alive.

"I . . . I c-c-c-command you! I c-c-c-command you to . . . obey me!" I yelled in the weakest, stuttering, cracked voice, which was also the bravest I could muster.

The chuffing sound grew louder, letting me know they had no such plans to obey.

For a moment I entertained the idea of pushing even more essence into the ring, but then I remembered *exactly* where I was.

The middle of a graveyard with literally hundreds, if not thousands, of skeletal remains surrounding me. Pumping more essence into the ring was likely to have dire consequences not just for me, but for the entire D.C. metropolitan area.

The shakers! I thought. *I can use them!*

The only problem was that the shakers were both in the right pocket of the leather coat I was wearing. They were impossible to get to without lowering the hand currently holding the ring.

There was no doubt in my mind that I'd never wrap my fingers around them before one of the skeletons treated my neck to the *serpent special.*

Out of all the convenient options, I eyed the door, which I'd so stupidly shut ten minutes earlier. It'd been hard to pull it closed, but maybe it'd be less hard to push open now that I'd already opened and closed it. Maybe the rust on the hinges had given away enough to make it easier now.

My mind was racing to give that plan some merit and I came to the conclusion that it was actually my *only* option at present.

Without thinking any more on it, I bolted across the crypt. The skeleton with the missing jaw was at the far corner and the others were seated on their bunks with only a narrow space to jump down and clamber after me. They could only do that one at a time.

I didn't even bother to slow down as I neared the door, intending to throw all of my weight and momentum against it to get outside, ahead of the undead in the tomb. If I broke my shoulder, so be it. It was better than one of them snapping my neck.

Hearing the clanging of trinkets right behind me, I knew the skeleton that'd worn the ring was nearly on top of me. I wasn't going to make it, and even if I did, what then? I'd get the door open, and they'd all pour out to attack or chase me, and these undead moved shockingly fast. If a miracle happened and I somehow made it out of the tomb before they caught and killed me, I didn't know that I'd be able to outrun them, especially since I had to climb a hill to get to the Rover.

Still, it was more than the chance I had standing still and waiting for them to attack and kill me as a group.

Fueled by sheer terror I launched myself for the door, turning my body in midair so that my shoulder would take the blow. I squeezed my eyes shut, bracing for impact when there was a loud, groaning sound of metal on stone and I continued to sail through the air well past where I should've hit the iron door.

Tumbling to the ground, I next heard a shout, and the sound of crunching bones. Landing on my side knocked some of the wind out of me. I managed only to get to my feet by sheer will.

Looking behind me I saw a tall figure with broad shoulders pummeling the skeletons one at a time as they came at him. Their bones shattered and splintered on impact, and only one or two continued to move feebly once sections of them hit the ground.

By my count there'd been six skeletons in the crypt, but it seemed like double that littered the ground because bones were flying and bouncing everywhere.

I stood there, hunched over, cradling the side I'd landed on, watching in awe as the last of the skeletons was picked up by its feet and thwacked against the side of the crypt, sending even more bones skittering around to clack against the stones.

Finally, his chest heaving from the effort, the figure turned to me, his fists still clenched, and a murderous look etched onto his face.

"Dex!" I cried, limping over to him and throwing my arms around his torso.

Panting against me he gave me an awkward pat on the back. "Hello, Dove. Fancy meeting you 'round these parts. Come here often?"

And then he began to chuckle, and I did too, and before I knew it, we were laughing hilariously and hugging each other tight.

I'd always liked Dex, and now I think I adored him. Leaning back away from him, I asked, "Are you hurt?"

He held up a bloody fist. "Nah. Cut myself on a skull, but otherwise I'm right as"—he paused to look skyward at the downpour soaking us through—"rain."

"What're you even *doing* here?" I had a pretty good idea but I wanted to hear it from him.

He thumbed over his shoulder toward the hill, on the other side of which I'd parked Gib's Range Rover. "Ursula sent me. Said you might need a bit of watchin' over."

I lay my forehead on his chest, beyond grateful to my best friend and to him. "You keep saving my life like this, I'm going to owe you one."

He laughed again. "We should get out of this rain, eh?"

I nodded and I began to head toward the path leading up the hill when I noticed Dex wasn't next to me. Looking over my shoulder I saw him gathering up all of the bones near the crypt and tossing them inside. He paused in the doorway, then he entered and reappeared with my phone, its flashlight still on. After shutting the iron door and the gate, he trotted over and handed it to me. "Don't want to lose that. You'll need some way to tell Ursula how I saved the day, and that's earned me a massage when she's feeling up to it."

"Oh, do not worry on *that* front, my friend. I plan to sing your praises to her for *decades*."

He grinned and motioned me forward. We were underway and now so soaked that it didn't matter if we hurried. "Whose crypt is that, anyway?" he asked, thumbing over his shoulder again.

"Lavender's."

"Ah. Yeah, I expect that thieving sheila won't be needin' access to it anytime soon."

"Or . . . ever again."

He nodded. He'd no doubt heard the whole story. "Mind if I come back here and take a look at what remains?"

"Be my guest, Dex, but watch out for serpents. It's best to come armed."

He flexed both biceps. "Always do."

I chuckled, and the act of simply laughing felt wonderful.

"How'd the dead alive themselves?" he asked next.

I thought about keeping the ring a secret, but knowing how dangerous it was, along with also knowing that Dex and his partner, Esmé, worked for Elric, I decided to level with him. Taking it out of my pocket, where I'd hastily shoved it as Dex was demolishing Lavender's ancestors, I held it in my open palm and said, "This was the culprit."

He paused and then hovered his index finger and thumb above my palm. "May I?"

"Of course, but Dex, remember that we're in the middle of a *graveyard*. Don't push any essence into it, okay?"

His brow shot up as his finger and thumb continued to hover above my hand. "A necromancer?"

I nodded.

"Oy," he said, blowing out a breath. "That's trouble."

"It is. One hundred percent, trouble with a capital *T*. Want it?"

He grinned and lifted the ring from my palm. "Necromancers are only trouble if you're powerful enough to give 'em a good jolt of essence. I'm guessing you pumped more than a thimbleful into this trinket, eh?"

"I'll say. At the time a six-foot serpent was just about to eat my face, so the trinket inadvertently got a dose of adrenaline-fueled power before I even knew I'd done it."

"Adrenaline essence is always the most powerful. Still, to wake up a graveyard, you'd need a lot more than that, but raising six of those piles of bones is still impressive, Dove."

"I'm glad it wasn't more. I had no idea they'd attack like that."

"If they'd been *your* long-dead family members, they wouldn't have. You could've commanded them to go right back to sleep. Waking up any undead you're not related to only causes chaos, unless you're *one* powerful mystic. The dead gotta respect you to obey you, even with a necromancer."

"Then why do trinkets like that even exist?" I asked him.

He turned the ring over in his palm, continuing to inspect it. "Like I said, to cause chaos."

I shuddered. "And like *I* said, you want it?"

He chuckled again, trying to pass the ring back to me. "Elric would pay a pretty price for this. You should take it to him."

I pressed my lips together, refusing to take the ring from him. "I can't. At least not right now."

His brow rose. "So, the rumors are true?"

"Yes. We've split up."

He shook his head. "His loss, Dove. Still, he'll pay to take this out of circulation, and necromancers are all in the level ten and up range, which means it'll also curry favor for me and Esmé. I'll turn it over to him as soon as I can. What do you want in return?"

A slow smile formed on my lips. "Funny you should ask . . ."

An hour later, after a quick stop at Dex's warehouse for a trinket swap and a change of clothes for him, and a brass button for me, which, when held close, dried my sweater and Ursula's jacket making them look like new, we were parked at Gert's bar and headed inside. I'd shared with Dex what'd happened at the FBI field office and my belief that there was at least one mystic infiltrating—and killing members of—the FBI.

He'd agreed that we had to get to the bottom of this quickly before more mystics and unbound agents were murdered.

At the bar, Dex held the door for me, and we walked into a large open area that was neatly kept and smelled of liquor and comfort food. My stomach growled. I couldn't remember when I'd last eaten anything.

"Sexy Dexy!" Gert called from the door leading to the kitchen.

"Gert, you gorgeous sheila. Come give us a hug and don't make us beg!"

I couldn't help but laugh when Gert came hurrying from the doorway to throw herself into Dex's arms. It seemed like everyone had a crush on the man.

Well, everyone but me and his partner, Esmé—if rumors were true.

Gert and Dex made a show of hugging it out, and then he gave her a great big kiss on the cheek and set her down.

"I've got some chili bubbling on the stove, Dexy. Can I bring you a bowl?"

"You always know what I need, Gert," he said with a wink. "Dovey, love, you hungry?"

"Famished."

"Oh! Dovey," Gert said, placing a hand on her heart and feigning surprise. "I didn't see you there."

In my pocket something vibrated at the same time that in my mind the words *Why'd* she *have to come along?* echoed. I blinked. What the heck?

To Gert I simply held up my hand and waved.

She smiled warmly, which put me at ease. "Make yourselves comfortable and I'll be out in a jiff." As Gert turned away, more words floated into my mind. *"He hugged me! I love that man!"*

"Dove?" Dex asked.

I shook my head, and the small vibration in my pocket settled. "Sorry, what?"

"I asked where you'd like to sit?"

I put my left hand in my pocket and used my right one to

point to the barstools at the corner of the bar. "There. Is that okay?"

"Works for me," he said, moving quickly to pull out one stool for me and the other for him.

Meanwhile, my palm had closed around the nutmeg grinder, and with a bit of surprise I realized that the essence I'd pushed into it an hour or so before had activated the trinket. It was a think truther.

I felt almost giddy. Think truthers are rare little trinkets indeed, as they need to be quite powerful to access the mind of a mystic. No doubt Lavender had missed the small treasure in her mad scramble to empty her cache of the more valuable trinkets, and I was now the richer for it.

Deciding to test its strength, I once again pushed a bit of essence into the grinder and, after taking my seat, I asked, "So what's the *real* deal between you and Esmé?"

Dex, who'd been leaning over the bar to treat himself to a pint of beer, dropped the mug he was holding. It slipped from his grip, but before it could hit the floor, he flicked his wrist, muttered something and the mug came back to him. I gave the man some credit. Retrieval spells are tough to pull off in the moment as they require a lightning-quick mind and reflexes.

"Nice," I said, pointing to the mug he put back under the spout.

He offered me a lopsided grin. "I've had plenty of practice fetching back the occasional pint."

Once he'd filled the mug, he asked, "What can I offer you, Dove?"

I smirked. He was trying to change the subject. "Coffee," I said, pointing to the pot that'd just finished brewing. Dex reached across the bar and lifted the pot and a mug from the back counter, poured me a cup, and slid it over. "Thanks. Now, back to my question—"

"Did Ursula ask you to ask me?" he interrupted.

"No. She would never. She'd ask you directly herself if she weren't afraid of the answer."

Dex grunted and took a swig of his beer. "It's complicated, Dovey."

I wish it weren't, but it is, a little voice in my head added.

"How so?"

Dex sighed. "If Esmé weren't my partner, it'd be less so." *And if the Flayer weren't in the picture, it'd be less so for her too.*

My eyes widened. Esmé and Petra's lieutenant? No. Way!

I winked at Dex. "So, the heart wants what the heart wants, eh?"

He shook his head, like he was deeply troubled about it. "There's history between me and Ezzy that makes seeing her only as my thieving partner . . . difficult." *Impossible.*

I wondered what history he specifically meant, and I would've asked but I doubted he'd tell me. "What does that mean for you and Ursula?"

Dex took a long sip from his beer and wiped his mouth with the back of his hand. "It means she's one of the best, kindest, and most beautiful mystics I know, and she deserves someone better than me." *But it'd kill me if she left me. I love her, but it's not fair to let her know how I feel while I'm paired up with Ezzy.*

Gert appeared from the kitchen carrying a tray loaded with food. Placing a heaping bowl of steaming chili in front of Dex, along with some deliciously smelling cornbread, she shifted over to me and set down a plate of gooey, homemade lobster mac and cheese. A favorite of mine.

I grinned. Gert's greatest talent, besides her cooking, is her ability to know just what her customers *really* wanted. She'd often ignore what they ordered and bring them a secret craving instead. Most of the mystics who frequented her bar understood the system, and most didn't even bother looking at the menu because Gert would serve them up something delicious every time. "How'd you know?" I kidded.

She grinned with self-satisfaction. "Every girl going through a breakup should get treated to her favorite comfort food." *Poor Dove. It was only a matter of time before Elric threw her over for a new one. The bastard.*

I quickly turned my focus on the plate of food in front of me, doing my level best to hide my shock and hurt feelings. Gert had obviously heard about my breakup with Elric, but the last part of her thought was a surprise. Had *Elric* already found another woman to replace *me*? I mean, he had always had a string of women he spent time with . . . but his favorite for as long as I'd known him had been me, and only me.

Had I been so blind by my attraction to Gib that I'd missed the signs that Elric had already been moving on? And who *was* he now favoring?

Had it been Tove? Was that why she'd been murdered?

"So what brings you two scoundrels by?" Gert asked, taking a seat behind the bar to cross her arms over her ample chest and consider us expectantly.

Dex chewed a moment on his spoonful of chili, pointing to the bowl and rubbing his belly. He washed it down with another swig of beer, then said, "Can't we just come in to have a good meal and spend time with one of my favorite girls, Gert?" *She reminds me of Mum.*

I nearly choked on the bite of mac and cheese. If Gert knew that Dex looked at her like a surrogate mother, she'd be shattered. She *lusted* after Dex, and he played his part, flirting with her, but his true feelings were far from what she was hoping for.

"You okay?" Gert asked, cutting a sideways glance at me.

I coughed for a moment, took a sip of coffee, and nodded. "Fine. Sorry." Pointing to my own plate, I added, "It's so good it's hard not to gulp it down."

She grunted in agreement but looked quite pleased by the compliment.

While I was recovering myself, Dex said, "We're here to see if you've heard any rumblings about a mystic using the Crushing Curse."

Gert widened her eyes slightly and nodded. "You're talking about what happened to poor Tove."

Dex nodded. "We are."

"Nasty business that. Everyone thinks it was Elric, but I can't see it."

"Why not?" I asked. I couldn't see him doing that, either, but I wanted to hear her thoughts.

"Because if he'd used it to kill her, he never would've dumped her body someplace for the unbound to find. That's a second mess he'd have to clean up. No, if he wanted Tove out of the picture, he'd just have Jacquelyn introduce her to that blue dragon of hers." *That freaky beast. Thing's a psychopath who'll kill someone important someday.*

"So, who do you think's behind it?" Dex pressed.

"Don't know. But if I shared my thoughts, what'd be in it for me?" Gert's smile spread ear to ear in anticipation of a new trinket to add to her collection.

I eyed Dex meaningfully and he wiped his hands on his napkin before fishing around in the messenger bag he'd brought in with him. "How's this?" he asked, holding up a silver-and-copper, barrel-shaped cocktail shaker.

Gert nodded and made a circular motion with her hand. She wanted a demonstration. Dex leaned over to the beer spigot and poured a bit of beer into the shaker. Then he turned to me and asked, "Favorite cocktail, miss?"

I tapped my chin thoughtfully. "I never turn down a well-poured cosmopolitan."

Dex nodded, capped the shaker, shook it, then motioned to

Gert to hand him a cocktail glass. She did so and he poured the contents of the shaker into the glass. Instead of beer, however, out flowed what looked to be a perfectly blended cosmo. Grinning ear to ear, Dex said, "Have a sip, Dove."

Curious, I reached for the glass and took a tentative sip, expecting to taste beer, but what lit up my taste buds was in fact an exquisite cosmopolitan. "Delicious!" I proclaimed.

I handed the glass to Gert, and she took a sip. And when the drink hit her palate, her eyes practically bugged out of her head. She wanted that trinket baaaaad.

"Does it work with water?" she asked.

Dex poured the rest of the drink into a second cocktail glass and took a sip, smacking his lips and nodding in approval. "It used to. Now it needs just a little something to get it started. Any cheap alcohol will do."

I could practically see the dollar signs behind Gert's eyes. She'd save a fortune in liquor costs while still serving superior-tasting drinks. The shaker was a bartender's dream.

"All right," she said. "You've got yourselves a deal."

Dex grinned and winked at me. Offloading the necromancer to him had been as good a deal for him as it had been for me. The shaker was perhaps only a level four, but it would prove quite useful to Gert.

"Whatcha want to know?"

She'd directed her question at me, which reminded me just how sly she actually was.

"Whoever is wielding the Crushing Curse is killing not just a mystic, but the unbound's FBI agents. Four high-ranking agents have been murdered so far, and I believe there's a mystic within their midst who might be responsible."

Gert nodded but didn't reply right away. I took the opportunity to get my phone out and show her the photograph of Elisabetta.

Gert studied the photo. "I've never seen her before, Dovey. Which means she's either not a mystic or she's new in town."

"She's definitely new in town."

Gert frowned, and there was a troubled look in her eye.

"What do you know?" Dex coaxed.

Instead of answering him, Gert shifted away from her seat behind the bar and moved over to an array of utensils.

I always admired the flatware that Gert served with her meals. Each fork, knife, and spoon was an antique. Most reflected the styles of centuries past and were always fun to use and remember bygone eras.

Today, she lifted a fork from the middle of the jumble and brought it over to us. As she drew close, I could see that it was a two-tined, sterling silver baked potato fork, circa late nineteenth century. Gert placed it carefully on the bar between us, effortlessly balancing it on its two tines. I saw the small shimmer of light yellow essence slide from her palm into the fork and an instant later I felt a shift in the pressure around us, as if we'd suddenly been transported into a much smaller space than her wide-open bar.

"A cloaking trinket," I said, pointing to the fork.

"Yeah. And my best one. I doubt even Elric could hear our conversation."

Dex's eyes glinted with desire and Gert waggled her finger at him. "Ah, ah, ah, Dexy. Don't go getting any ideas."

He shook his head and sat up straighter. "Sorry, Gert. My thieving mind takes over sometimes."

Why couldn't he look at me like that? Oh, how I'd love to strip that boy naked and—

Quickly, I shoved my hand into my pocket, wrapped it around the trinket and pulled my essence back from the nutmeg grinder. Gert's voice vanished from my mind. There were some thoughts I really didn't want to be privy to. After clearing my throat, I nodded at her. "You were saying?"

"There's trouble brewing," she began. "Big trouble."

"We already gathered that, love. The dead FBI agents and Tove's crushed bones were our first clue." Dex spoke with a slight smirk.

"Oh, it's much worse than that, Dexy. Qin Shi's gone missing, and no one can get into the trinket vault at SPL."

I sucked in a breath, my hand flying up to cover my mouth. "What do you mean Qin Shi has gone *missing?*"

"No one but Elric can get in there, right, Gert?" Dex said at almost the same time.

Gert's gaze flickered back and forth between us, finally settling on me. "I mean, he's gone, Dovey, and no one's got a clue where he might be. Jacquelyn's been assigned to track him down, but so far, she's coming up empty. That she even came in here to see if *I* knew where Qin's hiding tells you how desperate she is."

Gert sniffed indignantly, curling her lip. The bar-owning mystic got along with everyone, bound and unbound alike. Everyone, that is, except for Jacquelyn.

The story goes that not long after Gert first opened her bar—right around the time of Prohibition, Jacquelyn had gotten into a drunken argument with one of Petra's old lieutenants, which then caused a ruckus. Somehow, one of her dragons had appeared from her dragon brooch and mayhem with a whole lotta destruction to Gert's brand-new bar had followed.

A hundred years and Gert's still bitter.

Shifting her gaze back to Dex, she added, "Elric's in Europe. He won't be back for another day or two. He's got some other mystics working on the problem but, so far, the elevator at SPL refuses to stop at the seventeenth floor. It'll go up to fourteen—and you'll get a face full of fire—or eighteen, but it won't stop at seventeen."

I shook my head, so troubled by this revelation. Ursula and I had seen Qin less than twenty-four hours earlier, which I didn't want to mention to Gert lest it get back to Elric that I'd been at HQ. Instead, I asked the obvious, "If no one can get to the seventeenth floor, then how does anyone know Qin has gone missing? Maybe he's just inside the vault working on something sensitive, and out of caution he locked off access from the elevator." To my mind, that seemed like a perfectly logical explanation.

"They know he's missing because of the Loupe," she said.

My brow furrowed. "The what?"

But, of course, Dex knew. "The de Boucheporn Loupe?" he asked with keen interest, and immediately I understood who and what they were speaking of.

Claude-François Bertrand de Boucheporn was a mystic— merlin to be exact—and a French nobleman in the late eighteenth century.

The merlin had been a friend and ally to Elric for centuries. Then, when civil war broke out in France, Bertrand had chosen to ride it out in his beloved homeland, naïvely thinking that his mysticism would protect him.

It hadn't.

Bertrand had been taken prisoner and sentenced to death at the height of *La Terreur*, when some 16,000—mostly un- bound—were executed via *Le Rasoir National*, better known on this side of the pond as the guillotine.

Hearing of his friend's capture—but detained in Prussia— Elric had dispatched another mystic to help Bertrand escape. The mystic he'd enlisted was the famed Chevalier D'Eon, who loved to mingle and hold diplomatic power within the un- bound's kingdoms, but D'Eon proved themselves to be an un- reliable ally to their fellow mystics. Later, it was rumored that the Chevalier had played a significant role in capturing the merlin and keeping him imprisoned—making sure he was kept away from anything he could enchant to gain his escape, something they never outright confessed to. Still, in the dungeons that held the French elite awaiting a turn at the guillotine, the chevalier had visited Bertrand and demanded that the merlin become their slave in exchange for his freedom. Bertrand had flat-out refused, so D'Eon had allowed Bertrand's execution to take place. Afterward, he'd then made off with a good portion of the merlin's trinkets.

Decades later, Elric had gotten his revenge for the betrayal and the death of his friend. D'Eon had died under suspicious circumstances—meaning they'd died of old age, which was almost unheard of for a mystic as young as eighty-two.

Right around the time of D'Eon's demise, Elric had been seen using a few new trinkets, all of them created by Bertrand. The most famous was the de Boucheporn Loupe, which was the last trinket Bertrand created and had cost him so much energy in its crafting that it had left him weak and vulnerable to capture.

The Loupe allowed a mystic to see through any wall, past any ward, down any tunnel, through any obstacle. It was an absolutely priceless trinket for its spying ability alone, and Elric usually kept it sealed deep within his trinket vault as it wasn't something he could afford to have end up in the wrong hands. To my knowledge it'd barely ever seen the light of day because any thieving mystic wouldn't hesitate to risk their life to have it.

"That's the one," Gert said, pointing a finger gun at Dex. "Jacquelyn's been using it to look through the ceiling of her floors and into the vault. Qin's not there, and he's not in his quarters or anywhere else at SPL."

"How'd Jacquelyn get the Loupe out of the trinket vault if no one could get in?" I asked.

Gert shrugged. "Had it on her, I guess. Either way, Elric knows Qin is missing. He's nowhere to be found, and no one knows why he's disappeared, whether it was of his own free will or the work of another mystic."

Dex grunted. "Can't imagine that anyone would get the jump on Qin Shi."

I couldn't, either, which was why I believed that Qin had locked down the trinket floor so that he could scurry off to try and recover the Casting Bead. I wasn't about to share *that* with Dex and Gert, but I wasn't nearly as worried about Qin as I might've been.

"How does any of this relate to the dead agents and Tove's murder?" Dex asked next.

"Maybe it doesn't," Gert said. "But there're rumblings in Europe that've got everyone nervous."

"Rumblings?" Dex and I said together.

Gert nodded, her expression grave. "Vostov's court is unstable. The old bastard's been trying to quell the rumors, but no one's believing him. Seems there've been mysterious deaths among European intelligence—some MI6 agents from the UK, one from Spain's la Casa, and a couple of unexplained deaths among the French DGSI."

Dex and I traded wary glances before he turned back to Gert. "How're they dying?"

"Different ways, but all of their murders appear to be through mystic means."

Fear formed a knot in the pit of my stomach. This was much bigger than I'd thought. If Vostov's court was indeed unstable, and some rebel mystics within his court were stirring up trouble, it could upset the global balance of power among the six courts.

It was a terrifying thing to contemplate, because the last time that'd happened was during the Mystic Wars, and thousands of our kind had either perished or become enslaved.

"How are Elric and Petra responding?" Dex asked Gert.

"So far, they're not doing much other than arguing about

how to respond. The Flayer's in a tizzy over it. He's acting as the messenger back and forth between them, trying to work out some sort of deal to respond in unison and present a unified front, but Elric's been stonewalling his wife, and no one knows why."

I asked the question I didn't want to ask, "Could Elric be behind the foreign unbound agents' deaths?"

Gert studied me a moment before she said, "No. I don't think so. But he hasn't appeared to be in any rush to flush out those responsible and help Vostov quash what's looking like a rebellion. He and Vostov are tenuous allies at best and Vostov's still furious at him over the loss of the Promise, so things are tense in Europe right now."

"This could get bad," Dex said softly.

Gert nodded gravely. "Yes, Dexy, it could."

"What about Kallis?" I asked next. "Gert, you know him. Do you think he has anything to do with all this?"

Her gaze swiveled to me. "He's definitely on my list of top suspects."

"So you believe he's alive?"

"You mean, do I think he survived the wrath of Vostov once he returned home without the Promise?"

"Yes."

"You're assuming he returned home, which I highly doubt. The most reliable rumor I've heard is that he fled D.C. and hasn't been heard from since."

"Is he powerful enough to try and unseat Vostov, though, Gerty?" Dex asked, sounding incredulous at the very idea. Which made sense since Vostov was nearly equal in power to Petra if not Elric.

Gert *tsk*ed dismissively. "Is Kallis powerful enough? No. Stupid enough? Yes. After all, this is the man that lost track of the Promise in the first place, right?"

Dex and I both nodded. And then I thought of a final ques-

332 / VICTORIA LAURIE

tion to ask Gert, but it unnerved me to even form the words. "Gert?"

"Yes, Dove?"

"A mystic has been after me since this whole thing started. She attacked Ursula, trying to get to me, and nearly killed her."

Gert leaned toward me; her expression was piqued with concerned. "Ursula all right?"

"Yes." Rubbing Dex's shoulder, I added, "Thanks to this big lug, that is. She's healing well and she'll be fine. I don't know who this mysterious mystic is, though, or why she's trying to kill *me*. She's not the woman in the photo I showed you, so I'm wondering . . ."

"If I know who's put out a bounty on your head?"

I nodded.

Gert made a puffing sound. "Dovey, there's a whole band of women that Elric keeps company with who've wanted you out of the way for almost two centuries. Top of that list is Petra. I'd start with her and work my way down."

"This started before Elric and I split up, though, Gert."

Something flickered in Gert's eyes. "Do you think that Kallis would like to see you killed off?"

I bit my lip. "He would. If he's alive, I think he would."

"Would he make your assassination a priority?"

I gulped. I was the reason he was on the run. True, I worked for Elric, but it was due to *my* actions specifically that he'd lost favor in Vostov's court.

"Yes," I said simply. I didn't know Kallis well, having only met him once, but during that exchange I'd witnessed firsthand how quick he'd been to kill a minion who'd displeased him.

Gert made a waving motion with her hand. "Then there you have it. You've got to assume that Kallis isn't only alive, but behind all of this."

At my back there was a puff of air, and a beam of daylight lit a narrow path through the center of the bar. We all turned to see a boisterous group of mystics—some I recognized from SPL—troop into the bar. They were here, no doubt, for an early happy hour.

Gert picked up the fork from the counter and I felt the dome of protection fall away. "Sorry," she said, motioning with her chin toward the incoming crowd. "Duty calls."

Dex handed her the silver-and-copper cocktail shaker and off she trotted to tend to her patrons.

Next to me Dex's phone emitted a vibrating sound, and he reached into his jeans pocket to pull it out and look at the screen. "Damn," he muttered.

"What's wrong?"

His gaze lifted to mine, but he seemed quite distracted. "Esmé needs me. I've got to run."

"Of course," I said, while inwardly wincing. Dex was built for a fight, and it'd been nice having him by my side the past few hours.

He slapped a large bill down on the counter, squeezed my shoulder, and headed out the door. Through the mirror set into the wall at the back of the bar, I watched him leave and wondered if I should stay here for the rest of the day.

Gert didn't mind a little arguing among rivals, but any threats of or breaking out of violence were immediately dispatched via a special staff she kept under the bar. Jacquelyn was the one who'd given it to her in a reparations agreement for destroying the bar last century. In the years since, at the first sign of trouble, Gert would haul that thing out and wave her arms like Gandalf doing his "You shall not pass!" thing, and the mystics involved would be literally tossed right out of the bar before they even knew what'd hit them, then, through the magic of the staff's impact on them, they'd never be able to enter again.

Whoever Kallis had sent to kill me—if he was in fact behind all this—she'd never get the chance in here. With a sigh I resigned myself to sit out the afternoon, trying to come up with a plan, and I'd just put my feet on the rung of the barstool to give me purchase while I reached across the bar toward the coffeepot when my own phone buzzed. Lifting it out, I looked at the screen and froze.

It was from Ursula and it read:

911! Call me!

CHAPTER 17

My hands were shaking when I threw money onto the bar, grabbed my purse, and fled Gert's. On the way out I somehow managed to tap on Ursula's number and the line barely rang before she picked up.

"We need you," she said, her voice flat but far from calm.

I fished out Gib's key fob and unlocked the Range Rover's doors. "I'm on my way! I'm just leaving Gert's. I'll be there in twenty minutes!"

There was a pause on her end before she said, "No."

I pulled the Rover's door open and hopped inside, punching the start button before I'd even buckled myself in. "What do you mean 'No'?"

"Meet us at Gib's. It's closer."

"How're you getting there?" I asked, completely forgetting she'd ordered a new car.

"The new Mercedes and my new phone both arrived. Grant and I will see you in ten."

I drove like a madwoman, weaving spells and Gib's SUV through the afternoon traffic. I didn't know what was wrong, but the tense note in Ursula's voice during our exchange had left me filled with dread.

I arrived at Gib's townhome ahead of them. Deciding not to

wait for them. I used the house key on his key ring to let myself inside, turning on the lights because daylight had already started to fade and it was still overcast outside.

After looking around I spotted a clay dish on a sofa table next to the staircase, and I assumed that's where he kept his keys, so I plopped them into the dish so that he'd know where they were.

My eyes grazed over the other items on the table, and it was then that I noticed a photo album with a gold title embossed on the cover. The title read: *THE STORY OF US*.

"Well, now I have to look inside," I muttered, pulling the album close and opening the cover.

There were a series of pictures carefully taped to the paper on the album, beginning with a photo of a much younger Gib in his UVA football uniform, holding a football with one knee on the ground, balancing on the other foot. I smiled at his expression; he was trying to look tough, but he couldn't quite pull it off. His eyes were simply too kind.

The picture below his must have been his wife, Julia. She was in her cheerleading UF uniform, a blue and orange crop top and miniskirt, posing with her foot on a football and holding a sign that said: GO GATORS!

She was such a beautiful girl, full of promise, wearing a smile simply bursting with optimism. She reminded me of someone I used to know, but I couldn't place who at the moment. You meet a lot of people in two hundred years.

I flipped to the next page and there were several photos of Gib and Julia, young and in the first budding stages of love during their college years. Poses of her riding piggyback outside a local bar, the pair riding a roller coaster, their hair blown back, wearing exhilarated expressions.

Another photo showed them unpacking moving boxes and a caption written underneath that read *OUR FIRST HOME!*

Other photos of them together and separately including one hilarious photo of a bearded Gib dressed as Princess Leia in the slave metal bikini outfit surrounded by other *Star Wars* characters. And then there was a breathtaking photo of Julia, walking a catwalk in a gorgeous, ruffled, fuchsia evening gown at what I suspected was a Christian Siriano fashion show.

The one next to that was Gib, also on a catwalk, muscles rippling, clad only in tight-fitting red, white, and blue bathing briefs that made me suck in a breath; he was so beautiful.

The page after that was a wedding photo; the couple exiting the altar, jubilantly happy. Julia's white strapless, drop-waist, taffeta gown, which made her look like a princess, and Gib was as handsome as I'd ever seen him in a classic black three-piece tuxedo, red-rimmed buttons, red silk pocket square, and black velvet bow tie.

Again, I was struck at how familiar Julia looked to me. I swore she could've been the sister of someone I knew. Maybe an unbound I'd met in the past decade, but I couldn't quite place her.

The slamming of car doors made me jump. Gib and Ursula were here.

I shut the photo album, placed it carefully back in its spot on the table, then sprinted toward the kitchen, quickly heading to the sink and reaching for a water glass.

The sound of the front door reached me just as I was filling up the glass from the tap.

"Dovey?" Gib called.

"In here!" I called back.

Ursula and Gib appeared in the doorway to the kitchen, and I had to pray that my cheeks weren't too flushed from having almost been caught red-handed, poking through his personal photo album.

Holding up the glass, I said, "Hope you don't mind that I let myself in, Gib, while I waited for you two to get here. I needed to use the restroom and then I was thirsty."

"Of . . . of course," he said. He seemed nervous, and I suspected it was because he thought I might've been going through his things—which I had. I felt guilty, but I couldn't worry about that now. There were far more pressing things to think about at the moment.

"Talk to me," I said when he and Ursula came fully into the kitchen.

She came around to stand next to me, and her posture was rigid. She was spooked or rattled about something, and it jangled my own nerves to see her in such a state.

Gib stood on the other side of the counter, his eyes darting back and forth between me and Ursula while neither one of them spoke.

"Guys?" I prodded. "What's happened?"

Ursula cleared her throat and pointed at Gib. "Show her."

His gaze dropped to the floor. He now seemed defeated, or embarrassed, or ashamed, I couldn't really tell which, and I had no idea what was going on, but my alarm was growing by the second.

"Show me what?" I asked softly, doing my best to keep that alarm out of my voice.

His gaze shot back up to Ursula and she nodded. "Go on, Gib. Trust me. You have to."

But he was obviously reluctant and moved nothing but his eyes.

"Dovey will understand, Grant. I promise you. But you *have* to show her."

At last, and with a deep, weight-of-the-world sigh, he said, "The other day when I showed up at Ursula's, it was because I needed to tell her something. I would've come to you with it, Dovey, but I worried that . . . and I worry still that . . ."

"That what?" When he didn't reply I prodded a little more.

"Whatever it is, Gib, you can tell me. Or show me. I'll understand and I won't judge you, I swear."

His shoulders slumped and he cast his gaze downward again, but this time he lifted his hand, palm up, and said, "Ever since that day we solved the Ariti murders, I've been able to do *this*."

In the center of Gib's palm, a small, blue orb of energy formed and I inhaled a loud shocked breath. The orb quickly winked out. "I know," he moaned. "I'm a freak now."

I ignored him for a moment and turned my mounting panic on Ursula. "He's *bound*? Did *you* do this?!"

She shook her head vehemently. "It wasn't me, Dovey."

I was trembling from head to toe as a cascade of inevitabilities tumbled through my mind. Gib was bound. Elric had forbidden it. He'd think I'd gone against him and done it, or had someone else do it for me.

He'd kill Gib.

And perhaps me too.

No! I thought. *He wouldn't hurt me. But he might cast me out of his court.* I'd be banished, never allowed to set foot in his territory again, and even worse, I'd be completely unprotected from literally *any* mystic wanting to kill me.

Ursula grabbed my wrists and shook me slightly. "Hey," she said. "Dovey, don't go there. Neither one of us bound him, and we can vouch for each other."

"I don't understand what's happening here," Gib said. "What do you mean I'm bound?"

I opened my mouth and closed it quickly. Any explanation I gave to Gib about what'd happened to him would be betraying my promise to Elric. I couldn't do that and profess that I'd stuck to our agreement. "You have to be the one to explain it to him," I told Ursula. "Elric made me promise that I wouldn't tell him about our world."

"Who's Elric?"

Ursula ignored him for a moment and spoke directly to me. "If I remember correctly the choice of words he spoke to you—assuming you repeated the story to me accurately—Elric ordered that you would not bind Grant; that you would not ask anyone else to bind him; and that you would not teach an *unbound* Grant Isaac Barlow about our world." Pointing to Gib, she added, "He's clearly bound, Dovey, and not of our doing. You can talk to him about all of it without breaking your word to Elric, and trust me, I've peppered him with questions already to try and find the source of his binding without any luck. He's completely lost and totally vulnerable. He *needs* us if he's to survive."

I looked from her to Gib and back again. She nodded in reassurance, so I decided first to find out when and how this happened. "You said that ever since the day we solved the Ariti murders you've been able to summon an orb like that?"

His brows were still tightly knit together, but he answered, "Yeah. And it's not the only thing I can do. Remember earlier this week when we met for lunch and that vase fell off the table? I caught it without touching it. I know that sounds crazy, but I swear, I reached for it, would've missed it by a mile, and the next thing I knew it was in my hand."

I put my fingertips over my eyes. Someone had bound him and left him to figure it all out on his own. The cruelty of casting a spell on some poor, unsuspecting unbound, then leaving them to their developing magical abilities was tantamount to abuse. Bound mystics needed immediate guidance, and it was general practice that a binder would then mentor their protégé. Or provide a mentor for them if need be.

But whoever had done this to Gib had told him nothing. I wanted to hunt down the culprit and make them pay, because they'd essentially put a target on Gib's head. Elric would never stand for a permanent romance between me and Gib. He'd granted me a tryst, not a mystic's lifetime partnership.

"That day when you solved the Ariti murders," Ursula said, "did anyone sing a song to you?"

"Sing a song?"

"A poem."

"A poem?"

Ursula sighed. "Grant, I need you to focus for a moment. You wouldn't be able to call up your essence—"

"Essence?"

I pointed to his hand. "The blue orb of energy in your palm."

"Ah, okay, essence, I'm with you."

"You wouldn't be able to call up an orb if someone hadn't bound you first," Ursula explained.

"You mean like tied me up?"

Ursula sighed impatiently, which wasn't like her. "No. Not tie you up," she said while I moved out from behind the counter to the other side so I could pace off some of the tension coursing through me.

"Someone had to have sung you a rhyme, Grant. A song or a poem that when they were done left you feeling . . . different."

Gib was silent so long I paused my pacing and looked over at him. Finally, he said, "To be honest, my memory from that day is pretty jangled, Ursula. For the past couple of weeks, I've had nightmares of that day where I'm near this warehouse and I have the most intense urge to kill myself, and then I actually go through with it, but then that morphs into another dream where I survive my own suicide. I've been trying to separate the dreams from my memory of what happened before I made those arrests, but they keep getting mixed up and it's impossible to remember what's real from what I'm imagining."

I froze as Gib spoke. His memory was fine, in fact, it was *too* fine. He remembered the events as they'd unfolded, but I couldn't tell him any of that. Not yet, at least.

I caught Ursula's eye and offered her a nod behind Gib's back to let her know that's how the day had indeed unfolded.

She refocused on Gib. "All right, so after the arrests were made, did you get a visit from someone? A stranger perhaps? Someone you thought might've been speaking gibberish."

Gib ran an impatient hand through his hair. "No. I'm telling you, the only weird part of the day was when I was making the arrests."

"All right, I believe you," she said, backing off a bit. "How about now, though? Does a poem, perhaps, run through your mind when you first wake up in the morning?"

Gib shook his head vigorously. "I keep trying to tell you, no. The only song that consistently runs through my mind on repeat is my wedding song—"

He cut himself off, perhaps suddenly aware of the company in his kitchen.

"What song was that?" I asked.

He glanced over his shoulder sheepishly. "Aretha's 'At Last.'"

It was Ursula's turn to shake her head as she looked across the room at me. "It doesn't make sense, Dovey. He'd remember his binding spell. If he's this newly bound, the spell would be constantly running through his mind, over and over again. It would occupy nearly his every thought."

She was right. It took years before I stopped hearing my own binding spell running in the back of my mind on a constant loop. Part of the binding process, in fact, is to imprint the words of the spell forever on your hippocampus. There was no way that Gib could be bound and unaware of his binding spell. A mystic couldn't bind an unconscious person, either. The subject had to be awake and focused.

Still, I felt the need to test Gib's power, so I moved over to his kitchen table and lifted a glass-encased scented candle he'd put there.

"Hey," I called to him.

He turned to me, and I dropped the candle. Reflexively, his hand shot out and the candle hung suspended in the air, four inches off the floor, but a sheen of sweat had broken out across Gib's brow with the effort, and he seemed unable to move the candle up or down from there.

I bent and closed my hand around the candle, putting it back onto the center of the table. I then turned to Ursula and was about to tell her that whatever binding he had was fairly weak, when I realized she was staring with wide, horrified eyes at me.

"What?" I gasped, looking to my right and left but seeing no obvious signs of danger.

She didn't answer me, so I lifted my gaze again and saw that she was pointing at me. No, wait, she wasn't pointing *at* me, she was pointing to something on the wall just behind me. I turned to look at the wall, expecting to see a magical portal or some menacing magic at work, but the wall was blank except for a photo of Julia, which I now realized had been taken on her wedding day as her hair was styled the same way as in the photo album.

I glanced back at Ursula, who continued to stare with horror at the photo. "What's happening?" Gib asked her.

Her eyes darted over to him while her finger continued to point to the wall. "Who. Is. That?"

Without even looking over his shoulder, Gib said, "My wife. Julia. I called her Jules. She died three years ago."

Ursula came out from around the kitchen island, hurrying over to me, her face pale and her features strained. "Dovey," she whispered.

I took up her hand, fearful without understanding why. "Tell me."

"You asked about the mystic who nearly killed me last night."

I nodded. Ursula pointed to the photo of Julia. "*That's* her."

My eyes widened and I simply stared at her. "It can't be!"

Her own eyes narrowed with conviction. "It is. She's the mystic trying to kill you."

Gib moved closer to us. "I need one of you to tell me what the hell is going on. This whole conversation is freaking me out."

My mind was a flurry of tumbling thoughts, nearly making me dizzy with their frenzy. And then I turned and looked at Julia . . . really *looked* at her, and for the first time I saw the resemblance. She didn't resemble someone I'd known personally. She resembled Penélope Cruz—who was likely the actress that Ursula had mentioned was at the Museo Reina Sofia, quipping about her resemblance to Picasso's *Woman in Blue*.

"Gib," I whispered. "What was Julia's surname?"

"Kallis," he said simply.

I pulled out a chair from the table and sat down heavily. Ursula did the same and for a long time all we did was stare at each other, the impact of the sudden revelations hitting both of us so hard it made standing difficult.

"Did you know her parents?" I asked in a choked voice.

Gib moved to the table to rest his palms on the back of a chair. His expression was still worried, but he seemed willing to answer my question. "I knew her dad. Weird guy. Don't think he liked me much, but he adored Jules."

"He's European, right?" Ursula said.

Gib eyed her in surprise. "Yeah. He lives in Rome, but Jules was born in Spain. Her mother was Spanish."

I looked meaningfully at Ursula. "Spanish, not Italian." She nodded. Then I shifted my attention back to Gib. "When was the last time you saw him?"

"Nick?"

"Yes." Kallis's first name was Nicodemus.

"At her funeral. He wanted to give her a proper burial. He picked out her grave and her headstone, handling most of the arrangements because I was still in the hospital after getting shot and the explosion."

"Explosion?" Ursula asked.

"Julia was killed in a warehouse explosion. Or so Gib believes."

"What do you mean, or so I *believe?*"

I turned back to him. "Your wife isn't dead, Gib. She's very much alive. And, most likely, she's been alive for a *lot* longer than you have."

He stood there for a long moment, oscillating between wanting to say something and shaking his head. At last, he managed, "I saw her die, Dovey. I *saw* her die."

Ursula and I exchanged another look and Gib's impatience piqued. "Will you both just explain to me what's going on?"

I took a deep breath to steady myself. "Gib, there's a world you don't know about. A world that Ursula and I belong to that is going to blow up your perception of reality. A world where beings can become nearly immortal, and where magic is a way of life. And now, somehow, you belong to that world too."

He seemed to pale. "Are you . . . are we . . . are you talking about *vampires?*"

Ursula giggled and quickly coughed to cover it. Gib shot her a look like he wasn't in the mood to be made fun of. "Sorry, Grant. So sorry," she said, holding up an apologetic hand. "Vampires aren't real."

He held up his palm and that small blue orb of essence appeared again. "But *this* is, right? I feel like I'm losing my mind!"

I stood up and put a hand on his shoulder, forcing him to look into my eyes. "Gib, listen to me. You're not losing your mind. Your powers"—I held up my own palm and formed an orb of essence, then motioned to Ursula who mimicked me—"and ours are the same."

Gib stared at the three orbs in each of our palms before stumbling back a step. Under his breath he muttered, "How is this *real?*"

"We're called mystics," Ursula said. "Wielders of magic, enchanters of trinkets. We cast spells, barely age, never suffer from disease, and most of us are quite beautiful."

She smiled at that last part, and I did too. Some levity was necessary right about now. But Gib hardly looked humored. Instead, he looked terrified.

For the next twenty minutes Ursula and I talked to him about the mystic world, but there was so much to tell him and the disbelief that kept flashing across his features told me he wasn't able to take a lot of it in.

The one thing we couldn't convince him of, however, was that Julia was alive. And that she was murdering his fellow agents. And that she'd tried to murder both me and Ursula and might be out to murder him too.

"No," he kept insisting. "No way. I *know* my wife. Even if I *hadn't* watched her die, I'd tell you that she isn't capable of any of the things you're accusing her of."

"Her father is a well-known mystic diplomat, Grant," Ursula told him. "Nicodemus Kallis works for the Court of Vostov in Rome. He was here only a few weeks ago on a diplomatic mission and lost a trinket that affected people you knew."

"What are you even talking about?"

"The Aritis," I said. "Nicodemus brought an enchanted ring with him from Rome. The ring was known as Pandora's Promise. Once exposed to the ring, the viewer would have an overwhelming urge to kill themselves by means they most feared. *You* were exposed to the Promise, Gib. That dream you keep having is a real memory. You *did* kill yourself."

"Then how could I be alive right now?"

"Dovey saved you," Ursula said simply. "She was fortunate

enough to have a trinket on her that allowed her to rewind time."

Gib put his head in his hands and was silent for a long time. Finally, he lifted his chin and asked, "Was it an emerald ring? In a black velvet ring box?"

I sighed with relief. He remembered. "Yes. That was it exactly."

"But Jules wasn't there," he insisted. "If I'd seen her, I would remember that too. And she wasn't there because she died, Dovey. I know it. I saw it. Her dad even came over from Europe to bury her. Why would he do that if she weren't dead?"

"I have a working theory, which involves Atticus Hearst."

His expression was utter disbelief. "What the hell does Atticus have to do with any of this?"

"I believe that Atticus might be a mystic too."

Gib pulled out a chair and sat down, anger simmering along his furrowed brow, and he simply shook his head at me. "No. No way," he finally said. "All of this is crap. You believe things that aren't true, and I don't know what the truth is, but it isn't what you're saying."

An idea came to my mind that was risky for sure, but we needed Gib to believe us about Julia still being not just alive, and a major threat to all of us, we also needed him to accept his new circumstance and let us help him adjust *quickly*. I also knew these next steps for him would be mentally destabilizing, and he'd be better able to handle it if it came from a man.

Holding up my palm in a peace gesture, I told Gib, "If you'll allow it, I'll be able to prove all of this to you, but first I need to know where Julia's remains were buried."

"Why?"

"Please trust me for now, Gib, and just tell me where she is."

He sighed, and I could feel the well of distrust opening between us. I could be on the verge of losing him over this, and I wasn't willing to let him go without a fight.

"Please?" I repeated.

He ground his jaw, but finally said, "At St. Paul's Rock Creek Cemetery. Near Manor Park."

I pulled out my phone and made a call, without explaining to either Ursula or Gib who I was calling. When the call was picked up, I simply said, "I'm sending you a pin. Meet me there. Come armed and bring the trinket. You'll know which one."

CHAPTER 18

It was late afternoon by the time we reached the cemetery. Gib had driven, and I'd kept a keen eye on the passenger side mirror.

We picked up a tail not long after we left Gib's house.

In the Range Rover it was just me and Gib. I'd insisted that Ursula return home. She couldn't be anywhere near what I thought might go down. She was still healing, which made her vulnerable, and that would prove distracting should things go south—which I fully expected.

Winding our way through the cemetery, I looked all around for any unbound who might be here visiting loved ones, but the late hour, just as dusk was falling, and the rain had chased everyone away. That was a good thing. The last thing we needed were more casualties.

I was worried about Gib, and I knew I'd be able to protect him only so far, but again, the circumstances were now quite dire, and this was the only way I could see to get us all out alive. I'd made sure he was wearing the watch I'd had Arlo enchant for his safety, which would repel a death curse when one was shot at him. I didn't know if it would repel only one death curse or several, and I could only guess we were about to find out.

Dex pulled up behind us as we came to a stop. He'd been our tail for the past forty minutes. On the ride over, Gib's emotions had been all over the place, if the expressions that flashed across his face were any clue. I didn't try to reassure him, because I couldn't. We could be heading into grave danger (pun intended) and there was no sugarcoating the risks.

When Dex had parked, I motioned for us to exit the vehicle. He did so without comment.

"Hey there," I called to Dex as he got out of his Mustang.

He flashed me a winning smile, then nodded toward Gib. "Who's this?"

"This is Special Agent Grant Barlow. You can call him Gib. He's newly *minted*, Dex, and could use some help in that department."

Gib eyed me sideways, clearly still uncomfortable.

"Ah," Dex said, rocking back on his heels. "In need of a mentor, eh?"

"He is."

"The binder?"

"Unknown."

Dex frowned. "Esmé's got a similar situation, so I'm familiar with the circumstance. He'll need to tell me his binding spell, though. Is he okay with that?"

"He doesn't know it."

Dex's eyes widened. "How's that possible?"

"No idea."

"How do you know he's a mystic then?"

I nudged Gib's arm with my elbow, then held my palm up and created an orb of green essence. "Show the man."

"I don't even know who he is," Gib protested.

"Someone you can trust." Gib hesitated, so I added, "He's going to be the one to explain it *all* to you, Gib. The magic. The history. The how-to's and the who's who."

Gib studied me for a long moment. I knew he wasn't angry

with me, per se, and I also knew that the confusion was getting to him. With a sigh and a slight shrug, however, he lifted his palm and created a small blue orb. It winked out almost as soon as he created it.

"That's a bit weak," Dex said, watching the display. "That the best you can do?"

"The best I can . . . buddy, I just created some sort of plasma energy *in my palm*, and I have no idea how I suddenly became able to do that. Or levitate objects, and yet here we are. Maybe you should show me how it's done and then we can compare notes."

Dex grinned, raised his palm, and created an orb the size of a dinner plate.

"Show-off," I muttered.

Dex's grin widened. "He asked."

I sighed. "Fair point. Anyway, I don't know how you'll formally mentor him if he can't tell you his binding spell, but he'll need your help, Dex. He won't last long without it."

"Can one of you please explain to me what the hell's going on?"

Gib's patience was clearly at an end.

Dex said, "Gib, is it?" Gib nodded. Dex stuck out his hand. "Dex Valerius. Welcome to the world of mystics. I'll be your tour guide."

Gib shook his hand and said, "World of mystics. I still don't understand what that means."

"It seems you've been enchanted, and no one told you. Odd, but we'll figure it out. Whoever bound you in a spell has made it possible for you to live a very long life and wield magic."

Doubt was etched all over Gib's expression, and he crossed his arms defiantly. "Exactly what kind of magic can I wield, Mr. Valerius?"

Dex scratched his chin and there was a humorous twinkle

in his eye. "From the looks of it, you can create a translucent, blue bubble the size of a gumball in the palm of your hand, so . . . Vegas awaits!"

I pressed my lips together, struggling to hold in a giggle; meanwhile Gib surprised me by giving in to a hearty laugh. Much of the tension that had stiffened his posture for the last hour evaporated.

"All hail the all-powerful Grant Isaac Barlow." Gib chuckled, adding a little palms-high hand pump.

We all laughed.

I knew then that Dex would be the perfect mentor. "We'll start lessons soon," he promised. "In the meantime, Dovey, how 'bout you let me in on what we're all doing here?"

I told him the short version of Gib's marriage to a woman named Julia, then the events leading up to her supposed death, and finished by telling Dex who her father was.

"Hmmm," Dex said. "The puzzle pieces are starting to fall into place, eh?"

"And then some. But Gib swears he saw his wife die—"

"Sounds to me like he saw her wounded, not dead. The building blew up after you got out of there, leaving her behind, right?"

Gib winced, like it physically pained him to be reminded that he'd left his wounded wife in the warehouse while he went to get help.

"She was gut shot, bleeding, and unable to move under her own power. I left her in there while I tried to make it back to the car. It was maybe four minutes between leaving her side and getting into the car that the building blew. No way she could've gotten out on her own or survived all of that."

Dex shrugged. "Oh, it's quite possible if she's a mystic, bloke. In fact, it's *probable* she survived if she's Kallis's daughter."

But Gib crossed his arms again, stubbornly. He wasn't buying it.

"He's not going to believe it until he sees it, Dex," I said softly, then motioned toward the graves surrounding us.

Dex grunted, taking in the area. "She's buried here, eh?" he asked Gib.

Gib pointed to our left. "Over there."

Dex pulled from his pocket the ring I'd gotten off Lavender's ancestor. "If she is, then we should make sure of that, don't you think?"

Gib eyed the ring nervously. "How?"

Dex held the ring up to eye level so Gib could see it up close. "This here is called a necromancer. It's a trinket that's so potentially dangerous, it's illegal to own among our kind. But Dovey plundered it earlier today—"

Gib eyed me. "Plundered?"

I shook my head. "Long story."

"—and gave it to me for safekeeping. With it, we can call your wife forward. If she is really dead and buried, that is."

"You want to *exhume* her body?!" Gib asked incredulously.

"In a way, but not the way you're thinking. No bulldozing required."

"Then what is required?"

"If it is your wife that's buried here, mate, all you need to do is stand over her grave and push that little gumball of yours into this ring, then call out to her and she may shift some dirt around or stick a hand up for a wave. Your essence is so puny, that that's the best I'd expect you could do."

Gib widened his eyes, paled, and even turned a bit green.

I eyed Dex sharply and mouthed, *Not helping!*

"Sorry," Dex said, tapping his chest. "My bad. I'm trying to explain that you're not going to come face-to-face with your wife's charred remains—"

"Oh my God," Gib said, turning away, and I really thought he might be sick.

I glared at Dex. "How 'bout taking it down a smidge, eh, big fella?"

He simply shrugged. "He might as well get used to talk like this, Dove. Mystics have conversations like this over tea and scones."

I sighed. I doubted that, even when he was an unbound, much phased the giant Aussie. Turning to Gib, I put a hand to his arm and said, "Hey, we'll be standing right there. If you put a little essence into the ring, call out for Julia—and it's important to use her full name, not Jules the nickname you called her by. After you formally call out to her, turn away and we'll tell you if anything happens, and when, or if, to look."

"This is all so crazy," he said, the hair at his temple wet with perspiration.

"If no one's buried in your wife's grave, or if an imposter is six feet under, then nothing will happen," Dex assured him, although I'm not certain it was very reassuring.

Gib gaped at us. "You . . . you want me to call forward her *corpse*?"

I looked him straight in the eye and didn't waver. "Yes."

"Dovey, there's no way I'm doing that."

I reached out and took his hand. "You have to. It's the only way to prove to both you and me that Julia isn't behind all of these murders. You've given enough details to make me, Ursula, and now Dex believe that your wife betrayed you—not with an affair, but by lying about who and *what* she was."

"She doesn't have to actually come out of the grave," Dex told him. "Once the ground starts churning, you can command her to go back to her eternal resting place, and she'll do just that."

I pointed to him. "Yes. That's true. If your wife is truly buried here, then commanding that she not come out, after she starts shifting the dirt of her grave, will be proof enough."

"And if no one comes out of the grave?" Gib said.

"If no one comes out, then the grave is empty," Dex said, holding up the necromancer trinket again. "This ring won't miss, mate."

Gib shook his head, clearly troubled by what we were asking him to do, which was more than understandable. "The sooner we do this the sooner we can all head back home," I offered.

He sighed heavily but held his hand out for the ring. "Fine. What do I have to do?"

Dex held the ring away from Gib. "Not yet. Lead us to the grave and I'll instruct you."

"This way," Gib said glumly.

We fell into step behind him, and I leaned over to whisper to Dex, "You're positive he can't wake up any other dead things in this graveyard?"

"To be honest, I'm a little worried there might be a dead squirrel or a rat nearby when he wakes the trinket up," Dex said, doing his best to look wide-eyed and terrified.

I elbowed him in the ribs. "Would you be serious?"

He chuckled, and with abs like his, I doubt he'd even felt my elbow. "You saw that orb, Dove. He's barely got enough juice to bring that trinket to life, let alone someone other than his dead wife—who's not even dead."

"You're probably right," I agreed. Still, my hand went to my right jacket pocket, where I'd put the shakers, and discreetly took one out, eyed it to see that it was the pepper shaker, then dropped that into my left pocket. I then tucked both hands into the pockets, wrapping my palms around both shakers—ready for anything.

The walk was farther than I would've guessed, but at last we arrived at a beautiful headstone in gray granite engraved with black lettering. It read simply:

Julia Kallis Barlow
2/14/1989—5/19/2022

The simplicity of the engraving surprised me.

Granted, at the time of Julia's death, she and Gib were struggling, but I was surprised he hadn't recorded any sentiment on the headstone given how much he seemed to love her.

As if he'd read my mind, he pointed to it and said, "I could never settle on a sentiment to describe her loss, how much I loved her and how sorry I was that I didn't do more to save her. I just didn't have the words."

I laid my left hand on his shoulder to show him my support and couldn't help noting his heartbroken expression. It made me want to rail against the mystic who'd so deceived and hurt him. If I was right, she wasn't the woman Gib remembered. Not even close.

Dex stepped forward next to Gib and held the ring up in front of them. "The same way you created that bit of essence, Gib, is how you'll activate the necromancer. Instead of creating an orb in your palm, you'll direct it into the trinket, and as you do that, you'll speak your wife's full name aloud and command her to rise.

"If the ground starts churning, we'll know she's dead. If nothing happens, then either the grave is empty, or there's an imposter's body in the casket."

"Or, *when* she doesn't rise from the dead, it'll confirm that this whole thing is some kind of insane level joke."

Dex pointed back and forth between himself and me. "Maybe to you, but not to us." He then pulled Gib's hand up, turned it over, and plopped the ring into his palm. "Remember, say her full name as you put some essence into the trinket."

Gib shook his head slightly and muttered, "I feel ridiculous," as he picked the ring up with his index finger and thumb, holding it up in front of Julia's grave.

"Humor us," Dex encouraged, and I squeezed Gib's shoulder in reassurance.

Dex leaned back slightly and eyed me across Gib's back. From the inside of his jacket, he pulled out a letter opener in the shape of a dagger and mouthed, *Just in case.*

I nodded. While my left hand rested on Gib's back for moral support, my right hand was wrapped tightly around the saltshaker, which I slowly lifted out of the jacket pocket, ready to hurl it at the nearest zombie should Dex be wrong about the strength of Gib's essence orb.

Meanwhile, Gib stared hard at the ring, squinting in concentration, but nothing seemed to be happening, even his brow had broken out into a sweat again.

"I . . . I don't know how to do this," he said after several seconds.

"What're you feeling?" I asked gently.

He lowered the hand holding the ring. "Nothing. I only know how to make that orb thing with an open palm."

I smiled. I'd forgotten how difficult it'd been to create and wield magic in my newbie days. Reaching over I took the ring then pointed at his hand. "We'll make it easy then. Palm up, and call up an orb."

Gib frowned, but he did as I instructed, and a small blue orb of energy lit up his palm. "Hold it there," I instructed, moving the ring slowly over toward his palm. "I'm going to drop the ring right into the center of the orb, Gib, and when I do, wait to feel a catch—"

"Catch? What am I catching?"

"You'll know it when you feel it," was all I could tell him, because he would as we all did. "When you feel the catch of your energy connecting to the power of the trinket, simply say Julia's full name and ask her to come forward."

"Okay, but you better do it now, Dovey. Keeping this orb lit is getting hard."

I dropped the trinket down on top of his essence . . . and it disappeared.

For a moment, nobody moved; we all simply stared at Gib's open palm. And then his orb of essence winked out and we lifted our gazes to each other in astonishment. "What just happened?" he asked softly.

"Where'd it go?" Dex asked in reply.

"How should *I* know?" Gib said.

I began to search the ground. "Maybe the ring hit his essence and bounced off."

Dex and Gib joined me, searching the surrounding area, but none of us could spot the ring. "He must've done something," Dex said, catching my eye when I glanced up at him.

"I didn't do anything except what you guys told me to do."

"Did you feel anything? Were you thinking of somewhere other than where we are?" I asked.

Perhaps he'd unwittingly teleported the ring to another location. It'd happened so fast that it was hard to pinpoint exactly what *could've* happened.

"No," he said, his eyes roving over the grass. "I wasn't thinking about anything except holding that orb and waiting for the ring to land in my palm."

I stopped searching with a gasp.

"What is it?" Dex asked, already taking a step toward me. "Did you find it?"

I shook my head as goose pimples lined my arms and the hair on the back of my neck began to rise. "Do you feel that?" I whispered.

"What?" Dex and Gib said together.

I pointed to the ground under my feet. I'd stepped onto the grave next to Julia's and realized that the dirt under my boots had begun to churn. And then I pointed to the graves nearby, where the grass was stirring, and small mounds were beginning to appear.

"What the . . . ?" Gib said, looking around while automatically drawing his gun.

And then I heard a sound that was like a blade being drawn from a scabbard. I looked over to see Dex, raising what had been the letter opener but was now a longsword with a blade nearly as tall as I was. "Get ready!" he warned.

Dex was well prepared for battle, and I hoped my trinket would hold up well against whatever hellish nightmare was about to erupt from the ground, but Gib had only a gun, and a bullet wasn't going to do much against a literal zombie.

"We need to run for it!" I yelled to Dex.

He glanced at me and then at Gib and nodded. "Go! I've got your back!"

I began to tug at Gib's arm, but almost immediately I felt something sharp scrape against my ankle. I cried out in pain as the thing gipped my ankle, squeezing fast and hard like a vise.

Looking down, I saw that a skeletal hand, jutting out from the dirt, held my ankle in its grasp. I pulled my leg, trying to dislodge it, but its grip was insane.

Out of the corner of my eye I saw Gib aim his gun at my feet and fire. Bone fragments flew along with some dirt, and I was able to wrest my foot away from the zombie. "We gotta get out of here!" I yelled.

Decomposing bodies and skeletal remains began to erupt from the ground. They made no sound, but the smell was beyond anything I'd ever encountered. Bringing my arm up to cover my nose was no help, either, and I gagged and wheezed on the stench.

I knew I was about to lose my lunch, and I did everything I could to hold back the urge, sweating and clammy from the effort.

Next to me, Gib raised his gun again and fired off a shot over my shoulder. Something crashed into my back, and I tried to fend it off, but I felt that viselike grip again, only this time it had hold of my wrist.

Turning, I came face-to-face with a skeleton wearing a muddy pink sweater, long blue skirt, and disheveled blue wig. The sight of something so hideous and so close to me momentarily stunned me. I froze in sheer terror of this nightmare come alive.

"Dove!" I heard a male voice yell. "Duck!"

Somehow, I managed to sink into a squat just as Dex's long-sword swooped clean through the skeleton, sending rib bones, vertebra, and the skull flying. I shook off the bony hand that'd clutched my wrist and turned again toward the sound of a gun firing.

Gib was maybe ten feet away and backing up in the face of three skeletons that'd cleared their graves and were reaching out toward him as they opened and closed their mouths like hungry beasts snapping their jaws.

Gib shot all three of them in the head, but other than a little recoil, the skeletons seemed to barely notice and continued to advance forward. "Dex!" I yelled, keeping my gaze on Gib. "Help him!"

"A bit busy myself, Dove!" he shouted back. I glanced over my shoulder. Dex was being advanced on by at least ten of the undead in all stages of decomposition. He began sweeping his longsword from right to left, but even he was giving ground to the threat when they fanned out and began to surround him.

And then I heard Gib bark in pain and my gaze whipped back to find him with an undead on his back, looping its bony arm around his neck. The other three skeletons in front of him quickly advanced, and Gib pulled the trigger on his gun until he was out of bullets while they all descended on him.

I was the only one currently not under immediate threat . . . but that was about to change.

A group of undead emerged from my left—a pack of them

coming toward me, their movements far more limber than expected, and more like spiders than zombies.

In horror, I watched them come at me while Gib's cries of panic and pain and the crack of Dex's longsword against bone filled my ears. Belatedly, I remembered the shaker clutched in my hand.

Sheer terror fueled the essence that poured out of me and into the trinket, I felt the catch and a soul-vibrating surge of power, and then my arm was high overhead, launching the shaker straight at the threat closest to me.

The golden and glass trinket flew like it had a mind of its own. Whipping in a semicircle, it connected with the head of the first undead, closest to my right, and its skull literally exploded, causing the body of the thing to fall with a thud to the ground.

The shaker then continued its arc, crashing through the curved line of all the undeads' skulls until it'd felled the whole group.

In the blink of an eye, it was back in my palm, and I felt the surge of power pouring through me again. It filled me with a fierceness and courage that I'd never before experienced. Pivoting, I launched the shaker right toward the group attacking Gib.

Just like before, my trinket blasted apart each skull, cutting through them like a torpedo through wooden rowboats. The now-headless corpses fell limply across Gib, and I raced toward him just as the shaker finished the job and came back into my palm. "Get up!" I yelled at him, while he lay on his back on the ground, his eyes wide with disbelief.

He sat up, his hand at his throat. He stared at me, lifted his free hand to point a finger toward a spot over my shoulder. "Dovey, look out!"

I dropped into a crouch just as a bolt of blinding white essence crashed into a nearby tree, boring a hole straight through it.

The tree cracked loudly, its bark beginning to whine as the

top half of it twisted from the lower half while the canopy began to fall right toward me. Panic once again coursed through my veins as I tried to think through my options when there was the sound of a loud *thunk* right before the back of my right shoulder lit up in pain so sharp that I cried out.

I sank onto all fours, unable to lift the shaker underneath my quivering hand.

The sound of more snapping, cracking, and splintering thundered in the air above me.

"*Dovey!*" Gib yelled. I managed to lift my gaze enough to see him trying to fight off two of the undead who had ahold of him by the legs and the waist, while another group of the hideous things closed in from behind. And I also realized, somewhat numbly, that the sound of Dex's longsword, striking bone, had gone suddenly silent.

"*Move!*" Gib cried, reaching one arm out toward me, his eyes begging me to get clear of the danger descending overhead.

But it was too late. The trunk of the tree splintered with a thunderous *crack* and a moment later I was buried under a mass of leaves and limbs.

CHAPTER 19

I was completely pinned down, unable to move anything but one leg. On top of me was the crushing weight of one of the three's limbs, and I couldn't see anything through the mass of leaves covering the rest of me.

My head rang and pounded at the same time. For a moment I was so dizzy I didn't know which way was up. Breathing was difficult but not impossible, a check mark on the pro side of a ledger where all the rest were cons.

Beyond the tree were the strangled sounds of someone dying. And I knew they were dying, having been around death enough times in my two hundred years to know a death rattle when I hear one.

"Hi, Gibby," a woman's melodic voice sang. "Miss me?"

The gurgle intensified but no words could be heard.

"Yeah, I bet," she said. "But you've moved on, so I guess you didn't miss me too much, huh?"

The gurgling was even more labored, more unsettling. Gib was dying. Dex was likely already dead, and I wasn't far behind either of them.

"Sorry that it came to this," she went on. "But we'll always have Milan, right? And Paris. And Barcelona. Those were good times."

I closed my eyes, trying so hard to quell the rising panic riding the adrenaline coursing through my veins. Whatever had struck the top of my shoulder was still causing a searing pain, but I could breathe through it if I focused. I had to get out from underneath this tree!

"We made quite a mess today, eh?" she said, as if she and Gib were just two old friends, catching up after a time apart.

My fingers fluttered, feeling for the sphere. It wasn't in my hand. It must've rolled away when the tree branch hit me. My right arm was pinned down at my elbow, so if the shaker wasn't within a few inches of my fingers, then it was of no use to me . . . or . . . was it?

My brain raced through the physics of an angle I hadn't even considered and, as long as I could keep my voice low, I might, *might* have a chance to save Gib's life.

I gathered what essence I could, held it close to my mouth and whispered,

> *"Shaker filled with salt of rose,*
> *Entwined with vines of gleaming gold,*
> *Heed my sound and clear command,*
> *Come to nestle in my hand!"*

There was a small rustle of leaves off to my left and a moment later I felt the cool metal slide into my palm.

It warmed immediately to my touch, and I sent every ounce of essence I could muster into the trinket while holding the image of Gib in my mind's eye. A moment later the shaker exploded out from my hand and from under the tree. Not two seconds later I heard the satisfying *crack, crack, crack* of bones, shattering about ten feet away.

And then the shaker was back in my palm, where I clutched it tightly, panting for breath, which was getting more and more difficult. The tree was constricting my chest, and I could feel that the wound in my shoulder was leaking quite a bit of blood. I was quickly weakening.

From the direction of where the shaker had taken out whatever undead were holding Gib down, strangling the life out of him, I now heard coughing and sputtered breathing.

"Neat trick, *Dovey*," Julia cooed as her footsteps approached me.

White-hot fury flooded me. I was going to kill that bitch, but I had to get free!

Not even a second later I got my wish. The heavy branch was hit with a bolt of essence that only *just* missed me. The limb that had me pinned blew apart, and I felt my lungs fully fill with air. I wanted to suck in oxygen for days, but if I lay here longer than a second, I'd be dead, so I rolled to my left, still somewhat covered by the branches and leaves, but I managed to get myself free from the tangle.

"There you are," Julia said with a laugh, just as I was about to get to my knees.

My right fist lurched up high overhead, causing me to scream in agony as the thing that'd impaled my shoulder lit up like it was on fire. I didn't even realize I'd released the shaker until there was a massive explosion over my head that sent me back into a face-plant on the ground.

My hand was still above my head, and the shaker slid easily back into my palm. I sucked in some air, tears rolled from my eyes, and I moaned in pain.

I waited to hear Julia snicker, or curse, or rail at me, but no sound of her came to my ears. With monumental effort, I managed to get to my knees, and I sat back on my haunches to look around. I saw Julia and Dex locked in physical battle. Dex had Julia's small frame wrapped in his arms, as if he was trying to crush her, but she was holding up the Casting Bead, desperate to keep it out of Dex's reach.

It should've been an easy conquest, even given that Julia

didn't have a scratch on her, while Dex was a wreck. He was bleeding heavily from a cut at his temple, one eye was nearly swollen shut, and what appeared to be an undead's rib bone was sticking out of his side.

Clutched in Dex's teeth was the necromancer ring. My eyes darted right and left to see the ground littered with dead bodies—none of them moving. Somehow, he'd gotten the necromancer away from her, and drained it of her power.

I wanted to shout out in triumph. Dex was reaching for the Bead—it was within his grasp when his hand suddenly jerked, and the cracking sound of breaking bones echoed in the otherwise silent air. Another snap followed by yet two more in quick succession caused a deep grunt of pain from him, and his face contorted in agony. I realized that Julia was using the Bead to invoke the Crushing Curse and Dex was as good as dead, even if he let her go, which he looked on the verge of doing.

A few feet away, Gib was on the ground, crawling forward, gasping for air. I could see he was trying to make his way toward Dex and Julia, but I didn't know which of them he intended to help.

It mattered little; *I* knew who to help. Sending every bit of essence I had left into the shaker, I braced myself, waited to feel the catch followed by my hand shooting up above my head. Blinding white searing pain caused my vision to double, but I didn't falter. The trinket left my palm and its aim was true.

The shaker collided with the Casting Bead, sending it flying out of Julia's hand while the shock wave blew Dex and Julia apart. He went sprawling backward, landed face down, and didn't move.

The shaker rocketed back to my palm with energy to spare. Catching it sent me tumbling backward, and whatever had impaled my shoulder just punched deeper into my flesh.

The pain was so acute that I couldn't even manage to take a breath in, but I knew I had to get to my feet. I had to get to the Casting Bead before she did.

Rolling onto my belly helped to push in some air. I gasped, got even more air, and felt strong enough to push with my left hand up to my knees. Clutching the shaker in my right fist, I curled that arm to my chest, holding it as still as I could, and managed to hop-crawl on my knees a few steps to just within reach of the Bead lying in the grass. Staring at it, I had to work out how to grab it. I was too weak to stand and bend over, and I couldn't hold myself up without my left arm, and the shaker was clutched in my right hand, which wasn't big enough to hold on to it and the Bead.

Making the only choice I could in the moment, I let go of the shaker and reached my trembling right hand toward the Casting Bead.

I was a nanosecond too late.

It disappeared as my fingers were closing over it, and not even a moment later I was blown off my knees to fly through the air and land flat on my back.

My head lolled to the side, and I watched dully as Julia wiped a spittle of blood from her mouth with the back of her arm, then got slowly to her feet, her hand firmly holding the Bead. She eyed me with such malice that I was surprised to still be alive.

"You just *will not* die!" she yelled.

"Julia," I heard Gib say weakly. "Don't. Please. Let her go."

She turned to look at him as if seeing him for the first time, and the expression that came over her was one of revulsion. "*How* did I ever love such a weak, pitiful excuse for a man? Even as an unbound, you're a joke. Dad told me not to marry you. I should've listened."

"I'm begging you," he groaned, inching to his knees.

"Oh, I know," she said, turning slightly away from me to fully face him. "And it's pathetic."

She began to raise the Bead, murder evident in her eyes. I gasped for air, felt a solid breath flow into my lungs and used it to cry out, "Gib! Your watch! Put your essence into it!"

His gaze flickered to me, then down to his wrist. But Julia had already raised the Bead toward him. A blast of pure white energy burst out right at Gib, and I screamed, "*Nooooo!*"

There was an explosion of energy that sent everyone sprawling: Gib, Julia, several of the corpses littering the ground. The shock wave washed over me, and while I felt it, I was already down, so it didn't affect me nearly as much as the rest.

Somehow, I rolled onto my belly and my left elbow and began to slowly crawl toward Gib's prone body. I knew Julia had likely killed him; he didn't have command of his essence enough yet to push it into his watch, and I didn't think the trinket I'd had Arlo enchant for him could withstand a full blast from the Casting Bead if the enchantment in it hadn't been fully awakened.

The explosion as her death curse hit him . . . was definitely enough to kill an unbound or a very newly minted mystic.

Tears rolled down my cheeks as I inched my way, painfully clawing the ground with my left arm and working my knees and hips in a weak shuffle forward while my right arm dragged behind. I knew I was both too weak to stand and too heartbroken to do anything other than crawl.

I stopped inching forward when I got close enough to see him clearly, still and lifeless, his chin resting on his chest while his back lay almost peacefully against a tombstone, which was smeared with blood that was leaking down it from the back of Gib's skull.

I waited and watched for his chest to rise and fall, mentally begging for it, but no air filled his lungs. No life still clung to his body.

I let out a sob, ducking my chin, choking on the grief. He was gone. I was alone and heartbroken, as much for losing him as for losing what could've been. Seeing that orb of essence form in his palm when Ursula had brought us together in his kitchen, there'd been a flicker of hope. Hope for more than just a mortal's lifetime with him. Hope for decades and centuries. A love that would both endure and grow through time. Hope for spending it with a kind and gentle man rather than a powerfully ruthless one.

"Pitiful," I heard her say. "Why Elric ever favored you I'll never understand."

I kept my head down as the grief was quickly overtaken by rage. I wanted to kill this bitch. I wanted her to feel even one scintilla of the agony I was in. I wanted her to suffer.

"He loved you," I said softly, buying some time. My right arm was tucked in at my side, down by my hip. Julia would only be watching my left hand, which was stretched out in front of me. If I could call the sphere to the hand at my side, I might be able to get off one last blast, but to do that, I needed to gather just enough essence to send for the shaker, which was somewhere off in the grass behind me.

"Of course he did," she said, adding a haunting laugh. "And in his final moments, he was sorry he did. Mission accomplished, wouldn't you say?"

I didn't reply. I was focusing hard and trying to find a way to hide the spell that needed to be whispered low enough so she wouldn't hear, but loud enough for it to command the trinket to my hand.

"And I'll bet you're pretty sorry he loved me too, right, Dovey?"

I closed my eyes, kept my face to the ground, feeling my essence form, and I was just about to begin to whisper the comeback spell when I heard a sort of splat. Then another. Then another.

Keeping my chin ducked, I glanced back and behind me. Julia was casually tossing my shaker up in the air and catching it, like a ball.

Clutched in her other hand was the Casting Bead and it glowed with power. "Don't bother calling this thing to you," she said of my shaker. "I've already ensnared it with the Bead. It's not going to come when you call it."

I turned my chin away, closing my eyes in defeat. I was about to die. There was no one to save me.

No one to save me . . .

No one to save me!

With my chin ducked I formed the words and began to whisper:

> *"Shaker filled with spice like night,*
> *Entwined with vines of golden light,*
> *Heed my sound and clear command,*
> *Come back to my outstretched hand!"*

I barely got that last lyric out before the worst pain I have *ever* felt hit me. It was like bearing the weight of the ocean on every part of my body. I was being crushed from the inside out. I couldn't move, breathe, or even think beyond the silent screams that were filling my mind.

I felt my toes snap, one by one, and each one brought its own unbearable agony. In the back of my mind, I *knew* I had to think beyond the pain and fight, but the torture felt like a hill too insurmountable for thought.

The bones in my feet began to snap, crackling like the snapping of branches, and I desperately begged to black out, but the magic of the Crushing Curse kept my mind conscious and alert to the searing, blinding pain.

It was driving me to the edge of madness.

My left ankle bone snapped, and a lightning bolt of searing hot pain bolted its way up my leg to my hip, along my side, up my torso, and out through my arm ending in the flinch of my hand.

Which was holding something round and metallic.

The pepper shaker had come back to me.

"When there's no one left to save you, that might do the trick."

Falcon the Wise's voice played in the recesses of my mind, hovering just above the mental screams ricocheting back and forth, pushing me closer and closer to the edge of madness.

All I needed was a spark. Just a speck of essence to push into the pepper shaker . . .

My left fibula and tibia snapped, and I jerked, my hand squeezing the sphere and . . . I . . . felt . . . a . . . catch.

The shaker warmed in my palm, pulsing with energy, and, with immense effort, I closed my eyes. Whatever was going to happen, would happen. If I survived to see it, good. If not. So be it.

The pressure on my right fibula intensified, bringing the bone to the breaking point, and in my mind I screamed anew. The shaker was a dud. There was no one to save—

A loud bang not unlike thunder undulated across the landscape, rattling bones and leaves and the very air, which crackled with energy.

The pressure breaking my bones ceased abruptly and for the briefest moment between the crackling of energy and what happened next there was nothing but silence. As if the world had paused only long enough for me to inhale a ragged breath.

And then, just above where my head lay, there was a splat, followed by a sizzling sound. Something bubbled near my left wrist.

An acrid smell filled the air, and heat wafted over me along with a long, low rumble.

I didn't know if I could move. Worse, I didn't know if I *should* move or play dead. But even if I did, I suspected it wouldn't fool the apex predator that'd just landed in front of me.

The smell and the sizzle of bubbling acid were the telltale clues. Priscilla, Jacquelyn's deadliest, and most unpredictable, dragon had appeared in front of me, and whether she was there to defend me or eat me was anyone's guess.

"Where did you come from, kitten?" Julia's voice said in a wavering tone that revealed how rattled she was to see the blue dragon appear in front of us.

Priscilla's rumble wafted from deep in her throat, and I heard her chomping lips, clapping together hungrily.

"Easy there," Julia said. Her voice sounded just a touch farther away. "Your dinner's at your feet, baby, and I've tenderized the meat for you."

Another splat of acidic drool fell onto the grass to my right, followed by the sound of burning grass and the acrid smoke that threatened to choke me.

"Gobble, gobble," Julia sang. I imagined her, waving toward my prone body, just waiting for the dragon to take a chomp so that she could flee.

And sure enough, I felt the heat of Priscilla's head, just above mine, and the wind of her breath as she took in my smell.

I've never considered what it would feel like to be eaten by a dragon. The first chomp would no doubt be excruciating, especially given the sulfuric acid of Priscilla's drool, but would it compare to the agony of my bones being broken, one by one? Would anything ever come close to that level of excruciation?

I guess I was about to find out.

I squeezed my eyes closed, bracing myself for the inevitable, but the next thing that happened was a surprise. Priscilla nudged my left shoulder with her snout, not violently, but enough to roll me onto my side. The pain of the bones in my legs and feet grinding together nearly made me pass out but, somehow, I survived the maneuver fully conscious. I found the courage to open my eyes and came nose to nose with the blue dragon, seeing her from an angle that I doubt anyone else in the world had and lived through to talk about it.

She was breathtaking. The iridescence of her cobalt-blue scales shimmered above me, and her jeweled golden eyes sparkled with mischief.

I waited to feel the fire of her spittle, but none fell on me, even though I swear she was wearing a dragon's grin.

"I've got a candy bar in the car if you're willing to help me," I whispered to her. "In fact, there's a whole bunch of Twix bars in my handbag on the front seat. Just for you, you sapphire beauty."

Priscilla's leather lips peeled back to reveal even more razor-sharp teeth. She was game.

"Kill the mystic, lovey," I told her. And with supreme effort I raised my left index finger and pointed it to where I thought Julia was standing.

The blue dragon lifted her head, following my inference and without any hesitation she spat a glob of acid over my body, straight at the menace that'd caused all of this chaos.

There was a scream and a tumbling sound. I lifted my head just enough to see Julia writhing on the ground, much of her left arm, shoulder, neck, and head smoking from the direct hit. My lips formed a snear. I wanted to watch her die.

Still, she surprised me when she rolled over and got to her feet; clutching the Casting Bead, she held it out in front of her defensively, and I could see her essence gathering around the trinket. Priscilla flew at her just as Julia unleashed a torrent of energy, and the dragon collided with the deadly bolt, using her wings like a shield, meeting the bolt and splintering it in a thousand directions.

I turned back onto my stomach, squeezing my eyes shut from the brightness of the blast, hoping none of those splintering bolts of energy hit me.

When the explosions stopped, I opened my eyes and saw Priscilla standing triumphantly next to the Casting Bead, looking every bit like the cat that ate the mouse, and Julia was nowhere to be seen.

I sighed, ducking my chin and blocking out the light. I was

alive . . . but broken. Gib was gone. Dex too was surely dead, leaving me and Ursula to grieve together.

A sob overtook me, and as much as I tried to tamp it down, I couldn't. I was in so much pain, physically and emotionally, I didn't know how I would stand it. Another sob shook me and the physical and emotional pain of everything that'd happened in this graveyard was bringing me back toward the edge of madness.

Something heavy plopped to the ground beside my head. Priscilla expecting her candy bar. Which meant I somehow had to get to Gib's car, retrieve my handbag, and offer it to her. The task felt impossible. Another sob escaped me. "I can't," I whispered to her, knowing the blue dragon wouldn't accept breaking our deal. What was it the merlin had told me? Something about being careful choosing when to use the pepper shaker trinket to call for help as there was always a price to pay.

"So be it," I said. I was powerless to change anything about what happened to me next.

"Dovey," a woman said softly. My breath caught, but then I realized the voice didn't belong to Julia.

I held my breath and turned my chin to look up. Jacquelyn stood above me, staring down at my broken form with concern. "The brooch," she said, pointing to a spot next to my head. "Hold it."

I was slow to understand and simply blinked up at her. She squatted down, lifted her dragon brooch, and placed it gently into my right palm.

I winced from a shock wave of pain—the brooch was far heavier than it appeared and pain was still radiating down from my shoulder to my fingertips, but then something incredible happened. Heat thrummed outward from Jacquelyn's brooch and radiated inward along my bones. The pain lessened inch by inch as the heat sought all the broken parts of me and mended them completely.

In just a few minutes, the wonderful heat ebbed, and then

the brooch felt only warm in my palm. I got to my hands and knees and sat back on my haunches. Something slid off my back and I looked to my right. A large bit of bone with a sharp edge and covered in my blood lay in the grass. I realized that, as Dex's longsword was cutting through the skeletons coming at him, parts of them had flown, and one piece had impaled me.

I picked up the bit of bone and hurled it away from me. Then I gave the area a good look around.

Jacquelyn was walking among the corpses—a general inspecting the casualties of war. She stopped when she got to Dex, squatting down to lay a hand on his back. She withdrew it a moment later. She then stood tall again, her expression hardened. Noticing his longsword, lying not far away, she picked it up and brought it to him, laying it down at his side.

She then turned her attention to me. "Better?" she asked.

A tear slid down my cheek, but I nodded. Holding up her dragon brooch, I asked, "Can you save him? And my friend?" I pointed over to Gib's body just a few yards away.

The lieutenant considered me for a long moment before answering. "No, Dovey. I'm sorry. I can't save either one of them. The brooch's power is limited, and you were the only one I could afford to save. I can't take the risk that I might need use of it soon."

A chill rippled the hairs on the back of my neck; trouble was brewing, and I suspected Kallis was at the heart of it. "Is Elric still in Europe?"

"Yes."

I pointed again to Dex. "Can you ask Elric if he could spare a healing trinket from his vault? Dex saved us all, Jacquelyn. He bought me time to call for help."

Jacquelyn eyed the pepper shaker still clutched in my left hand. She pointed to it and asked, "You called Priscilla using that?"

I nodded. "The Falcon's handiwork."

She grunted. "He's a masterful merlin. Not quite as powerful as Adolpho, but a very close second."

"The trinket vault?" I pressed.

She shook her head again. "Dovey, I'm sorry. No one can get into the vault until Elric gets back from Europe, and I don't know how long that'll be, but it's likely to be far too late by then."

I blinked. "Qin is still missing?"

Jacquelyn's expression was now both grave and sad. "He is. We have reason to believe he might've been kidnapped and is probably dead."

I gasped, and more tears fell as another wave of sorrow washed over me. Why should I survive but Dex, Gib, and Qin Shi all die? I stared down at the ground, feeling hopeless. A moment later, the brooch disappeared from my hand, and I looked up to see it pinned back onto the lapel of Jacquelyn's jacket.

"Who did all this?" she asked me, waving at the wreckage all around us.

I wiped at my cheeks. "Kallis's daughter. Julia."

Her brow shot up in surprise. Her expression was shocking because I almost never saw Jacquelyn surprised. "You're positive?"

I nodded.

"How?"

I pointed to the grass behind a gravestone where the Casting Bead was hidden from her sight. "There."

Jacquelyn went around the stone and stared down at the trinket. "By the gods," she whispered. Bending to pick it up, she asked, "Where is the mystic now?"

I pointed to Priscilla, who sat curled like a cat with her tail flicking, watching me intently. "I'm fairly certain your dragon ate her."

Jacquelyn's brow arched yet again. Turning to her pet she

held out her hand and Priscilla got up to plod toward her and rub her head under Jacquelyn's hand, like a giant blue kitty cat. I got up too. "I owe her a reward," I said. "I'll be right back." I wound my way through the graves to Gib's Range Rover, and when I reached the door, I leaned my head against it for a long moment, sobs of sorrow overtaking me. I wanted to curl into a ball and disappear from the world. *How* was I going to tell Ursula about Dex?

Opening the door, I reached across the seat and grabbed my handbag, pulling out my phone and the cache of Twix bars.

Biting my lip, I dialed Ursula's number before I could think too much about it.

"Dovey? Are you all right? I've been worried sick!"

I tried to swallow past the lump in my throat, but it was impossible. "Ursula," I said, my voice cracking. "You need to come to the cemetery. Bring Esmé."

There was a long, long pause on the other end of the line. "No . . ." she whispered at last.

I looked up toward where Dex's body lay and saw Priscilla's narrowed eyes, staring at me impatiently. "I'm sorry, my friend. Just come and bring her, okay? I'll explain what happened when you get here."

Her sob echoed out from the speaker, and I couldn't handle it. "I'm sorry," I whispered, and clicked off the call. I then turned and was about to put my phone back into my handbag when it moved.

I stared at it a moment, my heart in my throat, and then it tipped over and out wobbled Bits.

I cried out when I saw him, scooping him up and holding him close to me, crying onto his quills.

He didn't make a sound; he simply allowed me to hold him close. Then I lifted him up to eye level and said, "I have to feed a dragon. You stay here. I'll be right back."

I set Bits on the front seat and closed the car door, turning

back toward the now quite impatient dragon. As I was hurrying toward her and Jacquelyn, I felt something land on my
shoulder. It stopped me in my tracks. Daring to peek I saw
Bits, nestling in between the collar of my jacket and the collar
of my sweater. He wasn't about to be left behind.

"Fine," I told him wetly. "But do *not* let Priscilla see you. I
have no idea if she'd prefer a picklepuss to a Twix bar."

Bits squeaked and burrowed a little deeper under the collar.
Reaching throwing distance of Priscilla, I tossed her the candy
bars, and she caught them all easily, chomping down on them
as her golden eyes lit a little brighter.

Jacquelyn gave her pet another rub on the top of her head
and said, "I'll send a crew to clean up. You can go home now,
Dovey. I'll take it from here."

I was about to thank her but didn't get the chance. Jacquelyn touched her index finger to the brooch and she and Priscilla disappeared, leaving me all alone among the dead.

CHAPTER 20

I headed over to Gib and sat down on my knees, right next to him.

His chin rested on his chest, his skin so pale it looked blue, and his beautiful hair matted with blood. Taking up his cold, limp hand, I put it to my forehead and began to sob. "I'm so sorry!" I wept. "I'm so, so sorry, Gib!"

I should've done more to protect him. It was my idea to have him try to raise Julia's body from the dead. I was responsible. He was dead because of me.

"I'm sorry, I'm sorry, I'm sorry," I repeated, over and over again, keening and rocking back and forth. I didn't know how I'd ever forgive myself. "I'm sorry. Gib, I'm so, so sorry!"

"For what?"

My breath caught, and I stopped rocking, realizing that the hand that I was gripping was . . . warm and far from limp. In fact, it'd closed around my own palm, in a weak but steady grip.

Lifting my chin, I stared into gray-silver eyes, alight with life. "My head hurts," he said.

I couldn't speak. Gib had been dead. I swore he had. And then I saw movement near his lap and there was Bits, standing on Gib's stomach, staring up at him as if he were in a trance. "Bits!"

Bitty didn't react to my astonished call. He simply wobbled slightly, his head drooped, his arms and legs went wide, and he slowly sank right down into a sploot. He was asleep within seconds.

For a long moment I didn't know what to do. Did I leave him settled on Gib's stomach? Was Gib draining even more energy out of Bits?

Gib shuffled a little to get into a more comfortable position, still leaning back against the headstone. Putting a hand to the back of his head, he rubbed his hair, then brought his palm forward to stare at it in shock. "Holy . . . am I bleeding?"

Making a decision, I scooped Bits up into my arms before leaning over to inspect Gib's wound. I ran the tips of my fingers along his skull, looking for his head wound, but there wasn't one. Bits had healed him completely.

"You're fine," I told him, then realized what I'd said. Lifting his chin, I stared into his gorgeous eyes and repeated, "You're fine."

He reached up and wiped my tear-stained face with his thumb. "Then why're you crying?"

"Because I didn't think you were. I thought . . . I thought the worst. I thought you'd left me."

The hint of a smile played at his lips. "I'd never leave you, Dovey. Not willingly at least."

More tears formed, but these weren't made of heartbreak. They were made of hope. "You promise?"

"I promise." Gib then leaned forward and kissed me.

It was the first time we'd shared a kiss, and the first time I'd kissed any man other than Elric.

And it was wonderful—gentle and tender with a note of need. When our lips parted, all I wanted was more, but I then became acutely aware of where we were and what surrounded us. He seemed to wake up to that reality too.

"Wanna get out of here?" he asked me, his eyes dark pools of desire.

I looked off to his left, over where Dex lay. Then I looked back down to Bits, cradled in my arms. Maybe if he rested for a half an hour or so, I could bring him to Dex and see if Bits could also save him too. Gib's head turned in the direction I was looking and he sucked in a breath. He began to struggle to his feet, and I tried to stop him. "Don't," I told him, reaching up to grab his arm and pull him back down. I didn't want him to see that Dex was dead and ask questions about how he came back to life should Bits be able to help him.

"Is he gone?"

"No," I lied. "But he's badly injured. Help is coming, though."

Gib continued to stare at Dex's prone body. "If he's bleeding, maybe there's something we can do."

"I've already stopped the bleeding, Gib. We just have to wait here for help."

"Who's coming?"

"Ursula, and Dex's partner, Esmé Bellerose."

Gib's face remained worried, but he finally stopped staring at Dex like he intended to get up and check on him. He then looked all around and asked, "Julia?"

I bit my lip. "Gone."

He stared at me and a wave of understanding and emotions washed over him. "She had me so fooled, Dovey. For all those years she played me for a sucker."

"I'm sorry." It was all I could offer him, because what else could I say?

"Did you get the ring back?"

I shook my head. "Not yet. I'll find it. I think Dex might still have it."

Gib motioned to the litter of skeletal remains all around us. "Somebody needs to throw that thing down a deep well and add a couple of bags of cement."

I nodded. "Esmé will know what to do with it. She'll make sure it never sees the light of day again." She could get it to Elric the same way Dex would've.

"How're you feeling?" I asked him next.

"Other than having a headache from hell? Not bad. You?"

"I'm fine." He studied me for a minute, as if he wasn't buying it. "I swear, Gib. I'm fine."

I didn't tell him about Priscilla or Jacquelyn. I figured there was only so much his newly minted mystic mind could take in one afternoon, and we'd no doubt hit that limit before Julia had even shown up.

He laid his head back against the gravestone and closed his eyes. "Okay with you if I nap until the cavalry arrives? I can barely keep my eyes open."

"Sleep then. I'll stand guard."

A moment later his breathing was deep and regular. As quietly as I could, I got up and left his side. I couldn't sit still knowing the necromancer and my saltshaker were somewhere nearby.

Using my comeback spell, I had my saltshaker back in a few seconds, and then I moved over to Dex to see if I could find the ruby ring.

He lay stiff and motionless on his stomach, his face turned away from me. I squatted down next to him, making sure to hold Bits away from him as my little picklepuss was still fast asleep, cradled in the crook of my arm.

I laid a hand on Dex, and he was just as cold and lifeless as Gib had been. My gaze flickered back to Bits. Esmé and Ursula would be here soon. I didn't think it'd be a long enough rest for Bits to recover from saving Gib to also save the Aussie. "I should've waited to call them," I fretted. If I'd just delayed that phone call, maybe I could've sat here with Bits for the rest of the evening and given him enough time to recover to try and bring back Dex.

But then I also realized that Jacquelyn's cleaning crew would be here soon too, and there was no way to avoid an audience then. I didn't know what to do, so I did the only thing I could; I got up to look for the necromancer, finding it near Dex's pale face. His eyes were closed and were it not for the pool of blood near his rib cage where the rib bone from an undead had impaled him, I could've convinced myself that he was only sleeping.

I put the necromancer in my pocket and squatted down next to him again. "I'm so sorry, Dex. I don't know if I can save you, but I'll sit here with you until I know for sure."

Nightfall fell and the clouds above gave way to a few glimpses of the stars as the storm system finally moved on. Bits didn't emerge from his slumber, and I knew he wasn't recovered enough to save Dex.

With each passing minute, hope for Dex faded, and I was once again wiping away tears by the time Ursula and Esmé arrived. Their headlights appeared on the road near Gib's Range Rover and parked behind Dex's Mustang.

I got up and hurried toward them. I wanted to prepare both women for the scene. Two car doors opened, and the women emerged along with Esmé's puppy. "Oh, no," I whispered. No doubt the pup would find Dex dead and gone, and I didn't know what her little puppy brain might think of that, so I moved even more quickly to try to intervene, but the pup flew past me, her excited bark sounding in the dark.

"Ember! Stop!" I called, remembering her name. But she raced through the cemetery, headed straight for Dex.

And in the crook of my arm, Bits stirred, then popped his head up and sniffed the air. A second later, he vanished. "Oh God!" I whispered, stopping in my tracks. Ember's excited barks were closing in on Dex, and Ursula and Esmé were closing in on me.

For a moment I was stuck in the middle, undecided about which way to go. Stall them, in case Bits had teleported himself over to the puppy, or chase after the puppy to grab Bits before he could overtax himself by teleporting himself near Dex. If Ursula and Esmé saw what Bits could do—if they saw that he could bring the dead back to life . . .

Pivoting away from the approaching mystics, I made a decision and raced after Ember, knowing Bits was likely not far behind the pup. In my haste, I tripped over a body and went sprawling forward but managed to recover and take up the chase again. I called to the pup several times—if I could just get her to come to me before reaching Dex's side, I might be able to stop Bits from reaching him too and touching him, but the pup only had eyes for her master, and she flew toward him.

I arrived just as the pup was nudging her way under Dex's arm, where she curled up and didn't move. And I gasped when I saw that within the circle of her body lay Bits, curled into a ball himself.

Panting, I went to grab Bits, but Ember emitted a little growl and bared her puppy teeth. That stopped me. "It's okay," I told her. "I just need to get Bitty."

I tried again to reach for my picklepuss, but again the copper-colored pup with the startlingly green eyes growled at me, and I knew I'd lose a finger if I tried to get Bits away from her.

Ursula and Esmé reached us then, both out of breath, and I didn't know what was going to happen, so I simply turned and said, "Dex is hurt quite badly."

Ursula's eyes brimmed with tears, and she seemed to plead with me, looking for any sign of hope. I couldn't offer it to her, so I simply stood aside and allowed them to see to Dex.

From the ground came the sound of a grunt, then, "Oy."

I gasped and so did Ursula. Esmé dropped to her knees at

Dex's head, next to Ember and Bits. "D?" she asked, putting a hand on his shoulder. She then produced the same glowing trinket Dex had used on Ursula and laid it on his shoulder, where it glowed with bright, yellow light.

"Ezzy," he wheezed. Ember licked his face and thumped her long, thin tail. And, to my astonishment, Bits unrolled from his ball and waddled out from Ember to come to me. At my feet he stood up on two paws and chuffed. The sound he makes when he's hungry.

I bent down, scooping him up, and avoided looking at Ursula or Esmé, hoping they'd buy the idea that Dex had only been injured and not dead, and that Bits had had nothing to do with his recovery.

"What hurts?" Esmé asked him.

Dex pushed himself to all fours, twisting and grunting his way into a seated position. Ember hopped into his lap and continued to kiss him enthusiastically. "Everything," he answered. And then he literally pulled the rib bone that'd impaled him out of his side like it was a mere splinter and tossed it away, appearing none the worse for wear after it was out of his side.

He then blinked at the three of us. Pointing to Ursula and Esmé, he asked, "You two came together?"

"We did," Ursula said, and Esmé nodded.

"Oy," Dex said, rubbing his forehead. "That's trouble."

Esmé chuckled. I studied her and was struck by her beauty. She was a breathtaking woman with long black hair, porcelain white skin, a heart-shaped face, green eyes, and the svelte, muscular build of an athlete. It was no wonder Dex was torn between the two women. "No idea what you're talking about, mate," she told him. "Ursula and I got on just fine." Turning to me, she said, "Ursula told me most of what happened before you left for the cemetery. Want to fill me in?"

I reached into my pocket and pulled out the ruby ring. Handing it to her, I said, "Dex can fill you in. We should leave before Jacquelyn's cleaning crew gets here."

Ursula and Esmé adopted twin surprised expressions, but then their gazes traveled to the battlefield, and they quickly understood.

The three of us helped get Dex to the car, and then I woke up Gib and got him back to his Range Rover just as Esmé left with Dex and Ember to head back to their warehouse.

"I thought he was dead," Ursula said as we watched them go. "By the tone of your voice on that phone call, I thought . . ."

I shook my head. "No, my friend. He was just badly injured from that rib bone. Sorry I frightened you. I was dealing with a lot when I called you."

She nodded like she accepted that answer.

Bits chuffed again from the front seat where I'd set him down, and I pointed to him and said, "There's a new box of Cheerios at home in the pantry, Bitty. Why don't you head there, and I'll be home later to—"

That was as far as I got before Bitty disappeared. "Whoa," Gib said, staring at the spot where Bits had just been. "I don't think I'll ever get used to your world, ladies. It's a total freak show."

I reached for Gib's hand and squeezed it. Turning to smile at him, I said, "Honey, you ain't seen *nothin'* yet."

Ursula laughed and pointed to her car. "Would you like to come with me or are you up for the drive? You both look exhausted."

"You don't look a whole lot better," I told her. The wear and tear of the last three days had taken a mighty toll on all of us.

"I can get us home," Ursula said. "It's only a little over an hour. You two can sleep over and I'll take you home, Dovey, in the morning. Then you two can come back here for Gib's vehicle."

I sighed, exhausted to the marrow. Her plan sounded reasonable. Bitty would gorge himself on Cheerios, then he'd no doubt fall into the same deep slumber he'd fallen into the last time he worked his newfound healing magic, and we could all get some rest that much sooner.

I turned to Gib. "What do you think? I'm game if you are."

He ran a hand through the back of his hair, and again studied his palm, which came away rust colored. "Actually, ladies, I have a better idea. Julia's dad bought us an estate after we were married. The place is massive—ten thousand square feet and twenty acres.

"I've had it on the market for three years, but so far, no takers. It's fully furnished, plenty of room, hot water, and it's only fifteen minutes from here."

I pivoted my attention to Ursula. "I like his plan better."

She grinned, already moving to her car. "You lead, Gib, I'll follow. Dovey? Would you ride with me?"

"Of course," I said.

We followed behind Gib and on the way, I gave Ursula the short version of what'd happened at the cemetery.

"So, Priscilla *ate* Julia?"

I nodded. "Swallowed her whole. There was nothing left."

Ursula made an eww face. "You're lucky you got off with only owing a couple of candy bars."

"Don't I know it."

Ursula tapped the wheel and pointed toward the Range Rover. "How'd he take the news that his wife is dead now for real?"

"He's bitter, but only because he thinks their entire relationship was a lie."

"And you don't?"

"I'm on the fence. When Gib was still unbound, I fell for him too."

She smiled sideways at me. "The man is simply too adorable for his own good."

"Agreed."

Ursula was quiet for a moment and then she pointed again toward Gib's car and asked, "Do you think that's where she's been hiding out all this time?"

I was slow to follow her train of thought, then I realized what she was implying. "You mean, do I think she was hiding out at their old home?"

"Yes."

"It wouldn't surprise me. We'll see what we find when we get there."

As it turned out, it was only another few minutes until we landed at the estate, and Gib wasn't kidding when he spoke of its massive size.

The structure was Palladian—not my style, and, from what I knew about Gib and his love of minimal, mid-century modern, not his style, either, but perhaps Julia had liked it.

We parked and followed Gib up the steps to the front door, which he had unlocked within a few moments, and we stepped into a large and lofty foyer, with limestone tile dotted with smaller black diamond tiles at the joints and a white-and-mahogany double staircase leading to the second floor.

Gib walked in, set his keys on a round table in the center of the foyer, and pointed to his left. "I don't have anything stocked in the kitchen, but I can make a grocery run in the morning." Pivoting to the left and a hallway leading off the foyer, he said, "Game room, study, sunroom, and living area are down there." Then he pivoted to his right and pointed again to another hallway. "And two guest bedrooms and a library are down that hallway."

Moving to the stairs, he pointed up and began to ascend

the staircase. We followed behind. "Up here we have three more bedrooms, the master suite, and what used to be my man cave."

"Your man cave?" I repeated, smirking at Ursula.

He grinned over his shoulder. "I was a gamer once upon a time. Couldn't keep me off Fortnite."

"I'm sure Julia loved that," Ursula said.

He crested the landing and replied, "She was a bigger gamer than I was, if you can believe it. Anyway, in that direction—"

"Wait," I interrupted, as a puzzle piece that'd eluded me slid into place. "You said Julia liked video games?"

Gib nodded. "Yeah. She was good too. She had lightning reflexes."

I looked down the right hallway leading off the landing. Gib had switched on the lights, but that hallway was still dark. "I never noticed any gaming equipment at your place, Gib. Do you still play?"

He shook his head. "No. I left it all here when I moved out after finding out Jules was having an affair with Atticus. After she died—I mean, after I *thought* she died—I didn't take it outta here. Gaming had too many memories tied to it."

My heartbeat ratcheted up, and several more pieces of the puzzle seemed to want to slide into place. My mind flashed to the photo of Gib dressed as Princess Leia at the Halloween party, and the person standing next to him in the photo had been dressed as Darth Vader, with Vader's mask covering their identity. Another flash called up Julia in her cheerleading outfit at UFL, holding up the sign that said: GO GATORS!

"Was Julia's gaming avatar called Darth Vader-Gator?"

Gib's eyes widened. "Yeah. How'd you know?"

Ursula too was staring at me curiously, but I couldn't explain just yet. "Did she have a pair of those 3D goggles?"

Gib nodded.

Another flash of memory called up the image of Julia's headstone, specifically the date of her birth. "She was born on Valentine's Day?" I asked, my breath coming quickly while my mind raced to fit the clues together.

"Yeah. We used to joke that she'd never know if I forgot because I'd always show up on the fourteenth with flowers."

I put a hand to my chest, and then said, "I need to see where she slept."

"Dovey?" Ursula asked. "What's going on?"

I ignored her and pleaded with Gib. "Show me her bedroom."

Gib pointed to his left. "The master suite's down there."

I brushed past him and practically ran across the landing to the opposite hallway. Behind me I heard Ursula and Gib hurrying to catch up.

At the end of the hall, I could see an open doorway with a French provincial bed frame. The bed appeared recently slept in as the bedclothes were askew and both pillows had head-sized indents.

The colors of the bed coverings, the French provincial style . . . "All his favorites."

"When did that get here?" I heard Gib say from behind me.

"What?" Ursula asked him.

"That's not our bed."

My gaze darted about the room, looking for more clues. It landed on a vanity on the opposite wall from the bed. The vanity was adorned with a brush, a hand mirror, some nail polish, a tray of jewelry, and a small wooden box, exquisitely carved.

I walked stiffly over to it, my heart sinking, knowing what I'd find inside of it.

Ursula came up behind me, peering over my shoulder

when I stood in front of it. "Oh my," she said, and I knew she knew too.

I opened the lid and there lay a set of salt and pepper shakers, but these were different than mine: round spheres of gold with inlaid diamonds. I took one out of the box, held it up, and pushed a bit of essence into it, feeling a tingling sensation along my skin. I turned to face Ursula, and she stared at me in wonder. "Dovey," she gasped. "Your face looks like Petra!"

Gib too was staring at me in surprise. "What the . . . ?"

I turned back to the box, and lifted the other orb, but I moved the box as I did so, exposing a note card underneath. I pulled out the note card, the lettering never needing to be hidden, and read it:

> *Julia,*
> *Jewel of my heart. My diamond. My light.*
> *A trinket in the making for you. Take this*
> *to Falcon the Wise and he will enchant it for*
> *you with a magic as perfect as you are to*
> *me—my everything. Happy birthday and*
> *may all the rest be at my side.*
> *I love you.*
> *Elric*

I dropped the card on the floor, lifted the other shaker, and pushed some essence into it to see what it'd do. I felt the catch, which was barely noticeable, but coupled by more tingling, this time along my scalp. I put a hand to my head and felt the long strands of braided hair, wound into coils like a crown. Just the way Petra liked it.

A little more tingling sent a tickling along my lips and eyelids and, in front of me, Ursula's jaw fell open. "You're Petra!" she whispered.

I saw the hand mirror on the vanity and reached for it, lifting it to see for myself, but the face that stared back at me wasn't mine.

Or even Petra's.

It was Qin Shi's.

CHAPTER 21

It took surprisingly little effort to bring Qin out of the mirror. Ursula simply took the mirror out of my stunned hand, poured her essence into it, reached into its surface, and pulled Qin out.

The first thing he said was, "Got any food? I could use a snack."

I looked over at Gib. An errand seemed like a good idea. "We passed a burger joint not far from here, right?"

He nodded dully, his eyes almost glazed over after the magical displays unrolling in front of him. "Yeah."

"How about a food run?" Ursula asked him gently.

He nodded dully a second time and turned toward the door. "Be back in twenty."

He left the room, and I rounded on the ancient trinket guardian, so mad I could punch him.

Qin seemed oblivious to my anger. Nodding to Ursula, he said, "Potion Master," then to me he said, "Dovey."

"How do you know I'm not Petra?" I demanded.

"Oh please. You couldn't pull off her resting-beast face if you tried. Nice getup, though. Who made it for you?"

"That's not the question, Qin," I said angrily, holding up the shakers. "The *question* is, *who* was it made *for?*"

Qin looked around at his surroundings, taking in the room. "So you know, huh?"

"About Elric and Julia? Yeah, it took me a couple of years, but I'm all clued in now."

He frowned. "I'm sorry, Dovey" was all he replied.

"You're *sorry?*"

"For what it's worth, I never liked her. That's why Elric thought her gift to me was a good idea. He was trying to win me over with it."

"The gaming goggles," I said.

Qin nodded. "Neither one of us suspected her. Or the goggles. Who knew it was a very clever trinket?"

"Maybe as the *trinket guardian* you should've been able to cipher that out?"

Qin shrugged nonchalantly, completely unfazed in the face of my anger. "You win some, you lose some."

"I want answers," I growled at him.

He almost looked like he was about to play dumb when I held the Eleanor of Aquitaine's mirror up for him, pointing to it threateningly. "Okay, okay. No need to get huffy. Whatcha wanna know?"

"How much *do* you know?"

"Julia and I had some pretty good chats. She'd get bored and talk to me through the mirror. She knew she'd never let me out of there, and it was a way for both of us to pass the time. So I know it all."

"Then I want to hear *all* of it," I said simply.

Qin sighed. "The big guy's gonna have my neck for this."

"Ask me how little I care." I was so furious. So enraged for having been lied to all along about Elric's relationship with Julia. Qin had known. Jacquelyn had known. The Falcon had known.

Why hadn't I?

"It started a little over three years ago," Qin began. "Kallis decided to bind his unbound daughter. She'd just gotten married, and I doubt the girl knew anything about our world, but she learned quickly. And she *loved* it.

"Anyway, Kallis introduced Julia to Elric, hoping for a match to help his standing within his own court and Elric's and . . . well, sparks *flew!*"

I swallowed the lump that suddenly formed in my throat and beat back the tears that stung my eyes. I would *not* weep over Elric ever again, but damn, did the betrayal sting.

"They got serious fast. Julia hid her affair from her unbound husband by making all the clues point to his best friend—"

"Hold on," I interrupted. "*Did* she have an affair with Gib's best friend, Atticus?"

Qin shook his head. "No. She hated that guy, but she thought it a clever way to hide Elric's identity should her husband ever discover she wasn't being faithful to him.

"Anyway," Qin continued. "No surprise to anyone, he found out and left her, which didn't go the way Elric thought it would.

"Turns out, she was still emotionally attached to the unbound husband, and Elric couldn't stand it. He was afraid she'd figure out how to bind him, and then it'd be harder to justify killing him."

A jolt went through me and my anger brewed hotter. I'd thought Elric hadn't wanted me to bind Gib because he was jealous of Gib's relationship to *me*, when in fact he'd been jealous of Gib's relationship with *Julia*.

"Elric started to hint that he was going to have the husband killed and sold it like Julia's husband was a threat to his organization and his court and he couldn't have Julia so closely tied to the FBI, but she threatened to leave Elric if he did, so they worked out a compromise. They arranged to have Julia die in a gunfight, one that the husband wouldn't investigate, and it worked. It fooled him."

"Didn't fool us, though, did it?" I said, and Ursula rubbed my arm in support.

"Anyway," Qin said, tugging on his beard, "all was rosy for a year or two, but then Julia started seeing the unfairness of her relationship with Elric. She had to give up her husband, but he got to keep his other women? No way. So, she demanded that Elric get rid of his other women, and when he wouldn't, she retaliated by feeding her father information about Elric and Petra.

"Elric got suspicious, he wasn't naïve; he knew Kallis intended all along to use his daughter to spy on the Court of Dobromila-Ostergaard, but then feeding Julia false information to feed to her father got tiresome, and Elric wanted to send a message. He discovered that Vostov had given Pandora's Promise to Kallis for safekeeping, and that presented Elric with an opportunity he couldn't pass up."

Ursula and I both gasped. "You're telling me *Elric* was behind the trinket being stolen?" I demanded.

Qin shrugged. "Elric never told me outright, Dovey, but if I had to guess, I'd say probably."

Rage coursed through my veins like a tempest. "I almost *died* retrieving that trinket for him!"

Qin nodded. "We would've brought you back."

I looked skyward, my lips pressed tightly together. I didn't doubt Qin and Elric would've brought me back to life. They just never would've bothered with the unbound FBI agent who'd also nearly died.

"So why did Julia turn on Elric?" Ursula asked. "She's killing all these agents, and she murdered Tove. What's her endgame?"

"Now? The same as her father's. He wants to upset the balance of powers, so he's formed a little band of diplomats from other courts and they're infiltrating some of the unbound governments' agencies with newly bound mystics that they can control."

"To what end?" I pressed.

"If Kallis and his followers can take out enough unbound senior agents, and replaced them with the newly minted ones, then Kallis will have control over the unbound's investigative and spy agencies. That's power, Dovey."

My eyes widened, because he was absolutely right. I saw the vulnerability clear as day now that it was pointed out to me. Elric, Petra, and the other five courts had long resisted getting involved in the governing affairs of the unbound. The Seven had always thought it beneath them, and too risky an endeavor to start fiddling with the unbounds' power structures.

But Nicodemus Kallis, it seemed, had no such qualms. If he controlled both the unbound investigation agencies and their spy agencies, then he could put all of the six courts into tricky waters. Investigative agencies could begin to look into the affairs of the courts and start to pull back the veil. And if those investigations were spearheaded by bound mystics loyal to Kallis and others in his band, then Kallis could make things very uncomfortable for all of the court heads.

And if the courts began assassinating agents who got too curious, then the unbound were likely to throw even more resources into ferreting out the cause, because so many senior agents at each agency were being targeted and eliminated in ways that couldn't be readily explained.

"Kallis is a genius," Ursula said. "I never gave the man credit, but he's managed to find a way to threaten all six courts."

Qin nodded. "Exactly."

"And Tove?" I pressed. "Why was she killed?"

Qin pointed to the golden spheres I'd placed back in the box on the vanity. "Julia suspected that Elric had made the rounds to his other girlfriends on Valentine's Day. She heard that Tove got a set of salt and pepper shakers identical to hers, but the rumor was started by Tove. She put the shakers into Elric's head by showing him the new collection from L'Objet. Elric loved them, but he only gifted out two sets, one to you and the other to Julia.

"But Tove got wind of it because one of her spies was the messenger who delivered your gift, Dovey. So Tove knew you were given a set. Julia made her appointment with the Falcon, and instead of being gracious and allowing the Falcon to enchant her trinkets as he saw fit, she demanded he create for her trinkets that would make her powerful."

Qin eyed us with a bouncing brow, and Ursula traded a look and chuckled. "Being Petra's body double has some power to it for sure."

Qin pointed at her. "Exactly. He gave her what she asked for, but Julia went nuts. Elric was a little miffed at the merlin's enchantment too, but the Falcon can be such a temperamental mystic, and what's Elric gonna do? He can't punish his *merlin* for pissing off his girlfriend! The Falcon makes lots of important trinkets for Elric, and the last thing he needed was the trinket spigot turned off."

"I have a question," I interrupted.

"Only one?"

"No. Obviously not. But this question is about last night, when we came to see you right before we saw the Falcon. You were trying to warn me—but you got cut off. What were you going to say."

Qin's bushy white brows furrowed for a moment before he seemed to remember and snapped his fingers. "I was trying to warn you against accepting any other trinkets from the Falcon other than the ones Elric gave you. You didn't, did you?"

Qin eyed me with an earnest worry that was so rare for him. "Uh . . . no," I said, pointedly ignoring looking at Ursula. "I didn't. I only came away with the shakers."

"Oh phew!" he said. "The Falcon is known for giving away

a trinket here or there and expecting a favor in return, and the favor is *never* one you want to pay. There are ways to avoid accepting his little gifts, but it's tricky."

"How would one avoid accepting one of the merlin's gifts?" Ursula asked, and I could feel the tension radiating off her.

"Well, you could start by running and see how that worked out."

"Good plan," I said dryly. "We'll keep that in our back pocket should we ever have the need."

"I'm here to help," Qin said, rocking back on his heels, looking smug. "Now, where was I? Oh yeah, so the Falcon's enchantment for her trinkets were the last straw for Julia. She thought the Falcon enchanted her shakers on purpose to please Elric, so she started to secretly plot against him, first by getting him to give me the gaming goggles, then by stealing the Casting Bead and the mirror, and then by murdering all the senior agents at her husband's bureau.

"Before Elric could put the pieces together, he received Vostov's urgent call and headed to Europe, and the minute his back was turned, Julia kidnapped and tortured Tove into giving up her Valentine's trinkets, but Tove had no trinkets to give up, so she gave you up instead."

I turned away in disgust. The whole thing was so despicable to me. Reaching for the pair of trinkets in the box, I pulled my essence back from them, and felt my skin tingle, but slightly in reverse.

"Oh thank the gods," Ursula said, staring at me in relief. "Looking at Petra was starting to make my blood boil."

"Imagine if you were Julia," Qin said with a snicker.

"Tell us how you ended up in the mirror," I said, ignoring the quip.

"I was going through the inventory of the trinket vault when I found another trinket missing. A small thing, but it was important to Elric."

"What was it?"

"His wedding band."

My eyes widened. "He had a wedding band?" Neither Petra nor Elric ever wore a band to publicly display their marriage. It'd never occurred to me that there'd been an exchange of rings.

"Yes. And he keeps it in the vault because its only power is to make him irresistibly attracted to Petra. Without it, he finds her repulsive."

"And because it was missing, you knew it was Julia?"

Qin nodded. "Who else but a Petra look-alike would want Elric to be irresistibly attracted to them?"

"Did you tell Elric?"

"No. Before I had a chance, I had to investigate a theory for how Julia got into the vault without my knowing. That's when I sensed that the gaming goggles she gave to Elric to give to me might be a trinket that allowed her access. Just in case, I locked down the seventeenth floor and threw a little essence into the goggles. She was waiting for that and had me ensnared in the mirror almost immediately."

Ursula and I fell silent, both of us thinking through all that Qin had told us.

"Is that all you wanted to know?" he asked.

I shook my head as my mind raced through all this new information. "No, Qin. I have other questions, most importantly about Gib. It seems he's bound, but he can't remember his binding spell. How is that possible?"

"Gib . . . ?"

I rolled my eyes. "Julia's husband. The guy out getting you burgers right now."

"Ah!" Qin said. "Tell me how he came to realize he was bound."

I briefly described what Gib had described to me.

"So, after his encounter with the Promise, Gib was able to generate an orb?"

"Yes, but it's quite small," Ursula said.

Qin nodded. "Expected."

"Expected? Why's that?" I asked.

"Because he's not truly bound, Dovey. At least not in the traditional sense."

"I'm not following."

"I've seen this happen before—it's quite rare. An unbound is exposed to powerful magic from a trinket that is destroyed midway through the effect on the unbound. That powerful magic has to go somewhere, so it bonds with the unbound, rendering him or her . . . mystic-lite."

"What does that *mean*, though, Qin?" I pressed.

"It means that he'll have some of the benefits of being a mystic; he'll probably live a much longer life, and he won't die of disease, but his ability to wield real magic—cast spells, wake up more than the simplest trinkets, and get more powerful over time—will be limited."

For the first time in a very long couple of days, hope bloomed large in my chest. Gib would live a long life. He wasn't truly bound, but he and I could live for decades together if love developed and lasted between us.

From the first floor we heard a door open and close. "Food's here!" Gib called.

"Yay!" Qin sang, bouncing off toward the sound of Gib's voice. From the second-floor landing we heard, "Wow! This is a *nice* place! Has anyone ever slid down the banister?"

Ursula and I stared at each other with wide eyes a moment before we heard, "Wheeeee!" then a crash and a tumbling sound, followed by a whole lotta wood splintering.

"I'm ohhhh-kay!" Qin called. "And I'll fix that. I've got the perfect trinket for it."

Ursula shook her head and said, "Now I know why Elric makes him live at SPL. The little gnome is a menace."

"He is," I said, my thoughts quickly moving to other issues. "What're you going to do with all this knowledge, Dovey?"

"I'm going to confront Elric."

"Is that wise?"

"No. But that's not about to stop me."

CHAPTER 22

I rode the elevator to the eighteenth floor, surprised that I wasn't more nervous.

I'd left Gib's house after spending the day with him shopping for dog toys, a dog bed, food and treats, and then we'd picked Moose up from the shelter.

I'd never seen a happier pup.

Or a happier man. Correction: a happier mystic-lite man.

Gib and I had talked a bit about what his new way of life would look like, but mostly I felt like I'd be relying on Dex to show Gib the ropes. We stopped by Ursula's on the way home from the shelter because I knew that Dex was there. I'd seen a bit of a shift in him since Bits brought him back from the dead. I hadn't used my nutmeg grinder around him to be certain, but I had a feeling he was leaning a little closer to Ursula's side of the scoreboard than Esmé's. Word had it she was fine with that. She and the Flayer were supposedly into each other. I could see it. Esmé was into the bad boy over the good guy. I was feeling the opposite.

After leaving Gib's I'd stopped by my place to check on Bits. He'd been sleeping a lot lately, but when he was awake, he was full of swagger. He seemed to understand that he was now imbued with a new enchantment, and he seemed to like it.

I'd have to be very careful with how I allowed him to be around others in the future—but then again, it's not like I had a lot of say about where Bits went or what he did.

Hedgehogs are such stubborn beasties.

The elevator chimed as it passed the seventeenth floor, and I smiled smugly. Qin was back at his post with a brand-new set of gaming goggles that we'd made sure weren't enchanted. They'd been a gift to him from Gib and I, and, in the offering, I'd agreed not to tell Elric what Qin had told me about Julia if he promised not to tell Elric that he knew the details of Gib's mystic-lite enchantment.

The elevator reached the eighteenth floor and when the doors opened, Elric stood there looking calm, and gorgeous. "Tortel-duif," he said warmly, which caught me off guard.

"Elric," I replied, bowing my head, trying to hide my surprise. I hadn't expected him to be so cordial after he'd banished me from the building. "You knew I was coming by?"

"A little birdie told me," he said.

I didn't know who the "little birdie" was, but I didn't dwell on it. Elric had spies everywhere.

"Can we talk?"

"Yes," he said, waving me toward his office.

I followed dutifully behind and once inside the door I moved to a chair set to the side of the love seats. The message was clear. We were no longer a couple. By his choice *and now mine.*

Elric wore a smirk as he sat down on the love seat and began to pour some tea out into two cups of exquisitely made china.

He offered me a cup first, and I took it, then he lifted his own, sipping at it demurely and eyeing me over the rim. "My thieves tell me you were integral to acquiring the Eye of Lucia."

My brow furrowed. "The Eye of . . . who?"

"Lucia. The necromancer."

"Ah, yes. I discovered it in a tomb, and offered it to Dex and Esmé, knowing they'd get it back to you."

He smirked. "And pay them a handsome reward for it."

"Benefits of the job, I suppose."

Elric reached for a round jewelry box, made of gold and mother-of pearl inlay. Lifting it, he offered it to me.

"What is it?" I asked, setting down my teacup to accept the gift.

"Your portion of the reward."

I lifted the lid and eyed the most stunning emerald-and-diamond bracelet, with two lion's heads at each end. "Oh, Elric . . . It's exquisite."

"It suits you."

"Thank you," I told him, closing the box without asking him if the bracelet was a trinket and what it did. He was no longer in a position to ply me with gifts and his charm and have me believe his lies while accepting his double standards. I was no longer angry at him over Julia, but I did have my head on straight about Elric for the first time in the 180 years of knowing him, and I didn't really care what tempting trinket he might think to offer me. Our relationship had changed, far more than even the change that'd taken place the last time I was in his office.

"I need to tell you something," I began.

"Anything," he said, almost languidly.

I set the jewelry case aside and folded my hands in my lap. "Agent Barlow has been bound."

Elric's right brow arched. His expression hadn't changed but I could tell this displeased him. "You went against my wishes."

It wasn't a question. He thought he was stating a fact.

"Of course not. *I* would never betray *you*."

Elric sat forward and set his cup down on the table, folding his own hands into his lap. "Then, Tortelduif, tell me how this came to be."

I shrugged. "Perhaps you should ask his ex-wife, my love."

Silent seconds ticked by without either of us saying another word. At last, Elric broke it by saying, "You believe Julia bound her husband?"

I shrugged again. My binding spell wouldn't allow me to outright lie to Elric. But I could dance around the truth. "I did not bind him, Elric. And neither did Ursula, Dex, or Esmé. No one I asked bound him, and yet, he's able to form an orb of essence and shows command of some magical abilities."

"Did you ask him who bound him, then?"

"I did."

"And?"

"He doesn't remember."

Elric sat back again and crossed one leg lazily over the other. I had no idea what he was thinking, but thinking he was. "This is problematic," he said at last.

"On the contrary. I believe we can use it to our advantage."

"We?"

"Yes, Elric. We. SPL is facing precarious times. The FBI has been infiltrated, and senior agents have been murdered. What we need is a spy on the inside to let us know when trouble might be headed our way. Agent Barlow is the perfect candidate for that."

Elric's brow arched yet again, and he tapped the back of the love seat with his index finger, thinking my plan through.

"What's in it for Agent Barlow?"

"He's allowed a mentor—I think Dex Valerius is a good candidate—and also in exchange, Grant Barlow is granted his life. Which *I'm* hopeful will be quite long."

Anger flashed in Elric's eyes, and I wondered if I'd just overplayed my hand, but there was no going back now.

But then the flash was gone, and Elric went back to eyeing

me thoughtfully. "Do you know one of the things that I've always loved about you, Tortelduif?"

I smiled. "Tell me."

"Your ability to learn the nature of things so quickly, and to accept them as they are."

I bowed my head to him. "I had you as my mentor, my love. You've taught me well."

"Perhaps a little too well."

I lifted my chin. "Time will tell."

"It will indeed. You have your wish. The new mystic may be mentored—Valerius is a good choice—and he'll work for us. Informally, of course. You'll be his handler."

"I accept. Thank you, Elric."

He got to his feet and held his hands out to me. I took them and he walked me to the door. "It was good seeing you, my dove."

"You, as well, Elric."

I exited the office on trembling legs. I'd gotten everything I'd wanted out of the meeting, and then some if the new bracelet was to be considered. I tucked the box into my handbag, breathing a sigh of relief, when I heard a sound coming up from the bottom of my bag.

Reaching into it, I pulled out the money clip that Qin loaned me. I'd forgotten it was there, and only realized I still had it because right now, standing a foot outside the closed doors of Elric's office . . . it was chiming.